More By The Author

The Raven's Journey

Book 1: See Me
Book 2: See Me Revealed
Book 3: See Me Go
Book 4: See Me Believe
Book 5: See Me Overcome
Book 6: Hawk
Book 7: Ronan
Book 8: Stolas

Looking Through The Shadows

The Underbelly
After the Wreckage
We Always Fight

I S.P.I.

I S.P.I. Mischievous Magic (Volume 1)
I S.P.I. Spicy Sorcery (Volume 2)

Short Stories & More

Where Realms Collide
Unnerving Descent
Unnerving Eclipse
Unnerving Wicked
Super: Unexpected Heroes Arise
Rise Reflection
Rise Resurrection
Rise Revolution
Rise Recreation
The Space Between Us
The Pulse (The Haunting of Orchard House)

Michelle Lee on the Web

Michelle on Facebook at
tiny.cc/MichelleLeeWrites

or write to
MichelleLeeWrites@gmail.com

THE RAVEN'S JOURNEY
BOOK FIVE

SEE ME OVERCOME

Michelle Lee

BLUE FORGE PRESS
Port Orchard, Washington

See Me Overcome
Copyright 2020, 2022
by Michelle Lee

First eBook Edition August 2020
First Print Edition August 2020
Second eBook Edition May 2022
Second Print Edition May 2022

Cover photograph by Michelle Lee
Cover design by Brianne DiMarco
Interior design by Brianne DiMarco

ISBN 978-1-59092-889-9

For information about film, reprint or other subsidiary rights, contact: blueforgegroup@gmail.com

This is a work of fiction. Names, characters, locations, and all other story elements are the product of the authors' imaginations and are used fictitiously. Any resemblance to actual persons, living or dead, or other elements in real life, is purely coincidental.

Blue Forge Press is the print division of the volunteer-run, federal 501(c)3 nonprofit company, Blue Forge Press, founded in 1989 and dedicated to bringing light to the shadows and voice to the silence. We strive to empower storytellers across all walks of life with our four divisions: Blue Forge Press, Blue Forge Films, Blue Forge Gaming, and Blue Forge Records. Find out more at www.BlueForgePress.org

Blue Forge Press
7419 Ebbert Drive Southeast
Port Orchard, Washington 98367
blueforgepress@gmail.com
360-550-2071 ph.txt

For my family—
thank you for
always supporting me
in everything I do.

See Me Overcome

Michelle Lee

Chapter One

"Where am I?" I shouted into the darkness.

"I'm not here to hurt you." That mysterious voice was back.

"Right, because that's been my experience so far. Why can't I see anything?" I asked the disembodied voice.

"I'm not here to hurt you," he repeated.

"Okay, fine. I get it; you aren't here to hurt me. Where is here, and who are you?" I stood up, and pain smacked into me.

"You're in a severely weakened state; you should stay seated," he suggested.

"I'm losing my fucking patience here. Turn on a damn light so I can see who I'm talking to, at least." I sat back down, not wanting to admit I was dizzy.

The black started to ease up, and I saw the raven from earlier in front of me. "You're a demon, right? Your soul is muddy."

"I am. He was right in that it only takes one wrong

choice for an angel to fall. I was once an angel. Now I'm a prince of Hell."

I forced myself not to panic. I was in a room, or somewhere, I couldn't tell where, with a prince of Hell. Not the best news I've had all day. "So, where am I?"

"In between worlds. It was the only way I could keep you safe. I will return you," he promised.

"What about my friends?" I could feel Jax. I knew he was okay, well physically okay. I could also feel him freaking out.

"They aren't harmed. The animals are keeping them safe. Once he leaves, I'll return you," the raven demon said again.

"I'm okay, Zeus," I sent Jax.

"Where the fuck are you?" he screamed into my head.

"Not entirely sure, somewhere called in-between. A demon snatched me to keep me safe. So he says. The raven that was on my car earlier."

"I promise, I mean you no harm," he said once again.

"Are you reading my mind?" I asked.

"Gotta go, I think he's reading my mind. I'll be back." I slammed down my walls on everything, sealing myself up tightly.

"No. Your facial expressions are easy to read," the bird cocked its head at me.

"Who are you?" The other one wouldn't give me his name. "Is it true if I know a demon's name, I can hurt them?"

"While I mean you no harm, it isn't my intent either to tell you how to harm us."

"Are you a malevolent demon?" I pushed for information.

"If I were, I would intend to harm you. I am indifferent to what you call evil. I just am. I often help humans, share my knowledge freely when summoned."

"This is so confusing. One demon wants to marry me, you, are for some reason helping me, and others are trying to kill me. How am I supposed to know the difference?" I threw my hands in the air and winced a little at a faint stab of pain.

"Not all demons are bad," the bird hopped to the side a little.

"The other one down there sure seemed to be. Quite narcissistic as well," I replied caustically.

"You can't defeat him yet. You aren't whole. Close, but not quite. He once was worshipped as a God in ancient times; greed turned him dark. He is also a prince of Hell, a mighty powerful one."

"Is he the devil?" I felt a flicker of fear trickle through me.

"No, for your world, he would be considered very close to the top. If he were to take you as his bride, which he already has one of those, your power would become his, and he would be in a position to overthrow current leadership."

More than a trickle of fear slid in now. "That's the demon's end game? Domination?"

"I can assure you; it's not a game."

"What's in this for you? Why are you intervening in his grand scheme?" I felt pressure in my head, building steadily.

"I don't want him as a leader. I will admit to

wanting you for myself at first, though, for different reasons. I miss love, I'm lonely, and I would be happy to be invited back into the light."

"Heaven? I can't make that happen." Was I missing something?

"Your love has a purifying effect on souls, though, mine has been tarnished for so long, I don't believe cleansing it is possible. Mainly, your capacity to love drew me to you. It is that quality that I wish to protect. I have no issues with humans; the earth is a lovely place I visit often. It needs you."

"Thank you?" I wasn't sure what to think.

The demon sighed. "You still don't believe me?"

"If you were in my shoes, would you trust a demon that took you from your world?" I challenged him.

"You are correct not to trust demons as a whole. I am putting myself at risk to help you. And while I am not foolish enough to ask for your trust, I am asking that you believe what I am telling you as true."

"Belief equates with trust. Is it not enough that I don't disbelieve you?" I tried to summon the lightning, but I didn't have enough energy. Or I couldn't because it knew I wasn't in danger from this demon.

"For now, I will accept that. I will also tell you the demon's name so that you may learn what you need to learn."

"How will I do that? Is there a book on demons you are going to lend me?" I couldn't help the sarcasm. It was a direct result of the pressure in my skull.

"You have resources. The demon's name is Bael. He just left if you are ready, I will return you to your friends."

"What do I call you?" I tried it again.

"My name is for another time."

A wave of dizziness hit me, and before I knew what had happened, I found myself wrapped in Jax's arms. "Siren! Holy shit, are you are alright?" He looked me over, stopping at my torn up wrist.

How had I not noticed that before now? It looked mangled. "I'm not going to become a demon wife, we need to find a way to stop that psycho," I said, staring at my wrist and wondering why I couldn't feel the pain. That had to have hurt.

Taklishim stepped over and took my arm gently in his hands. "Where were you?"

"Somewhere he called in between worlds. He told me psycho's name, but not his own," I ground out.

"What did he look like?" He was staring at my wrist with an unfocused gaze. Oh, he was doing his healing thing.

"A raven, ironically."

"He put something on this to numb the pain," Taklishim said.

"That explains why I can't feel it then. Why is there so much pressure in my head?" My voice sounded faint.

"You gave me almost all of your energy, and you are dangerously depleted," Taklishim said, a little angry with me.

"Before I pass out, the psycho's name is Bael," I sounded farther away now.

"Jax, skin on skin with her," I heard Taklishim say. "Tama, I need your help."

I felt Jax's touch and relaxed into it, the pressure in my head easing slightly. I drifted for a bit while they were doing something to my wrist, and Onida pressed some of the magic juice into my hand, telling me to drink it.

Chapter Two

Jax held her while they worked on her, his mind racing fast and trying to process everything that had just happened. Jax had seen the wolf grab Airiella out of the air, and he knew that's what damaged her wrist. Taklishim had told him that the wolf was trying to protect her, and Jax had no reason to think otherwise. He was having a hard time with having seen her disappear right before his eyes.

That had shaken him all the way through. He knew she was okay because he felt her through the connection, but he had no idea where she was. Every time he tried to get a lockdown on her location, it was like she was right in front of him, but no one was there.

Since she'd shut down the connection between them, he couldn't get even a trickle of her thoughts, and she hadn't moved those walls once since she reappeared directly in front of him.

The demon she'd said was named Bael tried to force Taklishim into a standoff with the animals that Bael somehow managed to exert some control over a few. Taklishim refused to cross that line and hurt an animal. Tama had kept him and Onida safe.

Onida was now fully healed, and a little shaken. Tama was back to her person form, and Taklishim was still pulsing out the wild energy that Airiella had pumped into him. Jax shuddered, remembering the fury that had come over the gray Indian when she'd disappeared. Taklishim was damn terrifying.

It had all happened so fast. Jax needed to brush up more on Native American folklore. He had no idea what Taklishim had been doing to get all those animals to appear. He'd told Jax that the bear and wolf had been leaders of a nearby tribe. The size of them was something to behold and ultimately terrifying on a baser level.

He wasn't surprised that the wolf's jaws had shattered the bone in her wrist and tore up the muscles. Tama and Taklishim both were sweating at the effort they were using to heal her. He was also thankful for whatever the demon had put on her to keep her from feeling the pain.

He was sure that would have traveled through their connection to all of them. More so than the emotions that had already made the rounds. Onida had taken the liberty of calling them to calm them and reassured them all everyone was okay. She left out the wrist part.

"Jax, it's finished. Don't let her use it for a few days," Taklishim told him. "No training with Ronnie for at least a week. The bone healed but is weak, the same with the tendons. They need a chance to rejuvenate." Taklishim stepped back so Onida could wrap it to keep it stable.

"I'll have an easier time herding cats than I will attempting to keep her from doing anything she sets her mind to," Jax told him.

"I can hear you, you know," she said weakly, her head still lolling around in his lap.

"I know, Ells," Jax rubbed her neck gently.

"Then listen to me, Raven, don't use that wrist. And don't do that with your energy again," Taklishim's voice thundered.

"If I couldn't kill him because it was a trap for me, then at least you could have," she argued. Jax held back at laugh at her logic.

Taklishim didn't find the same humor in it that Jax did. "Raven, neither of us could have killed that demon. Especially not if it's Bael."

"Who the hell is Bael?" she sounded drunk.

"Probably second in power to Satan himself," Onida said from behind Jax. "He has a little control over shifters, and he has the power of invisibility."

"The one that took me said it was because Bael wants me to help him take over Hell."

"You said the other one was a raven?" Onida knelt next to them.

"Yes. His soul is a muddy color, not dark like the psycho's was. Still darker than all of us, but not black," Airiella's eyes were glossy.

"What?" Tama looked confused.

"She can see souls now," Jax clued her in.

"Yep, all the colors, everything. It's exhausting." She sounded drunk.

"What was in that water you gave her?" Jax was a

little amused.

"The healing stuff she's drunk before, but I added a little pain killer to it," Onida smiled. "Airiella, thank you for coming after me."

"I'll always help you guysh," she slurred.

"If the other demon was a raven, and knew enough about plants to numb that wrist so effectively, I think he's Stolas," Taklishim looked at Onida for confirmation.

"I think so too. Not many demons have the plant knowledge that he has. If that's the case, we are pretty lucky. Stolas isn't a bad demon as far as demons go," Onida agreed.

"He's lonely. He likes my love," she said sleepily.

"Okay. It's time for me to get Airiella home if it's alright that we leave?" Jax looked up at them questioningly. "Not sure how long it takes to get there from here, and we need to be on that plane tomorrow."

"It's fine. We can do more research on the little info Airiella gave us, you've got a bit of a drive ahead of you. She should sleep most of the way. I can put her out all the way if you want?" Tama asked him with a gentle touch.

"No, she's not in pain. If she falls asleep on her own, that's fine. This way, if she talks or becomes more coherent, I can try to find out if there's anything else she didn't mention and pass it along." Jax shifted, stretching a bit before he stood.

Taklishim propped her up against himself as Jax stretched out his legs a little. "We are far more prepared now that we know who we are dealing with and his name. Keep hope, Jax. Bael is by far our biggest problem. The council, we will work on from the inside. The lesser demons' you guys can handle. She's a fierce warrior in her own right."

"I'm a bad bitch," she mumbled, and Jax laughed.

Taklishim helped Jax get her in the car, and Onida brought out another bottle of what Airiella called magic juice. "It's not laced," she informed him.

Taklishim held him back from getting in. "When she fed me her energy, it was the most powerful feeling I'd ever felt. She has a deep well, and in the wrong hands, it would be catastrophic. She needs to be very careful about what she does not to cross any lines that Bael draws. He will be trying to trick and trap her at every chance he gets. We don't know what will make her fall since we don't know the full extent of what she can do yet. We essentially know nothing when it comes to her. It's guesswork."

"I understand. Can you do me a favor and fill in Father Roarke? I don't want to make calls since I'm driving, and after this morning's little episode, I need to be careful," Jax asked.

"Consider it done. We'll be in close contact."

Chapter Three

Ronnie sat there with his hands steepled in front of his face, his arms leaning on the table as he listened carefully to everything Father Roarke was telling them. He filled them in on the events of the day as he heard them from Taklishim, filling in the missing pieces Onida hadn't told them.

"The second most powerful demon in Hell wants Airiella as his bride?" Mags was stunned.

"Yes, which, no, that's not good news. But, lassie, she also has another prince trying to help her. Don't give up hope," Father Roarke cautioned.

Smitty had taken notes, and Ronnie glanced over at them to see what points he had written out where they needed to focus. He'd underlined Bael and Stolas; he figured that was where they would start. Try to learn as much about them as they could.

"Is there a way to defeat him?" Ronnie asked.

"The same as any other demon, it will just be magnitudes harder. Bael commands sixty-six legions of demons, it's said," Father Roarke' words casting a pall over the group.

"Taklishim said she was hurt, and healed now?" Smitty asked.

"Yes, keep in mind though that he also said no training her in fighting for at least a week, son," Father Roarke added to Ronnie.

"We have to leave on shoots next week anyway," Aedan said. "How much of a possibility that any of these legions he runs will show up while we are on location?"

"I'd say the odds are pretty good on that," the priest said quietly.

"Are they all as strong as him?" Ronnie wondered.

"Oh, goodness, no. There will be some strong ones, yes. The most likely scenario will be Bael sending out the lower level demons who are more disposable to him."

"Disposable demons," Mags said sarcastically. "Worse tampon commercial ever."

Ronnie snorted. "Only you would take it there, Mags."

"What do we do now?" Smitty changed the subject.

"Learn," Father Roarke told them all. "Train."

"You just said she couldn't train," Ronnie interrupted.

"She can't, but you can," Aedan butted in. "*We can,*" he amended.

Ronnie rolled his eyes. All he wanted to do was scoop her up and hide her. Not that it would do any good with a demon that could pop in wherever he wanted. "At least they will be back with us tomorrow."

"Speaking of that, Aedan and I will be picking them up, you two stay here," Mags stood.

"What? Why?" Ronnie glared at her.

"Because! I know that you two will hog her time once she is back and we want to at least spend some time with her, even if it's only driving in traffic," Mags put her hands on her hips in that stance Ronnie knew meant not to argue with her.

"Fine," Ronnie gave in, and Smitty just laughed. "Guess that means the rest of the day we will spend training then," he grinned evilly at Mags. "Get your bow and arrow, Robin Hood."

"I'm more like Legolas or Hawkeye," she retorted.

Ronnie laughed; he'd give her that one. She was damn good. He grabbed a sports drink and headed out, hoping that Winnie was around tonight to fill her in. She probably already knew, if she was friendly with Onida.

innie popped in, "Yes, I know," Winnie told Ronnie as she appeared that night.

"Any new information to add?" he hoped.

"No. Knowing who it is adds a whole new element of scary. I'm hopefully out of his line of influence. But I also know that nothing is impossible, and I shouldn't consider myself out of reach. I think he used to be good at one point, though humankind easily fed into his ego and changed his course. I hear different things," Winnie spoke fast.

"Same as what we find on the internet, I'm sure," Ronnie picked at lint on the blanket. "I need to wash her sheets for her before she gets home," he said absentmindedly.

"Well, you might want to get going on that since she's back tomorrow," Winnie snickered.

"I get the feeling that everything is different now. I can't put my finger on what it is either; it's bugging me."

"It *is* different now. Different doesn't mean bad." Winnie stroked a finger over his hand, making him shiver.

He stood and started stripping the sheets off her bed. "Yeah, I know. I'm probably feeling insecure. Hard to say. Sometimes I feel like we are on a crash course with a meteor, and the clock is ticking fast."

"It kind of does feel that way. Let's just hope that with Stolas involved that the outcome won't be the cataclysmic event we keep imagining. He's pretty powerful himself. It can't be only him that doesn't want Bael in the head honcho role."

"No more visions?" Ronnie would take anything at this point.

"Not recently. All has been quiet on that front."

"Is Onida doing okay? Hang on, let me go start this, I'll be right back," Ronnie darted out of the room.

Winnie looked around; it was apparent Ronnie had been staying in there. He needed to clean up a little better. She made a mental list of things for him to do.

When he walked back in, she crossed her arms and looked at him. "You need to clean up. Pick up the dirty tissues, take the garbage out, put clean towels in the bathroom, and wash the rugs. Clean the toilet too."

He chuckled. "Yes, dear. Onida?" he reminded her.

"She's okay. Airy's blood did wonders for her. Taklishim wasn't too happy about that. He was also pretty bent out of shape about the energy thing she did with him.

He told Onida Airy was reckless."

"I doubt Airiella would agree with that. She did what she thought was best for those she loves. I'm guessing she stepped right into the danger zone?" The probability of that was very high.

"I wasn't there. I only heard Onida's side. She said that Airy's powers were off the charts and that the only reason Taklishim didn't exhaust himself into the danger zone healing her was because of all energy she fed him," Winnie fed him the information Onida had shared.

"Do I want to know how bad of an injury it was that it took that much to heal her?"

"Onida said it was bad. From a doctor's perspective, she said it was almost amputated."

Ronnie cringed. "Fuck. It makes me want to know what that demon used on her that she didn't feel that pain."

"I had the same thought. I was also surprised that Jax didn't freak out. He doesn't do well with injuries like that."

"No, he doesn't. Has he changed that much in a week?" Ronnie wandered around the room, picking up the garbage and cleaning as he talked.

"Onida said the changes were remarkable. I guess that means he has. To me, he feels the same; his emotions are just stronger and more on an even keel. I feel less of the instability in him that was there before."

"The even keel would be a big enough change for people to notice," Ronnie replied. "Any luck on finding anything out about the Italian relative?"

"The word is spreading that I am looking for him. I'm holding out hope. Don't forget to do the bathroom."

"I won't, jeez. It's not like I peed all over the floor,"

Ronnie shot her a look.

"You're a guy, of course, you peed all over the floor," Winnie said sarcastically.

"I remember Jax leaving the toilet seat up once and not flushing the toilet. He remembered it as you screamed, when your ass fell in," Ronnie laughed. "He was so sure you were going to break up with him for it, he almost ran out of the house."

"Yeah, I remember that. You also laughed so hard you almost peed yourself."

"Almost. I didn't, don't start rumors." Ronnie shook his head as he remembered the stark fear on Jax's face when he realized why Winnie had screamed. "Almost thirty years of memories with him. I hope he has changed and gotten more stable. I can't lose him any more than I can lose her."

"Neither of your stories ends soon. Don't let that be a worry in that pretty head of yours."

They reminisced as Ronnie cleaned the bathroom and changed the laundry around and washed the rugs. She'd be back tomorrow. Even if things were different, they would be together and not in separate states.

Chapter Four

edan rechecked his watch, "Jesus Mags, what are you doing? Come on, the flight is on time, and we need to get going."

"I'm almost ready, five minutes," she called out.

"You said that fifteen minutes ago. We are just going to the airport," Aedan almost tapped his foot and managed to refrain.

She walked out of their bathroom, all dolled up, and Aedan gaped at her. "What? Don't I look good?"

"You look like you are going on a date," Aedan stared in shock at all the hair and makeup.

"I'm happy they are back, and I felt icky. I wanted to look better than I felt," Mags pouted.

"You look hot. You always look hot. You are gorgeous," Aedan piled on the flattery. "Let's go."

Mags narrowed her eyes at him but followed him out of the room. Aedan grinned when Smitty whistled when she walked into the kitchen. "Looking hot, Mags."

"See? That's how you should have reacted," Mags pointed out.

"I told you that you were hot," Aedan argued, grabbing the keys. "Move that fine ass of yours."

She grabbed an apple and her purse, "Better. Lead on."

"I told Jax we would meet them in baggage claim since she had to check a suitcase. I guess her mother sent her back with a suitcase full of cookies," Aedan said as they exited the highway.

"Cookies are a good way to add some calories," Mags smiled.

They found a spot and rushed into baggage claim, hoping they weren't already there waiting. He didn't spot them yet and found where their baggage was supposed to come out. He flipped around as he heard Mags squeal, and his breath caught in his throat.

There she was, the woman who had changed all their lives. Mags practically leaped on her and was planting kisses all over her face. Jax smiled from beside her as Mags turned her attention to him. Airiella stepped into his arms while Jax was swinging Mags around in a big hug.

"I missed you," she murmured into his ear.

"I missed you too. I'm so glad you are back," Aedan squeezed her tight. "Jax looks pretty amazing. You've brought my brother back from the brink," he felt tears stinging his eyes.

He pulled back, and his eyes roamed over her face. "You still look tired. The grief, I imagine, will be there a while." He carefully pulled her arm to check her wrist. "Feeling okay?"

Airiella gave him a soft kiss. "Stop worrying. I'm fine."

Aedan chuckled as Mags pulled Airiella away from him. "If he gets a kiss, I get one too," Mags planted a big kiss on Airiella's lips.

"I'm going to grab the suitcase," Jax told Aedan. "Here, take these, so the willful one there doesn't try to do what she isn't supposed to."

Aedan smothered a laugh at the look on Airiella's face and took the bags from Jax. "Flight okay?"

"Yeah. Taklishim upgraded us to first class. No screaming kids or thumping on the back of my seat, so I didn't have to strike anyone with lightning. I'd say it was a good flight," Airiella gave a crooked smile.

"We are drawing attention," Jax warned, walking up fast. "Let's go." Jax put his arm around Mags, leaving Aedan with Airiella.

She grabbed his hand. "Thanks for coming to get us."

"Did you think Mags was going to let you take a cab back? She flat out told Ronnie and Smitty they had to stay home because they were going to hog your time once you were back. All that feisty in her has quadrupled with these added hormones."

Airiella laughed, and it was music to his ears. He hadn't realized quite how much her absence had affected him. "As much as I miss being near my family, I missed you guys just as much. It feels so good to be back with you." She leaned her head on his shoulder as they walked back to the car.

"Mags made Ronnie take a bath with your bath salts," Aedan told her.

"Why did she do that?" she asked with a small laugh.

"I think to be evil. We were all pushed to the limit and at breaking points. Ronnie ran so fast, and so far that he cramped himself up. He needed a bath to try and relax the muscles. And because he had been stupid, she added your salts to it. Her excuse was the smell would soothe him. Really, though, I think she just wanted him to smell like a girl."

Airiella laughed again. "Damn, I missed you guys."

"Ditto."

Smitty felt like a kid on Christmas Eve waiting for Santa to show up, he looked out the window so much. Ronnie finally pushed him outside, and they sat on the front porch. His body started humming, and he knew she was close. Ronnie had the same reaction.

They both stood, their eyes glued to the drive. Smitty held himself still as their car came into sight, holding back from bolting to them. Jax was out first, and Smitty saw the differences in him right away with the way he carried himself, and the natural smile on his face.

Then he held his breath as she came around the car and broke into a run. She launched herself at him as she had done to Ronnie at the funeral. He caught her mid-air and swung her around in a big circle as she smothered him in kisses.

"Baby girl," he croaked out. "I've never been so happy to see anyone as much as I am right now."

"Can I stay with you tonight?" she whispered in his ear.

"Fuck yes," he groaned and reluctantly let her go.

Smitty didn't feel one ounce of jealousy as Ronnie snatched her up the minute he let her go. She clung to him as he kissed her passionately. She wanted to stay with him tonight. He couldn't stop the grin that lit his face.

"Smitty, man, it's good to see you," Jax embraced him.

"Longest week ever," Smitty clapped him on the back. "You almost look that guy I used to know twelve years ago."

"Almost. The change in me feels fantastic." Jax dropped his voice after checking to make sure Airiella's attention was on Ronnie. "I have a few things I need to talk to you about."

Smitty nodded slowly. Jax made it apparent he didn't want Airiella to know about it, Smitty didn't know if this was bad or good. He grabbed the suitcase from Jax. "Come on, welcome back."

They went in, leaving an emotional Ronnie outside with Airiella. "I think that was the longest any of us has been separated in a very long time," Jax dropped on the couch.

"No joke. It didn't feel right. Shit got tense, bro," Smitty admitted. "By the way, Father Roarke will be here in a bit."

Mags sat next to Jax. "I have a lot of nagging you to make up for; I hope you are prepared."

Smitty felt another grin light him up at the sound of Jax's laugh. It was light, none of the darkness coloring it like they had gotten used to hearing. As cheesy as Smitty thought it sounded in his head, he had to admit that hope was being restored with the two of them back now.

R onnie set his angel back down on the ground. "Did I succeed in kissing you like I was missing you, angel?" Ronnie asked in a rough voice as she wiped the tears from his face. He'd felt the dam inside him break once she was in his arms.

"Definitely," she smiled.

"Let's not experiment with distance again," Ronnie advised. "It fucking sucked."

He sucked his breath in as she slid her hands up under his shirt. "Major suck factor."

"Jax looks like a new person," Ronnie kissed her again.

"Jax has made some huge steps," she mumbled as she buried her face in his neck. "I hope you aren't offended, but I asked Smitty if I could stay with him tonight."

"Nope, not at all. I'm happy to have you close and not two states away," Ronnie told her honestly.

"The color of your soul is beautiful," she whispered. "Sorry for being clingy; I don't want to let you go yet though."

"Do you hear me complaining?"

"No. Jax really missed you and couldn't wait to see you again. And I'm here hogging all your attention," she buried her face in his neck for a moment.

"He'll be fine waiting a few more minutes. I missed him too. It felt so wrong to be so far away from you both. I ended up sleeping in your room the entire time." He breathed in her scent and sighed in happiness.

"Do you hear me complaining?" she fired back at him with a smile. She used her sleeve and dried the rest of the tears from his cheeks. "Better?"

"Better. Let's go in," Ronnie shot a glance at her wrist as he gently took her hand. "Still hurt?"

"A little, not bad." Her voice was a little off when she said it.

"I heard you had Taklishim all bent out of shape," Ronnie told her as they entered the house.

"Let me tell you, that man is scary as hell when he's pissed and in his warrior mode. Holy shit, I would not want to cross him."

"Was that after you doped him up with your energy?" Ronnie asked as they came into the room where the rest were sitting.

"Yes," Jax cut in, "it was. She's right. Dude is one scary mother fucker."

Ronnie walked over to Jax, who stood and folded him in a hug. He felt the stab of tears threatening again and managed to hold them back. "I'm so glad you're back."

"If you two are going to kiss, let me get my phone ready first," Mags smirked.

Jax flipped her off as he sat back down. "I'll just hide all the cookies Ells has in her suitcase and not share with you," Jax shot her a look.

"Ells?" Ronnie looked over at Airiella. "Isn't that what your friend Chrissie called you?"

"Yes. My family calls me that. My grandparents call me, Ella." She came over and sat on his lap. "I don't care what people call me."

"It suits you. You'll always be an angel to me," he held her tightly as they all caught up and enjoyed the closeness of being together again.

Chapter Five

Mags finished setting the table and got dinner placed out and ready to go. She thought she did an excellent job. Everyone's spirits had improved now that Jax and Airy were back, and they felt like a family again. She went to the bottom of the stairs and yelled, "Dinner!"

Aedan was the first down to see if she needed help getting it all set out. She'd already done it all. Ronnie and Smitty were down next, and they all stood there waiting until a teary Airiella was led down the stairs by a doting Jax.

They weren't used to seeing Jax like this, and they were all a little stunned until it hit Ronnie that she had been crying, and that got him in motion. "What's wrong, angel?" Mags heard him ask.

She just shook her head in response and looked at

the table Mags had set. "It looks beautiful, Mags. Thank you for cooking dinner."

Mags came around the side of the table, "You sit here by me, sweets," Mags told Airy. Whispering in her ear, "You okay, love?"

"Yeah. I was talking to my nanie. The loss hurts, Mags," she whispered back.

Father Roarke walked in then, "Ah, lass, you are home now. It's mighty good to see you." He stepped over and wrapped Airiella up in a hug.

"Hi, Father. I'm glad you are joining us." Airiella sat where Mags told her to. Father Roarke on her other side, to the unhappiness of Jax, Ronnie, and Smitty, who were acting like they were in a timeout corner.

Airiella seemed a little off-kilter, and Mags's heart went out to her. "Dish up, guys! It's a celebration dinner to welcome Airiella and Jax back. I wanted to have a full-on dinner like her family did, while Aedan and I were lucky enough to be there and spend time with her wonderful family." Mags looked down at Airiella, "In honor of your grandpa."

Airiella teared up, "Thank you, Mags."

She didn't take a whole lot of food, and Jax had told Mags she needed to eat to regain some of her energy back. "You aren't eating very much," Mags commented.

"Not because it's not good, it's delicious Mags. You did a great job," Airiella was quick to reassure her.

"Then, why not? I know you need to restore your energy." Mags pushed her plate closer to her.

"I know. I'm just adjusting again, I think. My heart feels heavy, yet at the same time happy to be back with you all."

"Grief takes time, sweets." Mags noticed that all three of the men across the table had their eyes glued to Airiella. "Your guardians over there are watching, at least pretend to eat a little more. I'll do my best to distract them for a minute."

Airiella smiled, "I know they are. Good luck with that."

Mags stood up. "Aedan and I have a little announcement to make," Mags took Aedan's hand and waited until everyone was looking at her and not Airiella. "At my doctor's appointment yesterday, we learned something new about this little bundle of joy." Mags rubbed her hands over her belly.

Airiella narrowed her eyes at Mags and gasped, covering her mouth. "I think Airiella just figured it out." Mags looked over at Jax, "You and your little friends next to you are going to be some busy uncles. It's triplets, not twins."

Mags giggled with glee at the look on the three faces staring back at her. Jax's mouth was hanging open, "Three babies?"

Aedan laughed, "I repeated that statement more than once. Glad someone else is where I was."

"Holy shit, Mags!" Smitty came around the table to hug her. "That's incredible!"

Aedan squeezed her hand and helped Mags sit back down. "Also, I wanted to let you know we've chosen the names."

"Please don't let it be a color," Jax joked, but Mags saw the love shining in his face.

"The girl baby, we are naming Angel Gwendolyn," Aedan said, looking at Airiella first. Mags saw the tears fall.

Aedan looked over at Jax, who had his own watery smile on his face. "One of the boys will be Jackson Giuseppe," he said, looking at Jax, who upon hearing his name dissolved into tears, and next to Mags, Airiella gasped.

"You are naming him after my grandpa?" she whispered, her voice hoarse.

Mags held her hand, and Aedan spoke. "He was an amazing man. Both Mags and I thought naming him after his uncle and your grandpa would give him a great chance to be amazing in his own right."

Mags saw Ronnie put a hand on Jax's quaking shoulders. "The other boy we decided to name Ronan Arthur," Aedan said quietly, and Mags saw both Smitty and Ronnie look up in wonder.

"Ronan?" Airiella whispered, looking at Ronnie. "Your name is Ronan?"

He smiled at her and nodded. "Did you think it was Ronald?"

"I did. Ronan is a much better fit for you." Her eyes held a small sparkle in them.

Ronnie was coming around the table and scooped up Mags. "Thank you for that."

Likewise, Smitty was coming around the other side to hug Aedan. "It's an honor."

Mags sat back down, "We couldn't think of a better way to show you all how much our family means to us. These three babies will have the names of the best people that I know." Mags leaned over to say into Airiella's ear, "See? I told you I would distract them. Now eat a little more, please."

Airiella smiled and kissed Mags's cheek. "Thank you."

iren, I'm worried about you, I heard Jax say in my head.

I'm okay. I think everything is catching up with me. Everything feels different now.

I'll miss you tonight. Even the sound of his voice in my head was sexy.

I already miss you. I'm where I should be, and you are only thirty feet away. I love you, Zeus.

I love you too, baby. Shut down the link between us, he needs your full attention.

Are you sure? I liked feeling connected to Jax when I wasn't around him.

That he needs your full attention? I'm positive. If you need me, open it back up.

Will you spend some time with Ronnie? I think he needs you.

I'm already with him; he sent me.

Why am I so scared to not have you in my head?

I don't know, siren. I just know the team feels fractured, and all the team needs some time with you. Smitty and Ronnie are the worst of the bunch. For tonight, I've got Ronnie. We'll switch tomorrow night.

I had no idea what was wrong with me. I finished my shower and threw on one of Ronnie's t-shirts I had stolen from his drawer. His scent wrapped around me made me miss Jax more, which didn't help matters any.

Baby, you've got to shut down the connection, or I'm going to be unable to stop myself from charging in there and carrying you off. It's our first night apart in a week; we'll both be fine. We'll see each other in the morning. Let's heal our family up, love.

I know you're right. Can I have a kiss from you though? I pleaded.

I've been standing outside your door for the last minute, waiting for you to open it.

I flung the door open, and there he was, a sexy smile on his face. "Jax," my voice came out deep and throaty.

"Siren, don't use that tone," he warned and dipped his head to give me one of those kisses that made me forget everything. At some point in the past week, Jax had taken over my world. It hadn't changed the way I felt for the others; that hadn't diminished at all. He just became that much more.

"You're killing me with these thoughts," he whispered into my mouth.

"I'm sorry," I tried to stop them.

"Don't be sorry. It means more to me than I could say, to know how much I mean to you. I also know that these two are falling apart. As much as I want to be greedy and not share you, it would be bad for all of us." He patted me on the ass. "Go say goodnight to Ronnie."

He gave me a little push towards Ronnie's room, and I knocked lightly before entering. "Ronnie?"

"Angel. Everything okay?" he met me halfway across his room.

"Yes, I just wanted to say goodnight to you," I murmured as he raked his gaze over me.

"Did you steal a shirt?" he teased.

"Maybe," I buried my face in his chest. "God, I have no idea what is going on with me. I'm all over the place."

Ronnie kissed the top of my head. "As much as I need you, Smitty needs you more, angel. And I really do want to spend some time with Jax. A kiss goodnight would be spectacular, though," he tipped my chin up.

"Yes, please," I begged.

He granted me my desire and lit me on fire with his lips. "You look good in my shirt." He too patted me on the ass and pushed me towards Smitty's room. "Go. If you don't go now, you won't leave, and I won't let you."

"Love you, Heracles."

"Tomorrow night, Eros will be taking over," he promised with a naughty smile.

I shut down the connections with everyone, but Smitty, and softly opened his door and slipped in his room. He was stretched out on his bed wearing only boxer briefs, his soul shining bright with the colors that made him so magnificent. Heat pooled in my belly; he was a sight to behold.

"Baby girl, get your ass over here, please," his gravelly tone licked at the flames inside me.

I crossed the room and practically jumped into his arms. It felt right, as I sighed at the feel of this sexy man. He rolled and settled on top of me, the hard planes of his body molding to my soft ones.

"There were nights my brain tried to convince me you were nothing but a dream, but my body remembers every curve of yours," he kissed me, "the taste of you," he kissed me again slower, and more profoundly. "The smell of you," he pressed his lips to my neck and breathed me in.

I dragged my nails lightly down his back, his body shivering at my touch. "I missed you, Smitty."

He groaned. "I was sure I was losing my mind, baby girl. How do we do this blood thing? I want to get that out of the way and claim my little piece of you."

"We have to be vampires for a moment," I said, my face a blank mask of seriousness.

"I have to bite your neck?" Smitty pulled back and looked shocked.

I giggled. "No. When Jax and I did it, my lip was bleeding because I had bitten it. He bit his and made his bleed. I used my finger for my cousin's baby and to help Onida."

"Did your lip hurt?" his eyes were smoky looking.

"Um, no, I was rather preoccupied with other things," I tried not to blush.

"That I can do," he growled, reaching between us to pull off Ronnie's shirt. He drew my knees up on either side of his hips and skimmed his fingers over my calves. "These curves are etched in my memory, baby girl."

"You still have clothes on," I reminded him breathlessly as he ground himself against me.

"I know, otherwise this would be over way too soon." He licked and nipped his way down my body. "If I'm too rough, tell me."

"Be rough," I gasped as he licked into me, my body arching into him.

He wasn't rough, but he was aggressive and played me masterfully. He was hitting the notes that had me chomping right down on my lip to keep from screaming out as he licked me into more than one orgasm. I wanted him to the point of begging him and trying to pull him up me.

He finally stood and started to take off his underwear, the second he got them past that glorious cock I batted his hands away and sucked the head into my mouth, teasing moisture out of the tip. "Shit, you made me bite my tongue," he swore.

"Perfect," I pulled him down into a kiss, and he lay over me and slid right in, the room bathed in blue light as our blood mingled.

"Fuck me, baby girl, is that you in my head?" Smitty breathed into me.

"I am fucking you, and yes, it better be me in there," I panted, pulling him down into me harder.

He chuckled and rolled us over to let me take control. I shifted a little, leaning back to take him in deeper. "I won't last long like this," he warned me.

"Touch me," I pulled his hand to my body. His fingers made my body jerk, both of us groaning.

I went slow, grinding my hips into him, and the closer he brought me to the edge, the harder I rode, trying to time it, so he came with me. Soon I was slamming my hips down on to him as his relentless fingers drew another shattering orgasm out me. He followed me over the edge and pulled me down into a kiss that left us both trembling as lightning struck somewhere outside.

Once our breathing slowed, "Was the lightning you?"

I smiled. "Yeah, that happened when Jax and I completed the blood thing too."

"I have you inside me now?" he looked ridiculously happy at that.

"You did before, too," I said, kissing him softly.

"You had me from the start," his face suddenly serious.

I know that; I tested out the connection.

"Oh my God," Smitty's eyes went wide. "Can I do that too?"

"Try," I splayed my fingers out over his chest.

I love you; he sent me.

I love you, too.

"How far does that work?" he put his hand over mine.

"I was able to talk to Ronnie that way when I was home. It took a little bit of effort, but it was okay. You will probably be able to hear my thoughts now too. That's a two-way street, though. If I am paying attention, I'll be able to hear yours too."

"If you are paying attention?" Smitty asked, smiling.

"I try not to listen. It gets distracting, like seeing souls. It's a lot to take in, and when Jax and I were back at home, there were times I wasn't sure who was thinking what. I had to figure out how to shut down that connection, so only my thoughts were in my head, which is plenty enough."

"Seeing souls is a distraction?" Smitty stood up to grab a washcloth to clean us up.

As he wiped me down, my thoughts scattered at the contact, and he started laughing and crawled back in bed. "Okay, I can see how the thought thing is distracting. You'll need to teach me how to close that down, so I still have some secrets from you."

"Sorry. Jax told me I broadcast loudly," I blushed.

"Yeah, those were pretty loud, but it also made me feel happy to know how I affect you. Tell me about seeing souls," he prodded, pulling me into his side.

I shifted to lay my head on his belly, facing him so he could see my face. "It is just as distracting. I see all these colors that I instinctively know what they mean. I can see dark spots where something you felt scarred you happened, and while I can't see what it is, I can also tell if it's something that happened to you or something you did. I don't know how to explain it."

"Is it something you can turn off?" he wrapped his fingers around mine.

"I'm learning. It took a little bit. I had to walk away by myself at the beach and try to figure it out. Jax's soul is similar in color to mine. Yours is as well, but I can see more differences. You have a pure soul, there isn't any hate, and your colors are beautiful. There's this spot that is a brilliant purple that tells me how intelligent you are. There's red around your heart, well, all the colors really, and while each color has a bad aspect to it, yours are radiating the good."

"My soul is pure?" Smitty's voice was quiet.

"Yes, it shines bright and warm," I smiled easily, the rhythm of his breathing a soothing thing.

"I think Ronnie and I can feel and see demons," Smitty said. "Is this something we get from you?"

"Maybe? I don't know. When Jax and I connected, I felt the group connection change. We all got stronger. Now that we are together, it will be something that we learn about as we go." I wish I had all the answers for him, and now that I was here talking with him and touching him, I realized exactly how much I had needed this.

"It's kind of crazy, how okay I feel right now compared to how I was feeling earlier," Smitty pulled me back to him.

"You can feel how much I need you, right?" I asked.

"I can. It's rock-solid, and I admit, I love it. I also have to say that it made me feel stronger about Jillian, and somehow that makes my head tell me I am betraying one of you."

I traced his lips with my finger. "You aren't

betraying either of us. Jillian is your forever."

Smitty stilled beneath my touch. "You can see that?"

"I can now. I couldn't, before. It doesn't bother me, Smitty. I'm happy seeing that you have her."

"I don't know that I want to give you up," Smitty put a hand possessively on my hip.

"Why do you think you would have to? That bond is permanent. Only death breaks it."

"What if she wants us to be monogamous?" Smitty worried.

"I don't need sex with you to feel the bond. It's just a bonus. I could just as easily curl up next to you on a chair and feel the same closeness as I do now. Or simply hold your hand, or hug you."

His chest shuddered. "Really?"

"Yes, really. Did you think that sex was the only way?"

"I didn't know. I'd been wrestling with giving one of you up because I didn't think I could keep going with both of you," Smitty admitted.

"Oh, Smitty, why didn't you tell me?"

"I don't want to give you up. This little bit of you that I have is precious. I admit the sex is pretty phenomenal too, and sometimes I need it," Smitty stroked my cheek.

"I had a hard time tonight, myself. I desperately wanted to be with Jax, and I also wanted to be with Ronnie, and you. It's hard sometimes. Whatever you decide is fine with me. Whichever way we go, it doesn't change this link. I'm always going to need you, Smitty."

"It took being away from you for me to see that I needed you. After this, seeing your thoughts and feelings on a deeper level gives me the security my brain didn't have. For now, we go on as we have been. I promise to talk to you if things need to change."

He pulled the covers up over me. "You'll always be my first," I kissed his chest, my eyes heavy.

"Sleep, baby girl. I've got you tonight," Smitty said softly, and I let my eyes close as he pulled me up to his chest, his arms wrapped around me.

Chapter Six

Ronnie knew things were changing. After his talk with Jax last night, he now knew how much. It was a shock to him at first, but Ronnie was on board all the way. He also understood why he would be using Aedan as his go-to person for things involved, and he hoped that Airiella didn't see in his head to these things that Jax wanted to be kept private from her.

He'd also been more than impressed at the changes in Jax. One week had altered him entirely, and Ronnie couldn't be happier about it. They still had an uphill battle ahead of them with the demons and the remaining dark energy in Jax. He had no illusions about that. He knew it would be less traumatic now.

Ronnie put them through a good training session in the morning, keeping Airiella to lower body and foot movements, so she didn't use her wrist. She'd, of course, argued with him about it, her temper flaring, and he proved he could be just as stubborn as she could, to the amusement of the rest of them.

His heart soared a little as he watched Mags and her pregnant belly; she was going to name a baby after him and Smitty. He'd been ecstatic at the news. He was slowly starting to feel the team mend from the separation, his angel working her magic on all of them.

He didn't miss the way Airiella stayed close to Jax during training, either. Now that they were settling down in the TV room to go over the Franklin information they had gathered, Ronnie felt a little off-center. She sat next to him, with Jax on the other side of her.

"Most of this will be new information for you two," Ronnie said, leaning forward to grab the folder he'd put on the table.

"Ronnie and I were able to come up with two viable names from the mine fire that could be related to you, baby girl," Smitty added, sitting on the floor in front of them.

"After we narrowed it down to those two names, we both feel it's the one with the last name Rosati," Ronnie placed a printed photograph of the man on her lap.

"The name is very similar to my grandpa's," she admitted. "Spelled differently."

"Ronnie had some good insight on that," Smitty looked up from his papers.

"When people immigrated over from Europe, they had to check in with officials on Ellis Island. English officials at that and language barriers were a common thing. Phonetically the name Rosati to an English person could be written as Rosetti. It's a well-known fact a lot of names became shortened because they couldn't pronounce them."

Airiella nodded, "I agree."

Bolstered, Ronnie continued. "Marco Rosati left his family in Italy when he came here. Given that your great grandparents immigrated over in the early 1900's it stands to reason that your great-grandpa might have been the brother of Marco."

She looked confused for a moment. "We only said, Grandpa Rosetti. Wasn't his name Gabriele?"

"Yes," Smitty pulled out the family tree Ronnie had asked him to print out. He handed it to Airiella and she traced the name of her grandpa. Ronnie felt her grief, raw and exposed. A living, breathing thing inside her.

He cleared his throat, trying to choke back the emotions that wanted to pull him down. "From what we have been able to find so far, it seems Marco came over here as a punishment for something. We don't know what yet, but Father Roarke was able to find a couple of documents he had translated through some contacts of the church. Marco was seen as somewhat of an outcast back in their home town. From what he could decipher, Marco may have been an empath."

Airiella gave him a startled look. "Really?"

"Based on the descriptions in a couple of documents, the local priest had written about a possible demon possession because Marco knew when people were lying. They thought that was the work of the devil," Smitty bluntly said, ripping off the band-aid.

"I'm surprised they didn't accuse him of witchcraft then," she said, her expression sad.

"One of the letters did," Ronnie went on. "There were only two letters about it, and saying that he was to be shipped over here to work to keep his family safe. There was also mention that the girl he intended to marry was pregnant out of wedlock. We aren't sure if that is what got him in trouble or not. Father Roarke said that would have been a big issue back then, and especially in that area."

"I can understand that. I don't know how it relates to me, though, or how the council thinks they can use it against me to hurt you guys or me."

"If they hurt you, they hurt us," Jax broke in.

"Exactly. If the council pisses us off enough by hurting you, the hope is we will step out of line. More specifically, I believe they are trying to get Jax to step out of line, and then they can oust him," Ronnie filled in.

"Degataga uncovered enough to know it's the council behind the Franklin site. Also, that Asher will be joining us on that location," Smitty leaned back on his elbows.

"Asher? The medium guy, right?" Airiella looked thoughtful.

"Yeah. Asher is not a fan of yours," Ronnie said gently.

"I'd think it was Dr. Stone who was the bigger threat," Airiella tapped her fingers.

"He is. We think that Dr. Stone is manipulating Asher," Aedan spoke up.

Ronnie saw Jax playing with the ends of Airiella's hair and her eyes went out of focus for a moment. He smothered a smile. "When we put all this together as a whole, we can make assumptions about the direction they are taking this. With Asher being involved, it's logical to believe that he is going to try to talk to your ancestor and paint them as a witch or something equally as bad to discredit you. Not that being a witch is bad, we just know how it will play out on TV with viewers believing they were wrong about the hero that saved us."

"Wouldn't the easier course of action be, to just fire me?" Airiella pointedly asked.

"Stone is vindictive, he'd want to humiliate you first," Jax spoke softly, his tone hinting at anger.

"Whatever Marco Rosati did or didn't do doesn't have a lot of bearing on me. That was over a hundred years ago. How would that embarrass or humiliate me? I'm not seeing a connection. I mean, I see the connection because I am related to the guy, just not how it could hurt me."

"We are still working on it. Onida is trying to find Marco on the other side. She's hoping she can get more information from him that we could work with to figure out the puzzle. Maybe you could ask your family, see if any old pictures or stories are lying around in a forgotten box somewhere," Ronnie said carefully.

He felt the flare of grief and knew by the rigid postures of Jax and Smitty they did too. Jax buried his hand in her hair and stroked her scalp. "I can ask my nanie or my dad to look." She looked at Ronnie, the loss fresh in her eyes. "My grandpa was the last of his family. Any knowledge he might have had died with him." By the end of her sentence, her voice was hoarse.

She leaned back against Jax, and Ronnie was once again astounded by the changes in him. The rest of the group closed in around her, offering comfort through their touch. "Maybe this is their angle to hurt her," Mags suggested. "Stone is a psychiatrist, right? What if he just wants to keep this loss fresh in her mind to keep the wound bleeding?"

"Fuck, that would be cruel," Smitty breathed out.

"Mags might be on to something with that," Aedan said carefully. "What better way to hurt an empath than through their emotions. I'll talk to Degataga about it."

Airiella pulled away from them, "I'm going to go to my room for a little bit. I'll see you in a couple of hours."

Ronnie felt his heart lurch at the slumped set of her shoulders. He looked over at Jax questioningly. "She told me to stay here for a few minutes. She needed to be alone."

"Nope. Not happening," Mags stood. "Give me a least an hour with her before one of you bombard her."

They got back to work, Ronnie and Smitty researching more, not only on Franklin and Marco Rosati but also on their upcoming locations. Jax went over the research for the forthcoming sites making his notes. Aedan talked to Degataga, then Taklishim, filling them both in.

After a couple of hours, Jax left to check on the girls, and Mags came back down. "She's okay. Hurting, of course, it's still fresh for her. She's curled up with Jax right now, might be the cutest thing I've ever seen, the way he's taking care of her. Anyway, I'm hungry, any requests for dinner? I'll go grab something."

"She loves Mexican food, how about that?" Smitty offered up.

"Sounds good to me," Ronnie added in.

"I'll go with you, honey," Aedan said, taking Mags' arm.

Ronnie knew there was nothing cute about the way Jax felt for their angel. His emotions ran intense and deep, and the connection between the two of them ran even farther. He looked over at Smitty, "Do you feel better after last night?"

"I do, way less crazy now and more solid. Airiella

has moments of absolute passion; then, I can feel the grief, especially when she slept. She would dream of her grandpa and cry in her sleep, then she would settle down, and it was her usual bottomless well of love," Smitty described.

"Does it amaze you the same way it does me, that Jax can deal with that grief?"

"Yep. Thought for sure that would bring that shit right up out of Jax. Especially after the way he was when Winnie died."

"You aren't concerned about it at all?" Ronnie didn't want to doubt his friend, but it was a concern at the front of his mind.

"I was before last night. Not now. I see the changes in him; he's overcome quite a bit. If you are still worried, go check on them," Smitty told him.

Ronnie did just that. He found Jax propped up, one leg off the bed, the other curled around and under her, their angel resting against him. Mags was right; it was sweet. He'd never even seen Jax this way with Winnie.

Jax smiled at him and nodded to the chair. Ronnie sat in the chair, and with one smooth motion, Jax scooped her up and set her down on Ronnie's lap. "She needs you," he whispered in Ronnie's ear.

It was a whole new Jax. Ronnie's arms automatically wound around her as he mouthed "Thank you" to Jax.

She snaked her arms around Ronnie's neck, "Don't let go."

"Not a chance in hell of that, angel."

He sat with her like that until he heard Mags call them down for dinner. "She went and got Mexican food, are you hungry?"

She nodded. "Sorry about that. I find I have moments of overwhelming sadness."

He stood, setting her gently on her feet. "Not something you need to apologize for."

He led her downstairs and had a quiet dinner, she didn't eat a lot, but she did eat more than she had the night before. She also made sure she was touching him the entire time, even during her long goodnight to Jax.

"Any special requests, sweetheart?" Ronnie asked her as they climbed the stairs.

"Yes. Can we go swim under the stars?"

Ronnie's heartbeat began a staccato rhythm. "You bet. Go change; I'll put my trunks on and grab us some towels."

His blood was pounding through his veins at breakneck speed at the thought of her in the pool. He was already hard and trying to control it because it might not be what she wanted or needed right now.

It's exactly what I need, he heard in his head.

He stopped trying to control it. He was ready and met Airiella in the hall in under a minute flat. She was wearing his t-shirt again, and he grinned like an idiot. "It looks way better on you than it does on me," he told her.

He jumped in the pool and held his hands out for her to jump in. She shook her head no and sat on the edge, her eyes lit with a fire he'd only seen in them when she was with him.

The lights in the pool flickered on, and he knew Jax was behind it. She started to pull off his shirt, and that's when he realized she had nothing on underneath it. He groaned and pulled off his trunks as quickly as possible, tossing them up and out of the pool.

"Lay back," he instructed her as he pulled her closer to the edge.

She did as he asked, and she was at the perfect level for him to taste, his very own dessert. He licked up her slowly, a groan slipping through her lips. "Wait, angel, is anyone in your head right now?"

"No, it's just us. You and me, Eros."

Ronnie moaned this time. She undid him with a few words. He took his time with his tongue, alternating between licks, sucking, and flicking, wringing multiple orgasms out of her until Airiella was mewling under his ministrations. She was begging for him.

"Ronan, please," she cried, "I need you in me."

Ronnie growled in pleasure, hearing his full name on her lips. "Say my name, angel."

"Ronan." She sat up and slipped down into the pool. "Ronan, I love you."

He crushed his lips against hers with a bruising force, then tasting blood, he backed off and deepened the kiss, moaning when her hands started stroking him and playing with his balls. He pulled her hand away and whispered, "Wrap your legs around me."

She did and gasped as he slid in slowly; the buoyancy of the water allowing her to set the pace. She went slow, clenching around his cock rapidly as she sucked on his neck and over to his shoulder. Ronnie was going crazy with each squeeze.

He held her hips and lifted her off him and drove back in hard over and over, her own legs helping. She bit his shoulder when she cried out at the start of her orgasm, and Ronnie pumped fast, his own crashing around them as multiple lightning flashes struck down around them.

It wasn't the pool lights that were making them glow blue; their blood mingling was cementing that bond in place. He kissed her softly, her body still holding his inside her, and he carried her up the pool steps and sat them both down on one of the chairs. He wrapped towels around them, moving her off him so they could both lay back and watch the stars.

"Was that the blood bond thing?" he asked her gently.

"Yeah, sorry. I didn't realize I bit you that hard."

"Let's call it a crime of passion," he joked. "It didn't hurt me, angel."

"You can see my thoughts now," she warned him. "It's dangerous up there."

"Can you block me? Can you see mine?" Ronnie asked quickly.

"Yes, to both. I won't intrude. I'll also teach you all how to block the noise, or close the connection down."

Ronnie put his chin on her shoulder. "Why would we want to shut it down?"

"Because maybe some thoughts are private, for you only. I've done it a few times to Jax when I needed to sort through it all. Or like now, when I just want it to be us. And it gets overwhelming hearing multiple people in your head."

"I won't hear them, will I?" Ronnie worried.

"I think it's just me, you will hear. You can try talking to the others that way and see if it works."

"Maybe later. Right now, I just need to be with you," he kissed her neck. "I've never liked the way my name sounded until I heard it from your lips."

"I love the name, Ronan. It's perfect for you," she

murmured.

"Do you have any idea how much I have missed feeling you against me?" He hugged her tight.

"I do. I missed it just as much. If Jax hadn't been with me, I would have lost my mind without you."

"Part of me wants to ask if he has replaced me now, but the other part of me says he hasn't after what just happened between us. Plus, I can see right into your head right now and I know I'm not replaced. I will say that the changes in him are fantastic. He's a different person."

She shifted and moved sideways, hanging her legs off the side of the chair. "I can't replace you. Feel those feelings inside me? Those are for you."

"I know, angel. It's humbling."

Chapter Seven

I'd made up for the lost time and spent the nights with each of my new family; things were starting to feel normal again. The draw to be with Jax every second was overpowering, and I gravitated to him every time he was around.

Everyone noticed it, and I tried to pay attention to see if jealousy was rearing up. So far, it hadn't. We were due to leave tomorrow for the next location, Father Roarke now coming with us. It was somewhat of a security net to have him there. I also felt like I was putting the priest in danger.

I'd taught my bonded guys how to block their thoughts from me or shut down the connection. None of them had, and I'd left myself open while around the house so they could get used to it. I had been practicing turning off the soul sight, which is what I now called it because that was still a lot to take in. I'd been avoiding going out in public because of it.

Jax and I were in a training session with Father Roarke catching up on the how-to of fighting the lower level demons. It was more for Jax than for me since I could light them up with lightning, but the information was helpful.

I'd also been practicing with my abilities using the guys as the villains. I was mostly practicing using the elements and calling up that ring of blue fire that had given a shield of protection from the high-level demons.

Mags, in particular, loved it when I created little tornado storms around them, they couldn't get through. She'd even had me call rain down on Aedan while he was trapped because he'd made her mad. Jax and Ronnie had fallen over laughing when I dropped it all and he came out looking drowned.

The temptation was calling to make it rain on Father Roarke so that I could go sit down for five minutes; Jax snorted next to me. *I'm tired!* I sent him.

I know you are. Sorry for keeping you awake so late.

I'm not. It's worth it; I'd do it all over again if I had to. Spending time with Jax was one of my favorite things to do. When we added Ronnie, it was a close second.

"Father Roarke, we need a five-minute break, please," Jax requested. I could have kissed him.

The priest nodded to us, and Jax came to check on my wrist. It was sore and a little swollen. Our training session with Ronnie in the morning was the first time I had been allowed to use it a little. Even with it wrapped and supported, it had still hurt.

I noticed something odd out of the corner of my eye.

The demon raven appeared in a tree sitting beyond the fence of the backyard. My alarms hadn't triggered; he wasn't a danger to us. It was still unsettling to see him there. "Jax," I whispered so Father Roarke couldn't hear, "look. That raven," I nodded in the direction it sat.

"The one that said he saved you?" Jax tensed up.

"Yeah, not the demon that tried to kill you guys."

"Why do you think he's here?" Jax put a protective arm around me.

"I don't know. He's not here to hurt us; I can tell that much."

"I can hear you, light one," the raven called out. Father Roarke spun, ready to battle at the deep reverberating voice.

"Demon," the priest hissed.

"Easy, Father. He's not here to hurt us, or my spidey sense would have told me." I stood up from the chair, Jax, at my side.

"Are you always in raven form?" I sauntered toward the fence.

"It is one of my chosen forms, though I do use others," his voice boomed.

"I know your name." I didn't mean for it to sound like the challenge it had.

The raven flew down to the ground and transformed into a man right before my eyes. Why was he so damn good looking? Jax went rigid next to me.

"I've seen him before. He was at the hospital, watching you," Jax said, his voice tight with anger.

I looked back at the guy. "Is that true?"

"You think I'm good looking?" he smiled a slow sexy smile.

"I thought you said you didn't read my mind," I remembered him telling me that.

"I'm not, it was in the appreciative look on your face when I took this form."

Really, siren? Jax wasn't amused.

I ignored him for a moment. "Why are you here, Stolas?"

"You *do* know my name. Impressive. I came to warn you, also to check on your injury. I noticed the medicine man healed you."

"You came to check on me? A prince of Hell, checking on me?" Disbelief colored my tone.

"I see you are still in the stage where you don't believe me." He shrugged. "Bael is sending some of his minions after your friends in a couple of days. Be prepared."

"Can you not come on this land?" I crossed my arms and looked at him.

"No. There are protections in place here. Even if I could, I still mean you no harm. I would ask you not to repeat my name. I don't want him to know it is me that is helping you," Stolas requested.

Father Roarke had come up on the other side of Jax, his face a mask of fascination. "Why are you helping her?"

"She's lovely. It would be a shame to see someone as wondrous as her fall to the dark side. Her light is coveted and desired by many."

"You said you wanted to own her," Jax's voice was hard.

"I did. That's when the angel first came to my attention. I told her I wanted her for my own; this is nothing new," Stolas said casually, as if it didn't matter.

"What changed? Why wouldn't you want her now?" Jax challenged.

"I still do. It would be foolish to believe I didn't. As I told her, I want her love. I'm lonely."

I wasn't comfortable with this conversation. "I'm right here. You can both stop talking about me like I'm not."

"Ells, he's still a demon," Jax warned.

"You're right, he is. I do believe he doesn't want to harm me. My alarms would have gone off if he did, but I don't trust him."

"You want to. I can feel hope inside you. It pulls me to you." That slow sexy smile came back.

"You want her light," Father Roarke said on a whisper.

"I did. A small part of me still does; I will admit that. I also know the risk involved for her by being with me. And like I said earlier, I don't want to see her light destroyed. It keeps humanity alive in me," his tone was honest and gentle.

"Is this information you bring going to cost me?" I stepped closer, holding a hand up to Jax to keep him still.

Siren, he warned.

Trust me, Jax. I truly believe he won't hurt me. It doesn't mean that he won't hurt either of you. Stay back.

"No. I don't work that way. I give this to you freely," Stolas nodded formally to me.

"Why?" He was right; I did have hope that someday I would be able to trust him.

"I'm drawn to you." Stolas reached into his pocket and pulled out a piece of paper and handed it to me. "Give this to the medicine man. It was what I used to help with the pain of your injury."

"Is this Latin?" I stared at the paper, confused.

"It is. The medicine man will know what it means."

I slid the paper in my pocket. "Thank you. Taklishim had wondered about that."

Stolas had a look of need on his face. My senses were already open, and I quickly sorted through the tangled emotions around me. It was need and loneliness too. "I do wish to help you," he said quietly this time.

Do you trust me? I asked Jax.

Yes, siren, I do.

I held my hand out to Stolas as I filtered my senses and did something to the energy around me to keep a barrier between him and the men behind me. Pure longing spread across his face as he looked at my outstretched arm.

"Take my hand," I told him gently.

"I can feel you are doing something to the energy around you," he hesitated.

"I won't hurt you. I'm protecting those behind me. You only said you didn't wish to harm me," I reminded Stolas.

"I won't harm them either." He slowly raised his arm and took my hand.

Instantly I felt the void in him that wanted to pull the light from me. I blocked it and instead filled him with love. I took nothing from him because I didn't know what that would do to me. I did what I used to do for Jax when I couldn't pull that darkness from him. I gave him enough love so that he could battle the dark on his own.

Rapture filled the demon's face, transforming it into something more beautiful than it was before. The void in him was significant; I knew I couldn't fill it all the way, I was able to shrink it. I watched his soul go from a muddy brown to a lighter shade.

Siren, your wings are out. You might need to stop, two more feathers dropped.

Stolas himself pulled back with some difficulty. "If I had a soul left to sell, I would sell it to have you. That was a dangerous gift for you to give."

"Love is worth the danger. Love is my strength." I turned and held my hand out to Jax, who took it and stepped up next to me. "Jax loves me enough that he didn't stop me from doing that. He trusted my judgment. I can guarantee you, he didn't like it, and he warned me when I needed to stop. Love will always win. Love isn't something that you can force. I gave that to you freely, just as you gave me that paper and your warning."

"I am worth that risk, then?" Stolas asked in wonder.

"I don't believe you don't have a soul. I do believe it's damaged. No amount that I could give you would change that. I do, however, believe that everyone deserves love, and I have some to give," I tried to clarify. His need called out to the empath in me, and the angel inside me didn't argue. Nor did my raven try to stop me. "I could feel that void in you trying to pull from me; I was also able to stop it. I think the risk for me is my energy is still low."

He nodded at me. "It is." He pointed to the feathers that Father Roarke now held in his hands. "Don't let those fall into the wrong hands."

"What will having my feathers accomplish?" I asked out of curiosity.

"It's a piece of you. A piece of what you are, the feathers carry your essence. The wrong hands can use them to harm you." Stolas was entirely free with the information.

"Bael won't win a battle with me." I leaned against Jax. "Hurting those I love will reinforce my need to destroy him."

"Light one," the demon's tone was soft, "it is in destroying him that you risk falling from grace."

"Maybe, but I was given this power for a reason. Who I share my light and love with is for me to choose. I will never choose to share it with someone who wishes harm on others. I gave that to you freely in the hope that you will remember that there is still good to find here."

Stolas looked at Jax, "You are lucky. The stars spoke of you both; they hadn't decided when you met if it would be true or not."

"Have they decided now?" Jax asked defiantly.

"They have. However, I will not tell you. It's for you to figure out."

"Why do you guys always speak in riddles?" I asked, frustrated.

"I've been around for thousands of years. Some information I will gladly share, other information like prophecy and destiny, it is not for me to divulge." Stolas crossed his arms across his chest.

"Are those that are coming for us going to be hard to kill?" I went back to his warning.

"For you, no. For the rest, it may take a bit of work."

"Will it put my soul in danger to kill them?" I asked, pushing for more.

"That is a better question. It is of my opinion that it will not. The intent is to cause harm. To you, to the others." Stolas sounded sure about that.

"If that is the case, why would destroying Bael make

me fall? He isn't doing this out of love."

"No, obsession, not love. He doesn't wish to harm you himself. That is the tricky part. His intentions are for others to do it to weaken you, so you give in to him."

"Ridiculous. It's still a bad intent," I argued.

"I must go. I will be watching."

In the blink of an eye, he disappeared. In the next breath, he was back. "That was fast."

"You must finish healing to beat him," he said quickly.

"I'm assuming you aren't talking about physically."

"Correct."

I nodded, reaching back for one of the feathers in Father Roarke's hand. I held it out to Stolas. "You want me to trust you, and I'm having a hard time with that. If you show me this feather every time you appear and it's still safe, I'll get closer and closer to that trust you seek."

"Are you sure you want to give me that?" Stolas's hand shook.

"No, but I'm willing to take a leap of faith." I held my hand still, waiting for him to take it. He did so, very slowly and gently.

"I will treasure this always." Blink, and he was gone.

"Siren, was that a smart move?" Jax asked, pulling me into his side.

I shrugged. I had no idea. "We will see. Stolas appears to be an ally. I think we need those. We now know this next location will have a demon attack, and we go in prepared. We also now know that he can't come on this property, and Mags is safe here. I'm willing to hand over a feather for that peace of mind."

Father Roarke remained silent but held the other

feather out to me. I pushed his hand back. "Keep it, Father. It's a piece of me that you are allowed to have."

"You honor me, lass."

Thank you for trusting me, Jax.

I didn't like it; you were right about that. But I do trust you.

As we walked back, I held his hand, "Well, time to call out the team and get them prepared."

"Aye, lass. This training will be for them. I dare say, nothing can prepare them for the real thing."

Chapter Eight

Winne gaped. "Are you sure?" she asked Onida. "Yes, it's him. He's not dark; he has the same light Airiella has. They can't get to him there."

"But you found him?" Winnie paced, chewing on her nails.

"I did. Asher won't be talking to him unless he chooses to come forward. As of yet, I haven't convinced him he needs to. He's afraid of that place, and of the one that started the fire," Onida informed her.

"What can I do?" Winnie wanted to help.

"Nothing right now. I can take you the next time I go to see the spirit. Maybe the two of us can convince him. We can try to ask Airiella's grandfather to come with us."

"I'll ask Ronnie if there are specific questions that we can ask to find out more of the story. They don't have a lot to go on, right now. It's all assumptions." Winnie felt a tremor of excitement. "I'll talk to her grandpa."

"That's a great place to start," Onida touched Winnie's hand softly. "You are a beautiful soul. It would have been a pleasure to know you on the other side."

Winnie blushed at the unexpected compliment from Onida. She'd been a little different since the situation with the demon. She could smell a little Airy on her now too. The angel's blood had done wonders for the usually distant woman.

Winnie went off in search of Ariella's grandpa. She'd been able to figure out his usual spots for hanging out. Winnie hoped today wasn't the day he got creative and branched out. He liked to watch over his wife; usually, that's where she was able to find him.

Sure enough, there he was, in his spot on the chair he used to sit in all the time. "Hello sir, do you remember me?" Winnie spoke softly, not wanting to startle him.

"Ella's ghost friend? Right? Sorry, but I don't remember your name," Giuseppe apologized.

"Winnie. I came to ask you for your help." Winnie shook his hand.

"Help with what?" Giuseppe Rosetti was curious.

"Unraveling the reason some people want to hurt your granddaughter."

Giuseppe leaned forward in the chair, making it move slightly. Winnie saw that Airy's grandma saw the movement. "How could I be of help?"

"I need to find out if you remember anything about an ancestor of yours. He's how they are going to try to hurt her in some way. We just don't know their angle, so we are trying to figure it out. Our friend Onida has found his spirit over here, and we are going to talk to him soon. Would you like to join us?"

"An ancestor of mine?" Giuseppe furrowed his brow. "Which one?"

"Marco Rosati," Winnie said immediately. Maybe he did know something.

"That isn't ringing any bells with me, can you give me more than that?"

"He immigrated over from Italy in the late 1890s to work in a mine. A city that no longer exists called Franklin. We know that he possibly left a pregnant woman behind, that he was accused of witchcraft and thought to be a bad person."

"Kid, all of my ancestors came from Italy. There was more than one bad one from that group. Let me think about this. Find me tomorrow, or whenever your friend is going to go visit him."

"Thank you, sir."

Winnie left thinking about the conversation, hoping she hadn't offended him in some way. She didn't venture into any of the areas where the darker spirits were. She knew they were looking for her. Onida had told her she could be injured still. That wasn't high on Winnie's list of things to do as a ghost.

Aedan froze where he stood. "Jesus! Are you sure, Ronnie?" he spit out.

"Yeah, I can see them. Smitty can feel them. Outside this shop in the crowd, three demons are watching us," Ronnie said as if he was reciting the weather forecast.

Airiella was by Jax in the other room. There were way too many people around for her to use lightning. "Can't you talk to her in your head?"

"Yes, right now hardly seems the time to interrupt her thoughts. Besides, she has me blocked right now so she can watch for threats from inside," Ronnie shrugged.

"We can go out the back," Smitty said. "I don't feel anything back there."

"Well, that demon guy did tell her it would happen, guess he wasn't lying," Aedan mused. "I'd rather there not be a crowd of people to watch anything we do."

"Let's be smart about it then, and go out the back. Let the demons bring the fight to us on our terms. Limited people on the shoot location to see anything that happens," Smitty advised.

"I agree with Smitty. We don't have to walk into them out there," Ronnie crossed his arms, looking back out front. "The other thing to remember is, these are people that the demons are possessing. We don't need to kill them. She just needs to get them out of the bodies."

"I know. But Airiella glowed the last time that happened. Do we really want that to show up on the internet? Look how many people are already snapping pictures of us through the windows," Aedan pointed out.

Ronnie suddenly burst out laughing, both Smitty and Aedan giving him raised eyebrows. "Dude, did you finally lose it?" Smitty asked caustically.

"I'm picturing Aedan running out into a crowd of people swinging his medieval demon sword shouting, die demon scum!" Ronnie bent over laughing.

"Haha, funny." Aedan scowled.

They heard Airiella snort from the other room. "See? Even she's laughing."

Smitty bit his lip to hide the smile. "How about we

go out the back and text Father Roarke the three you see, and he can slide into the crowd with his holy water? No one gets hurt that way. No medieval sword is slinging." He tried, but couldn't hold back the chuckle of laughter at the end.

"You guys are children," Aedan said, pulling out his phone. "Which three, Ronnie?"

Ronnie described them, still grinning. "You'd find it funny too if you removed the stick from your ass."

"Why aren't you more worried about this?" Aedan sent the text.

"I am. But the demons are out there, we are in here. We have options, and we have the badass angel with us. Don't you think she would be out here if there were an immediate threat of danger, trying to save us?" Ronnie challenged him.

"Your badass angel just said, damn right she would," Smitty grinned.

Aedan grinned. "Okay, fine. I'm relaxing. Also, I see our sneaky priest in civilian clothes joining the crowd."

"We are as prepared as we could be, Aedan. Chill," Smitty patted him on the back.

"It's unnerving," Aedan defended himself.

The three stood there watching while trying to make it not look like they were watching. Jax came running at the first inhuman scream from one of the demons that had just gotten doused with holy water. A few seconds later, two more screams added to the confusion in the crowd outside.

Aedan shifted his stance, "Are they still there?"

The store employee came out, "Are who still there?" She looked up at Jax with wide eyes, grabbing his arm. "This weird stuff out there is what I was telling you. It scares me; I hate being alone."

Aedan smiled as Airiella gently removed the girl's hand from Jax's arm. "It's okay, there's nothing out there but people," her words telling him the demons were gone. "You are perfectly safe." Jax stepped out of reach.

Aedan damn near laughed when she switched her attention to Ronnie. "I'd feel better if you guys stayed here," her hand now on Ronnie.

Ronnie moved before Airiella could intervene. "No dice, kid. I've already got the most amazing woman."

"We will be leaving through the back," Smitty pushed Jax ahead of him, trying to keep him out of reach of the girl's grabby hands.

Aedan thanked her for her time, and they scrambled to get out of there. "Interview worthless?"

"She spent most of her time touching Jax," Airiella retorted.

"No one wants to see the jealous angel make an appearance," Smitty joked.

Jax grinned. "You should have heard the thoughts flying through her head. Man, it was so hard not to laugh." Jax turned to Aedan. "That one was pretty worthless. She had a few interesting things to say, but mostly she wanted to hook up with one of us."

They all felt the surge of energy from Airiella. "Hey, easy," Aedan out a calming hand on her. "She never stood a chance with these guys."

"Oh, I know. I still didn't like it," Airiella crossed her arms and leaned back in the seat, possessively leaning against Jax. "Sorry about that little display back there. It usually doesn't get to me."

"I didn't mind in the slightest," Jax dropped a kiss

on her head.

"Ronnie had a nice save back there," Smitty added.

"Oh, I didn't need to be unblocked from her head to know what our little angel was thinking," Ronnie laughed. "From the moment we walked in the door, and she tried with Smitty first, our girl had a fierce look on her face."

Aedan texted Father Roarke they were back in the car and waited for him to join them before they headed to the next interview. Once the priest was in, they set off. "The holy water took care of them?"

"Yes. Those were the lowest level of demons. Watchers, mostly," the priest answered, a smug smile on his face. "I admit, that was kind of fun."

Aedan felt a trickle of fear. He sensed the bigger ones would be later and not quite as fun.

We got through the rest of the interviews with no incidents, but I had an alarm going off in my head for the past five minutes. It was a quiet one, but it was still present. We pulled up to the hotel, and as we were getting out to check-in, I halted them all.

"Something is off. Please let me check us in." I met all of their eyes and climbed out, Jax hot on my heels.

"You aren't going in alone, siren," he started to argue.

"Fine, but let me talk. Please," I requested nicely.

I walked up to the front desk switching to my soul sight vision, and the colors made my step falter a bit. Jax steadied me, and I smiled at the clerk. "Reservations for Shadow Seekers. Do you have extra rooms available by any chance?"

The guy smiled brightly at me. "I know we have the suites available. Let me check for you." He typed in something and nodded. "I have the penthouse open, there are three rooms in there, or I have a two-room suite that sleeps 8."

"Can you switch all of our reservations to the suite? Please? We have a lot of work to do tonight, and all the room shuffling gets tiresome." I felt out his energy and sensed his hesitation. I pulled the uncertainty from him quickly and fed into his need to be helpful.

"If there's a loss of money, charge the same as you would for all the other rooms," Jax added.

The clerk nodded, "It will take a bit of finesse; let me go grab the manager."

He stepped away, and Jax looked at me, "You feel danger, don't you?"

"Yeah. I'd rather have us all together in the same place if something happens. I don't want to go yelling down the hallway pounding on doors," the investigation in Kansas came to mind.

"Will two rooms be enough?"

"There will be at least two beds in one of the rooms if it sleeps 8, and I am guessing a pull away or hide-a-bed. We will make it work. It will be less private for Father Roarke, but safer." I turned my back to the counter and looked at the car with the guys in it.

The clerk and the manager came back, both with smiles, and I repeated my request, adding Jax's suggestion about charging the higher rate if they were concerned about losing money. I should have known that was what the concern would be, Jax nailed it.

"Since it's a last-minute request, we will have to

charge the rate for all the rooms," the manager said apologetically.

"That's perfectly understandable," Jax said calmly. They got us squared away, and we went back to the car to park and help unload all the gear.

"Change of plan, guys, I'll apologize now. I switched our reservations to a suite that will hold all of us. I'd rather forgo the privacy to keep you all safe. I've got an alarm in my head going off, and instinct says to stay together," I told them as we unloaded.

Not one of them argued. When we got to the suite, we found that one room had two beds, the other a king bed, and a murphy bed in the open area. Father Roarke offered to take the murphy bed, Aedan and Smitty took the room with two beds. Jax, Ronnie, and I would share the other one.

"If it's awkward for you, Jax, Smitty can stay with Ronnie and me. We've shared a bed before," I offered. I knew he wasn't big on sharing.

"We've shared a bed too, it's fine. You get the middle, though. Ronnie is a cuddler, and I don't want to be cuddled by him," Jax smirked.

"Um, hate to break this to you, tough guy, but you cuddle too," I chucked him under the chin.

Father Roarke started laughing, "This will be an interesting night, at least."

"Sorry, Father." I wasn't really. Nothing sexual would be happening, so I wasn't embarrassed. "We stick together from here on out. If we need to leave the room, we all go. The alarm is still going off, but it's kind of distant sounding. Let's figure out what works for everyone for dinner, and we go as a group. Please," I added, so it didn't seem like I was pushy.

"I trust your instincts, angel. I'll eat anything you guys think sounds good," Ronnie answered, setting bags down in our room.

Smitty agreed. "I have zero reasons not to trust you."

Aedan laughed, "Didn't you call her a badass angel?"

"That was Ronnie, not me. I just relayed the message from the said badass angel."

Father Roarke smiled, "I sincerely hope that you guys never lose this closeness. It warms my old heart."

"You aren't that old, Father," I hugged him. "Why don't you pick where we go for dinner?"

"A burger sounds good to me," he admitted. "I haven't had one in a long time."

"Smitty, find us a burger place?" I turned to look at him as he was already searching on his phone.

"On it, baby girl."

After eating and going over everything again, we all went to bed. I woke up in the middle of the night, my senses on high alert. The air was too still. One arm and one leg were on top of Ronnie, Jax curled up behind me, his arm around my middle. Both were still sound asleep. It wasn't them that woke me up.

Smitty? I sent out quietly. I didn't want to wake him if he wasn't awake.

I feel it too, baby girl, he answered immediately.

Demon? Shit. I was hoping whatever was causing that alarm would wait until we were out of the hotel.

I don't know; I feel something. It woke me up.

Me too, I replied. I slowly moved my arm off Ronnie

and tried to move my leg without waking him. He'd always been sensitive to my movements. Come to think of it, Jax was too.

Aedan is still asleep. I'm going to check on Father Roarke.

NO! I unintentionally yelled my thought out. Damn it. I woke them both. I felt their breathing change immediately. *Sorry, Smitty. Now I woke up both of them. Sit tight. Don't leave that room.*

"Angel?" Ronnie whispered.

Shh, I sent to them both, hoping I could do that and that it worked.

What's going on, siren?

Can you both hear me? I tried.

Yes, came the dual answers.

Can you hear each other?

No, they said in unison.

It almost made me laugh. *Something is happening, it woke both Smitty and me up. I'm going to check. Please stay here.*

No way in hell, are you going out there without me, Jax sat up.

Please. I can handle whatever it is. If I can't, you both can come running.

I moved out of the bed slowly, crawling to the bottom of the bed. I'd left the room door cracked open just in case, and I peered out into the darkness using soul sight. Father Roarke appeared immediately, and not in the bed. He was at the other end of the suite.

Was that what I heard? Is Father Roarke moving around? That wouldn't have woken Smitty. I pulled the door open and stepped out slowly, my eyes racing to try to see what was with us. The air felt oppressive the farther I moved away from the room.

I crept slowly towards Father Roarke, my steps silent. It was then I noticed that the room was unnaturally dark, the hall light not even filtering in from the crack under the door that was so typical in hotel rooms.

Angel, you'd better be keeping us informed if you want us to stay put, Ronnie warned.

Something is here, but I can't see it, I sent to all three of them. *Father Roarke is against the wall on the other side of the room from where his bed is. It's dark in a way that it shouldn't be, and the air is heavy out here.*

I moved three steps closer to the priest. The air was not only oppressive; now, it was ice cold like I had stepped into a bank of snow. Oh fuck, something was in front of the priest. Why couldn't there be a light switch on this damn wall?

Baby girl, there's a demon in that room with you, Smitty warned.

It's in front of Father Roarke. It's darker there and cold. So cold.

I called the lightning to me, begging it to save the priest from whatever fate the demon was trying to impose on him. I called the air asking for help in pushing the beast away from the priest. I opened myself fully to both elements, the lightning sending electricity thrumming through my veins so loud in my ears it was crackling.

The first traces of the air started up, the still air moving to let me know it was ready to do as I asked. I pushed out my energy, imagining the demon getting thrown across the room and the air gusted. I jumped to the middle of the room to stand between the priest and the minion of Hell.

Get Father Roarke out of here, someone!

I let the lightning build inside me; my blue glow slowly lighting the space around me. My eyes adjusting, I found where the demon was and stepped closer, cornering it. I knew it was Smitty coming after the priest, and I quickly told Ronnie and Jax to stay put.

The moment Smitty shouted, I knew I made a mistake. There was more than one. I heard the thud of a body hitting the wall and Ronnie's soft gasp.

I've got Father Roarke, Smitty told me.

Jax, don't you dare move from that room. Something just hit Ronnie, and I've got another behind me.

I had immediately moved to the threat and saw the dark spot in front of Jax move. I sent another blast of air to blow it back towards the other one. *Where's the fucking light switch?* I asked them all.

By the bathroom door, Ronnie sent. *I'll get it; it's close to me. Close your eyes, so it doesn't blind you.*

Eyes closed, do it, Ronnie, I sent to all of them, so they knew Ronnie had it. I focused the air on staying around the demons so they couldn't move, adding a little electricity to the mix so they wouldn't try. Well, they wouldn't try it more than once, at least.

Jax, I need pants, or anything to put on my lower half, please.

Does that mean you are letting me out of here? He wasn't happy.

Hurry, please. I added desperation to my tone, hoping it would breakthrough.

I opened my eyes, slowly letting them adjust to the sudden light and felt Jax behind me. "Lift a leg," he said gently and slid a pair of shorts over my foot, "now the other."

"Thank you. I need to take the trash out," I told Jax.

"Will you let me come with you?" his tone was pleading.

"Please check on Ronnie and make sure he isn't hurt. I'll bring Smitty with me for backup if it makes you feel better."

"It would make me feel better if I was with you," Jax's tone was soft.

"I know. Please stay here with Ronnie," my energy was building too fast, and I needed to release it.

"Take Smitty," he conceded, stepping back.

Come with me; I sent Smitty.

"I heard, baby girl. Let's go. I'll check the hall to see if anyone is out there." He stepped into view and poked his head out of the door. "It's clear."

I directed the mini tornado in front of me, herding the demons out of the room. "There's no more hiding in there, right?"

"No. It was just the two," Smitty held the door to the stairs open for me.

The electricity was snapping as the demons kept bumping into the wall of the air around them. I smelled the sulfur smell as it burnt whatever their skin was. Hopefully, the sprinklers wouldn't trigger. That was my reason for taking this outside. I didn't need the lightning to burn down the hotel.

We made it outside reasonably quickly, and after checking for people and cameras, I released the lightning that had been building in me right into the air surrounding the demons and closed it in on them. I saw Smitty had a knife in his hand, and I held my hand out for it.

"No, baby girl, let me do it," Smitty commanded me.

"Smitty, no."

"You won't win this one; I'll do it. What better way is there for me to learn how to help," he insisted.

I did not argue with him. I sent another wave of lighting at the demons, their screams muffled by the air, and I let go of the hold on the air. There was no hesitation in Smitty at all. He stepped up and slammed the knife into the heart of the one closest to him and twisted hard, leaving nothing but a pile of ash in its place.

He moved to do the same to the other when it struck out, and Smitty slammed into the building behind us. Rage flooded through me, and before I had a coherent thought, I had my hand wrapped around the demon's neck, sending streams of lightning through it.

"Let me finish it, baby girl," Smitty's voice came from behind me.

I let go of it, and it crumbled to the ground, weak. The palm of my hand was burning, and my body was vibrating with energy and anger. Ready to lash out again at the slightest of moves it made. I didn't let it go until I saw it turn to ash, and I was in Smitty's arms.

"Put your wings back in," he said quietly into my ear.

I focused the energy still running through me, and before shutting it all down, I thanked the elements for their help. It never felt right to me unless I thanked them. With the rush of energy now gone, I sagged and tried to protect my hand from touching anything.

"Let me look at it," Smitty told me as he led me back up the stairs. I held out my hand. It looked like someone had poured acid on it. "This was after you touched it?"

I nodded as we walked back in the room, and Smitty sat me on the couch. "Let me see, siren," Jax asked in a restrained voice.

I held my hand out for them all to see since they now all crowded around me, Father Roarke going to his bag and pulling out a jar of something. "Degataga sent me this; he said you might need it."

The priest rubbed it gently on my palm, and the effect was instant numbing and cooling relief. "I can't believe you went out in public in that outfit," Ronnie tried to joke to lighten the mood. "Jax usually has way better taste in clothes than that."

"It's your shirt," Jax gave a ghost of a smile.

"Airiella, are you okay?" Aedan asked.

"I'm fine," I told them all. Truthfully, I was exhausted.

"We felt the rage, what happened?" Ronnie sat next to me and wrapped gauze around my hand.

"Smitty, are you hurt?" I looked up at him. "Take your shirt off."

He pulled it off, gingerly, and his back had several cuts and was starting to bruise already. "I'll take care of him, lass." Father Roarke began to smear some of that magic gel on his back.

"Angel?" Ronnie prodded.

"Smitty killed the first one, and the other sent him flying back into the building. That's when the rage got me. The next thing I knew, I had my hand around its neck, sending lightning through it."

"Touching it did that?" Father Roarke looked surprised. "That didn't happen at the funeral, and you touched them then too."

"Are there different types of demons like there are levels?" I asked.

"I don't know. I suppose it's in the realm of possibilities. Maybe they had abilities or were covered in something. That is new information," the priest sat down.

I felt the shakes start to come on and knew the initial terror I had felt at feeling someone in our room was going to hit. "Father Roarke, I'm apologizing in advance for my language," I told him quietly. I looked up at the guys as the tremors hit, "Someone, please fucking hug me." My voice started to shake too.

Ronnie gathered me to him, and Jax crowded in on the other side. "They were in our room," I whispered roughly. "They know my fears." I closed my eyes and knew Ronnie got what I was implying about someone being in my room. I felt it in the way he held me tighter.

Siren, talk to me, baby. Why are you shaking like this?

"You can talk out loud, Jax. It's okay. You all deserve to know if I'm going to fall apart every time this happens."

Please don't let me go, Ronnie. I can't open myself up to this without you.

Having you in my arms is a comfort to me as much as it is for you. I don't plan on letting go.

"In case you don't remember in Kansas when I flipped out over someone being in my room, that's a big fear of mine."

"I thought you were freaking out over almost being killed," Aedan knelt in front of us.

"That might have been part of the after-effects, but

the initial freak out was because someone was in my room. After he broke up with me, my ex would sneak into my apartment at night while I was sleeping. He'd pick the lock on my bedroom door and slink around in the dark to purposely scare the hell out of me. His end game was wanting me to come crawling back to him, telling him how much I needed him and how scared I was without him."

"Mother fucker," Jax swore. "I remember now."

Please can we go to bed? I felt tears pricking the back of my eyelids.

Of course. But I want you to stand and walk there on your own. Face it. Don't let this keep beating you, siren. Jax pushed gently.

I stood up, my legs shaking. "Father Roarke, maybe put some holy water around the door frame, so if they try to come in, it will hurt them."

"I'll set traps, lass. Go, rest."

I hadn't let go of Ronnie's hand, and I didn't plan to. I'd walk to the room on my own, but he was coming with me.

Aedan hugged and kissed my cheek. "Good call on being in the same room. Try to get some sleep."

"Take care of Smitty." I walked over and kissed Smitty gently, pulling Ronnie with me. "Thanks for the help."

Do you want me in there with you two? Jax asked, noticing I hadn't let go of Ronnie.

Yes, I need you close, or nightmares will get me. Please come with me.

Jax came up on my other side and took my wrist, looping his arm through mine, trying to be careful of the bandaged hand. They walked me into the room, undressed me and put me in the bed, each of them on either side of me, holding me while I shook until I fell asleep.

Chapter Nine

Jax woke up before Airiella did, her position reversed from how it had been when she had fallen asleep. Her head was on him now, her face pale and marked with dried tear tracks. He didn't think it was possible to love someone as much as he loved her. He'd been furious with her for leaving him in the room last night.

He'd known she was hurt, and seeing Smitty help her back in hit him like a sledgehammer to the gut. Then when she'd started shaking, his fury vanished only to be replaced by worry. After explaining her reason for the shakes, the rage returned but not at her. He couldn't believe he'd forgotten that.

The first time she'd cried in her sleep that night took him right apart because he saw the replay in her head. He knew Ronnie saw it too because they were both tense and grinding their teeth. He had a hard time falling back asleep after that. He'd managed short bursts of sleep, but now he was just awake.

He shifted carefully out of bed without waking her and saw Ronnie watching him. He motioned Ronnie to join him and patiently waited while Ronnie slid out of bed too. They went out into the main room of the suite and found Father Roarke awake as well, tending to Smitty's back again.

"We shouldn't leave her alone in there," Ronnie said quietly.

"Smitty can go in once Father Roarke's finished." Jax saw Smitty nod and noted the pale, drawn look on his face. "I don't think he got any more sleep than we did."

"Not if you saw her nightmares too," Smitty mumbled.

"Isn't there a gym here?" Jax looked at Ronnie, who nodded. "Let's go work out a bit. I need to lose some of this aggression before our day starts."

"Yeah, I'm with you on that," Ronnie clenched and unclenched his fists.

"We'll go in with Smitty and grab our bags," Jax stood patiently and waited until the priest finished his care.

They snuck back into the room, and Jax fought the temptation to crawl back into the bed. He grabbed his bag instead, and they waited until Smitty was wrapped around her, his tight face easing with the contact. Jax felt better at having him there with her, and they slipped on some workout clothes and left Father Roarke to oversee them.

"Do you want to find that fucker and beat his face in as badly as I do?" Jax asked.

"Damn right, I do. I have since Airiella told me about him." Ronnie didn't wrap his hands or put gloves on.

He just started hitting the bag, his moves powerful and precise.

Jax pulled him back, though, and wrapped his hands. "If she sees your hands all fucked up because you didn't protect them, she will know why. It'll hurt her."

The look Ronnie was giving him threw Jax off. He just continued wrapping Ronnie's hands and then laced his gloves up. Jax finished and reached for his wraps and found himself locked in Ronnie's embrace. Jax didn't care who saw, this was his brother, and he needed comfort the same way Jax did.

"I hate what he did to her. I fucking hate it. Every time she has flashbacks like that, it feels like she's getting gutted. Out of all them that hurt her, used her, beat her, he was the worst. He is the reason it's so hard for her to let us in. He's the reason she doesn't ask for help." Ronnie had angry tears running down his face as he bled out her secrets.

"She hasn't talked about him to me," Jax admitted, letting Ronnie vent.

"She won't either. I had to force it." Ronnie let Jax go and stepped back, delivering a giant blow to the bag that sent it swinging. "Even then, she talked about it clinically. You felt the emotions she let go of from the rape; this is even worse."

"How can it be worse than that?" Jax remembered the staggering emotions she let go of on the beach.

"The rape scarred her permanently, for sure. This ex, what the asshole did, he fucking broke her from the inside, using words, psychological abuse, breaking her down over the years. If that helpful demon is right and she's not healed yet, it's this ex that's still her hold up. I despise violence; you know that. Yet I still want to beat the fucker until the prick begs for mercy. I want to feel his bones crack."

Nothing could have shocked Jax more than that admission from Ronnie. It gave him a little better understanding of the damage she had inside that could trigger this response in his closest friend. "What did he do to her?"

"She'll tell you in her own time. She'll downplay it too. The abusive boyfriend with the golf clubs? That was a cakewalk in comparison. The ex-husband and ex-best friend and his stalker son? That was bad and caused PTSD. This ex used every event from her past against her. To break her down farther, giving the insecurities fuel to burn and growing them into these giant beasts so that she depended on him to help her through it. He wasn't helping her. He was destroying her."

"How can I not see that?" Jax asked, astounded.

Ronnie was like poetry in motion, his form perfect, his strength effortless. "You do see it. She just doesn't recognize it for what it is unless it's explained to her. She buries that shit deep. You saw it last night first hand in that delayed reaction from that fear of having someone in our room. It's deep-rooted. You saw it in Kansas when you dragged her out of that room and held her while she broke down. You see it when she reacts to someone getting bullied, constantly needing to build others up because she knows how it feels to be so broken. Those are a reaction to what she's been through," Ronnie punctuated his words with blows on the bag.

"She told you all of this?" Jax still hadn't moved.

"Some of it she told me. The rest I've been able to

piece together from what I know of her past and her reactions to things now, and what I've seen when she's sleeping. Sometimes when she's feeling vulnerable, she lets things slip. I don't react to them, or she would close up fast. I see it all."

"She told me you were her safe zone. You'd never let her fall," Jax hoped the words would ease some of what was eating him up.

"She's right. That's why I was struggling so much when you both were gone. I knew she was falling, and I wasn't there." He spun in a graceful arc and delivered a kick that sent the bag reeling. "I had to trust you would catch her." He faced Jax. "You did. I'm so glad you did."

"She still needs you. I'm not you. She told me you would try to protect her from the fire, or find a way for her to get around it safely. That me, I would take her hand and walk through it with her."

"She's right on that, too. I know the differences between us, and I know we balance it out for her. I know if she chooses to be with you, it's because she knows I would try to stop her. Just as if I know that if she chooses to be with me, she needs to feel safe. I just fucking hate it that the dick still has this power over her. It takes her down so fast and hard, and there isn't shit we can do about it." Ronnie made a combo move that Jax admired.

"We are there to get her through it." Jax stepped over to the speed bag and started hitting while Ronnie worked out his aggression. Ronnie's words playing through his head as he looked back at how she reacted to some things and began to put pieces together the way Ronnie had. "Every time she's running into danger to protect us, it's tied to emotion from her past?"

"Switch," Ronnie called out, and Jax moved to the bag to go through Ronnie's routines. "Yes. She doesn't want us to be hurt or to experience the pain she has."

His skill in fighting was nowhere near what Ronnie's was. Ronnie was in a class of his own. Jax gave it his best until his body was shaking with adrenaline and muscle fatigue. Ronnie still looked like he could go for another couple of hours. Jax sat down and let Ronnie finish, his thoughts all over the place. "Think we will have more encounters?"

"Guaranteed something happens at the shoot tonight. Most likely to be directed at you or me," Ronnie added.

"I figured whatever happened next would be one of us." Jax stood. "Are you done?"

"No, we need to do a cooldown, let's use the treadmills for fifteen minutes, a light jog."

Jax groaned. "I'm gonna need a nap before we go out today."

"You and me both, bro," Ronnie said with a small laugh.

Chapter Ten

Smitty woke up thinking he was in the middle of a wet dream, only to find it wasn't a dream, and Airiella's hand and mouth wrapped around him. The sight almost had him coming immediately, and she slowed down, feeling his reaction.

The chances of someone walking into that room were pretty high, and it added to the excitement of the moment. The gleam in Airiella's eyes told him she knew, and she loved it. The moment she started to massage his balls, they tightened, and he lost it, his cock jerking as she sucked him dry.

"Shit, baby girl. I don't know what made you do that, but it's the best way I've ever woken up." He moved to pull her up, but she stood, grabbed a bottle of water off the dresser, downed it, and then came back to the bed.

"Didn't think you'd want a morning breath, cum

kiss," she smiled, then kissed him. "I think maybe all the life-threatening, dangerous situations make me horny. Besides, you looked so yummy I wanted to taste you."

"How's your hand?" he pulled her arm up and tried to peek under the bandage.

"It doesn't hurt. How's your back?" Airiella threw the question back at him.

"Tender, but I'll live. Jax and Ronnie aren't back yet?" He hadn't heard them, but then again, his attention was laser-focused on her as he woke up.

"I think if they were, they would have been in here. Where'd those two go?" Airiella nestled into his side.

"They needed to work off some aggression," Smitty hedged around the truth a bit.

She narrowed her eyes at him. "What aren't you telling me?"

"I'm serious. Both went down to the gym to work off aggression. That's what Ronnie said."

"Okay, let me reword this. Why were Ronnie and Jax feeling aggressive?" she asked again.

Smitty found himself backed in a corner. Even if he hid his thoughts, she would know he was lying. "You, uh, had some nightmares of the flashback sort that were kind of loud in our heads."

He felt the exact moment her walls slammed down into place. He hated the distance she'd forced around her. She physically pulled away from him, sitting up and moving away. "Which ones?"

"Baby girl, you don't have to hide it from us."

"Which ones, Smitty?" she repeated, her voice tormented.

"Ones about why people coming into your room

bother you. Scenes from your ex, I am guessing. They were dark," he gave her what she was looking for, and it pained him to do it.

She put her head in her hands and shook a little bit, rocking back and forth. "I'm sorry. That means you guys didn't get much sleep, did you?"

"Stop it." Smitty grabbed her legs and slid her over to him. Pushing her hands away from her face, he tipped her chin up until she looked at him. "Stop. He has no power over you. Fight this. Let us in, let us help you."

Her eyes shimmered with unshed tears, but she kept her walls firmly in place. "I'm trying." She moved and crawled over into his outstretched arms. He didn't care what she said about not being fragile; when her scars showed like this, he felt how thin that barrier she hid behind was.

He understood precisely why Ronnie and Jax had been feeling so aggressive. "Don't apologize for hurting. Stop thinking it's your fault we didn't sleep. We are together in this."

Jax burst into the room then. "Ells, what the hell?" he sunk on the bed, his eyes wide with fear.

Ronnie moseyed in a bit slower, "He flipped out when the connections shut down."

Smitty gently nudged her towards Jax, and she went willingly, clinging to Jax's neck as he wrapped her in a hug. Smitty tried to push against those mental walls; all she did was close her eyes.

"Angel, stop shutting us out. I already know, we all saw it, we all felt the fear. There's no reason to hide. Come on, sweetheart. Drop those walls. How do you expect to heal if you won't allow that wound to bleed?"

She turned her face into Jax's neck, her hair falling over her closed eyes. Smitty reached over and brushed it back from her face. "Whether your walls are up or not, baby girl, we can feel every tear that falls from those beautiful eyes."

He got through because he felt the walls lift and the anguish that traumatized her seep out. He watched amazed as Jax absorbed it all. Smitty felt his heartbeat turn erratic at the way Jax cared about this woman. It was a completely natural and powerful love. He'd never been surer about something as he was that Jax and Airiella belonged together.

Jax's plan he had shared with Smitty earlier in the week came to the front of his mind. He vowed to talk to Jillian soon because he knew then that the future had changed for him.

Ronnie stood in the corner Airiella had marked and waited to see if a voice would come through the spirit box answering his question. The old hotel had a definite creepy vibe, and he had no issues imagining the colored past being true. He was in the room where the girl who had hit on them, claimed to have been molested. A ghost that molested and then haunted her dreams.

He could hear Jax down the hallway in the room where a murder happened, trying to provoke the spirit of the murderer. He wasn't sure that was the best move he could make, and he could feel the edge coming out in Jax's voice.

Airiella was down in the base camp in the manager's office with Aedan and Father Roarke monitoring the cameras. She'd argued with them all about Aedan being out in the hotel by himself because she couldn't communicate with him the same way she could with the rest.

Ronnie couldn't argue against her logic, and he loved that she was channeling Smitty's reasoning, and he couldn't argue it either. Smitty himself was down in the basement out of contact with both him and Jax, Airiella, their only go-between.

Are you sure you felt the energy in this room? He asked her.

I did. It wasn't malevolent, though. Aedan says to join Jax, that his body language is worrying him. As for that room, I think the girl made up the story to get close to you guys. Before you ask, yes, it might be jealousy talking.

Ronnie grinned at the camera and blew her a kiss. He stepped out into the hallway and followed Jax's voice. He saw something weird at the end of the hall and stepped to the side, standing against the wall.

Angel, can you see the end of the hallway on the camera?

Yes, nothing is showing there.

No sooner than she had finished the sentence, he heard Jax shout and a loud thud. Ronnie bolted down the hallway and heard Airiella yelling through the connection.

Get out! Get out of there! Back to base, everyone back to base!

Shit. Too late. Jax was on the floor near the doorway, and there was a strange man in the room. Ronnie had never seen this guy before. He slowly squatted down and hauled Jax out into the hallway, lightly smacking his face, trying to him wake up.

He heard the pounding of feet racing towards him,

and Ronnie knew who it was then. "You're Bael, aren't you?"

"Ah, my bride to be figured it out, did she? How nice," the demon Bael mocked.

"She's not your anything. You are one delusional demon if you think that." Ronnie drug Jax farther away even though he knew it didn't matter; they were right smack in the danger zone. Both of them.

"You are proving to be more resilient than I expected," the demon moved towards them.

A glowing wall of blue appeared before him filling the doorway. Ronnie reached his hand out and skimmed his fingers over the surface of it, mesmerized. It felt like his angel. He looked back over his shoulder and saw her standing there, wings out and glowing.

Suddenly the demon was no longer in the room. "Bael's gone."

"No, he's not. Invisibility, remember? He's somewhere. Hang on a second," her eyes went unfocused for a minute.

Instead of the glowing wall in front of him, there was now a bright ring around him and Jax. "Um, angel?"

"He's behind you," she said, her voice angry.

"Impressive. You can see me." The demon reappeared right where Airiella had said he was.

Angel, can I move with this stuff around me? What is it?

Shield. I don't know if you can or not, try it.

Ronnie grabbed Jax under the armpits and hauled him closer to Airiella, the blue ring around him, following. He kept going until he was right next to Airiella, and she was in the ring with him. Unfortunately, the demon had followed him and was now right outside the blue circle.

"You have no animals here this time protecting you, what's your plan now? Give in, come with me, and I'll spare these two humans." He held out his hand to Airiella.

Ronnie watched, stunned as she stepped forward. "Angel," he called out.

"She is mine, you sick fuck," Jax called out weakly.

Bael laughed, a sound that made Ronnie's stomach roll painfully, and he found himself unsteady on his feet. He dropped to the floor next to Jax and tried desperately to get his bearings. The hallway was spinning.

"See? Airiella Raven, I don't even have to touch them to get to them. You can't keep them safe. Come with me. Save them."

Give me your hand, Ronan. Ronnie held out his hand and grabbed Jax's with his other. He felt energy flood through him, his vision clearing and strength like he'd never felt before pumping through his blood.

Get down the stairs to the others, stay together, arm yourselves. Do not argue with me. Ronnie had never heard her tone like that before. She was downright pissed. Jax looked like he was going to protest, and Ronnie pinched him, shaking his head no.

GO! She yelled. *He's trying to get Jax to lose control. Fucking go now!*

Ronnie yanked Jax hard towards the stairs. His anger rearing up, and this enhanced strength he had almost knocked Jax right down the stairs. Smitty was halfway up the last flight of stairs, and Ronnie shoved Jax at him.

"What the fuck, dude," Smitty stumbled as he caught Jax.

"Get him out of here," Ronnie whispered.

"If you stay, she's at risk," Jax grumbled.

"She's at risk no matter what I do," Ronnie argued vehemently.

The hotel's walls started to shake, and Airiella's voice reverberated through the building, amplified to levels that made his ears feel like they were bleeding. The entire hallway above him was glowing blue so brightly, his eyes hurt. His retina's feeling like they were burning.

"You are not welcome here; leave now, Bael," Airiella boomed.

"How is she doing that?" Smitty plugged his ears. Only Jax looked like he was fine.

"Every soul in this building belongs to the light except you. Go back to the shadows, Bael. You are not welcome here," Airiella's voice thundered so loudly pictures fell off the walls.

Father Roarke was almost to them, reading from the bible as he climbed the steps, his hands shaking. Aedan right behind him looking like he was going to be sick. Ronnie didn't hesitate. He dropped to the ground and crawled back up the few stairs he had gone down, pulling out a throwing star from his pocket.

He peeked up, trying to spot the demon, but the glow was too intense, he couldn't even see Airiella. With her voice bouncing off all the walls, he couldn't even pinpoint her that way. He knew they were all in mortal danger. The overpowering smell of the sulfur was making him nauseous.

The demon's voice was now as loud as Airiella's, but the tone instead, of her commanding and powerful one, was one that had them all retching violently. "I will not be denied what is mine!"

A putrid and vile burst of energy slammed through them, making them heave; those standing now fell down the stairs in a tangle of limbs. Ronnie, already on the ground, felt the weight pushing him down into it further. A thud sounded just ahead of him, and the glow was gone.

Two feet in front of his face was a lump of feathers. "No!" He screamed trying, to get to his feet.

The priest started chanting louder. Ronnie, able to see now, took careful aim with one of the stars and threw as hard as he could, scoring a direct hit as it embedded into the demon's chest. The roar that bellowed from its mouth made him lose all sense of direction and blinded him.

He frantically pushed himself forward, feeling for the feathers he had seen. "Angel, wake up, sweetheart," he begged.

The next roar that shook Ronnie down to his bones came from behind him. A voice as familiar to him as his own. The demon had woken that dark energy in Jax. He and Airiella were directly between the two.

Chapter Eleven

I kept hearing Ronnie, but I couldn't make out his words. What the hell had happened? I listened to the raven cawing at me, her tone persistent. I couldn't get my mind focused, it felt fuzzy, and the alarms in my head were ringing so loud I wanted to scream.

Then I felt Jax. He wasn't in control; Bael had woken that energy up. The guys were down, hurt. Help me, raven, I said to her. I knew I couldn't fight both of them. She kept pulling me towards Jax, and all I could do was crawl.

Airiella, help Jax, I heard Onida's voice. *Don't go after Bael, not while you're hurt. If he gets control of Jax, you'll lose him.*

"Oh, fuck no, I won't lose him." Anger surged through me, and without asking, the lightning responded and filled my body. I felt the air around me react to the need in me to protect Jax. Something flew past me, and Bael roared that eardrum-shattering roar again that made me want to puke.

"Feet, don't fail me now," I begged, using the wall to pull myself up. My gaze finally focused enough to see Bael pulling throwing stars out of his chest and throwing them back at me. The air caught them, dropping them harmlessly to the floor.

"You see this? How easy it is for me to beat you? I will take them all from you until you give me what is mine."

"There is nothing here that is yours," I yelled back. "Nothing."

Jax stood in the middle of the hall between Bael and me, his body rigid as he fought against the energy that had taken over him. I knew he was fighting it; I could feel it. *Pull it, siren, before he makes me hurt you.*

No, Jax, no. Fight it, baby.

Pull it! Please! I can't hold him back!

Fuck. I reached for that darkness in Jax, and I tried to go slow to make sure it didn't hurt him. Bael wasn't giving me time. Jax turned to me, his eyes no longer his own. *I love you, Jax,* I sent right before I pulled.

I pulled until I saw Jax had control again. "I got it, siren. Stop."

I nodded, the sick feeling in me more potent than ever with the demon's power behind it. I took whatever good energy I had left in me and pumped it into Jax, our connection flaring to life, the air surrounding him pushing the demon farther back.

"Please go back to the group," I begged him, my voice weak as I fought against the energy in me. I could feel the pain in Jax, but he was still conscious, and I counted it as a victory. I pulled everything I could to me, feeding it to the lightning in me that was zapping at my insides trying to kill off that energy.

Instead of using it for myself, I flung it at Bael, hoping it would cause enough damage to him to at least get him to leave. I didn't care if I burned the hotel down at this point. If he didn't go, we were all dead. I couldn't do much with that dark energy in me.

The deafening roar that shook the building told me I'd hurt him. I saw two more stars go flying past me, and I used the last of my energy to send another bolt of lightning at him. He disappeared in a puff of sulfurous smoke. The hallway was now smelling like egg farts.

I fell like a sack of rocks dropped from a cliff. "Ronnie grab her, to the basement now," distantly I heard Father Roarke ordering Ronnie around.

I tried to make my wings as small as possible. I didn't have the energy to make them go away. "Jax, is he okay?" I whispered as Ronnie gathered me to his chest.

"I'm fine, siren. I can deal with this pain," Jax promised me.

"Jesus, Jax, you don't want to see what's about to happen," Ronnie choked out, a few of his tears falling on my face.

I couldn't get my breath enough to get full sentences out. "Not safe. Stay together. Only, chance," I panted out. The pain was tearing me apart inside. It felt like I was bleeding out, sounds becoming distant, my strength, gone.

"Fuck! Father Roarke, we need to do something now! She's dying!" Ronnie screamed, jostling me as he flew down the stairs.

I felt panic rip through Jax, Smitty, and Ronnie as

Ronnie laid me on the ground. *Airiella, give Jax your blood,* Onida's voice came through again. I couldn't talk.

Jax, Onida says to take my blood, I sent out, hoping he heard me. I felt him kiss me. It was only then I realized my mouth was full of blood; I was choking on it. He pulled away from me, his eyes anguished, and a silent scream erupted from me. The only sound I made was a gurgling sound as the pain became all I knew. I sent out the last thought of thank you to the elements for helping me.

Jax's eyes were the last thing I saw. I felt Father Roarke trying to dump holy water down my blood-filled throat, and I didn't know if that would work. I couldn't swallow. Blackness swept across my mind; the last sound I heard was the snapping of my bones.

Jax didn't understand what was happening. "Stay in control, Jax, don't lose it," Ronnie had a hold of him.

Her blood fixed the physical pain in him, but it did nothing to ease the mental and emotional torment of watching the love of his life die. Because of him. Again. The sight of her bleeding out, her bones breaking even though nothing was touching her. He was dying with her. The pain she was feeling bleeding through their connection as her blood spilled from her mouth; way too much blood.

"Believe in her, Jax," Ronnie's voice broke, just like Jax's heart.

"She's gone," he whispered. "I can't feel her." Anguish pumped through him faster than the blood that had spilled out of her.

Aedan lay crumpled at her feet, sobbing. Smitty a shadow of himself trying to console him. All of this was his fault. He told her to do it. "Stop, Jax," Ronnie tried again.

"Stop? She wouldn't have done this if I hadn't told her to," he felt unhinged. "There was demon energy in that shit she pulled!" he screamed wildly.

Father Roarke worked over her still and broken form, trying to get as much holy water in her as possible. He poured it over her, praying the whole time. Even the priest's hands shook, and tears fell. "She'll come back. She'll come back," Ronnie repeated, his grip tight on Jax's arm.

"What have I done?" Jax collapsed and tried to crawl over to her, Ronnie holding him in place. "Let me go."

"We can't interfere," Ronnie whispered again, choking on the sob that was trying to work free.

"She didn't do anything she wouldn't have normally done," Father Roarke said kindly. "She did what she thought was best."

"She told me no, I pushed her," Jax sobbed, hysteria licking at his brain.

"If she said no, it was because she thought it would kill you," Smitty said numbly. "Ronnie's right. She'll be back as long as we don't give up on her."

"She's dead!" Jax screamed again.

"Yeah, she is," Smitty agreed. "Just like before."

They sat like that for fifteen minutes before Jax saw the blue glow flicker through his swollen tear-soaked eyes. "What's happening?" he heard Aedan's rough cry.

"Her body is trying to heal itself," Father Roarke's reverent tone filled the basement. "It is both a blessing and a curse to see," was his gentle warning.

The tears never stopped falling from Jax's eyes as

he bore witness to something he would never be able to explain, and couldn't take his eyes off of her. Way too slowly, her bones snapped back into place as the blue glow became steadily brighter. The sounds torturous and painful to hear.

Her body started to rise off the floor, and Jax felt his jaw unhinge at the sight she presented to them. Father Roarke's words of it being a blessing fleeting across his mind. Her long hair pooled in a pile of curls on the dirty floor under her bothered him for some reason. He wanted to hold the silky strands in his hands; they didn't belong on the dirty floor.

Ronnie's hand tensed on Jax's arm at the movement he made; he shook his head. "Not yet."

"She's still not breathing," Aedan commented in a voice that didn't even sound like him. "Is this hurting her?"

"Would it hurt you if you had to feel your organs get torn apart and then try to stitch themselves back together through sheer willpower?" came a voice from behind Jax.

As one, he and Ronnie stood, spinning around. Ronnie, immediately going to throw a star at the appearance of the man. Jax knew who it was; they'd met. Ronnie didn't, and as he drew his hand back to throw, the man shifted into a raven before their eyes, and Jax caught Ronnie's hand before he releasing the star.

"What the fuck, Jax?" Ronnie barked.

"That's the demon that helped her," Jax said softly. He turned his back to the raven, watching Airiella instead.

"What are you doing here?" Ronnie demanded.

"The same thing I've done from the beginning, trying to help," Stolas responded.

Jax glanced back in time to see him shift back into

human form. "How?"

Stolas walked over to Jax and handed him the branch of a plant. "When she wakes, break the wood and let the sap fall into her mouth, crush the leaf, and put it in there as well."

"It takes a long time for her to wake, days last time," Ronnie replied caustically.

"Let me rephrase that then; when breath comes back into her lungs," the demon said with a bitter smile. "I am on your side."

"Will she come back?" Jax asked the demon.

"She will, the damage internally is bad." Stolas had a grimace on his face.

"You said she was stitching herself back through sheer willpower?" Aedan looked sick.

"Yes, this isn't divine intervention. Not entirely. It is the angel's love for you that is putting her back together. There are divine powers at work as well; that is what allows it to happen. The work to do it is hers. It is why it takes so long for her to wake. She takes and uses the energy given to her to bring her back to life to repair the damage done. The time spent in what you have called a coma is where she is resting, trying to regain that energy. It is not an easy process for her, and a reason she is so sought after. The power of hate can only match the power of love; even hate stems from love."

"What will that plant do?" Ronnie asked, looking at the branch Jax held.

"It will wake her, giving her the energy she needs for you all to leave here. It's not safe to stay long. She injured Bael. He will send others after you all."

"How do you know so much about this?" Jax was

curious. His eyes were traveling between her floating body and the demon.

"She's not the first angel I've encountered, though she is the first to have as many connections and as many abilities as she does. The others could regenerate as she does, their pool to pull from much smaller than hers. It took them longer, and they were easier to kill."

"There's a limit on how many times she can come back?" Jax kept pushing.

"With her, I am not sure. The others, yes." Stolas leveled a hard look at Jax. "You need to be wary around Bael. If he gets more control of that entity inside you, there will be no stopping him. That, combined with the energy he infused to gain control, literally destroyed all the organs in her. Without her, your world will fall to him."

"Then how do I lose this shit?" Jax challenged him.

"That answer lies within you. Airiella did what she needed to do to stop this from going further." Stolas disappeared without a trace.

"Do you trust him, Jax?" Ronnie moved closer to him.

"Trust a demon? No. Not at all. I do trust that he wants to save her. At least, I trust that he wants her alive long enough to make sure the other one doesn't come into power," Jax reworded it.

"Then, we just accept what he says on goodwill?" Ronnie was skeptical. Jax didn't blame him.

"The first time she encountered him, he saved her from Bael. The second time was at the house in Cali, and he talked to her. Both Father Roarke and I were there. He even offered up whatever he used on her to keep her from being in pain. He wrote it out and told her to give it to Tak.

I'm willing to take a chance with this. He told us we aren't safe here."

"My trust is in you, not him. If you think it's safe, then do as he says," Ronnie gave in.

"Do we have enough filmed to make an episode?" Jax asked, keeping his eyes on her.

"No. I'm guessing you aren't leaving her, right?"

"Correct. Can you and Smitty finish up? Aedan can stay here in case more show up and help defend her." Jax glanced at Aedan, who could only nod. He was in a state of shock, Jax thought.

"Smitty, how much more do you think we need?" Ronnie shot a questioning look at him.

"Maybe half an hour. Um, I'm pretty sure all the cameras recorded everything that happened. The static ones, anyway. We have one camera in the hallway from Hell, and one right here, then the ones we placed in those rooms."

"Shit," Jax hadn't even thought of that. "It's great for information purposes. We can send it to Taklishim and Degataga. It might help them with gathering info on the demon. His energy might have knocked out the power supply."

"Let's finish filming enough to make the episode." Ronnie headed to the doorway. "If more demons are coming, I'd rather not be a sitting duck."

"I'll pull the memory cards off the camera's upstairs as well. Actually, I'm going to pull them all. We can ask the crew waiting outside to do the teardown so we can make tracks as soon as Airiella is ready," Smitty added, following Ronnie.

Father Roarke had moved over next to Aedan. "Are

you okay, son?"

Aedan looked over at Jax; his face was gaunt-looking and haunted. "I get it now what they were saying. That'd I'd have to see to understand, and that I wouldn't like it. I get it."

"At least this time, you saw less of the physical torment she endures," Father Roarke said gently. "The screams are awful."

Jax shuddered, remembering the scream that ripped through her at the beach. "It was worse when she did this when Ronnie was there?"

Father Roarke nodded. "In the physical sense. I don't think it was as bad internally. The end result is the same. Traumatic equally, in different ways. She didn't drown in her blood last time."

Aedan broke down again, "How do you do this, Father?"

Father Roarke put a gentle hand on his shoulder. "It's not easy, son, but what you see there is a miracle, and it restores my faith."

Jax tried to blink back more tears as the priest talked; it was pointless. Nothing would erase that memory from his mind. Nor the fact that she did it for him. He paced a little to pass the time as his thoughts swirled. He had to let go of the guilt. Smitty had been right, he realized, her telling him no was because she was afraid of hurting him, not what it would do to her.

Father Roarke was also right, which means Stolas was too. She did what she had to do. She'd never been concerned for herself once. She knew what was going to happen. She'd even tried to take it easy on him. If he gave in to this guilt that was trying to pull him down, he'd feed right into that darkness that was hungering for it.

He glanced at his watch at the same time he noticed her glow getting brighter. It'd been forty minutes since the guys had left them. They should have been back by now. He hoped that didn't mean they'd encountered more demons and were lying up there hurt somewhere. Or worse.

"It shouldn't be long now," came Father's Roarke's soft voice. "When the glow gets brighter like that, she's closer to breathing. That's been the case the past couple of times, anyway."

The door to the basement thudded open, and Jax heard the thuds of footfalls, Ronnie and Smitty bursting into view. "The crew is doing teardown. I've got all the memory cards and made sure there is no trace of what happened on any of the recording cameras. The computers are inside my locked backpack, the passwords to get on them changed," Smitty said in a rush. "No change?"

"The glow is brighter," Aedan responded slowly.

"She's close then," Ronnie knelt beside Aedan. "You okay, bro?"

"Not really," Jax heard Aedan's quiet response from across the room.

An ear-piercing, shrill scream tore through the room. One so filled with tormented pain, Jax's heart stopped beating for a moment. Airiella was back, though not awake. Her body was lowering back down to the floor as she coughed up the blood left in her throat after that scream.

Jax raced over to her, snapping the branch and tearing off a leaf and crunching it in his hand. He saw one drop of liquid form on the end of the broken piece, and he held it over her mouth and gently placed the crushed leaf under her tongue. Once the drop fell, it was just a waiting game.

"Can we move her now, Father?" Smitty stood, his face pale.

"That scream never gets easier, son," Father Roarke nodded.

Smitty took the broken branch from Jax and put it in a baggie. Ronnie, whose face had also paled at the scream, stepped closer and went to lift her right as her eyes popped open, wild and full of panic.

Chapter Twelve

edan stumbled back at the look on her face, his body still shaking after the scream that he thought had given him a heart attack. "Airiella?" he said softly.

"We have to leave now," she tried to stand but couldn't.

"Angel, can you make your wings disappear?" Ronnie tried.

Jax was behind her, propping her up. Aedan stepped closer and put his hand on her, hoping the connection they shared would help, while Smitty went around to the other side and did the same. It took a few minutes, but the wings finally disappeared, and Ronnie scooped her up.

Aedan walked over to the camera in the room, grabbed it, and pulled the card out of it as they climbed the stairs and handed it to Smitty. He checked the memory on the camera itself and found nothing. Footage like that would end any semblance of a mundane life she might have. Not that what he had seen was normal.

He was walking next to Jax, who looked as shell shocked as Aedan felt. Yet there was also a fire in him that Aedan hadn't seen since high school. "Doing okay?" he nudged Jax with his elbow.

"About as much as can be expected after watching someone you love horrifically die for you," Jax snapped.

"She's back," Aedan felt pathetic. He didn't have anything to offer as consolation. "It's not your fault."

"I know. I need to figure out what Stolas meant when he said the answer was inside me, so she doesn't have to go through that again."

Aedan saw the new strength in Jax. It also became apparent to him just how much Airiella meant to him. He'd already known from the things Jax had asked him to do. It was a lot more visible right now, the depth of it all. Aedan's life had shifted, as well.

Ronnie felt thoroughly shaken. "Angel is going back to the hotel safe?" He didn't believe it was, especially considering her blood-covered state. "Shit. Father Roarke, her blood is all over that place!"

"I know, son." Father Roarke looked at Smitty as they got in the SUV. "Find me a catholic church, phone number, name, and address, please."

"No hotel," she whispered in answer to his question.

Father Roarke was on his phone, talking urgently and quietly to someone in charge. He relayed the address

Smitty gave him and waited. Father Roarke told Smitty to drive to that location, as Smitty tensed up. "There's a demon close."

Ronnie started looking around, and Airiella tensed in his arms. "No angel, don't use any more energy right now. Stay still. Please, sweetheart."

Smitty took off like a bat out of hell towards the church address, and the priest was back to talking into the phone, his tone brokering no argument from whoever was on the other end. "There is a cleanup crew headed to the church to take care of the blood."

"What if they don't get there in time?" Ronnie asked, worried.

"They will," Smitty responded. "The demons are following us."

Jax swore. Airiella reached for Jax's hand, her movements slow. Ronnie knew they all felt the pain that was battering at her; it wasn't just him. She held Jax's hand and curled into Ronnie's chest, her blood-stained face tense and exhausted.

Smitty pulled up to the church, and they found a closed metal gate. "Honk," Father Roarke told him. Airiella started against Ronnie as the horn blared, but it worked, the gate rolled open then closed behind them.

Father Roarke led them inside the church, someone closing the door behind them and locking it. Ronnie heard the gasp as he walked by carrying Airiella and was then led to a room that had a bed. He set her down gingerly and accepted a basin of warm water and a washcloth.

He looked at the older man who must have been another priest and thanked him. Jax pushed his way through, lifting her head and sitting down, her head on his lap. Ronnie looked at the priest, "Are spare clothes lying around anywhere?"

"Yes, I'll go get one of the robes." He quickly left the little room, Father Roarke, following.

Ronnie started to gently undress her while Jax cleaned her face, the water in the bowl rapidly becoming red. Smitty took it from him and found a sink to dump it in, refilling it with clean water and rinsing the washcloth out.

Aedan took the bottle of bleach Father Roarke came back with and poured a little down the drain. They worked as a team to get her cleaned up, then cleaned themselves off. Before they put the robe on her Ronnie asked, "Angel, can you bring your wings back out? I want to see if they need cleaning as well."

She opened her eyes back up, and he saw the agony brimming in them, but she did as he asked. They filled the entire span of the room, and they heard the gasp from the other priest once again. Father Roarke took over ushering the bewildered man out of the room, back on his phone again.

"I'm sorry, angel; I know you are hurting." Ronnie found a few broken feathers and even more coated in blood. Between him and Jax, they got her beautiful wings cleaned up, and she made them disappear again with some difficulty. Jax held her up while Ronnie slipped the robe over her.

Jax lay down on the bed, pulling her on top of him and made room for Ronnie next to him. They both lay there on the narrow bed holding her, neither of them willing to let her go. "Rest now. We've got you, love."

Smitty's heart shredded as he looked at the three of them laying there on that tiny bed. He was of more use getting to work than he was lying there with them. He strode over to the bed and dropped a kiss on her face. "Love you, baby girl. Aedan and I are going to go destroy these clothes and see what else we can do."

Her weak smile almost shattered his resolve and made him stay. *I love you,* he heard in his head. Even that way, her tone felt small. He took in a deep breath and forced himself to walk away with a nod at Aedan.

Smitty gave him a moment to kiss her forehead before giving him a glare that made him hurry. "What can we possibly do?" Aedan asked.

"Call Taklishim and fill him in. Find out what Father Roarke is doing and make sure this secret is safe, copy those memory cards on CD's and get them ready to send to Taklishim or Degataga, whichever one. Destroy these bloody clothes, make sure that hotel got cleaned properly, get an envelope we can mail that branch in, to either Degataga or Taklishim." Smitty pulled out one of the stars Ronnie had hit the demon with, which had a small amount of blood on the blade. "See if either of them can do something with this blood that can help us."

"Damn, Smitty. Does your brain ever slow down?" Aedan asked in awe.

"Nope. Especially not after seeing her die again. I'd give up sleeping forever if it meant I could keep that from happening again." Smitty had wrapped plastic around the star to keep the blood uncontaminated, and he wanted a baggie to put it in as well.

"Yeah. Um, about that. I want to apologize for my

behavior with you for that," Aedan said with deep sincerity.

"I told you that you'd need to see it to understand." Smitty felt no joy at the admission.

"You also told me you hoped I'd never have to; I get it. Airiella's going to be okay, right?"

Smitty knew how hard this was for Aedan. Hell, it'd been earth-shattering for him, and he wasn't as scientific-minded as Aedan was. Not to the same degree anyway. "Be prepared for nightmares. Yeah, she will be okay. It takes time. It makes more sense to me now why it takes so long. I didn't know she was doing it herself."

"I can't even begin to imagine what that takes. That demon said there were some divine powers at work. It gave me hope that my kids won't be born into a world run by demons. Still, Smitty, shit." Aedan stopped walking. His face pinched, "She drowned in her blood."

Smitty closed his eyes, trying not to picture it again. "We've got to move past it. Trust me. I know how hard it is. But we don't have time to waste right now. Don't think about it."

Aedan choked back tears. "I can't *not* think about it."

"She's still with us. Do you want to destroy the clothes and I'll call Taklishim? Or would you rather the other way?" Smitty didn't give him a chance to dwell on it.

"Fuck. You call him. I'll take care of the clothes."

They both walked back out to the SUV, where Smitty grabbed his backpack, and Aedan grabbed the matches from Airiella's. Smitty smiled slightly. *Your hiking pack with all its gear is coming in handy now. I'll never make fun of you again for always bringing it,* he told her.

He heard a quiet laugh in response. He went back

into the church and wondered where Father Roarke and the other man had gone. Smitty assumed it was the priest of this church. He walked around, looking behind all the doors until he found them in an office in the back.

"Is there a room where I can set up my computers and do a few things?" He looked at them both. Father Roarke's face was a careful mask of neutrality, his phone in his hand. The other older man's face pale and disbelieving.

"Two doors down on the left is a little conference room for parish meetings," he told Smitty pointing.

"Thanks." He nodded at Father Roarke and left them. He got everything laid out on the small round table and pulled out his phone. He winced at the time, but something told him Taklishim already knew something had happened and would be up. The phone hadn't even finished its first ring.

"Is she okay?" Taklishim's tone was rough and held a sharp edge.

Smitty blew out a breath. "She's recovering with Jax and Ronnie right now. In pain and exhausted, but she will be all right."

"Fill me in," he demanded.

"Did you know?" Smitty asked in return.

"Onida has a weak link to her through her blood. She knew some of it, and immediately when she died." Smitty heard the medicine man draw in a harsh breath. "It took her a long time to breathe again. I was scared. Onida was scared."

"We didn't have time to call, and there are more demons out there still after us. Currently, we've holed up in a church Father Roarke pulled some strings to get opened to us," Smitty filled in.

"At least you didn't go back to your hotel, that could have been bad for a lot of people."

"That's the thing; I almost *did* go back there. Airiella told us it wasn't safe. That's when Father Roarke stepped in." Smitty launched into breaking it down Taklishim, finishing with the fact that they had it recorded.

"Can you e-mail it to me?" Taklishim asked quickly.

"Nope. Not doing that, sorry man. No way am I chancing this landing in someone else's hands, especially with the council going after her. I'll burn it onto CD's to send you. What about this plant Stolas gave us?"

Taklishim paused, "Degataga would be a better one to send that to, his knowledge on those exceeds mine. He can work with Onida on that."

"Okay, the last thing, Ronnie hit Bael with several of those stars. One has blood on it."

Excited and explosive cursing came from the phone. "Send that to me. Smitty that is beyond impressive that you got that."

"Now what? Father Roarke said he got a cleaning crew to go to that hotel to clean her blood up. Aedan is outside burning her blood drenched clothes. It's still on ours, but we don't have a change of clothes to switch with since our clothes are still at the hotel. Where do we go from here?" Smitty needed a direction pointed out.

"Wait. Let Airiella recover. You are safe there for now. Father Roarke specializes in demons. He will get you guys back out of there safely. I trust him," Taklishim said, much calmer now.

"I do too; he loves Airiella. He's also in danger because he's with us. Feels wrong to me." Smitty rubbed his tired eyes.

Taklishim chuckled at that. "He'd be in danger too if he was out doing what he does for the church. Let him work his contacts. He might need a copy of that footage, so make an extra one. Smitty, you did good. Make your copies and get some rest. Was this time as bad as before?"

"Worse, in some ways. Scratch that, worse in all the ways. At least there was only one scream. I think Aedan is traumatized, and Jax, well, I don't know what Jax is. He's different."

Taklishim softened his tone. "Watch out for him. It might hurt to hear this, but she means more to him than she means to you."

"No, that doesn't hurt, I know it's true. I know you weren't implying Airiella doesn't mean a lot to me. I just can't tell what the impact on him was. I can only tell he's different." Smitty ran his hand through his hair. "I'll get this stuff out to you today. I'll overnight it. Text me Degataga's address if you can. Will you fill him in, or do I need to call?"

"Tama said to send it all here, she just hung up with Degataga, and he's flying out," Taklishim changed his mind.

"That makes it easier. Will do. Thanks, Tak."

"Take care."

Smitty hung up the phone. He hadn't noticed Father Roarke come into the room, and he almost fell backward out of his chair when he spoke. "Tell me what you need."

"Immediate need is a box so I can package everything up to send to Taklishim after I copy these cards. We'll need clothes before we leave so those wearing her blood can destroy the clothes. Other than that, I need direction. Airiella probably needs some ibuprofen."

"Can you make me a copy of the part in the hallway? I've taken care of the ibuprofen part," Father Roarke patted Smitty on the arm.

"You don't want all of it?" Smitty was surprised by that.

"No, son. I don't want all of it getting out. Proof of her being an angel is enough to get things moving on my end. That hallway, if it recorded, will show the demon and her wings. That alone will be enough to get hearts pounding and people taking action. A warning, the church is *notorious* for leaks. So, if you can do anything to narrow that scene down to just enough for proof, that would be great."

"Let's get started on that then," Smitty fired up both computers.

"Let me go ask the priest for a box, some tape, and if he knows anyone that can run out to get clothes for you lot."

"Thanks, Father." Smitty pulled out the blank CD's he kept with him for backup purposes and the memory cards. He got to work.

Chapter Thirteen

She's okay," Winnie promised Airiella's grandpa for the twelfth time.

"She was here!" Giuseppe was inconsolable.

"That happens, sometimes," Winnie skirted the truth a little. She'd been a little more than scared this time around.

She'd been startled when Airy appeared, even more so when Airy didn't know who she was or what was happening. It had taken a long time for her to come around. She'd received some severe damage. Winnie tried not to cry in front of Airy's grandpa.

"She's okay?" The message seemed to be sinking in that Airiella wasn't still on their plane.

"She is. She's back where she belongs, in the arms of her team." Winnie spoke without thinking about that one.

"What does that mean?"

"They are taking care of her," Winnie answered quickly.

"Is that boy with her?"

"Jax? Yes, he is." Winnie felt around Jax's emotions and knew without a doubt that Airy was with him. She could feel the vibration of his love for her and the need he had to protect her. Winnie could also tell that Ronnie was with them both. She'd felt a different vibration in him since they'd gotten back, one that he got when he was around Ronnie.

"She's not supposed to be here," he said. His voice adamant as if Winnie had any say in the matter.

"It's a temporary stop while she does what she needs to do," Winnie tried to explain. "Are you going to come with us to talk to your ancestor?"

"I suppose. Who is the ancestor again?" Giuseppe asked, the distraction working.

"Marco Rosati. Surely you've heard of the name?" Winnie tried to push him gently.

"I hope my wife doesn't think I'm being unfaithful talking to all these pretty young girls of Ella's."

Giuseppe was charming. Winnie couldn't help but like the older man. "I won't rat you out."

"I had an uncle Marco, but I never knew him. He died before I was born. I think he died before my dad even came here."

Finally! Information. "Do you remember any stories about him?"

"No. My dad didn't talk much about him. He was several years older than my dad. Don't dawdle, young lady, let's get this business over with," Giuseppe tapped his foot impatiently.

Winnie snickered and called for Onida. "He's going to join us," Winnie smiled when Onida appeared.

"Who are you talking to?" he cocked his head and gave Winnie a strange look.

"Can you see the hawk?" Winnie gestured.

"I'm not blind, of course, I can see it. It's quite large."

"That's Onida. She's a friend of Airiella's."

"That can't be true; the girl is terrified of birds." Winnie saw Onida shift out of the corner of her eye. It wasn't often that happened on this side. "My sight must be failing me because that big bird just turned into a beautiful naked Indian lady."

Onida smiled, pulling on some clothes she had stashed here. "You are a charmer, sir. My name is Onida. It's a pleasure to meet you."

"I don't want an explanation for what I just saw. It's enough that my granddaughter is an angel and was here when she wasn't supposed to be."

"You saw Airiella here?" Onida had a concerned look on her face.

"She didn't even know who she was!" Giuseppe exclaimed. "How can that be?"

"It was bad, Onida," Winnie whispered to her.

"It was, I'll admit that." Onida turned back to Giuseppe, "Do you speak any Italian?"

"Sure do. Well, I can understand it. I've forgotten how to speak it."

Winnie didn't know how that was possible, but she wasn't going to argue with him. It had been hard enough to convince him to come after he saw Airiella. "Did your uncle ever learn English?"

"How would I know that if he died before I was born?"

"Sorry, good point. You can be our translator." Airiella's grandpa had a fire to him. He was a strong man, and she certainly saw him in Airiella. "She takes after you, you know?"

"She's a good girl. She was always different than the rest of us. So quiet. She saw everything that one. Ella learned faster than the rest too. It's always the quiet ones you have to watch out for; they sneak up on you. Boy, that girl could cause trouble when she wanted too," he whistled and got a distant look on his face.

"That, I have no problem believing. Your granddaughter has an incredible spirit," Onida told him.

"Most beautiful spirit I have ever seen in all my years, except my wife, of course. It always bothered me she was hurt so much by so many. Out of all my grandkids, I was so sure she would be a mother, and a darn good one too. Broke my heart when she got cancer. It sure changed her. I told her mother that it should have been me, not her," he reminisced as they trudged along.

How much he loved Airiella was obvious. She had that effect on people. "Make sure to remind her what I told her, would you?"

"What's that?" Onida politely asked.

"He will come back to her," was his simple answer.

"Who?" Winnie asked.

"She'll figure it out," he insisted.

Winnie shot a confused look at Onida, who only shrugged. "We'll tell her."

Onida sat down on a large rock, "This is where he

will meet us."

"There's nothing here," Giuseppe stated the obvious.

"This is where he chose, he feels safe here," Onida responded kindly.

They didn't wait long before Winnie saw a handsome man coming up to them. "Is that him?" she asked Onida.

"Yes. Mr. Rosetti, this is your ancestor, Marco Rosati," Onida introduced them.

"He looks like my dad," Giuseppe said in wonder and held out his hand.

Marco rattled off a bunch of Italian words Winnie had no chance of understanding. She looked at Onida, "Do you understand him?"

"I do, but it's because I am not hearing him in Italian. In my head, it just sounds like English."

"That's a useful trick," Winnie was jealous. This man Marco was dreamy. "Do ghosts get hookups?"

Onida burst out laughing; it was probably the only time Winnie had ever seen her do that. "He is handsome. I'll give you that."

"Young lady, that is very inappropriate," Giuseppe chided.

"What did he say to you?" Winnie flushed.

"He was asking me who my father was. He does speak some English he said, but not much," Giuseppe translated.

Winnie looked thoughtfully at Marco. "Hello Marco, my name is Winnie." She held out her hand, and Marco took it, kissing the back of her hand and bowing. Winnie loved it. The men in Airiella's family sure had the charm gene going for them.

"Oh, for the love of Pete! I hardly think this is the time for flirting," Giuseppe groaned, but he smiled as he said it.

Onida held her hand out to Marco, "May I?" He gave her his hand, and Onida took Winnie's with her other hand and connected all three of them. Winnie felt her palm grow warm and threw a curious look at the mysterious woman. "You should be able to understand him now. Might come in handy later," she winked at Winnie.

"You can understand me now, no?" Marco said.

Winnie almost swooned, his voice was a deep baritone and that accent! "Yes, I can understand you, it's a pleasure to meet you."

"How can I be of help?" Marco smiled.

"Your great-great niece is in danger, and some not nice people are trying to use your spirit to harm her," Onida started.

"She knows of me?" Marco sounded surprised.

"She does now. What we want to understand is what happened in your life that someone could use to try and hurt her," Winnie said.

"I would not hurt her," Marco misunderstood.

"Not you, people who know of you wish to harm her," Giuseppe intervened. "My granddaughter."

"I still bring shame to the family?" Marco asked sadly.

"If you ever did, I never heard about it," Giuseppe turned grave. "Why do you think you brought the family shame?"

"We sit, please," Marco plopped himself right down on the ground. Onida moved off the rock so that Giuseppe could sit there, while Winnie and Onida joined him on the ground.

"Will you tell us your story?" Winnie gazed at him, loving the twinkle in his eyes.

"A story?" he sounded confused.

"Not a story, your history," Onida clarified. "He won't understand our vernacular. Try to speak properly, and it will translate better," she told Winnie.

"This will help?" he asked timidly.

"Yes, it will help," Giuseppe answered.

"Very well, I will share. Your granddaughter, she is like me?" Marco looked at Giuseppe, who got a blank expression on his face.

"What do you mean? She is an angel, are you an angel?" Giuseppe raised both his eyebrows in surprise.

"If I were an angel, they would not have sent me away," Marco's expression grew grim.

"Sir, there's something lost in the translation. I think he was referring to his ability to feel what other people feel," Winnie tried to explain to Giuseppe. She looked over at Marco, "His granddaughter's name is Airiella. She is an actual angel. In answer to your question, yes, she is like you."

"Angel? And a witch?"

"Witch?! She's no witch!" Giuseppe growled, getting to his feet.

Onida put a hand on his arm. "He's not calling her a witch. He thinks that is what he was."

"Yes, they told me I was a witch," Marco nodded.

Winnie's heart broke a little at his expression. "You weren't a witch. You are what we call an empath."

"I don't know this word," Marco shook his head this

time.

"An empath is someone who knows what other people are feeling." Winnie wasn't sure how to explain it in terms he would understand.

"Yes, I know things. You feel happy with me," Marco told her with a smile.

Winnie blushed. That was one way to put it. She was confidant he wouldn't understand what she meant if she told him he was hot. "Attracted. Happy, too."

He got a gleam in his eyes at her words, "Attracted. You like me."

"Yes," Winnie said honestly.

"At home, I scared them. I knew when they were not honest. No one would talk to me. At school, I only had one friend; she was the daughter of a wealthy man in the village. She was never scared of me. I loved her."

Winnie saw the path Marco was heading, at least this part of the story. It was similar to Airiella's in that people shied away from her because she knew when they were lying. Or when they were sad or angry. She knew it all. Airiella hadn't been called a witch, but they *had* called her a freak.

"Lena's father did not like her talking to me; when he caught her, he punished her. I wanted to marry her. She gave herself to me. We were going to leave and start our lives somewhere else. We planned in secret and saved money." Marco gestured to his stomach, "Lena was with my child. Her father found out. He killed them, Lena and my baby. He left her body at the door of my family's house, and told the village I killed her so I wouldn't have to marry her."

Marco's eyes filled with tears at the memory, and Giuseppe drew in a sharp breath. "He wanted the village to condemn me to death. A life for a life he told them. He told them I was a witch and had put her under a magic spell so she would lay with me."

"I did hear this story," Giuseppe breathed out. "I assumed it was a myth. Something my parents told me so I wouldn't do something dishonorable."

Marco pointed at himself. "I brought shame to my family. My father bargained with a traveler for passage to coast to get on a boat for America. He was ashamed, but he did not want me dead. I arrived very sick and with no money. I only spoke Italian and made a few friends in the town where I landed. I did not know they were bad."

"Bad?" Winnie asked, caught up in the tragic tale.

"Criminals. I was arrested and sent West to work in a coal mine as punishment. I was sad and lonely; my love was taken from me, my home gone. At the mine, there were other Italian's; they talked to me. We worked long hours, sick all the time in our lungs, back-breaking work. I had heard one of the men talk about setting a fire. They were angry that men of color were coming to do their work. I tried to tell the boss about the danger; he wouldn't believe a criminal like me."

"Oh no," Winnie felt tears spring to her eyes.

"The man knew I had told. They beat me the day before the fire. It hurt to move, and I still had to go work. They followed me to make sure I didn't tell, threatened me, the other Italian's that talked with me. I knew they were telling the truth; they wanted to hurt everyone. They told the boss I was doing the work of the devil, and they docked my wages. That night, I stayed away from everyone. I heard them still. They all spoke of me doing the devil's work."

"What does that mean?" Winnie asked, her heart

broken.

"They called me a demon." Marco lost himself in the memory, his eyes haunted by the pain of his past. "No one wanted to work near me the next day; I was alone. I smelled the fuel and heard the explosion, the screams of the men. There was nothing I could do. I tried to escape, to help the other's escape. They knocked me over trying to get out, screaming that I did it. So many died. I died, disgracing my family."

"You didn't disgrace us," Giuseppe said softly. "They did talk of you. They never said your name. My father mourned for you."

"My life was lonely. My death is lonely."

"Well, I'm here now, and I'm your family," Giuseppe smiled. "You don't have to be lonely anymore. We have others here, and together we will find them."

Winnie flung herself at Marco, sobbing as she hugged him. "You have me, too; I'll be your friend."

"That would make me happy," Marco seemed embarrassed by the display of emotions. "Will you tell me of your granddaughter, the angel?" he asked Giuseppe.

"It would be an honor," the elderly man said.

"Marco, they are going to use a spirit to try and contact you," Onida told him gently, his story affecting her as well. "You don't have to talk to them. If you want to, that is fine. Can I ask you a favor?"

"Yes, please. You have given me much," Marco graciously offered.

"If you choose to answer the call, will you please take Giuseppe and Winnie with you?"

"Of course, yes, if they don't mind," he acquiesced readily.

"I don't mind at all. It's my family they are trying to hurt. You and Airiella both," Giuseppe retorted.

"I'd love to help you any way I could," Winnie gushed. "I'll also help you not to say things you shouldn't say."

"Thank you, Marco. If you don't mind, I will take my leave now. I believe I have the information I need to help Airiella. Winnie and Giuseppe will keep you company. If I can be of assistance in locating your family for you, please have Winnie contact me." Onida stood and shook Marco's hand before shifting back into hawk form and taking off.

Marco had an astonished look on his face. "Don't mind her, she's mysterious," Winnie said with a smile.

"You are my nephew, then," Marco shook his head and looked back at Giuseppe.

"Yes, indeed, I am. I can fill you in on everything I know," Giuseppe offered Marco.

"Wonderful. And you, you will be my, what do they say, girlfriend?" Marco smiled at Winnie.

Giuseppe chuckled, "He works fast."

Winnie blushed. "Sure, why not? I'll be your girlfriend." She kissed Marco's cheek, and his face lit up with a brilliant smile.

"This is a good day," Marco beamed.

Chapter Fourteen

I woke up disoriented. I had no idea where I was other than between Jax and Ronnie. I still felt battered, though I didn't sense any immediate danger. The room I was in was dark, and the air was chilled. I wasn't cold; it was hard to be cold when pressed between these two. They radiated heat.

I desperately wanted a shower, and I had to pee. Moving was still painful and would be tricky. I didn't have a lot of room to maneuver. No matter what I did, I was going to end up waking one or both of them up by moving.

"I'm already awake, angel," Ronnie said quietly. "I'll move and help you up, then show you where the bathroom is. Come on. I've got you."

"We're both awake, siren. Don't step on Smitty or Aedan," Jax's warm breath tingled against my ear.

"Where are we?" I had a vague recollection of

leaving the hotel, everything after that was a blur of pain.

"A church near the hotel. Father Roarke reached out for help," Ronnie helped her around the men sleeping on the floor.

"How long have I been out?" I hoped it hadn't been days.

"About ten hours after we got settled on the bed," Jax stretched. "Not nearly enough time for you to recover."

"They left some food for us in one of the rooms down here. There's a small shower in the bathroom, and Father Roarke had someone get us some clean clothes," Ronnie led her to the bathroom. "We'll go after you."

I was slightly embarrassed that I didn't think I could get the robe off of me. My arms weren't working very well. Jax dropped a kiss on my lips. "I'll help you."

"Thank you." He let me pee and came in after the shower started and helped me get that robe off.

"I'm so sorry, siren," Jax had tears in his eyes.

"I'm not." I gave him a swift kiss and slowly got in the tiny shower. Thank God there was no step up.

I stepped under the spray and saw the white floor turn red as the blood rinsed from my hair. I winced, remembering that I had aspirated on my blood. As soon as the water ran clean, I felt Jax turn me around and start to shampoo my hair. I was not about to argue because it felt damn good. He turned me again when it was time to rinse, then repeated the process with conditioner.

He tenderly washed me and helped me feel clean again. I was putty in his hands and let him lead me where he wanted me. Soon he was swapping places with me handing me off to Ronnie to dry while he showered. Between them, they thoroughly pampered me.

Ronnie got me in clean clothes and led me out to sit down and eat some food while he showered. Jax sat down next to me a few minutes later. I looked at him warily. "No, we aren't going to talk about it." I sighed in relief at his statement.

"Thank you again."

"You haven't eaten much," he commented.

"My stomach isn't quite up for it yet. I had a little."

"I'll leave a note asking for something a little gentler, oatmeal, maybe?" Jax thought out loud.

"Oatmeal would be good," I started to feel drunk.

"Easy angel," Ronnie steadied me as he came into the room. "Not up for food yet?" he asked as he saw my plate.

"Did you guys drug me?" I slurred.

"No. You just need more rest," Jax touched my cheek in concern.

"Eat, Jax. I ate while she showered. I'll take her back, come in when you're ready," Ronnie helped me stand and scooped me up as I swayed.

I felt awful. I knew there was no point in arguing. I didn't have the strength to even stand on my own. "Why don't my arms work?" Shit, why didn't my tongue work?

Let's not wake the guys up. Smitty has been busy all day. Do you remember everything that happened? Ronnie sent me.

It's there, but my brain is fuzzy.

Don't push it then. You still need time to recover. Ronnie sat me down and slid in behind me on the narrow bed, pulling me against him.

If I still need to recover, why am I awake?

Stolas showed up while you were, um, out. He told

us we needed to get out of the hotel and gave Jax a branch of something he said would give you enough energy to wake up so we could leave. Ronnie filled me in a little.

I see. I kind of saw, honestly, I was still too out of it to grasp a whole lot. I got snippets of what Ronnie said in weird little flashbacks; it was all jumbled though.

You were in rough shape, angel.

That I can believe, based on how I feel. Jax blames himself, doesn't he? I only felt a little guilty for telling on him.

You nailed that on the head. He's doing better than I thought he would be, considering. There's some sort of new stability to him, a different type of strength, Ronnie fumbled for words. *He hasn't left your side.* He threaded his fingers through mine, *Go back to sleep.*

I was halfway out by the time he finished his sentence.

J ax felt that she was falling asleep; he was relieved. He had been hungry but quickly lost his appetite as his mind replayed the events over again. He didn't want to remember it all, just the words Stolas had been saying.

Jax! She shouted in his head. *Where's my necklace?!*

He jumped, almost tipping the chair over. Airiella's voice was frantic, and he tried to calm his racing heart down. She had scared him. *Which necklace, baby?*

The necklace you gave me, it's not on me! Her voice was borderline with panic.

I have it in the pocket of Smitty's pack. The clasp broke. It's okay, love.

I was terrified that I lost it. Are you coming back?

I will soon unless you need me now. Airiella didn't sound like her usual self, and that worried him.

I'm worried about you.

You're worried about me? Why? Jax was confused.

You feel different.

Bad different? He hoped she wasn't picking up on something attached to him.

No, not bad. Just different.

I'm working on being the man you need, siren. After last night a few things inside me shifted. I feel stronger. Maybe that is what you are picking up?

Could be. I love you.

I love you too. Airiella sounded tired again, the panic seemingly over.

Jax stood and paced the small room. The answer was inside him, the demon told him. He felt like it was a trick. The only thing inside him was the darkness, which was significantly smaller thanks to the love of his life.

He paused as that sank in, the love of his life. Love wins. Was that the answer? She was already the answer to so many things; he didn't think that was it. He found it easy to admit that she was it for him; that was a huge change. There would never be anyone else. What was he missing?

His pacing was interrupted by the arrival of Father Roarke. "You should be resting, son."

"Probably. My brain won't slow down. Stolas said the answer was inside me. I can't figure it out. My best guess was love. Part of me doesn't want to believe that she is the answer to making that darkness go away. That price she pays is way too steep. I want that to stop. If the answer to making it stop is in me, what is it?"

"Have you slept at all?" the priest asked.

"A few hours."

Father Roarke sat down and picked at the fruit salad that Airiella hadn't eaten. "Well, if you don't think it's Airiella, what else have you come up with?"

"Nothing. That's it. That's the whole problem."

"There's a subtle change to you since last night. Are you not feeling okay?" Father Roarke observed Jax.

Jax slumped down in a chair across from the priest. "Airiella said the same thing. Am I coming off as not okay? Honestly, I feel more me and stronger than I ever have."

Father Roarke cocked his head to the side and studied Jax. "Maybe that's your answer. Do you feel like you are all the way healed emotionally?"

Jax thought about it carefully. "I think I'm close. Really close. I'm not sure what's left."

"Why do you think you are close?"

Jax gave him a quizzical look. "You don't think I've changed?"

"Oh, I do. I just want to know what you think." Father Roarke smiled gently.

"I'm stronger. More open-minded. Less angry. I can control my emotions better and see things clearer. I can admit my feelings. I told Airiella I loved her. I can admit that everything that happens is not my fault. I'm starting to believe that I'm worthy of her."

Father Roarke remained quiet though he nodded. He steepled his fingers and raked his gaze over Jax's face more than once. When the priest closed his eyes, Jax wasn't sure what to think of that. "In that list you just gave me, did you notice that you didn't mention Winnie?" he finally said.

No, Jax hadn't noticed that. "Winnie? You think the

answer is Winnie?"

"That's not what I said. I noticed that you didn't mention Winnie in the list of things that have healed in you. Winnie is a pretty big one. Do you still blame yourself for her death?"

Oh, did he? "Is that it?" He stood and paced the small area he occupied. "To finish healing, that part needs to be done. And then what? The darkness disappears?"

"I don't know that it will disappear, but it will lose power. Have you ever said goodbye to Winnie?"

"I buried her, Father." Jax ran his hands through his hair in frustration. He knew the priest had hit on something, based on the feelings that were running through him.

"You may have buried her, but you are still holding on to her, to the guilt."

"Am I? I'm not sure I am. Though the more we talk about this, the more my heart feels like someone is using it for a punching bag. You could be right. How am I supposed to go about this?" Jax dropped back into the chair and rested his forehead on the table.

"Ask the other's how they communicate with Winnie. Airiella has brought her back to them. It could be as simple as you talking to her as if she were right here in the room with you. It's the symbolism of letting go. The closure that it gives that will allow you to heal. Forgiveness is a powerful tool."

"Figuratively speaking, Winnie is my demon that I need to slay in order to win the battle." Jax thunked his head on the table a few times. "If Airiella hasn't healed yet either, what's her figurative demon?"

"I can't answer that for you, only she can. However,

since she has several demons after her, figurative and literal, demons might not be the best analogy to use."

Jax barked out a laugh. "Right you are. We need to talk about that too. This is your area of expertise. What could we have done differently to have had a better outcome?"

"The obvious answer is to heal yourselves, so you are better prepared to fight. Defensively speaking, I've never dealt with one of the princes of Hell. Much less two that are on opposite sides of the field. These lower-level ones that Bael keeps sending after you guys, you are more than qualified to dispatch them back to where they came from."

"Is he beatable?" Jax was afraid of the answer.

"I assume so. I'm under no illusions that it will be easy. Bael triggered that energy inside you easily enough. She can hurt him as we've seen, and Ronnie got a few good hits in with those stars of his. All it did, however, was buy us time to escape. That's not an outcome we can hope for every time he makes an appearance." The priest's answer was candid and frightening.

"I don't think we can count on Stolas to give us a handbook on how to beat a prince of Hell." Jax had to trust that Father Roarke was at the top of his field. "Have you requested help?"

"I have. In the morning, the few that are above me will receive the remarkable footage that we sent of Airiella and Bael. The small snippet we sent should be enough to light a firecracker in their hiney's. At the very least, we will get more specialized weapons. The best outcome will be the top researchers will be put on this and find us something useful in those archives."

"Yes, that would be helpful," Jax snorted.

"We have the churches brilliant minds on this, Jax. We will get through it."

"I can't lose her again, Father. I only just found her. We have no other choice but to get through it. That's the only option for me. I fear that if I lose her, I lose me." Jax felt like every cheesy rom-com movie ever made, but he also meant it.

"Never lose hope, son. She has continued to give me a reason to keep it alive." Father Roarke stood up. "In the morning, Taklishim, Degataga, and the church will have irrefutable evidence that demons are at play. And that the first angel of her kind is here to help us. From here on out, it all changes for all of us. Get some rest. When it hits the fan tomorrow, and it will, we will at least be ready."

Jax nodded and stood. He wasn't ever going to be ready to see Airiella go through that again. Jax walked back to the little room they were all crashed in and made his way around the sleeping men on the floor and eased on to the sliver of bed she left for him. At the feel of her arm snaking around him and pulling him closer, he allowed a small smile.

Chapter Fifteen

Aedan clutched the phone to his ear, "She's not recovering as we had hoped." Aedan was honest with Taklishim as he paced back and forth behind the church.

"Because she woke too soon?" Taklishim wondered.

"I don't know. Airiella's having moments of complete forgetfulness, then a few minutes later, it's total clarity. Physically, it's still hurting her to move. Jax is trying not to let it show how freaked out he is. Ronnie and Smitty are hovering like helicopters. Even Father Roarke is concerned."

"Yes, he's told me. It's not even been two days yet, and Airiella was out for that last time. Give it time, Aedan. In the meantime, Degataga is here; we've received Smitty's package and are going over everything. Onida made contact with Airiella's ancestor and has a load of information to share."

"Should we do a conference call when she wakes up?" Aedan glanced at the door of the church.

"I think so," Taklishim agreed.

"Okay. Now, Jax said he mentioned to you his secret plan?" Aedan kept looking back to make sure that he was alone.

"Yes. You have a prospect?"

"It seems good to me. This Ben guy checked it out and said it hits all the points Jax wanted. If you get a chance in the next week, would you mind taking a look? I'd like a second opinion of someone I know." Aedan heard his phone alert him of a text message.

"Sure, Tama and I need to head south a bit for a tribal meeting this week. Send me the address."

"Thanks. I appreciate it. Hang on." Aedan looked at his phone. Ronnie was letting him know Airiella was awake. "She's awake. Ronnie just texted me."

"Give me ten minutes. I'll call back."

"Got it." Aedan hung up and texted the address before forgot and headed back inside. He ran into Smitty first.

"Conference call with Taklishim, Tama, Onida, and Degataga in ten minutes," he informed Smitty. "Tak said Onida made contact with Airiella's ancestor and has information."

"Fuck. Finally, a break in something," Smitty heaved a giant sigh.

"Yep. I'll go find the others." Aedan headed to the small room where they had all slept. He found all the rest of them there. "Conference call in ten minutes. Onida has information for us."

He looked closer at Airiella; her face was pale and drawn tight. Her eyes looked dull, none of that usual spark she had. A trickle of fear swept through him again that she wasn't alright. They needed a break and bad.

Father Roarke passed him on the way out of the room, "Don't lose hope."

I didn't feel right; I remembered everything now, at least, but I still felt sick inside. I forced more oatmeal down my throat to appease Jax and Ronnie and hoped it stayed put. I needed fresh air and didn't think I was going to get any soon.

"Raven, are you with us?"

"I'm here," I answered flatly. Taklishim's voice held concern.

"Airiella, I'm flying to California. I'd like to check you over myself," I heard Onida say.

"We aren't in California," I told her.

"We will be leaving in a few hours," Father Roarke interrupted. "The church is allowing us a private plane."

"Any catches?" Smitty asked.

"They are sending someone to meet Airiella tomorrow. She might need to make her wings show up," Father Roarke shrugged.

"Whatever," I answered. "I'll do what I need to do."

Jax had his eyes glued to me. He knew I wasn't okay. I couldn't hide it from him. "What have you learned, Onida?" he asked, watching me.

"Marco Rosati is indeed her ancestor. He told her grandfather, Winnie, and I, his story. It's quite tragic, and it gives us several angles to pursue as a course of action the council is going after. It could be any or all of them. Marco had gotten accused of a murder he didn't commit, witchcraft, and his family helped him escape the town and death sentence the father of the murdered girl announced necessary. Over here, he fell in with what I believe was mafia or some sort of organized crime and arrested. As a punishment, they sent Marco West to work in the mines. While there, he overheard the plans of people plotting a fire due to racial and political unrest and tried to warn the others, but Marco's claim got ultimately discredited. The people behind the fire accused him of working with demons, and they set him up to take the fall for the explosion and fire."

"Holy shit," Ronnie exclaimed. "That's indeed a lot of angles. None of them good."

"Who committed the murder he got blamed for?" I asked.

"The father of the girl. He caught Marco and the girl, Lena, in the act, so to speak. They had been planning on running away and getting married. She was pregnant with his child."

"Oh, my God." I was horrified. That poor man. "You said you spoke with my grandpa?"

"Yes, we took him with us to talk to Marco. He asked me to remind you of what he told you."

"What was that?" My eyes teared up.

"That he will come back to you. He said you'd know what it meant."

"I don't though." I swallowed the sob that was trying to choke me. "Is he okay?"

"He's fine, Airiella. He was happy to meet Marco. Also, Winnie is now Marco's girlfriend."

I could have sworn I heard a smile in Onida's voice when she said that. I was intrigued, but I didn't feel well enough to follow through with the questions that peppered my brain.

"You saw Winnie?" Jax spoke up. I wondered how he was taking that.

"I've been speaking to her for a while now," Onida confirmed.

"Okay," Smitty interrupted. "Looks like we focus on finding out which angle the council is going to try to use against Airiella."

"If they are bringing in Asher, I'd think they are going to go after the demon angle, and murder rap, possibly organized crime. Those would be the things in their eyes that would hurt Airiella now, or cause the public to have a bad opinion of her or her family," Jax said.

"I think Jax is right," Taklishim said. "Especially the demon part because of the show. It ties in."

"Can Asher force Marco to speak to him?" I wondered out loud.

"There are ways to force spirits to talk, and it would mean that he is in communication with some dark forces. Asher doesn't strike me as someone brave enough to venture there," Tama commented.

"Stone wouldn't have that problem," Ronnie added. "He could be doing the dirty work and forcing Asher somehow."

"Degataga, are there any side effects of whatever that plant was that Stolas had me use?" Jax focused his gaze back on me.

"I don't know yet, unlikely any dangerous ones. The recipe Stolas gave for the topical pain solution he used on

Airiella is brilliant. If Airiella isn't feeling well, it's likely from the demon poison she pulled that was helping to activate that energy in Jax. Onida will be able to tell if that's what it is. I can join her if you'd like."

"I was poisoned?" I didn't remember that part.

"I need to watch the footage again more slowly. Something happened there; I'm just not sure what," Taklishim said carefully.

"Two heads are better than one, no offense Onida," Jax broke in.

"None taken, Dega is welcome to join me," the words were friendly, but I was picking up on something in her tone that told me there was more there.

"Smitty, the blood on the star is perfect. Kalisha said she thinks she can come up with something that will hurt Bael with it. We are looking at a few other avenues as well," Taklishim continued.

"What blood?" I felt like I was missing vital information.

"Yeah, what blood?" Ronnie sat forward.

"I grabbed one of the stars you hit him with, there was blood on it," Smitty explained.

"Is it possible that his blood got in Airiella?" Jax asked. He was like super Jax today.

"It's possible, I suppose. I didn't see one of those hit Airiella. As I said, I need to re-watch all that footage."

"If it did, what does that mean for me?" I needed to know this information.

"I'm not sure. Between Onida and Degataga, they should be able to figure it out. There's a lot about you that we just don't know."

I was back to feeling like a science experiment. My

head started buzzing loudly, and the room got fuzzy for a minute. I blinked slowly, trying to bring it back into focus, though it only made me dizzier. The damn buzzing was so loud I couldn't even hear them talking anymore. I didn't feel my head hit the table.

Fuck! How soon will you guys be in California?" Ronnie exploded out of his chair and was gently checking Airiella's head.

"We will leave at the same time as you do. Did something happen?" Onida asked rapidly.

"That thud you just heard was Airiella's head hitting the table," Jax responded. "She's out cold."

"I'll call and ask if we can leave sooner," Father Roarke stood and left the room.

"I'm going to go put all our stuff in the car," Smitty followed him out with Aedan trailing after, looking back worriedly over his shoulder at Airiella.

"She is not okay," Ronnie's quiet statement filled the room.

"She's not," Jax agreed.

"Do you guys know how to get ahold of Stolas and ask him what the hell is wrong?" Ronnie fought to keep from shouting.

"I'm sure he's watching already," Tama replied. "He's invested in her."

"We will see you soon. We'll meet you at the house," Degataga interrupted before Ronnie could find some smart-ass comment to fling out there.

"Thank you," Jax told them and gave Ronnie a look.

"What? You can't possibly tell me this doesn't worry

you."

"It worries me plenty. If Onida is flying out here to check on her without us asking her to, that tells me something is wrong. I just can't afford to lose my shit like that." Ronnie looked closely at Jax's face watching for signs that he was losing control and didn't see any.

"The thought of losing her fills me with panic on a level I've never felt before. I've watched her die twice now, and each time I wanted to go with her." Ronnie knew his tone was wild and crazy-sounding, and he didn't care.

"Do you honestly think that I don't feel the same way?" Jax sounded scared.

"I don't know what to think. I don't know what to think about anything right now." Ronnie bent and carefully lifted her into his arms. "I've carried her so many times now that I don't feel right if I don't have her weight in my arms. Yet the flip side of that is I'm sick of her getting put in the position of needing it."

Taklishim's voice came from the phone. "I'm still here. Onida wanted to know if she had a fever."

"I haven't taken her temperature, but I can tell you she's been warm and dry," Jax answered, grabbing Aedan's phone. "She's hardly eating or drinking."

Ronnie felt like a total asshole then. He hadn't even noticed that she'd been warmer than usual. "What do you mean dry?"

Jax shot him another look. "Look at how narrow that bed is, and there were three of us crammed on it. Both you and I were hot as hell and sweating. She didn't sweat once."

"Jesus, I'm sorry, Jax. I'm not trying to be an asshole." Ronnie walked out of the little meeting room and back towards the bedroom, Jax relaying more information to Taklishim that Ronnie hadn't picked up on at all.

When Jax turned back to them, the phone wasn't in his hand, and Ronnie assumed he'd hung up. Jax saw everything where it concerned Airiella. Ronnie only saw the worry he had for her. He started to apologize again when Jax held up his hand for Ronnie to stop.

"Don't apologize. I get it."

"Did one of the stars he threw back towards her wing her?" Ronnie suddenly asked.

"I don't know. I don't think so, and it was hard to tell with so much blood on our angel. Her head slammed into that wall pretty hard though when whatever he did sent her flying backward."

"Do you ever think about quitting the show now?" Ronnie was afraid to ask and afraid to tell Jax he felt like being out. He wanted to take Airiella somewhere safe and just take care of her.

"All the time. I see what it's doing to Airiella, to all of us. I also know that she would hate it if we stopped. She truly believes we are doing something good and helpful with the show and proving that things we can't see, exist. Fuck, we are literally living a life that proves it all exists, and we can't say anything."

Ronnie leaned over her inert form and breathed her in. "It's been so long since I've seen you like this. It's taking me a bit of getting used to; I trust your decisions where she is concerned, where *all* of us are concerned. I'm just having a harder time, not panicking."

"Shit, Ron," Jax sat down next to him. "You've been taking care of me for the past twelve years. It wouldn't surprise me if I gave you PTSD. You're entitled to your fear.

I'm not trying to take over. Who I was before Winnie's accident, and who I was after her accident, neither are the same person I am now."

"I see that. I keep expecting you to revert to that Jax before the accident, which isn't fair. I'm learning. A lot has changed."

"A lot had to change. It still has to change. Through all of you, I am becoming who I am supposed to be. I don't expect any of you to know how I will react or what I will do when I don't even know myself. All I am sure of is that I want to be someone she can be proud of, someone she wants to call hers."

"Well, *that* was a sign of the idiot from the past twelve years," Ronnie said sarcastically. "She's already proud of you, Jax, and she already calls you hers."

Jax grinned, "I know. She calls you hers too."

"She's right, I am."

Airiella suddenly groaned, and as Ronnie glanced down at her, he noticed her face was ghostly pale. He recalled Jax saying she was warm and he felt her head, it wasn't warm, it was hot. "She's got a fever."

"We need to get out of here." Jax flew through the room, calling for the priest demanding to know when they could leave.

Ronnie knelt on the floor, bringing his face close to his angel's. "Don't you dare leave me, angel. We are going to get you back, Onida and Degataga are going to check you out. You fight this, whatever is happening. We love you."

She opened her eyes, "I love you too, Heracles. Where's Jax?"

He felt a pang in his heart. "Checking on when we can leave, do you need me to get him?"

"No. Can you take me outside, please? I want to see the sky." Her eyes closed again, and her request worried Ronnie, though he didn't know why, maybe because it sounded like a final request.

"I'll take you outside, but you have to promise to stay with us," Ronnie countered as he stood to lift her again gently.

"I'm not going anywhere," she whispered.

"He truly loves you, angel. I hope you mean that." Ronnie dropped a kiss on her burning forehead.

"I love him more than anything," she said right before her head lolled against his chest. His heart panged again. He wasn't jealous; he only wanted someone to love him that much.

I do love you that much.

He carried her out to the front steps of the church and sat down with her in the fresh air. Tears stung his eyes. He'd known from the start Jax was the one for her, but he wasn't ready to let her go yet.

Chapter Sixteen

iriella, you need to wake up now," Onida told me.

"I'm talking to you, aren't I? What do you mean I need to wake up? This headache is a bitch."

"Look around you. What do you see?" Onida demanded in a brisk tone.

"Nothing. Where am I? The last thing I remember was being on the phone with you all. Where's Degataga?" I didn't think I was going to like her answer.

"You are in the spirit world, Airiella. Not fully, you are straddling the lines between the worlds. I need you to wake fully up so you can drink the mix Degataga has made so we can work on you."

"Work on what?" I had no idea why I was acting so obstinate.

"Your brain is bleeding. Between Degataga and I, we can fix it without taking you in for surgery, but I need you to wake up first. Also, these two men won't leave your side, and they are driving me crazy."

"Fine. How do I wake up?" I asked.

"Open your eyes," Onida said drily. She tapped my head.

I opened my eyes to see Jax and Ronnie hovering at the foot of my bed. Wait, I was back in California? Onida said my brain was bleeding. "Can't that kill me?"

My question startled Jax and Ronnie, and both were in motion before Degataga stopped them. "Yes, it can kill you. Drink this please," he handed me a water bottle with green colored water in it.

"You two need to let us be," Onida glared at them both.

"If you think I'm leaving here, you are delusional," Jax crossed his arms.

"Ditto," Ronnie mimicked Jax's stance.

"Sit back there and don't speak then. At all. We need concentration and silence," Onida crossed her arms and looked formidable.

Degataga chuckled and felt my head. "You are still warm. What we will do won't hurt you, but if we don't do this soon, we won't be able to fix it without taking you in for surgery. Jax said you impacted the wall of the hotel pretty hard with your head."

"Airiella, it's delicate work, but it's also incredibly urgent. Drink that mix down as fast as you can. It will put you out," Onida told me gently. "Do you trust us?"

"Of course, I trust you. I wouldn't drink green water if I didn't trust either of you. Will it make this headache go away?" I chugged the water down.

Degataga lifted the amulet that Kalisha made me off

my neck and patted me on the hand. "Relax."

Angel, this is serious. Do whatever they tell you to do. I love you; Ronnie's voice filled my head.

I love you too, Ronnie.

Siren, I won't leave this room. I promise you, Jax said next.

I love you, Jax.

I love you too, baby.

My brain started to fuzz out, and I grabbed Onida's hand. *Take care of them if I die.*

You won't die, Airiella. Doing this will be exhausting for us, but you won't die.

I opened my senses up, and after I grabbed Degataga's hand, I pumped my energy into both of them until I saw them both start to glow, which happened at a good time because suddenly, I was out cold.

J ax winced. "Good thing Taklishim isn't here, that move would have pissed him right the hell off," Jax whispered to Ronnie.

"What the fuck did she do?" Ronnie whispered back, swallowing his gasp.

"She gave them her energy. That's what she did to Taklishim that first time we saw Bael when it zapped all her strength out of her." Jax remembered how fierce it had made the warrior. Onida looked equally as intense right now while Degataga looked stunned.

"Quiet, both of you. Yes, that would have pissed Tak off, but if she hadn't done that, it would have been harder for us. Before you ask, no, I didn't know she was going to do it." Onida shot a look over her glowing shoulder at them.

"You knew she could do this?" Degataga still had a shocked look on his face. "It's the craziest high."

"Let's get to work," Onida ignored him, all business as they both fell silent and went into a trance-like state. After about an hour, Jax noticed that their glow had faded away, and both had a subtle sheen of sweat on their face.

Two hours after that, they finished. Degataga handed Onida a bottle of something that she drank down fast while he drank his own. "We will need to rest. Is there a room we can use?"

"You can use both of ours; they are the connecting rooms directly across the hall. We will be staying in here," Jax stood, slowly stretching. He half expected an argument from Onida. "Is she okay?"

Instead, she stood over Airiella and wiped the hair off her face. "It is nice to be able to return the favor of saving you. Rest," she whispered over the still form. "She is. She just needs the rest she never gave herself last time. I imagine she won't wake until morning." She gave a gentle nod to Jax and Ronnie and left them there.

"Want to take turns eating?" Ronnie asked.

Jax shrugged, he wasn't starving. "Go ahead; I'll sit here. You can let the rest know that they are finished on her, and what Onida said."

"Want me to bring you anything?" Ronnie gave Jax a look. "Changes aside, I still know you, and know that means you aren't leaving here."

Jax gave a soft laugh. "You got me there. Sports drink and water maybe. I'm not hungry."

"Mags won't let that fly. I'll find something for you, so she won't barge in here and demand that you go eat." Ronnie stretched out a few more times, and they both heard a buzzing noise and checked their phones. "Not mine."

"Not mine either," Jax put his phone back in his pocket. "It's Airiella's. Should we answer it?"

"Who is it? I don't want to tell her family about this," Ronnie asked nervously.

"Chris. Do you know who that is?" Jax frowned, trying to remember if he met anyone with that name.

"Her friend in Kansas that we visited. I'll answer it. She might remember me."

Jax handed the phone over and stretched out on the bed next to the greatest love he'd ever known. "If you can hear me in there, I love you, and I'm patiently waiting for you to come back to me."

He ran his fingers through her hair, finger combing the tangles out as he hummed mindlessly. He skimmed his fingers over her face and ran his hands down her arms. He decided that once Ronnie came back, they could dress her in one of Ronnie's t-shirts that she loved to wear so much, so at least she would be comfortable.

Now that Jax thought about it, he'd bathe her first. He changed his mind; he was hogging her. Jax would ask Ronnie if he wanted to bathe her. He'd caught the expressions of longing on Ronnie's face. With that decided, he was content to sit and watch her sleep, keeping his skin on hers.

"I'm in the same rabbit hole you are, love. Soon, I hope to prove it to you in a way that leaves no doubt in your mind. Thanks to you, I'm almost healed inside. I think there's only one thing left in me that I need to address, which is the biggest of them all: Winnie. After you are awake and I know you are okay, I'm going to try to talk to her and sort out this mess in my head. All that leaves me with is you. Which, if I'm honest, is all I really want anyway."

He kissed her cheek gently. "Everything about you draws me in from your stubbornness and sarcasm to your absolute conviction that everyone deserves love. Your fierce spirit that hides the soft and vulnerable parts of you that you share with so few people is the most beautiful thing I've ever encountered. The way you so selflessly step right into the dark places inside me and pull me right back out without regard to your safety manages to undo me every time. The fact that you see something worthy of love in me, and you work so hard to show me tells me without words how much you love me. For me, there's only you."

Jax pulled her hand into his and massaged her palm and fingers. "The way your skin feels on mine is pure magic. There's no cure for this addiction I have for you, and I don't ever want there to be. I'd walk away from my life for you. I'll walk through every fire of your choosing right by your side and go head to head with any demon to remain with you."

Jax heard Ronnie clear his throat. "Am I interrupting?"

"No. I was just talking to Airiella. It made me feel better."

"It was quite touching. I didn't mean to eavesdrop." Ronnie walked in and set down a baggie of almonds and grapes, the sports drink, and water on the nightstand. "Was all of that true?"

Jax opened up the sports drink and took a big gulp. "Every last bit of it."

"Those are forever words."

"Yes, they are. Airiella's that for me. I don't think I've ever told her that, because it scares the shit out of me to admit it. But it's true." Jax refastened the cap. "Should we give her a bath?"

"Sure. Our angel would probably appreciate that."

"Think we can sneak into our rooms to get some clean clothes? Grab one of those shirts of yours that she loves to wear so much."

"Funny thing about that," Ronnie grinned. "There's no one in my room. I peeked in yours, and they both lay curled up around each other."

"Seriously?" Jax felt his jaw drop open.

"Yep. I'm quieter than you; I can grab you a clean pair of sweats. Give me a minute."

Jax couldn't help but grin. Onida seemed so distant to Jax, never really showing a whole lot of emotion. Of course, he never attempted to get to know any of the council before Airiella came into the picture. He wished them well if something was between those two.

Ronnie came back in with a pile of clothes. "Easy enough. They are out cold."

"Let me shower super-fast first; then, we can get her undressed while the tub fills." Jax stood up.

"Wait, you aren't bathing with her?"

"I thought you would." Jax stepped into the bathroom, leaving a stunned Ronnie behind with Airiella. It was the fastest shower he'd ever taken, but it got the job done. He came back out to find Ronnie had opened the windows in her room, allowing a fresh breeze to flow through.

"She loves the fresh air," Ronnie explained, he went into the hall and came back with four towels and set them in the bathroom.

They got her undressed, and Ronnie settled into the tub first. "At least you didn't scent the water with flowery stuff as Mags did," Ronnie laughed.

"I thought about it. Then I figured if we were both staying with Airiella tonight in here, I didn't want to get confused and cuddle the wrong person," Jax shot him a grin as he lowered Airiella into the water. She let out a soft moan and snuggled into Ronnie's chest. "Want me to leave?"

"No, you promised her you'd be here." Ronnie's face lit with happiness at how she melted into him. Jax thought for sure he'd be jealous at that, but he wasn't. She'd told him so many times of the differences she'd felt between the two of them he was secure about it.

"I need to talk to Winnie," Jax told him. The comment startled Ronnie. "Sorry. I do. I think it's the last thing I need to do to make things right inside me. Give me a fighting chance to make this shit in me weaker."

"Well, if that's the case, all you need to do is take the necklace off and call out to her. She appears to me when I do that. You have to take the necklace off, though. Otherwise it doesn't work."

"Is it safe to take it off?" Jax fingered the amulet.

"I only do it here in this house since Father Roarke told me that this property is safe. I'd assume the same for you. When are you going to do it?"

"After she's awake, and I'm sure she's okay." Jax handed him the washcloth he was pointing at, marveling at how pliable she was.

"Not wasting any time then?" Ronnie rinsed her off and slid her down a little to get her hair wet and shampooed it, massaging her scalp gently.

"I don't see any reason to. It's in all of our best interest for me to heal up. I can't help but wonder, with as far as Airiella has come, what does she have left to face?"

Ronnie pulled the plug of the tub. "Hold her up, while I stand."

Jax knelt and held her in place while Ronnie stood and turned the shower on, careful not to spray Jax. Jax released her when Ronnie grabbed hold of her and stood under the spray to rinse her hair off. Jax conditioned her hair while Ronnie held her, and then rinsed her off.

Jax grabbed a towel and wrapped it around her lower half. He picked up another to wrap around her upper body, and then the third one to cover her hair. Ronnie handed her over and finished his shower while Jax dried her off and put her back on the bed.

He stepped back in to grab the jasmine lotion he'd gotten her all those months ago and started rubbing it into her skin, thoroughly pampering her. When Ronnie came out, they put his t-shirt on her and laid her down in the middle of the bed.

"I think the only thing she hasn't faced is her last relationship. She's talked about it. She told me about the asshole, but it was in a somewhat distanced manner. She held back most of the emotions she was feeling," Ronnie answered Jax's earlier question.

"Was it one of the abusive ones?" Jax wasn't sure he wanted to know.

"Not physically. From what Airiella said, he's the one who hurt her the most."

"Emotionally, then?" Jax pushed.

"If she hasn't told you, then it needs to come from

her. I can tell you that the prick gaslighted her."

"Fucking prick," Jax fumed. "It's the ex that did the bedroom stalking thing, right?"

"Yeah. Let's not talk about it. Let's just give our angel some TLC and hope she wakes up good as new in the morning." Ronnie settled back into the bed and brushed her wet hair out while Jax ate the grapes Ronnie had brought up and a few of the almonds. His mind miles away.

Jax lay back, and she automatically curled up into his side. She reached behind her for Ronnie's arm, which she pulled across her middle. Jax's heart swelled and felt like it would burst from the emotions she brought out in him.

Chapter Seventeen

Winnie wasn't sure what to do. She'd never been called by Jax before. It scared her and made her giddy at the same time; she went to him but hadn't appeared yet. He was sitting in the garden on that bench where he'd had his first real talk with Airy.

He looked good and very different than what she remembered. To Winnie, he seemed more like a grown-up now than before Airy had come into the picture. He was still handsome, and she had to admit that the stubble looked very sexy on him.

She slowly materialized, so she didn't startle him. "Hi, Jax. You are looking good."

His face was a mask of shock. "Winnie," he let out in a startled breath.

"Why are you surprised? You called me here."

"I don't know. I guess some small part of me didn't

fully believe the rest could all see you. Maybe I didn't want to believe it because I couldn't. Finding you was the whole reason I started this journey. It took a total stranger I'd never even heard of saying she talked to you, and that's why she was with us," Jax blurted out in a breath.

"I tried. I knew you were looking for me. I couldn't breach the boundaries. It took Airy to make that happen. I was just as surprised as you were. I probably handled it better than you did, too," Winnie gave him a wink.

Jax laughed. "I'll admit, I was an ass. I didn't want to be. She stirred something in me from the start, and it scared me."

"Believe me, I know. I could feel the fear running through you. I also felt the rest. You don't need to justify your feelings to me, Jax."

"I'm not. That's not why I called you here. I wanted to see you with my own eyes. I wanted to talk to you."

Winnie's eyes shone with unshed tears. He indeed *was* better. "I'm glad you did. I'm going to tell you a little secret. When you told Airiella you loved her, the binds that were holding me here broke. I'm not hurting anymore, Jax."

Jax paled. "I created binds that held you here? You were hurting because of me?"

"You created the bindings, yes. It wasn't you that was hurting me. That energy in you was. It used to seep out from you into my trapped spirit. I tried for years to get through to tell you, and eventually, I gave up, resigned to being stuck. I felt everything you did." Winnie had to tell him the truth.

Jax blinked back tears. She saw them shimmering in his eyes. "I never meant to do that. I'm so sorry, Winnie.

That's why I called you here. I wanted to apologize for everything. I didn't know you were trapped."

"Hey! Look at me, Jax," Winnie demanded as the tears fell, and his eyes followed, dropping down. "If I had believed that you created those binds intentionally, I would have found a way to haunt your ass. I know you didn't mean to, I had no way to get through. It never worked with anyone, with any team I tried, professionals and amateurs alike."

"I'm trying so hard, Winnie. I want so badly to be someone worthy of Airiella. I think talking to you is my last hurdle." Jax looked away again. "I need to forgive myself, but after hearing that, I'm not sure I can. I never wanted to hurt you."

Winnie reached out and put her hand over his, watching as he visibly shuddered and then looked down at her side. "Jax, I never blamed you. It was an accident."

"If I had just not been a jerk, you wouldn't have taken off like a bat out of hell from Ronnie's house."

"All that means is I would have died another day in a different accident. I saw my death, Jax, it was a foregone conclusion. You didn't cause it. Yes, because of you, I was never with Ronnie in the way we both wanted. Maybe things would have been different if we had been, but then I still would have died, and he would have lost even more. It worked out how it was supposed to. I was angry that I never got to be with him, yes. Time has also allowed me to see that it was perhaps for the best."

"I'm so sorry, Winnie." Jax's shoulders shook with the force of the sobs he was trying to keep silent.

"It's not your fault Jax. Yes, you were a stupid boy scared to be alone. Do you think you are the first? There's countless over here who did equally as stupid things. Everyone makes mistakes. If it makes a difference, I forgive you. I've never blamed you; you shouldn't blame yourself."

"I don't know that I know how to stop. I felt guilty for falling out of love with you in the first place," he swiped at the tears on his face.

"I know. I felt guilty too. It happens. We were both young, and I think on some level we both knew we weren't the forever couple. No matter how much we told ourselves we were. It doesn't lessen the love we did have, then or now. I still love you, Jax. I always will. You are a part of me. I am a part of you."

"I do love you, Winnie. You're right that you are a part of me. I, too, will always love you. I *did* love you with everything I had back then. Fiercely. It's only now, with Airiella, that I can look back and see the holes. It adds to my guilt, and I know that it shouldn't. Relationships come and go. I felt so strongly that I failed you. Sometimes, I still do. I think that ultimately, I failed all of us. You, me and Ronnie."

"You didn't. Ronnie still loves you. I've never seen a closer friendship than the one you two share. It's awe-inspiring. Despite the ups and downs, it's never wavered." She wished she could wipe his tears away.

"I don't know about that. I pushed Ronnie to his limits. Now, there's Airiella. He's in love with her just as much as I am."

"That worries you?" Winnie wasn't shocked, she was mildly surprised, given that Jax knew how Airiella felt for him.

"In the sense that I don't want him to feel like I've taken another love from him. I know how she feels about both of us. She put it in pretty clear words for me. I also know she has this amazing capacity to love both of us. She needs both of us. I know what I want to do, Winnie, but I am also afraid of losing Ronnie."

"You won't. Airiella is his first real love. She isn't his last." Winnie understood where he was coming from with the concern. "You've gotten pretty mature lately. I see hints of the Jax I dated in you, the one after I died, and this new emerging person that's pretty incredible in his own rights. Trust me when I say that Ronnie knows the score with Airiella. It might sting a little bit, but Jax, Ronnie knew she was yours before you even met her. I told him I had seen her and you together before I died."

"I don't want it to hurt him. Not at all. I tried to imagine my life without her. I thought I would walk away and let Ronnie get the girl. It hurt so bad I thought I was dying."

"Let's just say I know he won't be alone," Winnie winked again.

Jax breathed out a sigh of relief. "I won't ask for any more details. It still doesn't help me forgive myself for putting you both through all that shit."

"I can't help you forgive yourself, Jax. I can only tell you I don't believe you have anything to forgive. Whether you believe it or not is up to you. You didn't kill me. Your wrong was in your attitude and fear, and I've got to say those are pretty normal things to have. You're human, mistakes happen."

"I know. Did Aedan tell you the names of his babies?"

Winnie squealed. "Yes! I was so excited. I told Airy's grandpa too. He was impressed and called Aedan a good fellow."

"So, you've talked to him then?"

"Yes, quite frequently. Guiseppe's a charmer. And he loves her so much; it's easy to see where she gets some of her characteristics. Oh, and his ancestor, Marco? He's super-hot and says he's my boyfriend now. I am *not* going to argue with him."

"Is ghost sex a thing?" Jax teased.

"I don't know yet. I've got to get around Marco's old-fashioned ways still. You'd think for someone that had premarital sex in Italy, of all the places, it wouldn't be such an issue. He still feels scandalized by everything he went through. The most I've gotten is a kiss that landed near my lips. With Giuseppe as a chaperone," she said wryly.

Jax laughed. "Then take matters into your own hands. Just don't tell me the details. Torture Ronnie with that."

Winnie sobered up. "Can you do it, Jax? Can you forgive yourself? You both deserve it."

"I feel better saying sorry to you. Saying sorry to myself is a little harder and might take some self-reflection that scares me to do, but I will. I *have* to do it, Winnie, I don't have a choice. She's everything to me. Everything." Jax leaned back on the bench and stared at the sky through the tree branches.

"Well, think of it this way. Ronnie has experienced love, I have experienced love, and now I get to do it again, and he's way hotter than you." She winked at his frowning expression. "I don't blame you. Ronnie doesn't blame you. We both believe in you, and you won the heart of a truly rare and exceptional woman. Plus, her grandpa likes you."

"I don't think poor Marco is at all prepared for an

Irish redhead," Jax commented.

"You are right on that one. I'd go easier on Marco if he weren't so hot and charming. The men of that family were all blessed with the charm gene, that's for sure," she fanned her face dramatically.

"Thank you, Winnie. For everything. Then and now." Jax tapped his chest. "You'll always be a part of who I am, no matter how much I change. I can't tell you how much I've missed talking to you like this."

"Let it go, Jax. Open those cage doors and let it go. I'm happy now, and you deserve that too."

Jax nodded. "I wish I could hug you."

"I can hug you! Be prepared for a blast of cold air!" Winnie threw her arms around Jax and smiled as his skin pebbled up. "I'm always around, Jax. We can talk whenever you want."

She popped out of sight and took a moment to watch whatever he was about to do. Her heart stuttered around in her chest as she watched him break down and cry again. He stroked the cross tattoo on his finger that he'd gotten in honor of her.

The emotions she picked up from Jax wasn't all pain. She hoped those were freeing tears and not guilt ones. She heard him whisper, "It's not your fault, Jax. Let it go." He honestly was trying. He repeated that mantra over and over again. After a while, she heard him utter, "Goodbye, Winnie. I love you."

At that, Winnie broke down in tears. He'd done it. She felt the freeing weight of grief ease from him in a slow trickle, his tears cleansing him now. It was bittersweet; she'd gotten so used to the feel of his grief it had become a part of her. She figured things with that energy inside him would get easier to deal with now that the power it used to feed on had diminished. With the release of that grief, Winnie herself, felt lighter.

Jax lay down across the bench and stared up at the sky. Winnie felt the changes inside him and did a happy dance, elation bubbling up. If Jax could be brave and face that, she could be bold and face that sexy new ghost that called her a girlfriend. It was time for her seduction to begin.

Chapter Eighteen

ven with Jax having closed off his connection to me, I still felt the weight of the emotions coming across, and it called to me on a deep level. I tried hard to let him have his space. I understood his need for it. He'd always given me the space I needed and waited until I was ready and went to him. Jax deserved the same respect.

I grabbed a book and decided to meet him halfway. I went and sat by the pool to read, Ronnie quickly seeing through my ploy, but he didn't stop me. He went to work with Degataga and Onida on plans to halt demon attacks, while Smitty and Aedan edited the footage of the investigation to send the studio.

I was impressed with Jax facing the last of his wounds inside. It was something I needed to do myself; I just didn't know how to go about it. Michael was a pretty big wound that still found ways to bleed. Aside from being in a different state than him, even if I had been at home, I wouldn't know how to go about letting that go. I didn't want to see him. I didn't even want to acknowledge his existence.

I got so lost in my thoughts that I didn't hear Jax's approach until he sat on the end of the chaise lounge I was on. "Are you pretending to read?"

I so badly wanted to pull his clothes off and mold that glorious inked up skin of his to mine. That need to be close to him never eased up, and easily distracted me. "I was thinking," I defended myself, pulling my thoughts away from where they had been heading with that train of thought.

"Are you sure you weren't coming out here to check on me?" he ran his hands over my legs.

"Maybe I was trying to get a little closer to you. I left you alone, though."

"You could have come out there. I was missing you anyway. How do you feel?" Jax looked me over.

"So much better. I'm only a little tired, and that's probably due to giving the healers my energy more than it is from the head injury. No more headache."

"No other residual effects from anything. Are you moving better?" Jax pulled the book from my hands and set it on the little table.

"Hey," I protested weakly. "I was pretending to read that."

He stood up and laughed, hauling me to my feet. "No more pain?" I shook my head in answer to his question as he lowered those yummy lips to mine. He scooped me up, one of his arms under my legs as he deepened the kiss.

I was lost. The next thing I knew, we were submerged in the water, clothes and all. I sputtered to the surface, "I can't believe you did that!" I shouted and splashed him. "That was a dirty trick!"

"It was so easy, too," Jax laughed.

God help me; this playful side of him was sexy as sin. That white t-shirt he wore so well molded to his body and became see-through. Just like that, I needed him like I needed oxygen. "You know, swimming with your clothes on is dangerous. They can weigh you down and exhaust you faster, which could lead to drowning. You should probably take them off to be safe."

He threw his head back and gave me a belly laugh that tickled my insides. "That was not subtle at all, siren. You've gotta try harder than that. I'm standing with my head above water. I don't think I'm in danger of exhausting myself." The gleam in his eyes told me I could sway him with a little effort.

My plans got derailed at the shout of "Cannonball!" Ronnie yelled as he splashed down in the water.

Quickly followed by a slower Mags who shouted, "Chicken fight!" and dunked Jax to climb on his shoulders.

Ronnie came up under me, putting me on his shoulders. "Hey! I can't fight a pregnant lady!"

"Chicken!" Mags called out. "Hey, I kind of like directing Jax around like I'm his boss."

"How is this is different from any other day?" Jax teased her.

"I'm pretty sure I'll never complain about having an angel's legs wrapped around my neck either," Ronnie tipped his head back, looking up at me. I bent to drop a kiss on his head.

"Not fair," Jax said with a smile.

"You had your chance, buddy," I grinned wickedly.

Trip him, make both of their asses fall in the water, I sent to Ronnie.

I'm way ahead of you there, angel. They don't stand a chance.

We were so intent on taking down Jax and Mags, I hadn't heard Smitty and Aedan get in behind us. At least not until I was squealing and falling backward into the water, spotting their grinning faces. I came up spluttering. "Cheaters!"

It became an all-out war, with Father Roarke, Onida, and Degataga smiling from a safe distance away. I knew they wanted to get back to the business at hand, but our little water fight was some much-needed downtime and bonding time.

Along with that, I felt the pure joy flowing through Jax, and it made my heart sing. He had healed up, and it looked phenomenal on him. We all had a new sense of hope filling us, something we had desperately needed, along with our having fun.

Jax and Ronnie were so finely in tune with me they knew when my energy was starting to run out. Between some unspoken command, they halted the war, declaring Aedan and Smitty the winners, as they had been the only ones able to get Ronnie and me down.

After volunteering for me and him to make dinner for everyone that night, Jax pulled me off of Ronnie. Together we went into the house and up to my room. "How are you feeling?" he asked me, pulling me in for an orgasm inducing-kiss.

"After that kiss or in general?" I said breathlessly.

He chuckled softly, "In general."

"I'm okay. Just tired. How are *you* feeling?" I ran

my fingers over his stubble, making him shiver.

"Like I'm good enough to be with you," he gave me a sexy smile.

"You always have been," I whispered, sealing my mouth to his while we stood there, making a puddle on the bathroom floor. "Shower with me?"

"That was my plan," he groaned into my neck as I ran my hands up his chest.

"By the way, you make plain white t-shirts look like the sexiest piece of clothing ever made. Even better when it's wet and see-through."

"I should enter a wet t-shirt contest then?" he smirked.

"No. I'd have to use lighting on everyone that looked at you."

He laughed again and started stripping off my wet clothes. "I think I like it when you are jealous."

Two could play at that game. "I wonder what Ronnie would look like in a white wet t-shirt?"

"Probably better than me," he didn't fall for it. He didn't need to. He knew how I felt.

"Damn, this new, healed version of you is harder to rattle. I'm not used to working this hard with you." I said it with a smile, so he knew I was kidding.

"If that was your goal, you should have picked someone other than Ronnie. I'd have fallen for it in a heartbeat, siren."

"Well telling me how to beat you kind of takes the fun out of it," I pushed his pants down off him and ran my hand down the inside of his thigh and back up, noting the hiss of breath between his teeth as I danced my fingers over the hard length of him. "Besides, I don't want to make you jealous. It's so much more fun to torture you this way instead."

"You are good at that," he moaned when I switched my fingers for my tongue. He hauled me up to his chest and lifted me, placing me in the shower and stepping in behind me. "And as much as I like that, I need to be buried in you. It's been a rough couple of days."

"I'm not arguing," I stretched up and kissed him under the spray of the showerhead. I opened my senses back up so he could feel the deep well of emotions he brought out in me and gave in to them. I went pliant in his arms, surrendering to the sensations of his touch.

A primal moan tore from his lips, and he spun me around, pushing gently on my back, so I bent over, his grip on my hips firm as he wasted no time and slid in fast and hard. I arched my back to change the angle, and he pushed his hand around to the front of me, his finger sliding across my folds before zeroing in on my swollen button.

He rubbed small circles over it in time to his thrusts, sending me crashing into a wild frenzy of an orgasm. He didn't let up though, he kept going, building the crescendo up again until I felt him swell up inside me, and we fell over the edge together, his body jerking wildly into mine. I laughed, seeing the blue glow of the bathroom.

"I'm never going to get enough of you, siren."

"Good. I kinda like you too," I smiled as Jax turned me, pulling me into a hug.

He tenderly washed me, massaging me as he went. I did the same for him, enjoying the closeness and alone time. All too soon, we were back with the rest of the group and back to business.

Chapter Nineteen

Aedan was exhausted. Two months had flown by in a whirlwind of locations, demon-killing, interviews, doctor appointments, research, and meetings. They were one month away from the two-day live show and back in California for the week. He was exhausted and happy to be back with Mags, who was now very large and doing quite well.

Jillian had just arrived, and she and Smitty holed up in his room. Mags was downstairs with a pile of road maps planning the little road trip she and Jillian were going to take to meet them in Washington for the live show.

She wouldn't be able to fly, but the doctor okayed the road trip, and surprisingly okayed the hike and camping trip. He had been fully prepared to argue against her going and was relieved that he didn't have to. Mags was over the moon happy.

Aedan was just as thrilled that she got to go; this was right up her ally of things she loved to do. He was also happy that he had a few moments to himself; to just sit in the quiet and reflect. He'd chalked up a few demon kills under his belt, and started to feel like more of an asset to the team.

Father Roarke had been firm that the guys kill the demons and not Airiella. He was all for it if that meant she wasn't running straight into danger or having to pull that energy from Jax and die. He didn't want to see that again. It still gave him nightmares.

He was taking his time getting used to the person that Jax had become. He knew that energy was still inside Jax because she hadn't pulled it since that last time, you couldn't tell though. Even in the tensest situations, Jax kept his cool and wouldn't let himself get pushed into that uncontrollable anger. Aedan had suspicions remaining that it would only take someone threatening Airiella do it; he didn't want to test the theory.

They also hadn't been revisited by Bael or Stolas. It was a blessing and a curse. He knew it was coming. Bael didn't seem like the type to give up, and he seemed to think that Airiella was his. He wasn't sure what to make of Stolas. There was something scary about him, yet he wasn't threatening towards any of them. He also came across as sad.

Aedan must have fallen asleep because the next thing he remembered was Smitty throwing open the bedroom door. "Wake up! I've got something!"

Aedan dragged himself out of bed and down to the TV room where he heard them all gathered. Smitty was mirroring his phone screen to the TV to show them. It was a scan of an old newspaper article that wasn't in English.

"You can read this?" Aedan raised his eyebrows at Smitty.

"No, you tool. I'm showing you the original so that you can see the date. 1891, this article is from a neighboring town to where Marco lived," Smitty rolled his eyes.

"What does it say?" Aedan was still tired and wanted to go back to his nap.

Smitty changed the screen to a translation of the article. It didn't exonerate Marco from the murder charge leveled against him, but it did call into question the girl's father. "This gives us ammunition against the murder rap if that's the angle they are trying to use."

"It's something," Aedan agreed. He glanced at Airiella, who was sitting with Mags, rubbing her belly. She looked intrigued.

"It backs up the story Marco told at least. How did you come across this?" Airiella continued rubbing Mags's belly. Aedan bit back a laugh at the look of rapture on Mags's face.

"Father Roarke talked to some of his contacts in that region of the country, and they did some digging for him," Smitty exclaimed. "It's the first thing we've found that corroborates his story."

"Did you doubt he was telling the truth?" Airiella was frowning at that.

"Nope. It's just hard to find evidence to support it, especially the witchcraft and demon angle. Not a lot of people wanted to talk about that in those days. Think about it, a staunchly devout Catholic village in central Italy. They'd want to cover it up."

"The demon angle didn't come into play until he

was working in the mine," Airiella pointed out. "You'd think here they wouldn't be so quick to cover it up."

"Very true. I haven't found anything online. Everything I've found talks about the fire itself, the loss of life, and that the person responsible died in the mine. I've uncovered many political unrest articles about them bringing in slaves from down south to cross the picket lines and work in the mine. And I've only found one article in what I think was a tiny publication that even listed Marco as a suspect." Smitty clicked through his phone until he found a picture of the article and put it on the screen.

"You think if there is something to be found, it will be via feet on the ground approach? Something physical?" Ronnie asked.

"Yeah. I think in this case, it will be our *only* shot of finding anything occult-related. I've asked a couple of the historical societies in the surrounding towns but haven't gotten great responses. It seems people still think it's taboo," Smitty shrugged.

"Maybe I can ask some of my family to dig around?" Airiella suggested.

"Would they be willing?" Jax leaned forward.

"I think my dad would. He'd be pretty thorough too. Look at all the information he dug up on my family tree," Airiella replied.

"If you don't think he would mind, that would be great," Smitty added.

Mags got up and came over to Aedan and plopped on his lap, "Ooof. Babe, you just crushed my balls," Aedan groaned.

The rest of the group cracked up laughing while Mags replied, "Good thing I don't need them then. It's not like I can get any more pregnant than I am."

"You were so nice and quiet over there with Airiella, what happened?" Aedan grumbled, shifting a little to get more comfortable.

Jax shook his head, smiling. "Wrong question, dude."

"You've been napping on the job while everyone else works. You looked like you needed something to do," Mags grinned.

Aedan poked her hard belly. "Looks like I've done enough."

Jax and Ronnie made their exit, not wanting to catch the ire of Mags. He saw Jillian go over and talk to Airiella, the two of them leaving together, while Smitty shut down his electronics and shrugged at Aedan. "You're on your own, man. Good luck."

"Shit. Am I in trouble?" Aedan looked up at his wife.

"No. It worked; I got you alone." She bit his neck.

"If you wanted that, you could have come up to the bedroom," he told her. "The ball crushing wasn't necessary."

"An unfortunate accident, babe. These kids are heavy, and they made my ass bigger."

"I think your ass looks fantastic. So do the bigger boobs," Aedan nuzzled her neck.

"I wanted you to rest, that's why I didn't bother you. Airiella's belly massage got me a little horny, and you looked all rumpled and sexy."

"You should have led with that. Now that my balls broke, I can't perform," Aedan teased.

"Really? What's that pressing into my ass, then?"

"No idea. Maybe you should investigate it," Aedan

grinned no longer sleepy.

"Come on, let's go make some noise," Mags stood, grabbing his hand and pulling him behind her. Aedan was happy to be back to their temporary home.

Ronnie ducked as Jax threw a jab at him. "It's on the market, then?" Ronnie asked Jax as they sparred for a workout.

"It will be within the week. I'm having my mom go over and get it ready. I gave her the go-ahead to hire some people to pack up what they think is necessary to show it."

"I'll call her later and tell her what's safe of mine to have them do too," Ronnie unleashed a flurry of kicks and punches that had Jax reeling backward.

"Damn. You gave no sign that was coming," Jax panted.

"Kind of the point, bro." Ronnie grinned. "So, do I need to sign something?"

"Not yet. Aedan's taking care of the paperwork part. He'll let us know when we need to do something. We need to tell the producers, though."

"Can't we leave that for Aedan too," Ronnie grumbled.

"Did you look at the pictures? This place is fucking huge."

"Yeah, I looked. It's impressive, all right." Ronnie dodged the kick Jax sprung on him and flew around in a circle with a kick of his own, Jax barely escaping.

"Am I out of shape, or are you just that much better?" Jax whined.

"Both," Ronnie laughed, he loved this new Jax. He

was easy going and relaxed most of the time, yet still had that fire to him that showed his edges and grit. He rolled with things much better and had laser-sharp focus when needed.

"I've noticed you've been on the phone a lot lately," Jax commented, throwing Ronnie's stride off so severely that Jax finally landed a hit.

"Cheap shot, damn." Ronnie rubbed his side. "Yeah. I have been."

"Care to let me in?" Jax sat down and laid back on the mat, sweat rolling off him.

"I guess; I'm not ready to say anything to our angel. So keep it between us for now. Please."

"Sure. Not a problem unless Airiella goes trolling through our heads, then you won't need me to be the one to say anything."

"She doesn't do that," Ronnie sounded nervous at the thought.

"Relax, dude, she doesn't."

"You know her friend Chrissie? I've been talking to her a lot." Ronnie fidgeted. He wasn't ready to give up Airiella yet; however, he would admit there might be something developing between him and Chrissie.

"Really? Why are you nervous about that?"

"I'm not ready to walk away from what I have with Airiella." Ronnie felt like a complete ass saying that to Jax.

"Why do you think you'd have to?"

"I don't think I can be a guy who can be with two women. Especially not one who is best friends with the other." Ronnie *knew* he couldn't. It also felt like the timing wasn't there yet. He still needed Airiella. She'd reassured him often that she would always need him, that wasn't too much of a concern for him.

"Okay, I hear you there. I couldn't do two women either. I don't have any interest in even looking at another woman. Even still, don't compare Chrissie to Airiella. It's not fair to either of them," Jax reasoned.

Ronnie wasn't comparing; he couldn't. No one was like Airiella, she was literally, one of a kind. Chrissie had a fire in her, similar to his angel, just in a different way. It had started when he'd answered Airiella's phone when Chrissie had called.

He had been the one to fill Chrissie in and pass along updates. He'd given her his number to make it easy for her since Airiella often left her phone somewhere other than where she was. It was clear why the two women were so close. They shared a lot of experiences and history. Ronnie himself had been surprised that he looked forward to talking to her.

It was only recently that he had felt Chrissie had shown some interest in him. She'd made it a point to tell him that she had no intention of coming between him and Airiella, something that tugged on him. He also really loved her kids and found himself asking about them with every conversation. She'd even sent him some pictures of them playing.

"I'm not comparing them. Both have a lot of similarities, but they also have a deep bond. It's funny to hear them talk. Chrissie can read Airiella like a book. Same with Airiella about Chrissie. I do think there's something there, but she's also in Kansas, and we are here. I'll explore it when it feels right."

"You know I'm not pushing you away from her, right?"

"I know. I don't feel like you are." Ronnie leaned forward against his knees to see Jax better. "I want something like what the two of you have. I'm not jealous in a bad way; I just want to feel that too. As much as I love Airiella, I know it doesn't even come close to what you feel for her. It's obvious anytime you are remotely in the same vicinity."

"She loves you, Ronnie. A lot. I'm not saying you shouldn't try; I'm only trying to make sure you know how deeply that woman loves you."

"I've never doubted it, Jax. Let me put it this way; when the three of us are together, she gravitates to you. I don't even know if she knows she's doing it. Even in her sleep, she turns to you. I want to be with someone that gravitates to me."

Jax sat up with a sad look on his face. "I'm sorry. I can give you alone time with her. I'm not trying to but in."

"Don't misunderstand me. Airiella's all but told me to come in with you guys. I know she wants me there too. As I said, I'm not ready to let go of her yet. It's always been more than sex with her, and there are ties I know won't ever be broken. I know that if I find someone else and she doesn't accept how close I am to Airiella, that won't be the person for me. Whoever I am with needs to trust that if I am lying in a bed with Airiella, it's because she needs me close, not because I'm going to sleep with her. That's not easy for a lot of women. It's also something that I am not going to ever let go of; I'm capable of being with her without the sex."

"You think Chrissie would be bothered by that closeness?" Jax rolled to his side to look at him.

"No, she's not at all. In fact, when we first met,

Airiella told me Chrissie would be in my future. Chrissie only smiled and told Airiella to test drive me first. I think, maybe, that's why I am allowing myself to see a possibility because she understands that bond between us."

"I'll say this for Jillian, now that we are on that line, she understands it too even if it took her a couple of days to get over her tantrum. The women of this group are pretty spectacular." Jax wasn't very close to Jillian, so the concession was startling.

"Well, now, you know. That's what all the phone calls are about, me exploring possibilities. We've been getting to know each other." Ronnie blushed, "She's pretty hot too."

"If I noticed, you can bet your ass that Airiella noticed all the calls too. You know this is something she would be happy about, Ronnie. You don't need to keep it from her."

"Yeah, I know. I don't want her pulling away though. You know she would, and I'm not there yet."

"She might, I can't say. She's always catching me off guard," Jax admitted with a smile.

"No shit, she's good at that. Thanks, man. I appreciate the ear," Ronnie stood and held his hand out to help Jax up.

"Anytime. I'd share Airiella forever with you if that's what you needed."

"Like she'd give you a choice in the matter," Ronnie shoved him playfully.

"You might have a point. Let me rephrase it; it wouldn't bother me because it's you."

"So, are you hoping this will all be over in time for her birthday?" Ronnie switched the subject.

"That's my plan."

"It's a good one." Ronnie closed up behind them. "What's for dinner?"

Chapter Twenty

I need your help," Jillian started as we walked across the yard to the carriage house. She requested somewhere wholly private, and that was the only place I knew of that we could achieve that.

I'm going dark guys. Need some alone time. I'm fine, nothing's wrong, I sent out to all three, so no one freaked out when I shut myself off from everyone.

All good, baby girl, Smitty responded first.

Thanks for the heads up, angel, Ronnie was next.

Aren't you with Jillian? I should have known Jax would notice.

I am, she said she needs to talk to me privately. I can't do that with you guys in my head.

Understood. Where will you go?

Carriage house. I have a feeling this is about Smitty, so keep him occupied. Please, and thank you.

On it. Love you, siren.

Love you, Zeus.

"I'm all yours," I told her as I closed the door behind us.

"I told Art about the rape in my past. You were right, he took it well and understood more than I gave him credit for." Jillian plopped on a chair.

"I'm glad you let him in."

"Along those lines, I also decided to stop seeing other people. I want it to be all him." Jillian's statement completely knocked me off balance.

"Really? Does he know that?" Flabbergasted, I sat on the couch and stared.

"Not yet. That's where you come in. I hope, anyway. I'm sure you've noticed I'm not exactly a traditional type of person."

Big understatement, I just nodded, though. I didn't know the direction Jillian was heading with this. "Go on."

She took a big breath in, "I want to propose to him."

I hadn't expected that. "Wow."

"I'm terrified," she admitted.

I could feel that she was excited too. "Understandable. How can I help? If you want to make sure our physical relationship is over, I am fine with that."

"It's not that. I understand the bond between you two. I don't have any issues with that. I also think I know him well enough that if we were to be married, he wouldn't do that anyway. First, I wanted to make sure you knew that I was okay if things continue with you as they are, also, to see if you would be okay if he decided not to continue that."

"Of course, I am okay with that. Our bond exists without the sex; I don't need that to maintain it. No worries there." I leaned forward to put my hand on her to help calm her a bit; she remained petrified. "You are still pretty scared."

"It's a huge step for me. Commitment on a permanent level and monogamy. Maybe even kids. I'm scared shitless." Her hands shook a little.

"Please don't be offended, but what made you come to this decision then?"

"In a word? You."

I was baffled. "Me?"

"Yeah. Art showed me the video of what happened with that demon. He was trying to help me understand why he freaked out being away from you. Because honestly, I thought he was exaggerating. Shit, Airiella. He wasn't. I didn't even want him to be away from you after that. Anyway, I saw how you protected them, stood between them and danger. I saw what you were willing to do to save Jax. It made me think."

"I wish you hadn't seen that. It's not an easy thing to see." I wasn't angry with Smitty for sharing it; I understood why he did it.

"Definitely a memorable thing," she said wryly. "It made me think about how I would feel if you weren't a part of their lives. They would have died without you. Which then made me think about how I would feel without Art, and that thought sent me straight into a full-blown panic attack. I haven't had one of those in several years."

I noticed that her anxiety went up again. I stroked her arm, "Would you like me to take that from you?"

She gave me a weak nod. "Please. It's distracting." I gently pulled it from her and sent her a calm feeling. "You are better than a drug."

"Glad I can help."

"Okay, on with my ramble then. I don't want to be without Art. If something were to happen to either of us, I'd like to die at least die knowing that we had committed in a way that left no doubt about our feelings. I see how you and Jax are, and frankly, I'm envious. He lets you be you; he doesn't try to control you, he's supportive, and that man worships you. It's kind of weird, because I've only ever known him as an asshole, but he's not, he's different now. Shit, Art is different now."

"I didn't change them, Jillian. It's always been who they are. Maybe I helped them be able to show it, but I didn't change them. No matter what they claim." It bothered me when they said I changed them. Well, Jax didn't say I changed him, he said he was transforming himself. Smitty only said what he had seen changed him.

"No, I'm not saying you changed them. You brought out things in them. Regardless, by the time I finished watching that video, I was half in love with you myself. Don't close that door on sex yet," she joked. "I may want a piece of that."

Now I laughed. That would probably freak Jax out. Not to mention, Smitty. He'd already told me he didn't want to share me with Jillian. "No promises."

"Do you believe I can make this work? Do I have what it takes?" she looked so worried about my answer, I hugged her.

"You are probably asking the wrong person. Mags is the better one to answer that than I am. All my relationships have been trainwrecks of the worst kind," I replied candidly.

"You can see things others can't. That's what I am

looking for, am I too fucked up to be married?"

My heart broke a little. "Jillian, you aren't too fucked up for anything. You will get out of marriage what you put into it. It's not easy, and it takes work. Why would you think you couldn't do that?"

"I know I can love him. I do already, with all my heart. He makes me a better person, keeps me sane, and has never tried to change who I am. Is that enough?" her face crinkled in worry.

"Only you can answer that. You both deserve happiness. Smitty gives his all, but even he has bad days. Can you handle him at his worst?" I tugged on her hand to make her stop picking at her nails and held it in my hand.

"Yeah. I can. The worst I've ever seen Art or talked to him was when he watched you die after your interview. I'm proud of how I came through for him on that. Now that I've seen it, I'm even more impressed he wasn't worse off than he was."

"If you can handle him at his worst, then you deserve his best. Is the flip true?"

"Well, to be honest, my worst was that first time meeting you. Art handled it, but he also laid down the law. I think that man can probably handle anything."

"That's your answer, Jillian. You don't need me to tell you anything. Trust your heart."

She laughed. "My heart is telling me to run and hide but to take Art with me."

I smiled. "I know that feeling."

"Can you help me with the rest then?" she asked.

"There's more?"

"I need him out of the house for a while. Art said they were going to talk you guys into cooking dinner for them again. By you guys, I mean you and Jax. I'd like to do it tonight." She pulled a box out of her pocket. "I got him an engagement ring, am I silly?" She showed me a platinum band that she had engraved on the inside with "Forever my heart."

"I think it's great and that he will love it." I handed it back to her.

"Before my mom died, she gave me the wedding ring that had been given to her by my grandmother," she pulled out another ring with a big solitaire diamond in it. "He doesn't even have to buy me one. I'd like to use this one."

"Okay. If you need Smitty out of the house, taking him away is probably not the best bet if you want me to make dinner. Having the guys get him out would work better," I started to think of a way to get them out without cluing them in.

"He probably wouldn't go for them. For you, he would," Jillian countered.

"He would, but it would also raise suspicion in him since you would be here and not with him. We may have to bring one of the guys in on this," I suggested.

She bit her lip. "Okay, then Jax."

"Really? I would have said Aedan or Ronnie, but I can make that work if Jax is your choice." Kind of surprised me.

"He'd never suspect I was in collusion with Jax."

Okay, that was true. *Zeus, can you come out here?*

Is everything okay? He was quick to reply.

Yes, I need your help with something. Come alone, say nothing to anyone.

On my way, siren.

"He's on his way." I smiled at her.

"That's a handy trick," she remarked.

"I can do it with Smitty and Ronnie too, but I don't intrude on their thoughts." I could feel Jax getting closer and stood up as he came in and directly to me, wrapping me in a hug.

"That. That's what I want," Jillian whispered.

"I'm hers," Jax moved away from Jillian.

I giggled. "Not you." I filled him in with as little detail as possible, loving the shocked look on his face. He agreed to get the three of the guys out after he admitted he already committed us to cooking dinner.

"That leaves you and Mags to do whatever needs doing. Jax and I will go shopping. Any special requests?"

Chapter Twenty-Seven

Smitty was beyond annoyed; this wasn't how he had thought his day would go. "Really dude? Why can't you go do this?" Smitty argued.

"I need some alone time with Airiella, plus, if you want us to cook, we will need to go to the grocery store. That's your trade-off," Jax replied testily.

Smitty was a bit taken aback at the tone; he'd been so laid back lately. He hoped that he wasn't arguing with Airiella. *Baby girl, are you and Jax okay?*

Is there a reason we shouldn't be? She answered immediately.

He's just got a bit of an attitude right now, that's all. He said he needed alone time with you.

I know he's tired, maybe that's it.

Smitty sighed. "We have a week off. We could do this another night. It doesn't have to be right now."

Aedan stepped in, "Might as well get it over with, between the three of us it will only take three hours tops.

Not all day like normal. Mags will like the girl time with Jillian anyway since Airiella doesn't get all girly."

Jax snorted. He loved that about her. "That is true. Painted nails on Airiella would last maybe a day."

At that, Smitty eased up. "I doubt even that long. She is the definition of low maintenance." He stood up but agreed to go to the studio. "Better be a damn good dinner."

"Has my steak ever let you down?" Jax smirked.

"Steak?" Smitty looked interested. "What else?"

"Baked potatoes, asparagus, French bread, and salad," Jax listed off Smitty's favorites.

"Holy shit. Deal. What about dessert?" Smitty was okay with this trade-off.

"That's up to Airiella."

"Fine. I trust Airiella. Come on, boys, my stomach is grumbling already. Let's get this shit done." Smitty strode out of the room, leaving a laughing Jax behind him.

"Asparagus. Damn that woman and making me eat vegetables," Ronnie mumbled.

"Whatever dude, you love vegetables," Smitty fired back. "Let me say bye to Jillian. Meet you at the car in five minutes."

He took off to find her and saw Mags already planted on his bed with an assortment of nail polishes out. "Girl time! Get your stinky ass out of here!" Mags shot him a look that he was afraid to defy.

"Just saying goodbye to my girl, jeez, relax woman." Smitty bent down, gave Jillian a quick kiss, dropped one on Mags's head, and got out as quickly as he could before asking him what color he liked.

He passed Aedan on the way and gave him a warning. "She's already got the polish out."

"Shit." Aedan stopped outside the door and sighed and went in. Smitty laughed and escaped, bumping into Airiella on the way down the stairs.

"What's for dessert?" Smitty cornered her and gave her a quick kiss.

"Mmmm, haven't decided yet. Why? Something you want?" she asked.

"Something chocolate." He knew Jillian loved chocolate, and maybe he'd get lucky tonight. He'd missed her. Last night hadn't been enough, he wanted more, and that had been his plan until Jax put a kink in it.

Airiella grinned. "Chocolate? Anything? You are leaving that wide open, you know."

"I trust you. I like chocolate. I like anything you make." Smitty was pleasantly surprised when she wrapped her arms around him and hugged him. "Love you, baby girl."

"Stay out of trouble," she warned him. "Love you, too."

Smitty lost himself in the routine work. They got the inventory done, recorded, and submitted to the producers with their list of equipment needed for the upcoming shoots and the live shows. They edited the last shoot and reviewed it all again before sending that off as well. They'd even included evidence of demons in that last one.

By that time, Smitty was truly hungry, and it'd been three hours. They set off for the house, and Smitty decided to stop and pick up flowers for the girls. He picked out red roses for Jillian, a variety of colors of roses for Airiella, and a bunch of flowers that looked wild and reminded him of Mags.

"Suck up," Ronnie said as he got back in.

"Hey, it makes Aedan look bad, so I'm all for it," Smitty joked as Aedan groaned.

He'd gotten the fifteen-minute warning from Airiella, so he knew dinner was close, and they got back with ten minutes to spare. He flew up the stairs, cleaned up for dinner as fast as possible, and got back down just in time.

He presented the women with the flowers and a bow to each, making them all smile and giggle. The other guys just glared. "Jax gets a pass; he grilled," Mags said.

"I'll do dishes," Ronnie piped up, looking sheepish.

"I'll clean the kitchen," Aedan offered.

"Totally, not fair. Airy never leaves the kitchen a mess," Mags crossed her arm. "Guess that means you'll owe me sexual favors."

Smitty burst out laughing. "Poor Aedan."

They sat down, and ate and Smitty noticed the women were all dressed up more than usual. Airiella must have gotten caught up in the girl time unwillingly. She was unusually quiet, for being nestled between Ronnie and Jax.

Are you sure you're okay, baby girl?

I'm perfectly okay. Stop worrying so much, Airiella told him, rolling her eyes.

Ronnie and Aedan started clearing the dinner plates, and Jax went outside to get a fire started in the firepit. Smitty wandered out after him, still concerned. "Everything okay, man?"

"Yeah, why?"

"Airiella was pretty quiet. Usually, you guys get her fired up pretty quick."

Jax laughed, "She's fine. Can't you feel her?"

"I can. I don't feel anything off, and I was just

concerned." Smitty sat down. "We got everything done. We can relax for the rest of the week."

"Great news. Did you make the demon part work without giving anything away?" Jax wondered.

"It turned out brilliant," Smitty patted himself on the back. "Even Aedan liked it."

"I knew you could do it. Be right back," Jax walked in the house, leaving Smitty outside by himself.

It was a perfect night, clear sky, warm, the sun was just starting to set. His belly was full, and he was with the people closest to him. The scent of jasmine floated on the breeze from the plant Mags had gotten for Airiella. The pool sparkled in the background.

Soft music started to play from the outdoor speakers, and he figured Jax had turned some music on. He tipped his head back, watching the leaves flutter as the wind teased them. Something he had become attuned to after being with Airiella so much. The little things in nature that so often got overlooked but were so peaceful and soothing.

I love that you have an open mind. Keep it that way.

He smiled at her voice in his head. Then his breath caught in his throat. Jillian was walking out the back door, looking like a vision backlit by the outdoor lights that someone had turned on. The short flowing skirt she had on accenting her long legs. He stood up, smiling.

"Hi, beautiful," he purred.

"Art," she started, her voice nervous sounding. "For so long, you've let me be me. You accepted me as I am, flaws and all, and still loved me. You keep me calm when I derail, and you share the excitement I have over silly things. Individually, we've grown so much over these years, and now I'm ready for something different."

His heart stuttered painfully in his chest. Was she breaking up with him? He started to panic; this couldn't be happening right now.

Easy, love, hear her out. Trust me. Listen to her words, her tone.

He searched Jillian's face and saw only love. "Okay, I'm listening."

She got down on one knee before him and held out a jewelry box. "Art, I want to see what we can become together as a family. I don't want others, only you. I'm ready for monogamy. I love you more than anything in the world. Will you marry me?" Tears sparkled in her eyes, and she smiled up at him.

His heart burst open as he dropped to his knees in front of her. "Are you proposing to me?" he whispered, his voice breaking.

She nodded, her hands shaking. Smitty took the box from her and opened it to see two rings. He pulled out the band and saw the engraving on the inside, "Forever my heart." His own hands started to shake, and he realized the implications and the importance of what was happening. He put it together. He took the diamond ring out of the box, too, noting that it was old.

"It was my grandmother's," Jillian said softly.

"Jillian, I will marry you," Smitty felt his eyes pool up with tears as he slid the ring on her finger and put the band on his own. "You all planned this, didn't you?"

"Not all of us, Aedan and Ronnie didn't know," she said quietly.

"I can't believe you did this," Smitty pulled her to

him, falling back on his heels. "You truly want monogamy?"

"I do. I'm ready for it. For you, for a family, and for forever. You don't have to change anything with Airiella either; I'm okay with it. We talked about it earlier," Jillian kissed him. Smitty felt the promise of her words in her kiss, and his tears fell.

"If you are giving me all of you, I am giving you the same," Smitty told her. "Equal partners. What about all the other stuff we talked about?"

"I'm on board. All the way, and that's not why I did this. I'm ready. I want you by my side, not some random person. Only you."

"Jesus. I love you, Jillian. I'm so happy right now. I don't know what to do with myself," Smitty kissed her, feeling completely whole.

"Congratulations!" Airiella cried, coming outside, Jax behind her with a tray of flutes filled with something Smitty guessed was sparkling cider.

"Dude. Your woman just got on her knees and had the balls to propose to you in front of us. Stop being a pussy, get up and kiss that woman properly, before I do," Ronnie said with a giant grin.

Smitty grinned back and stood up. "There's just one more test she has to pass," Smitty chirped. A worried look came over Jillian's face.

Baby girl, will you touch both of us and tell me what you see? He looked at Airiella.

You know I will, but you already know the answer to that.

I know, but I want her to feel it too. Are you sure you are okay with this?

Smitty, I'm thrilled for you. Of course, I'm okay

with it.

Smitty held out his hand to Airiella and the other to Jillian. "Take baby girl's other hand," he told Jillian. They stood there in a triangle, and Smitty loved the feeling of the energy that washed over him. Even better was the look of awe on Jillian's face.

"Is it real, baby girl?" Smitty asked quietly, needing Jillian to hear this.

"As real as it gets," Airiella said with a smile. "Don't let go yet; let me try something. I haven't done this since all these changes happened."

Smitty held still as he felt her energy charge through him. *Smitty, open yourself fully,* he heard her say. Smitty focused all his energy on being open, and it happened. He saw in his mind what she saw.

"Oh, my God. How is this happening?" he heard Jillian say.

"It's all Airiella," he whispered.

"What's happening?" Ronnie said impatiently.

"She's showing us what she sees," Smitty answered. "Baby girl, the only thing that changes for me is we no longer have sex. Everything else stays the same. Say it out loud, so these doofuses hear it."

"Nothing else changes, Smitty," Airiella agreed with a smile.

"Except maybe now I want to have sex with her," Jillian joked.

"Hey! I just got rid of one guy, I'm not trying to grow that list," Jax growled good-naturedly.

Mags was utterly emotional and threw herself at Smitty. "I'm so happy I can't stop crying. Somehow, I blame Aedan for this."

Everyone laughed but Aedan. "You all laugh, but it's true. I'll be in trouble later, I'm sure. Just wait, Smitty. When Jillian is pregnant, you'll feel my pain."

"I'm willing to talk about having babies, but please God, don't let it be triplets. There's not enough valium in the world for that," Jillian said with a straight face, which got Mags laughing finally, as she disentangled from Smitty.

"I'm going to get dessert; you guys be nice to Smitty. He'll have a wife soon enough to beat on him," Airiella quipped as she went in the house, Jax hot on her heels.

"I like the sound of that, I'll have a wife," Smitty gave a dopey smile that had Ronnie groaning.

"Whipped already, I'm the sole survivor," Ronnie sank into a chair in mock misery. "I've lost my wingman."

"Aw, poor Ronnie," Mags cooed, messing up his hair. "I seem to remember more than a few times you and your wingman crashed and burned."

Aedan snorted. "Oh, the stories I can tell."

Airiella and Jax came back out a few minutes later with brownie sundaes. "Damn, can I have two wives?" Smitty said, diving into his dessert.

"No." Jax's answer was swift and firm.

Thank you, baby girl. I'll miss our alone time, but I also feel that Jax is waiting patiently to have you to himself. I couldn't be happier right now.

We'll still have our time, Smitty, you're my Apollo. That doesn't change.

If you weren't okay with this, it wouldn't be happening. I need you to know that.

I do. Jillian talked to me earlier about it. Enjoy your moment. It took her some major courage to do that.

Smitty gave Jillian a chocolatey kiss. "Thank you."

Chapter Twenty-Two

Winnie was feeling the pressure of a deadline. There wasn't much time left before the group was back in Washington for the live show, and Winnie hadn't gotten any further into her investigation. Winnie and the others had thoroughly coached Marco on what he could say and shouldn't.

He hadn't met Airiella yet, and Winnie was hoping to introduce them before the show. She'd been trying to get through to Ronnie for a week but hadn't been able to. It was Mags who finally called her.

"Oh, my God! You're huge!" Winnie exclaimed when she popped into Mags's bedroom.

Mags burst into tears. "That's not what I wanted to hear!"

"Oh Mags, I'm sorry. You are beautiful, and so is this giant bellyful of babies! They've grown a lot! That's all I meant."

"I know," she said tearfully. "I can't seem to control my emotions these days. I wanted to ask if you'd watch over Jillian and me while we drive up to Washington."

"Naturally, I will. Is it safe for you to be traveling?" Winnie wondered.

"Yeah. I had a doctor's appointment yesterday, and she said all my plans are fine. I have a doctor to check in with up there if anything happens or concerns me. Did you hear? Smitty is engaged."

"What?!" Winnie cried. "He is?"

"Yep. Jillian proposed to him. It was beautiful. I blubbered like an idiot," she gave Winnie a watery smile.

"Mags, you are pregnant. Anything will make you cry."

"I know. I do not like that part. Onida said she thought that the birthing process for me wouldn't be as bad as my doctor thought, that made me cry. Airiella brought me a candy bar I'd been craving. I cried while I stuffed my face with it. It's ridiculous."

Winnie giggled. "Then there is me, opening my big mouth and calling you huge. I'm sorry."

"It's okay. I *am* huge. Even still, the doctor said I could do the hike and go camping. She thinks I'll deliver early but not that early."

"Onida knows you will be up there, my guess is she will be somewhere nearby just in case," Winnie said. "She won't intrude."

"I figured as much. I'm not worried about that. Just about the shows themselves. They've had so much activity lately. It's wearing on Jax and Ronnie, though their stubborn asses won't admit it," Mags angrily swiped at the stray tears.

"I've been trying to get a hold of Ronnie. I want Airiella to pop over here to meet Marco before the show. I'm not sure if he tried to come here if she would be able to see him or not."

"I'll tell her. Will you have her grandpa there?" Mags asked.

Winnie thought about it. "Would it hurt her too much to see him?"

"I don't know. I know Airy misses him. She calls her nanie all the time, and she looks sad when she hangs up. Maybe talk to her grandpa about it and see what he thinks. Is Marco cute?"

"He's so hot. Incredibly charming, and that accent is sexy," Winnie said dreamily.

Mags laughed. "Right? I love Italian accents. I have no idea why Irish is Airy's favorite. I'm Italian all the way when it comes to accents. She gets all glossy-eyed when Father Roarke drones on with a story. It's funny."

"Did you know Jax talked to me?" Winnie asked carefully, not wanting to reveal anything she shouldn't.

"Oh, yes. That was obvious. I'm glad Jax did that, he's so much healthier now. I nag him a lot less. Well, okay, I don't, but I don't have to do it as much. I just like to."

Winnie laughed again. "He'd be worried if you didn't. When are you leaving?"

"In two days. We are giving ourselves three days to get to Airy's house. It should only take two with Jillian driving, but we will play it a little carefully. Aedan wants us to take four, but I think that would drive me crazy. There's plenty of room in that SUV for me to lay flat if I need to."

"Okay. Then just call me before you leave. Pass my

message on to Airy, will you? Right now, I hear Marco calling me. I finally got him to relent, and we had sex. He's yummy, as Airy would say."

"You go, girl! Get that ghost ass. I'll tell her. See you soon, Winnie."

Winnie popped out and went to find her new boyfriend.

Jax was on edge and trying not to show it. So many things were happening at once. He had no idea how Aedan managed to stay sane through all this. They all signed the papers that needed to be signed, and Aedan was juggling it all, trying his best to keep Airiella in the dark.

Jax had numerous shopping trips to make on the sly and was finding it hard to get out unnoticed. Mags and Jillian were leaving the next day, and the rest were packing up this house to ship everything out that was personal because, after the live show, they wouldn't be coming back here.

Airiella thought they were shipping it all to Jax's house in Wyoming, and Jax was finding it hard to keep everything straight. He was even hiding things from Ronnie now; he needed a break. The filming season couldn't be over soon enough. Then they had a month break, and it was on to PR season.

First, they had to make it through these live shows. Jax's nerves were strung tight about those. Every time he thought about them, he got a sinking feeling in his stomach. He knew something was going to happen because of the council, but that feeling he kept getting was more insidious. He was figuring that there would be some sort of demon attack.

He couldn't figure out if the attack would come from Bael, or if it was something that Asher was going to try and conjure up to do the council's dirty work. He had a sneaking suspicion it might be both. Something about the whole Asher role rubbed him wrong. He thought that someone on the council, likely Stone, had figured out what Airiella truly was, and was now trying to out her on the live show. Maybe claim she was possessed because it fits in with the accusations about her ancestor.

He had no concrete evidence to support it. He had tried to get it, but the producers hadn't gotten any farther than he had in the digging. Jax's gut told him it was, at minimum, Stone and the money man that had it out for him. He needed to share his suspicions with the team, but he wanted Mags to be on her way first. Aedan had to be focused.

"Jax! Hey! There you are," Airiella jogged up to him. "I've been looking for you."

He felt the smile light up his face; she had that effect on him. "I come here to think." He patted the bench next to him.

"Care to clue me into these thoughts?" she nestled into his side.

"It's about the live shows. I have suspicions that I've been trying to find evidence on but haven't gotten any luck. I was going to wait and tell everyone after Mags left. Aedan will be worried about her, but I have a better chance of getting him to focus if Mags isn't here."

"That's probably true. I'm going to send my raven to watch after them; at least that way, I'll know right away if something happens."

"Smart girl," he kissed her on the top of her head. "Excited to be going home?"

"I am. Nervous too. I don't want to put my family in danger."

"We'll figure it out. Have you gone to meet Marco yet?" Jax rubbed her arm, pulling her closer.

"No, that was why I was looking for you. I need to do that. I wanted someone to watch over me since I'm not too sure about the whole being in two places at once. I couldn't find Ronnie either."

Jax tapped her head, "Did you try talking to him that way?"

"Yeah, he's got me shut out. Just like you did," Airiella's tone had a few hurt feelings in it.

Jax knew that meant he was probably on the phone with Chrissie. "Well, you have me. Want to try it here?"

"Might as well, I guess." She shrugged aimlessly.

"Anything I need to do from my end?" Jax asked cautiously.

"I don't know," she admitted.

Jax pulled out his phone and texted Taklishim. "I'll ask Tak."

Jax, can you hear me? I sent him.

Yes, baby, I got you. Are you over there?

I think so. There's no one here. Can you pick up my thoughts still, or are you just getting me this way?

I started to think about my surroundings. The spirit world, to me, is just all gray. It's the same as the living world in every other way; the colors just go away. I wonder if the spirits see this place as gray too?

I can pick up your thoughts too. Everything is gray there.

Okay, then I am not going to keep up dialogue this way if you can hear my thoughts, this took a bit of energy from me.

Are you moving around over there? Here you are still in the same place. I'm not quite sure what to expect.

I'm moving around a little bit right now, but I haven't strayed too far away. I could see vague forms on the bench in the garden, and I plainly saw the silver thread that connected me to one of them.

Be careful. I love you.

I love you, too.

"Winnie? Are you here?" I called out.

"Airy!" she popped in, right in front of me, scaring me so bad I fell backward on to my ass.

"Damn, Winnie. You gave me a heart attack!"

Winnie giggled, "Sorry. I didn't mean to; I have some people with me that I think you'd like to see."

"I don't see anyone," I grumbled, standing up. "Are you sure this will work? So far, you are the only ghost I've ever been able to see."

Winnie scrunched up her face. "They are here with me. Marco is trying to say hi to you; you don't hear him?"

I shook my head, sad. "I can't. More than Marco is here?"

"Yes. I have both of your grandpas here with me too. They wanted to say hi."

Tears pooled in my eyes, "Both of them are here?" my hand covered my mouth, and my voice came out in a whisper. "Grandpa Jack too?"

"He is. I'm so sorry. I thought this would work. He's

telling you he is so proud of you and what you've become. He says that he will always be at your ocean when you need to talk to him. He also said that he approves of Jax. I'm so sorry, Airy. I truly believed you being here would help you see them."

"It's okay, Winnie. He can hear me, right?" I was hopeful for that, at least.

"He can. We all can hear you. Marco wanted me to tell you that you are his beautiful niece, and he is happy to see you. He said you could trust him talking to the medium."

"Thank you, Marco. Please take care of Winnie for me, she's an extraordinary girl," I smiled through the tears.

Winnie blushed. "Your Grandpa Giuseppe is a very charming man. He keeps telling me to remind you that he will come back."

"Onida said that too. What does that mean? Who will come back?" I looked around, hoping for any clue that I could see him again.

"He said that you would know when the time is right."

"Sorry, Grandpa. I'm tired of the cryptic bullshit messages I keep getting. I know I'm supposed to have patience, and all things will make sense when they are supposed to, it's just wearing me out fast. Fighting demons isn't all that fun." I rubbed my eyes. "I miss both of you so much that it's all I can feel at times. Especially at the ocean, Grandpa Jack. I swear I can feel you hugging me when I'm there."

Winnie gave me a soft smile, "He said he is, and that he hopes you like the tide pools."

"Grandpa, I hope that you've found other relatives

here and have been able to set the record straight about Marco. It's kind of cool you get to meet these ancestors of ours and hear their incredible stories."

"He said that he had found his parents and Stephanie's dad. He's introduced Marco as well. Marco said thank you for sharing your family," Winnie relayed the messages.

"I wish I could see you all. I love you so much. I'm trying so hard to make you proud of me, and it hasn't been easy. The path isn't always clear, and all I can do is have faith I've made the right choice. I never asked to be given this task, and as much as I want to see you all, I hope I don't end up here soon. I want a chance for a normal life. One with Jax, where we aren't constantly worried someone or something is going to show up and try to kill either of us." I broke down in sobs. "I miss you."

"Airy...God, I'm so sorry. I didn't want to do this to you," Winnie cried.

I felt arms around me and expected to see Winnie, but I didn't see anyone. "Is someone touching me?"

Winnie nodded, biting her lip. "Marco gave you a hug."

"Thank you, Marco."

"Your Grandpa Giuseppe wants to see your wings," Winnie glanced next to her.

"Will that make them come out back in the other world too?" That would probably scare the shit out of Jax.

"Maybe, I don't know," Winnie shrugged.

They want me to show them my wings.

I heard. I've got you sitting up, so if your wings come out, you won't knock both of us on the ground. I'm sorry you can't see them. I can feel how much it's hurting you, and it's a little disconcerting to see these tears falling. Jax's tone was gentle and warm.

Thank you for taking care of me. My Grandpa Jack said he approves of you.

I concentrated and heard Winnie's gasp and knew the wings were there. I felt little shivers run up and down my spine and knew someone had to be touching them.

Holy shit, siren. Three different see-through hands are touching your wings! Jax exclaimed excitedly.

Can you see them? I asked, stunned.

I can see three hands! Don't move; I'm going to try and get a picture of this.

I held still, shivers running over my back each time someone stroked a wing. "Hey, whoever is touching me, Jax can see your hands. Maybe try and put your face against my wings and see if you can see him," I suggested.

Oh my God, baby! There's a face! Holy shit, there are three faces!

"Well that worked, Jax is going crazy. I'm glad someone got to see you at least," I smiled weakly.

"Light one, I've been looking for you," I spun around to see Stolas leaning against a tree.

"You've been able to find me other places, why not this time?" I couldn't help the frustrated tone that came out.

"There is some powerful protection around you, and I already told you, I can't get on that property. Here, I can find you, but you don't come here unless you die," Stolas answered smoothly.

Stolas is here!

Please tell me it's only him, Jax sounded worried.

Yes, so far.

I'm listening through you now, not sure how that happened, Jax sounded befuddled.

"Why can I see you, and see Winnie, but not the others?" I asked him.

"I don't know the answer to that. I came to tell you to be on guard. Bael is coming and bringing minions with him."

"When?" I demanded an answer.

"I'm not sure. it will be soon." He strode over to me and tapped the top of my wing. "Do you know the power these have?"

"The power to fly?" I asked sarcastically.

"Oh, I do wish I could keep you, so much fire in you. Yes, the wings can make you fly; they are also impenetrable. They will act as a shield," Stolas informed me.

"You mean if someone were shooting at me, I could let my wings out, and bullets wouldn't hit me?" I was a little surprised by that.

"Theoretically, yes. We don't have guns here. If Bael were to throw something at you, you could wrap these around yourself, and it wouldn't get through to your body, which is vulnerable. The impact will still hurt, but it won't be fatal."

"That can't be true, my wings were out last time, and I got thrown into a wall!"

"Were they around you?" Stolas asked point-blank.

"No, they were just out. Just like right now." Was that the key?

"Were there people behind you? Behind the wings?" Stolas kept up the questions.

"Yes, my team was behind me."

"Were they hurt?" Stolas was moving closer to me, and I backed up a step.

"No, I think a few fell down the steps because they got hit with a blast of energy."

"There is your answer. Your wings protected *them*. That blast should have killed them all." He stepped closer again, but I held my ground this time.

"This would have been useful information to have earlier," my tone was mild, but the meaning behind it wasn't.

"If you looked at the souls around you, you'd be able to see them," Stolas said quietly, his face next to my ear. "I am trying to help you. I also admit I do still want you. I am not stupid enough to believe I will have you. Your heart belongs to the one listening to me through you. Yes, I know he is listening; I can feel him in you."

"Then stop antagonizing him like that," I said and pushed him away from me. Or at least I tried to; he didn't move.

"There is another, of my kind, that wishes to help," Stolas let his lips brush against my cheek, and I held back a shudder. It felt wrong because it wasn't for the right reasons. "His name is Seir."

"How is it he can help?" I held my ground but allowed the lightning in me to come to life as a warning.

"He's a good demon, like me."

"Those two words don't belong together," I snipped. "I will admit that you have been helpful, but I also think you have a hidden agenda that you aren't telling me about."

He stepped away from me at that and gave my glowing blue form a wary look. "Light one, I do not wish you harm. I am willing to allow you to strike me with the light inside you if that will help you believe. I've told you my hidden agenda; I have not lied to you. I want you. I'm lonely."

I heard Jax growling in my head and felt his anger, which fueled the lightning. "My heart belongs to another, as does my soul. I don't want to strike you, Stolas. I'm glowing because you were too close and touching me without my permission."

"Then do as I said, look at the souls around you, and your wish will come true," he gave me a sad smile.

I switched to soul sight and immediately saw the three I couldn't see before. "Oh, my God. Grandpa! Grandpa Jack! I would recognize those souls anywhere!" I ran over to them and tried to hug them, and my arms only went through them. "Damn it. Let me try this." I held my palm up to their face and felt their familiar touches light my soul up.

I walked over to what must be Marco, whose soul shone bright and pure, very similar to my own. "Marco, it's a pleasure to see you. You have a beautiful soul."

Winnie's eyes were bright with fear and tears both. Fear for Stolas and happy tears because I could see Marco and my grandpa's. "He does, doesn't he?"

"Good choice for a boyfriend, Winnie."

I turned back to Stolas. "Thank you for that."

Stolas gave me another sad smile. "They are all lined up behind you like warriors."

"That's what family does; they protect those they love," I said simply. "They won't hurt you unless you hurt me."

"Do you honestly not see that I won't hurt you? I'm in love with you. I've not made one aggressive move against you." His voice was flat, and I saw the hunger in his eyes.

"I don't see it, Stolas, because I don't *know* you. I don't believe you will hurt me; I'll grant you that much. Though I don't know if I believe you are in love with me for the simple reason that you've made it clear you are lonely. That's not loving; it's needing."

"Those can be the same sometimes," was his quiet response.

"No, they are different. Love and need can go hand in hand sometimes, but the emotions are quite separate."

I reached out for his energy and found the one that said need, and I pulled it from him, startling him. I found the one thin strand that I had used last time to push love back into him and sent love over. "Do you see the difference now?" I asked softly.

"What was it you took?" he gasped.

"I took the need from you. You don't need me. You don't need to possess me; to own me. Love is something that should always get freely offered."

"When you've been where I've been for so long, the things you miss become the things you need," he said.

"That may be, but you have a strand of love in you. If you want to feel love, you need to give love. Real love is reciprocal. Why do you think I have so much of it? It's not because I'm an angel. It's because I freely give it, and those that love me give it back to me. If you want your soul to be better, work on that," I told him, feeling tired.

"What is there to love in hell?" Stolas blinked slowly and shook his head.

"Don't you go to earth frequently? There's plenty to love there. Aren't you a master of plants? Love the plants, love the earth that grows them, be thankful for them. Little things, Stolas. They add up fast."

"Thousands of years, I have survived, and a young angel schools me," he smiled bitterly. "I see the truth of your statement, though."

"Let me say this, then. I'm not saying that I won't ever grow to love you, I am saying that I will not fall in love with you. If you want my love, you have to work for it and give it back," I crossed my arms and glared at him.

"Am I not giving it back by helping you?" he seemed genuinely confused.

"To me, that is a kindness. Some would see it as you are serving your own purpose. I don't give love expecting to get it back. I give it because I can. Those that are experiencing real love do give it back. Do you see the difference? Kindness is a great start, but don't give out kindness expecting something in return, there's no genuine emotion in that. The greatest kindnesses are those often given to those who have no way to return the favor except in saying thanks. It's a good first step."

"At some point in my early life, that was something I understood. Less so now that I've seen the darker ways. You gave me love; I can feel it. Yet I also believe that you want something in return."

"I don't. I don't expect anything from you. That is the truth. I'll give you another truth; if you shine a light on the darker ways, they aren't as dark. Kind of like what I just did. Your soul isn't as dark now."

Stolas laughed at that. "This has been an enlightening experience."

I couldn't help but grin at the pun. "Okay, your warning was received, and we will be on guard. We have been on guard anyway."

"Yes, you have been. This time, Bael is once again coming himself. You aren't complete yet, and won't be strong enough to send him back fully. Remember, he has the power of invisibility, he could be around, and you wouldn't know," Stolas reminded me.

"I'm tired of hearing that I'm not whole. Just tell me what I need to fix, and I'll do it! All these mixed messages are frustrating." I felt like stomping my feet, but he was thousands of years old, and I'm sure that would seal the image of me acting like a child. "How do I stay careful if I can't even see him?"

"I can't tell you what you need to fix inside; I don't know. I can still see a crack in you, and that is what Bael will attack if given a chance. Your love, he has fixed his. The only way Bael can get to him is to try to get control of that entity inside him. With his soul whole now, that won't be easy for him to do. He still is at risk because it resides in him; until it's gone, Bael will use him as a tool to get to you. Use your sight to look at souls in situations where you feel something isn't right," Stolas advised sagely.

I swore under my breath; soul sight gave me headaches if I used it all the time. "Is the only way to get rid of it is by me pulling it from him?"

"I'm speculating on this, so take it like that only. If that energy is inside you, it puts you at risk; it can turn you to the darker side. When it's inside you, that is when you are most vulnerable and open for attack. If Bael can get that entity to take control, forcing you to pull it to save your love and keep you from releasing it, he wins. That's speculation like I said, but I've watched and seen; that is when you are most vulnerable. My advice is if you have to pull it from him, do it where you can release it quickly. Even if it kills you as it seems to do, he can't get to you. If you are dead, you are in the hands of the higher power that created you, and therefore protected."

"Stolas, *that* was useful information. Thank you," I stepped to him and embraced him lightly. "Now, who is this other demon that wants to be helpful?"

"Seir. He has a good nature to him and can appear anywhere at any time. He's happy being a prince of Hell. His good nature and willingness to help others got used for bad, so he fell. If you see someone on a winged horse, I believe your world calls them Pegasus, that would be him. He does not wish you harm."

"Okay," I drawled. "A Pegasus showing up would certainly draw unwanted attention."

"If I may point out, your wings do the same," his smile wasn't a mean one.

I pulled them back in. "Other than that, does he have any other characteristics I would be able use to identify him? At least I can let the team know he isn't there to harm us."

"I've been told he is quite beautiful to look at, like a treasure."

"That doesn't give me a lot to work with, Bael showed up looking insanely good-looking," I frowned.

"Perhaps I can give him this," he pulled my feather out of his pocket. "That should help identify him."

"Please don't. That is for you and you only as a sign of good faith and trust," I pleaded.

"As you wish." He pulled out another piece of paper and handed it to me. "Give that to your medicine people; if Bael's poison gets in you or one of your team, it could be fatal. This solution will draw the toxins out. It is in this that

Seir might be most helpful, some of these plants are hard to find. Seir specializes in finding things."

"How do they call him?" I put the paper in my pocket.

"I'll tell him to listen for his name. We have to be careful that we remain unseen," Stolas shifted uncomfortably.

I reached for his strand of love again and fed more into it. "Be well, Stolas. Thank you for your assistance."

"Word to the wise before I go, don't do that for Seir. He would take that as an opportunity to reciprocate in ways that wouldn't be welcome," he hedged.

"Understood," I smiled kindly, as Jax swore in my head.

"Light one, be careful. I'll be watching." He popped out.

I turned back to my family of ghosts, "Thank you for watching over me. I'll do my best to make you proud." I turned to Winnie. "Thanks for your help with this. I love you all."

I pulled on that silver thread and let it lead me back to Jax, who had me laying with my head on his lap again. I opened my eyes to see his gorgeous face staring down at me. "Hi honey, I'm home," I smiled.

His lips twitched like he was going to smile, but he didn't. "I'm guessing you fed Stolas love again, and that was what that warning was about?"

I sat up and nodded. "I do believe he is trying to help us; Stolas, that is. Not whoever Seir is. Though, if Stolas says Seir wants to help, I believe him."

"I feel like you are pimping yourself out for favors from demons," Jax ran his hands through his hair.

"He didn't ask for that. I did it to be nice. If it bothers you, I won't do it anymore." I put my hand on his and squeezed it gently.

"It doesn't bother me. I don't want there to be an expectation on Stolas's part that every time he doles out something useful, you are going to just hand over love to him," Jax tried to explain. It wasn't jealousy I felt, instead it was a feeling of concern.

I reached into my pocket and handed him the recipe Stolas had supplied. "We should get that to Degataga and Taklishim."

"Siren, you can't pull the darkness from me if it makes you vulnerable."

"Jax, I already knew it made me vulnerable. That's why it affects me the way it does. It only means we need to be more strategic about it. I'm going to do it if it's the only way to get it out of you. The best we can hope for is to do it in a controlled setting, the worst, well last time was the worst way to do it."

Angel! Where the fuck are you? Ronnie frantically shouted in my head.

In the garden with Jax, what's wrong? I stood up.

There's a fucking Pegasus in the driveway!

Well shit. More demons. How did Seir get in the driveway? I thought Stolas said this place was protected. *Tell him we don't need him yet.*

Why aren't you more freaked out about this? Ronnie swore again.

Stolas told me about him. We are on our way. Relax, he's not here to hurt us.

"Seir is apparently in the driveway," I told Jax as I tugged him behind me.

Chapter Twenty-Three

Ronnie was freaking out. "She said she doesn't need you yet."

"Yes, I'm aware. Stolas said she wanted to know how to identify me. I figured I would show my face so you all would know it."

"Holy fuck," Airiella said as she came out the front door. "Seeing a Pegasus in real life is quite something. I take it you are Seir? How did you get on the property?"

"Your wards are weakest here, easy enough to sneak around if you have the know-how. Getting in anywhere is a skill I have," Seir smiled.

"Angel, there's a lot I seem to be missing here." Jax walked up to him and put a hand on his shoulder. "A pretty boy on a flying horse seems to be a damn big one."

"You aren't so bad yourself," Seir told him with a sly smile.

"Oh my. I don't think Ronnie is interested in a sexual relationship with you, Seir. Why are you here?" Airiella took a protective stance in front of them.

"So that you can see my pretty face, as your friend called it."

"Okay, noted. You might want to leave before you draw attention that might not be so helpful to us. Flying horses aren't an everyday thing." Airiella's tone was a warning that Ronnie wasn't sure this new demon would understand.

"Should you need my assistance, you only have to call my name."

"It won't be me that needs your help. Stolas told me that you could help find the ingredients needed to make a recipe he gave me." Airiella turned to Jax and held out her hand.

Ronnie saw Jax pull a piece of paper out of his pocket, and he snapped a picture of it before handing it over. Ronnie felt the tension in his body reach lethal levels as she walked right up to the demon and showed him the list.

"Yes, I know where all these are. Allow me a few hours, and I will bring them back to you." He handed the list back to her.

"Uh, sure. Maybe after dark, so you don't stand out quite as much," Airiella suggested.

"As you wish." Just like that, the demon disappeared.

Ronnie sagged. "What the fuck?"

"You had me blocked; it's not like I hadn't tried to call you," Airiella turned. "Come on. We need to talk to everyone. I'm only going to go over this once. There's already way too much shit in my head to keep straight."

"You were with her, right?" Ronnie focused his eyes on Jax.

"Yes, I was. I heard everything, too, a nice new little trick that happened."

"Jesus. I was only on the phone for fifteen minutes. That scared the shit out of me." Ronnie rubbed his eyes. "I seriously thought I was hallucinating for a minute until he talked."

"Was the call good?" Jax changed the subject.

"What? Yeah, I guess. You are oddly calm for someone who just saw the same thing I did," Ronnie huffed.

"I knew there was a possibility he would show up. I didn't think it would be here though. Trust me; I've gone through a range of emotions in the past half an hour."

Ronnie studied Jax for a moment. He was the picture of calm and collected right now, but he could see signs of strain around his eyes a tad bit. Ronnie sat on the couch next to Jax as Airiella paced back and forth. Jax remained quiet and texted the picture he took. Ronnie guessed either Degataga or Taklishim.

When Jax's phone rang, Ronnie heard him say, "She hasn't started yet, I'll put you on speaker. Okay, you are on speaker now. Siren, say something to see if they can hear you."

"Hi, Taklishim. Just waiting on Smitty and Aedan."

"Hello Raven, we can hear you crystal clear. This is quite the recipe, Degataga said it wouldn't be easy."

"I don't think you'll have to worry about that," Jax answered giving, Airiella a look Ronnie couldn't define.

He felt like an outsider at the moment, and he

didn't like it at all. *Is this just the Jax and Airiella show now?*

Don't be ridiculous, you know that's not it at all. Jax was with me. I needed help, and I wanted someone with me while I went to the spirit world, and I couldn't find you.

Fuck. I'm sorry, angel. We need to talk after this.

All he got was a nod in response. She was irritated, that much he knew. As soon as Aedan and Smitty came in and sat down, she launched into her story, filling in all the blanks he had been missing, and provided some helpful information Stolas had doled out.

Smitty was frantically taking notes, and not one of the four council members interrupted once. When she finished, silence reigned king in the room until Degataga spoke up, "He's bringing you the ingredients?"

"That's what he said," Jax stepped in.

Now that Ronnie was all caught up, his mind was racing. "If you have the ingredients, will you be able to make it Degataga?"

"Yes. Stolas specifically said this would work against demon venom?" Degataga asked.

"Yes," Jax added as Airiella went and sat between Smitty and Aedan. Ronnie saw both men cuddle her and felt a flare of jealousy.

"Then you need it on your bodies when you go to the live shows," Taklishim's voice was firm.

"I'll overnight them once they are here," Smitty replied. "Will you all be at the locations?"

Ronnie watched Airiella's face; she looked conflicted. He only figured out she was talking to Jax when he made a noise and shifted, staring at her.

"We will, though probably out of sight," Tama said cryptically.

"Except me, I'll stand with Father Roarke," Degataga added.

Ronnie got it, which meant they would be in animal forms. They expected danger. "Did you know about Airiella's wings?" Ronnie asked.

"No. It doesn't surprise me. My suggestion to you all is that if Airiella tells you to get behind them, you do it. No heroes. If Bael himself is showing up, nothing good will happen," Taklishim sounded angry then. "That is why you won't see our faces."

Jax leaned forward. "Will this be a repeat of the last time we didn't see your faces?"

Ronnie was confused a moment until he heard Taklishim's reply. "If necessary, we'll bring in the others. We will try to handle it on our own. I don't want casualties. There aren't many of us left in this area."

Jax sighed. "Okay, fine. There's one other thing. I've been thinking a lot, and I have a scenario in my head that I've been trying to find supportive evidence to back it up, but I can't. Airiella is in my head, badgering me to share it. I wasn't ready yet, but as usual, her arguments are persuasive. I think the council might be trying to use Asher or his spirit guide, whatever, to call a demon. It's possible that Stone is using Asher, or blackmailing him to get him to do the dirty work. I know Stone has to be involved, and I suspect that the money man that is after me is with him on this. If Asher can call a demon and claim it's her ancestor Marco, and get it to say that Airiella is one too, or get it to admit what she is, or present enough danger for her angel to come out, it's on live TV, and she's exposed."

"Holy shit, that's underhanded. You might be on to something with that," Aedan sat forward. "We should have thought of that."

"The fact that Asher is going to be there is what was rubbing me wrong. I think one of them knows what she is and wants to expose her. If they can either reveal what she is or accuse her of collusion with demons, it casts doubt upon her in ways we can't fathom."

"Jax, you may have figured it out," Taklishim said quietly. "We haven't been able to get anything out of anyone. I know that someone is watching us. Chances are Father Roarke, too, but the church protects him far more than we are protected."

Ronnie's mind spun out of control. "What happens if she is exposed?"

"As a demon? It discredits all of us, and people can claim we are summoning demons to prove ghosts exist, or that we've sold our souls. The possibilities are limitless based on the imaginations of the viewers," Smitty replied.

Ronnie shook his head. "Exposed as an angel," he clarified.

"I'd have no chance at a normal life, ever," she said quietly, her voice sad.

"Angel, you don't have a normal life now," Ronnie pointed out.

"Let me try putting it this way, Ronnie," Tama's voice floated out of the phone. "You've seen the alien shows where they try to capture the alien and do experiments on it to learn more about it. It's not a stretch for that to be true. How much easier would it be for government or private think tanks to capture a woman? If her powers were exposed, people would be seeking her forever. The religious fanatics who want healing; those that worship the dark side would want her dead. Criminals would want her powers for nefarious reasons, to make them rich. Governments would want her to work for them. There wouldn't be anywhere she could hide. Every time she went to the grocery store, she would get swarmed by people."

Ronnie looked over at his angel and saw the tears streaming from her face. "If it means you guys would be safe, I'll take the risk."

"No, angel. There is nothing worth that. I wanted to know the worst-case scenario if the world knew what you were. Now I get it. We work from there. For starters, we can make sure you aren't on camera, that's something you can help with; if you have to show up, stay out of sight of the lens. You'll know where they are."

She nodded, grateful. "I can do that."

Ronnie hadn't failed to notice the anger rolling off Jax at the picture Tama had painted. "Jax, calm down. The more we know, the better we can plan. Do you honestly think I'd want that for her?"

"No, the thought of it makes me want to punch Asher in the face," Jax snarled.

"Onida," Airiella called out from where she sat nestled into Aedan's side. "Mags is leaving in the morning. I'm sending my raven with to watch over them. Can you communicate with her?"

"I can. I'll stay in touch," Onida promised.

"Thank you," Aedan said down into Airiella's ear. "That makes me feel so much better."

"We all feel it coming. Whether you are feeling it because you are picking it up from me or feeling it on your own, all we can do is work together. There are so damn many moving pieces at play here; we just have to trust each other," Airiella said, her voice firm. "Please, let me protect you if it comes down to it. I know you don't like it, but out of all of us, I have the better chance of surviving."

"She's right, guys," Tama agreed. "You have us as well. We won't let you lose her. If it comes to Bael, let her lead."

Ronnie saw that Jax was vibrating and put his hand on him. "Relax bro, she's a badass angel, remember?"

"If she has to pull the energy Jax, she will. Trust that we will make sure she can make it back to us," Degataga commented gently.

"Jax will be fine," Airiella said confidently. "He trusts in me to do what is right, and he has never held me back. He doesn't like it, and he's allowed to feel that way. Don't be hard on him for it."

Ronnie saw the utter faith Jax had for her in his eyes, and he knew she was right. Jax wouldn't stop her from doing anything she felt she needed to do, even if it killed him to let her. "We've all got each other's backs," Ronnie said, sliding his arm around Jax.

Angel, he needs you to be over here with him.

He's okay, Ronnie. Trust me. Let him work through it.

What if I need you over here with me? Ronnie tried again.

Airiella kissed Aedan's cheek, then Smitty's. She stood up silently, walking over and sat on the floor between his leg and Jax's, touching them both.

"We'll see you soon. Degataga and I will have this recipe ready for you when you get to the location. You *will* see our faces then. After that, only Airiella will be able to talk with either Onida or me," Taklishim told them, a finality to his voice that they hadn't heard before.

"I'll send you tracking once I get it," Smitty informed them, then they hung up.

"Brilliant deduction, man," Aedan said to Jax. "I think you are right."

"Yeah, there's a ring of truth to it," Smitty agreed. "Cold-hearted and flat out wrong, but I do think Jax is right, Asher is a puppet. His god is money and fame. The money man or Stone could have offered him a boatload of money, and he'd do anything."

"Aedan, can you let Mags know that if she sees the raven, it's me? Tell her to speak to it, telling her that they are okay. I'll hear her."

"I'll do that. I didn't know you could do that, send the raven away like that," Aedan had visibly calmed at that news. Ronnie didn't blame him. He was worried too.

"I can. No way was I letting her go without her," Airiella stood. "Smitty, go spend time with your fiancée; Aedan, your wife."

Ronnie winced. He knew what was coming. "Jax, I need to talk to Mr. Secretive here."

Jax gave him a look. "Told you to come clean." Jax took off fast, grabbing his phone.

She sat where Jax had vacated, her back against the arm of the couch and crossed her legs. "Did you honestly think she wouldn't tell me, Ronan?"

Ronnie slouched down. "I had hoped she wouldn't."

"Why would you hope that?" she sounded hurt.

"I'm not ready to lose you yet."

"Why does everyone keep assuming that they are going to lose me?" she threw her hands up in the air. "You should know better than that! Ronnie, you know how I feel about you."

"I do. I also know how you feel about Smitty. I watched as you agreed to stop seeing him as soon as his relationship with Jillian changed."

"Is that what you are worried about?" her jaw dropped.

"I just told you I was. In my heart, I don't feel like we're over yet. If I tell you that I am interested in your best friend, I damn well know for sure that you are going to back off and allow that to develop. I'm not there yet."

"Ronnie, Smitty *asked* me if I was okay with nothing physical between us. That was after Jillian already talked to me and told me she was okay if it still went on. She had no objections. It was Smitty's choice to end that, just as it will be your choice to end ours. You are correct, that if you do decide to pursue this and she agrees, that I will back off because that's just an awkward triangle to be in for all of us. I also know that you wouldn't want to be in it either. Be honest with yourself and stop hiding; this isn't you."

"It's not. It's not me at all, and I've hated every minute of it. Angel, please understand I'm not there yet. I do feel a change coming, but not yet. I still need you. I still need the feel of your body next to mine, on mine. I need to feel the passion in you."

"You still have me, Ronan." He loved the sound of his name on her lips. "Chris knows about this; about us. While she is interested, she also knows long-distance isn't completely feasible. When you both are ready, I step out. Hopefully into Jax's arms, but if not, I'll make do."

Ronnie wanted so badly to tell her Jax's secrets just

to allay her fears. "What are you doing about finishing up healing?" he hated to ask but needed to.

She stiffened, and Ronnie fought back the urge to pull her to him. "I don't know."

"It's Michael, isn't it?"

She nodded. "We aren't going to talk about this right now."

Ronnie internally flinched at her tone. It was one hundred percent an exposed nerve. "Okay. Will you stay with me tonight?" He could at least distract her and give Jax some time to do what he needed to do.

"I'd like that," she smiled slowly. Ronnie still saw the pain he'd caused under the smile, but it was a start.

Chapter Twenty-Four

Aedan was beside himself. "Damn it, Jax! I hate this!" Aedan shouted.

"She'll be okay," Jax tried to soothe him. "Airiella has her raven flying over the car, you saw her. She'll be able to communicate to Airiella if something is wrong. Either of them will. Also, come on, Jillian is a ball buster, do you think anyone is going to mess with her?"

"Is that supposed to help?" Smitty glared at Jax.

"Oh, come on. You guys know they will be safer than we will," Ronnie defended Jax.

"Aedan, you know Winnie is watching over them too, right?" Airiella said as she walked out the front door.

"Yeah, I know. That's just the love of my life, carrying my three unborn babies, that drove away while there are demons after us," he couldn't help the nasty sarcastic tone.

"She'll be okay. I believe I would have felt it otherwise since she's one of my connections," Airiella hugged him.

He shook in her arms, relenting a little. "I do believe you; it's still stressful."

"I know. So, let's do what we need to do here and get there. Mel will tell me when they arrive if we haven't heard from them by then. I can also look through my ravens' eyes and see them. I can tell you Jillian is driving like an Indy driver. They'll make good time."

Smitty laughed, "That about sums up her driving; that's for sure."

"Guys, pack up the gym, I'm going to finish in the kitchen, and one of you can make a food bank run with me."

Aedan dropped a kiss on Airiella's head and followed the rest to the gym. They got it packed up in a lot less time than it had taken Ronnie to get it set up. "Jax, everything is a go in Wyoming. When we get to the first location, the agent will be there with the papers for you to sign in person. Well, we all need to sign them. Since it's that guy's wife, we can say we are signing autographs for her."

"Thanks. One of you go with Airiella to the food bank, I've got to make one stop before we leave and if I go while she is here, she will never let me rest until I tell her why I went out," Jax told them.

Aedan volunteered. "I'm the only one here she can't communicate with; it makes more sense for me to go with her."

"Do you wish you had changed that?" Ronnie asked.

"No, what Mags and I have with her is enough. I'll have three kids because of her. I don't need to hear any more thoughts in my head." Aedan rubbed his chin. He was exhausted. "Think we should fly out early? Change up the scheduled plans a bit?"

"I thought of that, too," Jax said. "It would tip them off though that we might know something. If we stick to the schedule, it looks like everything is going to plan."

"Hide in plain sight," Smitty added. "Mags took the bow and arrow, right?"

"She did, and it's within reach inside the SUV. I don't want them at either filming location. That feels like it's asking for trouble," Aedan shifted from one foot to the other, nervous energy jumping around in him.

"I agree, they shouldn't be there," Jax turned to look at the room again before they left. "Aedan, you're up. Go and distract her so I can sneak out. If she asks, tell her I went to grab food for lunch. I'll come back with something to cover my ass."

"She'll be pissed you went alone," Ronnie pointed out.

"Then I'll bring back tacos, and she'll get over it," Jax grinned.

Smitty belted out a laugh. "Man, you are good. Go, we've got your covered."

Aedan headed to the kitchen with a smile. Jax had plans, and Aedan thought he knew what they were. "Airiella, are you ready?"

"Not quite. That was fast," Airiella answered while her head was in a cupboard.

"Well, you sent four of us in there. Have you heard from Father Roarke today?"

"No, should I have?" she was on a stool reaching for the stash of junk food Smitty had hidden on the top shelf.

"No, I was just wondering; he's been checking in

every day. I guess since he's with Taklishim, if something were wrong, you'd have known." Aedan reached around her and pulled the food down effortlessly.

"Bite me, you tall jerk." She smiled and nudged him as she got off the stool.

"What's left?" he smirked.

"The stuff in the fridge and freezer. I saved that for last, so nothing spoiled."

"Good call. I'll grab it, sit a moment," Aedan pushed her.

"Nope. My brain needs me to keep moving." She brushed past him and started loading up a box with the frozen items. She moved fast, and soon the fridge was empty too. "Okay, let's load up. I've already called and told them we were stopping by."

"Someone will be there then?"

"Yep. The food bank will give us a receipt, too, so you can do whatever you need to with that." She picked up two of the boxes and headed to the front door.

Aedan picked up the heavier of the boxes and followed behind. They made two trips and were on their way. She hadn't asked about Jax or even noticed that his car was gone. If she had, she didn't mention it. Times like this, he was glad she couldn't see his thoughts.

"Are you okay?" he asked her.

"Yeah, just feeling the distance from Mags. Jillian must be driving super-fast because there's a slight discomfort there now."

"I remember how it felt to be away from you. If Mags gets anything like how she was before, I feel sorry for Jillian," Aedan said dramatically.

"She's not that bad; it's mostly hormones and

pregnancy pain. It can't be comfortable to have all those babies in her," Airiella defended Mags.

Aedan laughed. "I'm willing to bet you that she asks Jillian for a massage."

"No bet, I know she will. That woman is not shy at all." He felt Airiella look at him. "You've got to be there for Jax if I have to pull his energy. He won't stop me, but I need to make sure he is okay, that it doesn't hurt him."

"We will all make sure he is okay. Do you think it will come to that?" Aedan worried.

"I don't know. If it doesn't, I want to do it while we are camping. The ocean will help me release it, coupled with the holy water; it may even keep me alive. That's my goal, at least, to do it there with a controlled, well somewhat controlled environment. Nature and the ocean will help me."

"Have you told Father Roarke that?" Aedan glanced over to see her staring out the window at the passing buildings.

"Not yet. I will. I want to talk to Jax first before I do. I won't do it behind his back."

Aedan glanced back over at her. "He'll do anything for you; you know that, right?"

"I do. I want it to be something he agrees with; it's his body, and it hurts him," she admitted quietly.

"Shit, Airiella, it hurts you way worse, and that's his hang up."

"Too many moving pieces," she whispered. Then in a louder voice, "We will get through this."

Each of them had a lot to lose if they didn't. Aedan didn't want to think about it. He pulled into the food bank. "Let's do some good and give our food away."

Chapter Twenty-Five

Ronnie went still, "He did what?"

"He's flying the boys and me out for her birthday. He wants to surprise her. I was hoping one of the nights I am there, you and I could go out to dinner. Ells can watch the boys."

Ronnie was stunned silent. "He didn't breathe a word of it to me."

"Oops, maybe it was a surprise for you too," Chrissie laughed. "Surprise."

Ronnie paced around the location while the producers were talking to Jax and Airiella. "This place feels weird."

"Which one are you at?" Chrissie asked him.

"Northern State. We came straight here from the airport. We have three days before the filming starts. Three days to get interviews done on each location. We leave here tonight and head to her place. Then we will do the interviews in that little town near Franklin. Then back up here, and then back down there. I think the traveling between the two will drive us all crazy."

"It's a lot of miles. What about it feels weird?" Chrissie tried to help him hone in on the feeling.

"The energy, it's not right. Airiella felt it way before I did. She said there wasn't an immediate danger." Ronnie sighed. "In answer to your question, yes, dinner would be great."

"I didn't ask. I kind of told you."

Ronnie chuckled. "So, you did. I'm used to it by now. Between Airiella and Mags, I just do what they tell me. Mostly."

"Good, means she's broken you in already," Chrissie laughed.

"Okay, Chris, I've got to run. Talk to you soon." Jax was walking towards him, and Ronnie slid his phone into his pocket.

"Well?" Ronnie asked.

"Let's do a quick walk around since we are here. We can film some of the locals if they agree to it, then we'll head back down to her place. Also, Taklishim just arrived." Jax walked back towards the gathering group.

"Father Roarke is staying where?" Ronnie pressed.

"He's got a hotel near Ells house," Jax told him.

"Can we all fit in her place? Didn't she say it was two bedrooms?"

"There's an office too. Smitty has an air mattress he had shipped there. Aedan and Mags can have the other room," Jax kept walking.

Ronnie felt like there were eyes on him. "Do you feel

it, Jax?"

"Yeah, I've been feeling it since we got here. Can't spot it."

"This blows. I'm so on edge right now I feel like I'm going to snap," Ronnie huffed out in irritation.

"I'm right there with you. With every person that looks at Airiella, I want to knock them out."

Ronnie was shocked at that, "You're jealous?"

"No, I'm untrusting. Every person here is a stranger that could be a demon in disguise."

"Whoa, bro. She'd know, remember? Take it easy," Ronnie slowed him down.

"I can't lose her, man."

"You won't. If you go off knocking everyone out that looks at Airiella, you might so chill. Trust our angel. She needs us, Jax. You aren't violent."

"Fuck. I know. I'm okay. Let's get this potion or whatever it is, and have it on us. It looks like today is a hiking day, and being friendly to locals."

"Yay us," Ronnie droned in mock joy.

I'd hiked here before, but it hadn't felt sinister and creepy then. It had felt like a ghost from the past with the old rotted-out buildings and berry vines taking over. Beautiful in its destruction and reclamation alike.

The uneven terrain was rough with my soul sight on, the colors leaching out of everyone blended, and I kept stumbling and rolling my ankles, even with my boots on. The other hikers we encountered were loving getting interviewed about the place, and just about every person we came across had a creepy story to tell. From witchcraft, voodoo practitioners, satanic cults, and angry ghosts to weird noises and vines that moved on their own.

I had no idea how Jax did it. He was a lot more introverted than he portrayed on TV, and I knew how much this drained him. But the public Jax never let it show. I was impressed until we got crazy fans. I wasn't even a celebrity like Jax was, and I still had some guy following me around asking me questions. Then his friend, the crazy female, jumped from each guy on the team, touching them, making inappropriate comments, and basically, setting my teeth on edge.

None of them encouraged her, and the producer Tom, that was following us tried to intervene. It didn't take a lot of common sense or a touch of genius to see the guys were getting irritated quickly. Yet, it wasn't until the barn structure that had vines falling in from the top of the roof, giving the place a surreal feel, that the crazy fans went too far.

I had walked in on the tail end of the group, trying to get a better read on the surrounding area when I was shoved bodily against the doorway to the barn. The crazy male fan started groping me painfully and was trying to suck my lips off my face. I couldn't get him off of me, and when I first heard the roar of anger, I thought it was Jax.

Nope. It was from Ronnie. Of all the people to lose their shit, it had to be the biggest and strongest one. I was thankful that he hauled the guy off me. One-handed no less, but with so many people around, I didn't want him to lose it completely. Unfortunately, it was a chain reaction. Ronnie's roar alerted everyone. Suddenly, there were four men between the nut job and me. All of them pissed, and Ronnie was still holding this guy with one hand.

To make matters worse, a crowd was gathering, and the female fan started to join the fray. This behavior was so out of character for Ronnie that I scoured him for signs something had gotten ahold of him. But his soul was utterly his. Nothing other than him registered with me. My danger alarms weren't even going off.

Not even when the female barreled into me, knocking me flat while accusing me of hitting on her boyfriend. Aedan reached down and lifted me to my feet and took an aggressive stance, putting me between him and Smitty. Jax's face was absolutely thunderous as he looked between Ronnie and this crazy female threatening me.

Poor Tom looked like he was going to have a heart attack, while Father Roarke simply stood there smiling. It was so sad it was comical. I started cracking up laughing, which only made the crazy woman angrier.

"Your boyfriend?" I laughed, bent over. "You were throwing yourself all over these already spoken for men that you don't know, while your boyfriend attacked me. Your boyfriend?"

"Fuck you, bitch! I know what I saw! You grabbed him!" She lunged for me, and I sidestepped, so she missed and fell on her face.

"Do not *ever* touch a female without their permission," Ronnie growled at the guy and dropped him. Suddenly, we found ourselves surrounded by about ten people, all confirming they saw everything that happened and that these two were behind it.

Then I felt it, the sense of danger I had been waiting for to show up. When I looked back at the two crazies, I could see the demons possessing them. The dark forms were entering into their bodies in a way that made me feel violated. Way too many people to do anything about it, and I shuffled over to Father Roarke, pulling him back.

Demons! I yelled through the connection to the guys who went on instant alert. *The crazy ones!*

"Father, those two are being possessed by demons, right now. There are too many people in here," I urgently whispered to him.

"Are you sure?"

"Yes, I just saw it happen." I turned sideways to look back, and they both had their attention on me. Their eyes, inhuman now, sent a chill down my spine.

"I see, lass. I'll handle it. You guys go on as if you would normally." Father Roarke moved away from me, and I found myself lifted and flung over the shoulder of one very pissed off Ronnie.

"Put me down," I told him, the blood rushing to my head.

"No. That fucker touched you, Airiella," Ronnie growled. I have never seen him this angry.

"Now he's possessed. Don't you think that maybe flinging me over your shoulder might cause a little scene?" I tried arguing.

"That is my intent. A distraction so that the priest can do what he needs to do."

"Why didn't you just say so? Instead of the caveman act?" I quieted down immediately.

"I'm pissed, angel. He's lucky I didn't do something else." He finally set me down and looked me over. "No one touches you. I'm not okay with that. Jax is *unequivocally* not okay with that."

"Jax didn't flip out and throw me over his shoulders!" I cried out.

"Sweetheart, if you think he wasn't about to lose his goddamned mind, you better think again."

Then I noticed I couldn't feel him. "Holy shit! He shut me out!" I looked back to where Jax had his eyes glued on me and saw the violence swirling around him. I tapped my head, and he let me back in.

I'm fine. Don't lose your cool; I told Jax once the walls were down.

I'm not okay. None of us are close to okay! This situation is out of control, and this fucker touched you without your permission. This possessed bitch had her hands on all of us; she grabbed our dicks. He had his mouth on you!

Jax, baby. I'm okay. I promise.

This shit ends. Stay there with Ronnie. Please. There was going to be no reasoning with him.

He shut me out again, and I looked back at Ronnie, narrowing my eyes. "What's he going to do?"

"I'm standing here with you. How should I know?" Ronnie wasn't budging either. Their reactions were frightening.

"Fuck. He said this shit ends." I jumped, flinching away when Ronnie started brushing the dirt off me. I guess some part of me wasn't ready for hands to touch me yet.

"You aren't fine, angel. Not if you jump when I touch you," the quiet of his voice and utterly calm of his tone told me everything I needed to know about where my gentle giant was, mentally.

"I'm not afraid of you, Ronan. You just startled me." I stood completely still while he finished getting the dirt and weeds out of my hair. Then he turned me to face him.

"Someone strange dude manhandling you that way

will *never* fly with any of us. Not ever. Even if someone knows you, that isn't okay. It shouldn't be something you dismiss so easily, either. Especially not with insane laughter." Ronnie's tone was lethal in the barely contained fury he was directing at the two culprits.

"Heracles, it was either laugh, cry, or punch them both," I admitted quietly. "I wasn't okay with it then, and I'm not now. But it also didn't send me into a blind panic like it would have before I healed."

"Jesus, angel. I wanted to break him into little pieces," he crushed me to him and I could feel the intense emotions vibrating through him. I slipped my hand under his shirt and let our connection soothe him. I didn't want to pull any of the feelings they were all experiencing. They were entitled to them. Ronnie was right, what had happened was a massive violation, and the aftermath hadn't quite settled in yet.

Come back here, please, I heard Jax's constrained voice.

"He's calling us back, but he doesn't sound happy," I warned Ronnie, letting him hold my hand and lead me back.

"Whatever he's done, just go with it. Believe me when I tell you that what just happened will have a lasting effect on him."

As we walked up, the crowd grew silent, and Smitty was filming. Jax reached out and drew me to him, his arm possessively around me. "Not only was the attack that just happened wrong, but those unwelcome touches are also a personal violation of her, myself, and the rest of our crew; several people were present to witness each of these attacks. Shadow Seekers as a whole, and I, stand here and ask all of you watching to stand against gross violations like this. Don't tolerate it. Help me put an end to it. How would you feel watching the one you love having that happen right in front of you?"

Jax ended his dialog with a sweet and gentle kiss, right in front of everyone. To my complete embarrassment, they all started clapping, and I felt myself blushing. I wanted to pull away, but he had me trapped against him, and my body wouldn't obey anyway. It was Jax.

He just claimed you and had this crowd publicly declare what they witnessed these two do, not only to you, but to us. Jax is a man in love, Smitty sent to me. *Aside from that, we all want to beat the shit out of this guy. Please tell me you are okay.*

I'm okay; I sent back to Smitty.

Okay? You kinda went a little crazy there with that laughter. You aren't okay.

Like I told Ronnie, it was either laugh, cry, or punch them. If I was honest, I still wanted to punch them both.

My vote is punching. I think Aedan's is too. He was shaking; he was so pissed. Jax was the smart one and used a public platform to call out the behavior. But he is quite assuredly, not happy. Is Ronnie okay? I've never seen him that mad before.

He said he wasn't okay. I looked over at him and saw he had a hold of his temper, but barely.

Let's finish this and get out of here, Smitty watched us closely.

I was all for that. I tried to veer away from Jax, but he wasn't letting go. That was a sure sign I knew he wasn't okay either, in case I had any doubts. Instead of arguing, I pulled him along with me to Father Roarke. "Did you fix it?"

"Aye, lass. Aedan and I will be sitting right here with these two until the police arrive."

I gulped. "The police?"

"Siren, did you honestly think I wouldn't press charges, or ask you to do the same? She had her hand on my dick like she had a right to be touching me. I can bet that you will have bruises from what this fucker did."

I squatted down in front of them but not within reach. "What the fuck were you thinking?"

The female spit at me. "Whore." I felt Jax start to react, and I squeezed his hand to stop him.

I shrugged. "From where I'm standing, it would appear that the name is better suited to you. What makes you think I would want him," I pointed at the guy, "when I have him? Oh, and him," I looked to Aedan, "and the other two as well."

Father Roarke chuckled. "Aedan will text you when the officers arrive; I'm sure they will want a statement. The rest of the crowd offered their names and numbers as witnesses, as well as Smitty filming them saying what they saw."

"You are good and screwed," I smiled at them. "Have a nice day."

I stood, and we finished the walk around the grounds, heading to the parking lot when Smitty declared they had enough footage for the pre-show. The cops were just arriving as he got to the SUV and started loading up the gear.

All of the guys gave their statements individually, leaving me for last. It wasn't my first time presenting myself to an officer about sexual abuse, which left a bad taste in my mouth. Despite the evidence against the previous claims, it was still my word against his.

I knew the routine and pulled off my outer layers before it was my turn, and when Ronnie went rigid next to me, I guessed he realized what I was doing. "I'm going to assume by the tension rolling off you that when you did this before, it didn't go so well?"

"No, it didn't." I didn't follow through with more details; it would only make him angrier.

"Jax's move was incredibly smart then. He has a minimum of ten witnesses on film and what we all saw and had happened to us. He won't let this lie if they don't believe you," Ronnie promised.

"I know. It's still not a fun process. I've healed, but the scars are still there, those don't ever truly go away. I wasn't lying when I said this didn't trigger those emotions, but it still wasn't a pleasant experience."

"One of us will go with you for support," Ronnie offered.

"They won't allow it. I'm fine." I knew I didn't sound fine. I was tired, sore, and starting to feel like my nerves were raw. The process of *this* was more triggering for me than the attack itself was. "It's clear to me that the demons are going to use my past as a way to get to me or to make you guys react. I think it's important not to give in."

"That would have sounded a lot better if your voice hadn't been so wooden," Ronnie pointed out.

"I serioiusly hate this," I leaned against him resting my head on his shoulder.

"I know, angel. I'm sorry you have to do it. You need to know, we won't tolerate this kind of behavior, especially against you." He kissed the top of my head and wrapped his arm around me. I must have had bruises on my back because even the slight pressure hurt, and I flinched.

Fortunately, a female officer came to get me before I had to answer any of the questions I felt bubbling up inside him. "Can one of the guys be with me?" I asked her.

"I'm supposed to say no, but if he doesn't speak, I'll allow it. Which one?" She was kind, at least. I pointed back at Ronnie, and she motioned to him to join us. As he came up, she told him, "She requested you, but I am going to caution you not to speak. Her statement needs to be her own words. And if I think you are upsetting her, I will have you escorted away." Ronnie gave a silent nod.

"Okay, hon, which do you want to do first? The statement, or the physical exam?" her touch on my elbow was gentle.

"I'd rather get the physical exam done with first if that's okay," I replied weakly. Shit, this was indeed triggering me.

I'm so sorry, angel.

Just keep me blocked from the view of others, please.

Officer Rodriguez was the name that I read on her uniform. She led me behind a makeshift wall of car doors they had formed to try and keep this private. I was thankful that I didn't have to go to the police station to do it. Small towns were a good thing sometimes, or it was Jax's influence. "Do you want him to be a part of this?" she gestured at Ronnie.

I nodded. Ronnie was my safety net. I might not have wanted him to see the bruises if there were any, but there wasn't anyone else I felt safer with, except maybe Jax, and he was still giving his statement. "He's intimidating enough to keep people away," I said with a weak smile.

"Looks more like a big teddy bear to me," she gave a little laugh. "I'm a fan of the show, so I know he isn't mean. Besides, I have a gun, and I don't intimidate easily."

"Well, he isn't trying to intimidate you, just the mob of people out there," I pointed back to where a crowd of looky-loo's gathered.

"I know, hon. I'm just trying to make you feel more comfortable. Let's start with the pants, go ahead, and take them off and if there are any bruises, I'll take a picture. Do you need help?"

"No, I'm just stiff," I heard Ronnie grunt, and then he turned around and dropped untying my shoes for me. I kicked them off, leaning against the seat of the SUV and tugged my leggings off. Ronnie backed up and blocked me from view.

"There's a good-sized bruise that's forming on the back of your left quadricep," she snapped a picture. "A couple of smaller ones on the right, and a small cut on your right calf." More photos got snapped as she cataloged the injuries. "Go ahead and put your pants back on."

At least this isn't a rape kit; I sent to Ronnie before even thinking about how that statement would sound to him. I saw him flinch. *Shit, I'm sorry.*

Don't be. Just something I've never thought about before. How violating this part of it is, as well, Ronnie's sent back, his tone hovering on a dangerous edge.

"Shirt, next, bra as well," Officer Rodriguez told me gently. "I know how awful this is, personal experience, and I'm sorry."

"It's okay. Not my first go around," I said numbly. *I*

need help with the bra; my shoulders are hurting.

Ronnie stepped forward and unhooked the back of my bra for me, his beautiful face a mix of anger and sadness. He shook his head slightly at me, letting me know without speaking, that he didn't want me to say anything.

"I'm sorry to hear you've done this before. Hold the bra to your chest for some privacy; I'll look over your back first." Of all the times I had done this, she was by far the best officer I'd gotten to work with for this part. "Your back is a mess; I'm sorry to say. You'll be sore for a while." She took several pictures and had me turn to the side, then the other before she asked me to lower the bra.

The wave of anger that radiated out from Ronnie rocked me back on my feet, and I almost stumbled, Officer Rodriguez gave me a concerned look. "Are you okay?"

"I'm fine. Tired," I offered the lame excuse.

Fingerprint bruises were evident over my breasts and rib cage. Times like these, I'm glad that my pain tolerance is so high. I knew he had used force when he groped me, but I am happy that I hadn't felt it the way I was now. My arms had a few bruises. She took her pictures and allowed Ronnie to help me get dressed again.

My gentle giant hadn't uttered one word the entire time, but I felt the storm brewing inside him. I didn't say anything to him. There wasn't anything I could say that would ease the burden. These emotions in him were triggers from his past in watching this happen to his mom. Now to me. If anyone could help him, it would be Jax.

Ronnie needs you. He's struggling hard with this; I sent to Jax.

I felt it. I'll come get Ronnie; I'll swap him out for Smitty.

I put my hand out to Officer Rodriguez and stopped her, begging her with my eyes to understand. I waited while Jax pulled Ronnie away, and Smitty stepped in, then let her go. "He was having a hard time seeing that," I tried to explain.

"I get it." She didn't push and led me over to where the other two men had been questioning everyone else. Smitty stood silently by my side as I answered all their questions three times in three different ways and left my contact information.

Tom had obviously pulled quite a few strings to get this done like this, and we were soon headed back to my house with a stop off to drop Father Roarke at his hotel. No one had spoken, and it was awkward and tense. I desperately wanted to pull it from them. Instinctively, I knew that would be the wrong thing to do, so I just leaned against the window and let my eyes close. Today had only been the opening act, I was sure.

Chapter Twenty-Six

Jax wanted to tear something apart. Furious didn't begin to cover what he was feeling. Ronnie had never been so close to losing control before. Jax hadn't been sure he'd be able to get him off that edge. After Ronnie had told him what he'd seen, Jax hadn't wanted to.

Smitty had been the only one able to reign in his temper, and Jax knew that was hanging on by a thread. The three-hour drive to her house had been painful, and upon arrival, Mags had whisked her away the moment she stepped out of the vehicle.

That left the four of them in the SUV; they hadn't gotten out. His biggest concern was Ronnie. He'd flat out cried when Jax had pulled him away. The words were spilling out of his mouth in a jumble. The marks and bruises she sported now, the haunted look on his face, mixed with the anger of having seen it happen.

"Alright, this isn't going to get any easier. This shit is just starting," Jax began.

"I don't want to talk about today," Ronnie interrupted him.

"She's okay," Smitty intervened. "She's sore, but it's not bad. Mentally it didn't push her over the edge. It might have pushed all of us over the edge, but she's still solid. We can't let this shake us."

Ronnie barked out a bitter laugh. "Go look at her chest and tell me she's still solid. Or her back. Or have her tell you in your head that it isn't a rape kit at least this time. I didn't even realize that the shit she has to go through *after* an attack is still a violation."

"What?" Aedan sat forward. "What do you mean?"

"She has to strip before a stranger after being sexually assaulted by a different stranger, in front of strangers. And then have pictures taken of what happened and asked to relive it all over again. Why did none of this occur to us? Aside from the fact that she hated every minute of it, she also had to confess to the cop taking pictures of her naked body that it wasn't her first time doing this. After she told me the previous times she had to do this, it didn't go well for her." Jax saw the angry tears slide down his cheeks again.

"Shit. No wonder Airiella's tired," Aedan mused.

Jax struggled to maintain his control, "We've got to hold it together. Today seems like an attack on Ronnie and Airiella. They are using our pasts to bring us down. It damn near did."

"If that's what the rest of this week is going to look like, I won't survive it. I'm about to break, Jax," Ronnie warned unnecessarily.

"I'm not going to let you go in there like this, Ron. You've got to calm down first." Jax was firm but gentle. "If she sees you falling apart, it's going to knock her off balance."

Ronnie broke down in sobs again. "You know what's even worse? Her thoughts when she asked if one of us could come with her was how safe I made her feel. Safe? Some puny, crazy dude attacked her right in front of me!"

Jax blinked back his tears. He knew. He'd heard it too, and he knew what it was doing to Ronnie. Hell, it was doing the same thing to him. "Then, let's blow up here, not inside."

"I think that's where you might be wrong, Jax. She's the only one that brings us back from the edge we are all on. It's when we are near her that soothes us, the connection we share. Maybe, even though we are all a little raw, we need to be next to her," Smitty suggested. "She already knows how we are all feeling. Even if we block her out, these emotions are heavy enough; we can't hide them."

Smitty is right, baby. I do need to feel you all near me.

Jax deflated. "Smitty's right. She just said she needed us all near her."

In a flash, Ronnie was out of the car, the door opened by Jillian, who pointed up the stairs. The rest followed a bit more slowly and came inside to find Ronnie carrying her back down the stairs. Mags waddling behind him.

"She's okay, Jax," Mags told him before she wrapped herself around Aedan.

Jax followed Ronnie's path down the hallway to find him and Jillian moving the tables around, so there was a large enough place in the middle of the room for them all to sit. Mags and Aedan trailed behind them, Jax noticing a jar of something in Mags's hand.

"Is that the healing stuff from Father Roarke?" Jax felt hopeful at last.

Mags nodded, handing it to him and sat down on the couch, stuffing a pillow behind her back. "I think Degataga made it. I used it on my back when I was hurting during the car ride." At Jillian's not so subtle cough, Mags revised her statement. "Okay, Jillian used it on me. That stuff is magic. So are Jillian's hands."

Smitty finally laughed, but he agreed. "Feel like stripping, baby girl?"

"Not particularly," she answered sarcastically. "I'm not a good dancer."

Ronnie was not in the least amused, and it stung Jax to know how much he was hurting. *He seriously needs you, siren.*

I know. Ronnie's still got me shut out, but I can feel it. I can't force him.

Bullshit. Ronnie's not doing anything, because he's afraid he'll hurt you. Don't give him a choice, Jax pushed back.

He tried not to smile as she patiently held a hand out to Ronnie, waiting for him to take it. Once he did, she pulled him down and propped the upper half of her body across his lap. "Can you pull my shirt off?" she asked him.

Jax lost his smile at the pained look on his face. Ronnie didn't refuse her and gingerly lifted the shirt off her while she held herself up. They *all* felt the anger wash over him at the sight of her now very colorful back and dark bruises on her sides.

"Pants too," he said, his voice thick.

"My legs are fine," she argued.

"How is laying like this not hurting the front of you?" he ground out.

Jax bit the inside of his lip. If the front of her looked as bad as her back did, it wouldn't only be Ronnie that was fighting for control of his anger. Jax held his breath, waiting for her response. She must have responded through their connection because she said nothing out loud.

Ronnie shifted and dropped butterfly kisses along her back as silent tears fell once again. Jax moved into position next to Ronnie, and Smitty took the other side. Both of them touching her arms. Aedan waited until Jillian was in place to rub some of the jar contents on her back since she took it from Mags; then, he sat where he could touch her leg.

Only Mags wasn't touching her. It was then that Jax noticed she was having a hard time getting up. He held out his hand, and she pulled herself up and slid down next to Aedan, once she added her touch the living room filled with a blue glow of the shared connection flowing freely.

Jax felt the tension bleed out of the room, and Ronnie finally relaxed next to him. Jax leaned forward and unhooked her bra, wincing slightly at the deep bruising. *Why didn't you tell me it was this bad?*

It doesn't feel that bad to me. I'm stiff, but not in severe pain. I'm guessing it looks a lot worse than it feels.

It looks fucking awful, siren. Jax couldn't tell if she was understating it or not.

I probably landed on rocks when she knocked me down. Honestly, I'm not in pain. Trust me; my pain tolerance is pretty damn high.

That's not a comforting thought. It means that it does hurt, and you just don't know it. Is Ronnie doing better? Jax cast a sidelong look at Ronnie and saw his eyes closed.

Maybe a little. Ronnie said he couldn't get the image out of his head of that guy grabbing my crotch.

Jax agreed with him on that one. The only thing that had kept Jax from falling into a blind rage was seeing that Ronnie was in one. Jax had been terrified that Ronnie was going to break the guy's neck. *He hasn't been like this since his dad got arrested.*

He's coming down, she reassured him soothingly.

How are you so calm? All of the guys had been thoroughly shaken by it.

I'll probably freak out after I'm asleep if it will happen. I didn't have any danger warnings, though I was pretty damn pissed that she kept touching you guys. I wanted to rip her arm off when I saw her grab your dick.

You and me both. It had given Jax a slight understanding of how violating it was to have an unwelcome touch in that manner. It hadn't been a good feeling.

"Jillian, you really do have magic hands," Airiella groaned. "Smitty's a lucky man."

Her warm laugh eased more of the tension in the room. Jax heard Airiella's phone ding with a text message, and he grabbed it and handed it to her. She gave it right back, and he looked at the screen. It was from her dad, a photo of an article he'd found.

"Holy shit, he found something!" Jax crowed and showed Ronnie, then Smitty. "Vague reference to satanic rituals being performed by the accused. Can I respond to him, siren?"

"Yep."

Jax was texting back and forth furiously. When he finished, he told them, "He's going to stop by with a photocopy of the article for us. He said it would be about half an hour." It was perfect for Jax. He wanted to talk with him anyway and let him know of his plans.

"Well, that undoubtedly means my bra and shirt go back on," Airiella quipped lightly.

"Damn, I finally get to touch you, and now your dad shows up," Jillian joked.

"Parents, always ruining the fun," Mags added. "I get to look forward to that."

"Siren, I'm going to tell him about today. I'd rather him hear it from me than someone who watches the show. That will be part of what's shown, and if someone recognizes you, they might say something."

She groaned. "I hate telling my dad that stuff."

"I'll do it, so you don't have to. I'm going to sit on the porch and wait for your dad. It'll give Jillian a little more time to feel you up and make Smitty jealous," Jax shot a grin at Smitty.

Chapter Twenty-Seven

I was going to be glad when this day was over. Jax had been acting withdrawn and odd since my dad left, and I couldn't figure out why. Jax had pulled Ronnie away, and they had another closed off discussion, I was starting to feel like a third wheel with them.

I ordered pizza and salad for dinner and was happy to see that Ronnie was perking up a little, but I was feeling caged and edgy. I didn't know if it was the trauma of the day catching up to me or that Jax was standoffish, and I wanted some time with him.

It didn't matter; my house was small. There was no room for me to have time with him. Instead, I decided to give an impromptu tour of the place and go out to the river for some nature time. They could either come with or stay behind. I didn't care.

"Okay, it's going to be a bit cramped since my house

is small, sorry, guys. Smitty and Jillian can have the office; they have an air mattress we can put in there," I said, pointing to the office and then the guest room down the hall. "Mags and Aedan can take the guest room since she's pregnant. It's five nights; so I can switch it up with you Smitty, we can take turns using my room, I'm fine with that. The bathroom is there between the two, linen closet for towels or extra blankets is here behind me," I said, tapping the door. "Obviously, this is the laundry room if you need to wash something before we head out."

Opening my bedroom door, "This is my room. I do have a big bed, so either Ronnie or Jax can both sleep here with me. Or just one of them and the other can have the couch downstairs, I don't care either way," I said looking at both. I knew Ronnie would want to sleep with me, Jax though, I guess it depended on his mood at the moment, I wasn't sure what was going on with him.

"Damn, girl! You've got a huge tub!" Ronnie shouted as he pushed past me into my room to drop his bag on the bed and looked in the bathroom. "Wait, I gotta take a bath?"

"There's a shower in there too," I said, pointing to the other end of the bathroom. Jax wandered in and glanced around. As if he was looking to see if it had changed. Then he dropped his bag in front of my nightstand. I saw Aedan and Smitty both raise their eyebrows at me as I caught their glances. I shrugged.

"Jillian and I will keep the office and air mattress the whole time; we don't need to switch, we like roughing it," Smitty said with a smirk and Jillian smacked him on the back of the head.

"I don't want to hear about your sex life," I shot

back at them.

"Guess Mags and me, are going to bed then, works for me," Aedan grabbed Mags and pulled her into the room and closed the door.

"Guess that means you get to hear their sex life," I tossed out to Smitty, laughing at his grimace.

"I'll just have to make more noise then," he fired back.

"On that note, I'm going to leave you love birds alone and take off for a bit, so I don't hear things I don't want to hear," I said, smirking. "You two can come with me if you want," I said, looking at Jax and Ronnie.

"Where to, angel? You know I'm in," Ronnie said as we walked out of the room. I pulled the door closed behind me, looking at Jax, who still hadn't said anything. I was a little concerned because he was working hard at keeping me out.

"I was going to head out to the river spot where this all started for me," I said quietly. "I need some nature that doesn't have crazy fans in it."

"I'll go," Jax said and walked past us and down the stairs.

"Where you first saw Winnie?" Ronnie whispered to me. I nodded. He grabbed my hand, "Let's go then."

"Is he okay?" I asked Ronnie.

"Yeah. Probably just the day is catching up with him. I didn't make it easy for him," Ronnie tried to shrug it off, but I felt something under those words. "I like your house. Can't wait to be in your bed."

"You mean with Jax?" I nudged him. "Should I leave you two alone then?"

"Jax couldn't handle me," Ronnie laughed as we

came down the stairs. "Isn't that right, Jax?"

"What's that?" he asked curiously.

"You couldn't handle me in bed." I almost laughed at the expression on Jax's face.

"I wouldn't *want* to handle you," he corrected.

"Come on, let's go," I grabbed my keys, remembering I couldn't get out of the garage since the rental was parked there. "Keys, please."

"I can drive," Jax said.

"Do you know where you are going?" I snatched the keys from him. "I'd like to drive, please." I had no idea why I was flipping him this attitude. He hadn't given me any; he was just distant. "Sorry. It's not far; it's just easier if I drive."

He put his hand on the small of my back as we walked out, and I knew I hadn't lost him. Maybe Ronnie was right, and it was catching up to him. "Is this the same river you did your naked rope swing?"

"No, this is the river where I met Winnie for the first time. The spot that ultimately led me to you guys. It's a peaceful spot where I can unwind," I told them as I drove. It wasn't dark yet, but it would be soon. Luckily, I hadn't taken my pack out of the SUV, so my flashlight was there. A headlamp too if I remembered right.

Is it safe for me to take my necklace off so I can talk to Winnie? Ronnie asked me.

Debatable. I don't think anywhere is safe for us right now. Go ahead and do it. I'll blast the fuckers with lightning if they show up.

I parked the car and got out, opening the back to rummage through my pack and find the lights, subtly holding my hand out for Ronnie's necklace and put it in the pocket of my pants. I'd give it back when we were headed back to the car.

We hadn't gone three steps when my phone rang again, my peaceful place interrupted. "Hi, Tak."

"Raven, I hate to do this over the phone. Kalisha is dead," Taklishim's voice raw with emotion.

I dropped the phone. Jax caught it before it hit the ground. "Taklishim, what's going on?"

Jax paled, pulling me to him and wrapping his arm around me as he listened to Taklishim. Ronnie reached for my hand, "Angel, talk to me."

"Kalisha is dead," I whispered, my fingers brushing over the necklace she had made me.

"Fucking hell," Ronnie growled, picking up a rock and throwing it.

I pulled away from Jax, handing him the flashlight and started walking towards the river. Ronnie scrambled after me. I led him to the log I had sat on and talked with Winnie the first time. "Sit here; this is where I met Winnie. Talk to her now. See what she knows."

He didn't argue with me. I didn't go far from him, still within sight distance for both of us. Me, so if he needed help, I was close. For him, so he didn't worry about me any more than he already had today.

I found an open spot at the edge of the river and dropped to the ground, guilt, and grief swamping me. I buried my face in my hands and let the tears fall for the beautiful and mysterious woman who had done nothing but help us and try to keep us safe. "Why?" I whispered.

Smitty's phone dinged with an alert while raiding the pantry for snacks, trying to stay ahead of Mags's craving curve. Jillian had told him she was hungry about this time every night for the past couple of nights, so she left stuff out on the counter for her.

He grabbed his phone to see a text from Airiella. Nope, it was Jax from Airiella's phone. Someone had killed Kalisha. Stunned, he stumbled back into the counter and heard Aedan thudding down the stairs. Smitty looked up as Aedan flew into the kitchen, "You get the message too?"

"Uh-huh, what the hell?" Aedan was just as shocked as Smitty was. "She's the best there is out there at protection. How could this happen?"

"I don't know." Smitty was responding to Jax when another message came through. "Apparently Taklishim called Airiella and told her, and she dropped the phone and walked away. He's warning us in case anything comes through the connection."

"She's alone?" Aedan practically shouted.

"Chill, I'm finding out." Smitty was texting furiously. "No, Ronnie followed her. Jax is going to try to look for her. He'll try to find out more. Said Taklishim didn't know a lot of details yet, but that it wasn't a natural death."

"No, shit. I'd say that's a pretty big warning to us." Aedan bit out. "This place is protected, right?"

"Yeah. Taklishim did it when she was back for the funeral. I'm more worried about them out there." Smitty scrubbed his hands over his face. "She was helping us, and I bet that's why. Fuck." Guilt washed over him, and he slid down to the floor. He'd respected the beautiful woman and her intelligence. She'd never been unkind to any of them. She didn't deserve this.

J ax's heart was racing at the news, and now he was standing alone in a small field with a trail running through it. He'd seen the way they had headed but finished up the call with Taklishim and texted Aedan and Smitty.

Airiella had already needed nature, so he wanted to give her time to herself. After that news, he didn't think any of them should be alone. He'd been a jerk the rest of the day after talking to her dad, and he regretted that. He had allowed his fears to take over his thoughts and pulled away from everyone.

Spencer told Jax that she might say no, and then Jax having to explain what had happened earlier that day. Ronnie confronted him about Chrissie, asking him if he was trying to push Ronnie into something before he was ready. It made him question all his decisions. Now, this.

Kalisha. She'd always intimidated Jax, even though she'd never been anything but friendly and kind to him. A woman of mystery, she seemed to understand things about him she shouldn't know, see the things he didn't want anyone seeing. Her beauty was almost unworldly, and she had been the absolute best in her field. Unsurpassed and always deferred to when she made a suggestion.

His eyes stung. In his gut, he knew this was because of Bael. Taklishim felt it too, though they didn't know how to confirm it. It wasn't like they could go to the police and tell them that a prince of Hell killed her. That would go over well.

He started wandering down the path they had taken, going slowly, and listening for sounds that shouldn't be here. It was a pretty wooded area, and in the distance, he could hear the river. If he had to guess, near the river is where he'd find Airiella. He came to a split in the trail and paused, trying to figure out which way they had gone.

His heart was pulling him to the right, so he went with it for no other reason than his heart told him to. He saw Ronnie first, in an idyllic little setting. It made him think of a fairy world; it was so lush and green. Ronnie pointed to a direction off on Jax's left, and he turned and saw her.

She was curled up around her knees, her shoulders shaking, right at the water's edge. She was in a small clearing not big enough to fit Jax as well, so he stayed back, between Ronnie and her, allowing each of them their space.

He'd instinctively known that she wouldn't be far from Ronnie. With the level of activity they'd been having, she would have been worried about him being alone. The attack today felt like it had targeted Ronnie more than it had Jax.

Jax leaned back against a tree and watched the woman who'd so easily captured his heart and soul. She was hurting right now. That was plain enough to see by the expression on her face and how she'd dropped the phone and left. He glanced over at Ronnie just in time to see him bolt to his feet, staring at Airiella.

Alarmed, Jax turned back and jolted when he saw Stolas standing there next to her. Airiella made a motion with her hands, sending a blue ring of fire around them, from Ronnie to Jax and back to her. To him, it meant she felt danger, and he made a move to go to her when he saw

Ronnie gesturing at him to stop.

Ronnie jogged over to him. "Let her be. She's shut us out. If she wants us there, she will tell us. I think the fire thing is an added layer of protection because she's distracted. I'm over there talking to Winnie if you want to join me."

"Nope. I'm going to stay right here where I can see her," Jax refused to move from this spot.

Winnie waited for Ronnie on the log. "He won't hurt her, right?" Ronnie asked Winnie as he sat back down.

"I don't believe he will. From what I have seen and understand, he's in love with her."

"Just what every angel needs, a demon falling in love with her," Ronnie ground out, kicking at a weed.

Winnie looked over at Airiella; this beautiful woman has borne too much in such a short time, and her heart went out to her. Winnie didn't know where Airiella's breaking point was, and lately, she'd been starting to worry that she was close.

"I love her so much, it scares the hell out of me, Winnie." Ronnie's confession confused Winnie.

"Why would that scare you? Love is wonderful. You don't honestly believe Jax is trying to push you out of the picture, do you?"

"No. I don't believe that. I said that more out of fear than actually thinking it to be real."

"Then, why are you scared? Explain it to me," Winnie requested.

"I don't know!" he cried. "Not entirely true. I'm so

afraid of losing Airiella, to demons, to death, to Jax. And I don't mean that I don't want her to be with Jax, I'm more afraid that she will pull away from me. I'm honest when I say I'm not ready for that. The love I have for her is the strongest emotion I have ever felt."

"She wouldn't ever pull away from you. She loves you just as much as you love her."

"I think the other part that's scaring me, is now that I've been talking to Chrissie, I realize I'm starting to fall in love with her. My brain is now open to me, accepting that Jax is her forever, and I'm not."

"Wait. You are afraid to fall in love with Chrissie?" Winnie's jaw gaped open.

"Kind of, am I stupid?"

"Yes. Sorry. Falling in love is such a wonderful feeling. With Airiella, you never have to doubt that you are loved. No matter what you decide, you will always have a place with her and with Jax. Even I know that. Jax has even told you that."

"Fears aren't rational, Winnie. Chrissie deserves all of me if I go that route. What if my body doesn't react to her the way it does to Airiella? I'll never stop wanting her and that feeling we have when I'm making love to her. I can't in good conscious be in a relationship with Chrissie and be lusting after Airiella."

"Don't you think you are jumping the gun a little bit here? You haven't even been on a date with her yet. On that same note, how do you know you are falling in love with her?"

"I look forward to her calls. My heart feels happy and light when I hear her voice. We can talk about anything. Her boys are wonderful. When I think of something funny, I think about texting it to her. Her spirit is that of a warrior, but she doesn't even see that." Ronnie's expression was somewhat dreamy.

"Okay, let me point out something totally self-evident here. You feel all those same things about Airiella; I already know that. You seem to be missing an important piece of this, while you are *still* feeling all those things about your angel, you are more excited to talk to Chrissie than you are to tell Airiella. What does that say to you?"

"That I'm desperate for someone to love me the way she loves Jax?"

"You're an idiot sometimes. That may be true, but it tells me you aren't falling in love with Chrissie, you are *already* in love with her and your heart has plenty of room for both women in it. I know you better than to think you are just worried about the sex aspect of this."

"I don't want things to change with Airiella, and I feel like they already have." Ronnie sunk his head.

"They haven't! It's only in your mind because your heart is loving someone else, and it makes you feel guilty. Playing the long game is good in some aspects, but right now, you need to focus on the short game and just get through this crap with the demons. I also believe that Airiella said the only thing that would change with Chrissie coming in the picture is that she wouldn't have sex with you once that happened. Stop worrying over nothing." Winnie had no idea where these thoughts Ronnie was having were coming from; they weren't like him at all.

"Sometimes, I feel like I'm trying to replace Airiella with Chrissie. To make Chrissie fit the mold, and that feels wrong."

"Why do you think you are doing that?" Winnie

sighed.

"I don't know. Both women have so many similarities I worry that I'm latching on because of that."

"I can't make you see reason. It sounds like you are making excuses and looking for a reason to talk yourself out of it. Airiella is your first real love. It's hard to let go of that."

"That's not true; you were my first love," Ronnie argued.

"You loved me, but we were never together. You've been with how many other women?"

"A lot," Ronnie said, ashamed.

"How many did you have an emotional investment in?" Winnie was trying to be kind in pointing this out, but he wasn't getting it.

"None," he admitted.

"She's your first. You fell fast and hard without looking back once. Now that there is someone you are feeling those same emotions for, the fact that they are strong enough to make you aware of them while you are still in love with Airy should be a pretty big clue that it's real, and it's a good thing."

"Shut up," Ronnie smiled when he said it. "When you point it out like that, I am an idiot. I'm not ready to not be an idiot, so let me have my idiocy."

"As long as you realize it. Your connection and bond tie you to that wonderfully complex angel out there, you won't ever lose that. It shouldn't even be a fear you feel. Chrissie is her best friend, and knows all about it and has zero problems with it," Winnie rolled her eyes for emphasis.

"Okay. I get it. I already admitted I was an idiot."

"Only reaffirming it. Your focus needs to be on surviving Bael. He's coming, and soon." Winnie wished she had more than that. "Kalisha's death was because of him. Because she had his blood and was making something Airy can use against him."

"Are you sure about that?" Ronnie focused on her.

"Positive. I'm also sure that is what that demon in love is telling her right now."

"Could you maybe not say that? It's not comforting."

"What, the demon in love part?" Winnie grinned.

"Yeah, that part. Who wants the dark forces lusting after them?"

"He won't hurt her. He's all but sworn it." Truthfully, Winnie found it sad. Unrequited love was painful. "He's put himself at great risk helping her. I believe that Bael has the power to end Stolas if he finds out."

"Is one less prince of Hell a bad thing?" Ronnie countered.

"Another would just take his place, it's not like there is a shortage of demons," Winnie pointed out. She gazed across to Airiella, talking with Stolas and Jax waiting patiently behind. Winnie wasn't about to tell Ronnie how scared she truly was. She'd had some terrifying visions lately; she knew the images weren't ironclad, especially with the way Airiella changed things. But the possibilities were enough to scare her stupid.

Chapter Twenty-Eight

I'm so sorry, beautiful angel. I truly am," Stolas knelt next to me and put a hand on my arm.

I expected to feel disgusted when he touched me, but I didn't. Maybe I was numb, or perhaps I was finally trusting that he wouldn't hurt me. "Did you know?"

"I did not. If I had, I would have warned you. You may be able to see the priestess still; she is stuck in between," Stolas looked sad at that.

"Why is she stuck?" I hated the thought of her being unable to enjoy whatever came next. "Is she bound?"

"No, she is not bound. I believe it was what she wanted. I think she wants to make sure the job is complete. If she's in between, she can get through; she's quite powerful. Her magic straddles a fine line between dark and light."

"You almost sound like you admire her," I

commented drily.

"I do, actually, quite a bit. I did not wish to see the priestess come to harm, nor did I want to see it hurt you like this."

"Your soul is lighter in color these days, less muddy," I wiped the tears from my cheeks.

"That's from you. Do you mind if I sit next to you?" Stolas gestured to the weeds.

"I guess ticks aren't really a concern for you, are they?" I tried for humor. I wasn't feeling it.

"Is that worry I hear in your voice? For me?" he sat down in the weeds, a little too close for comfort for my tastes, but he wasn't crossing any lines.

"Maybe? I don't know." I propped my chin on my arms and stared at the river flowing by, letting the energy flow through me. It wasn't washing the grief away as I had hoped, but I think that was my fault because I wasn't exactly letting go of it either.

"She was successful, you know. What she made can banish Bael from this world for good, possibly even weaken him enough that another could kill him."

"I won't be able to kill him?" Banishment was good, but justice for Kalisha was even better.

"It's possible, I suppose. Are you sure that's something you would want to bear?"

"I was attacked today, sexually assaulted in front of many people. Deeply hurting those I love. He killed Kalisha, someone who only wanted to help protect me and those I love. It's not a burden; it's justice." I was angry and heartbroken.

"I wasn't aware you had gotten assaulted, are you hurt?" Stolas sounded angry, and I turned my head to look at him.

He had schooled his face into a mask of casual indifference, but the fire in his eyes gave it away. "That makes you angry, doesn't it?" I dropped my knees down and pulled off my shirt, allowing him to see my back. In a move I couldn't explain myself, I showed him my breasts and the marks before putting my clothes back on.

I wasn't expecting the wave of fiery power that slammed into me as his expression went from indifferent to rage. "Angry is a good word for it, yes. Was it demons?"

"At first, no. I didn't sense any danger until after it happened. I saw two demons possessing the two people after the attacks."

"That doesn't mean that the thoughts and ideas hadn't been planted in them already. Are they dead?" Stolas was radiating a power I didn't want to be on the wrong side of, one I hadn't known he possessed since he always appeared so docile.

"Father Roarke took care of them. We were surrounded by too many people for us to do anything, really. Can you reign it in a little? You are making my wings itch to come out, and if that happens, we won't be having this conversation alone."

"I am sorry, my dear. It's not often I lose control like that." The heavy feeling around me eased up some. "I believe my feelings for you are deeper than I had thought."

That admission made me uncomfortable. "Stolas, we talked about this."

"I will never impose my will upon yours, and I'm quite aware of how you feel about these two humans that wish to charge in here and rescue you. It was nothing but a simple explanation for the release of the power like that."

The sad look on his face tugged on my heartstrings. In this form he was extremely handsome. It still didn't change the fact that I didn't feel the same way for Stolas he felt for me.

"It doesn't mean I won't be your friend, Stolas. I still love my friends," I reached out and took his hand. "I trusted you enough with one of my feathers."

"A treasure I keep close to my heart," he smiled softly. "I came because I wanted you to know that I didn't know about Kalisha. Her death unleashed many unhappy gods upon us; it was not her time. I knew this would hurt you, too. I had hoped that telling you she was in between would give you some comfort that you might be able to see her still."

"Thank you for telling me." I knew if Kalisha needed to get through to me, she would. I would make a note to tell Onida and Winnie both that she was there.

"Bael is coming. If I learn more, I will tell you. I believe your grey warrior has the weapon she made. Please take care." Stolas kissed the back of my hand and stood.

"Stolas, wait." I stood up too, not wanting Jax or Ronnie to hear this. "Can they hear me?"

"No, not right now. Once I leave, both will be able to. Why?"

"I'm willing to die to make sure they don't. If it's between those two or me, do your best to help those men, please. I have a chance of coming back. They don't," I begged him.

"You are asking a lot of me. I desire to protect you."

"I know. But if you want to protect me, then knowing those men are safe is the best way you can do that. It also guarantees you a spot in my heart."

"You are magnificent." Stolas raked his gaze across

my face. "I would have done it without the guarantee of earning even a small space in your heart. You have my word that if I can do something to keep them safe, I will. Please find a way to fix that crack that's left."

Grateful for his offered help, I again took his hand and pushed love at him in gigantic quantities. "Thank you. Without them, I would cease to be."

He pulled his hand back quicker than I thought he would. "Your love makes me both weak and strong." He smiled again, "All you have to do is ask when you need me." He reached into his coat pocket and pulled out a small container. "Have them put this on your marks."

I looked down at the small container, and when I glanced back up, he was gone. I slid it in my pocket and sat back down. I felt Jax come up behind me. "Stand up siren, just for a moment." I stood and he sat in my place and pulled me down onto his lap. "I couldn't stay away from you any longer."

I leaned into his arms. "Kalisha died because of me," I gave back into the grief.

"You don't know that," he started to say.

"I do. Stolas told me she died because she had Bael's blood. She made a weapon that will banish him from here for good and weaken him enough that another prince could kill him. He thinks it might be possible for me to do it, he didn't know."

"That was a shitty thing to tell you," Jax grumbled.

"No. Stolas didn't know; her death upset him too." I wasn't about to tell him about the promise I extracted from Stolas.

"He's quite powerful. What was that about?" Jax finally asked me after we'd sat in silence for a few minutes.

"He didn't know about the attack earlier today either. He was angry about it," I explained. I looked up at the night sky knowing that soon this would be over, one way or the other. "Kalisha, if you can hear me, I vow to get justice for this wrong done against you."

Behind me, I felt Jax shudder. He felt the power of my words and tightened his arms around me, staying silent. We sat there for a while longer, and I finally let the earth energy wash away the grief. I thanked it and the universe for its assistance and stood. "Let's go."

Chapter Twenty-Nine

R onnie looked down at the cheerful comforter on her bed and felt a smile tug on his lips. "Do you want me to go sleep on the couch?" he offered to Jax.

"Don't be stupid, and don't let her hear you say that. You belong here just as much as I do," Jax had stripped down to his boxers so his clothes wouldn't get the bedding dirty, just as Ronnie had done as soon as she went to shower.

"I just wanted to give you an opportunity for some time with her," Ronnie was secretly happy at Jax's answer.

"I know. I'd rather spend the time with both of you," Jax answered carefully. Ronnie heard something in there under his tone.

"What exactly are you saying?" Ronnie knew, but he wanted to hear Jax say it.

"She wants both of us, at the same time. I know

you've heard the same thoughts I have every time we are together," Jax shifted uncomfortably. "I'm willing to give it a go if you are."

"I'm good with it; it's not really up to us." The statement floored Ronnie, he'd never expected Jax to be willing to try. "I'll admit to being shocked."

"I'd only consider this with you. No one else," Jax was emphatic in his swift answer.

"Jax, if it makes you that uncomfortable, why are you suggesting it?" Ronnie was sure it would have happened between Smitty and him before this would have ever happened.

"To help you understand, I'm not trying to push you out. There's no one other than Airiella that's closer to me than you. With everything we are facing, this feels right."

"I feel like there are several jokes that I could be flinging around right now. I'll go easy on you. I understand what you mean. Let's just see where the night takes us." Ronnie was overwhelmed by the emotion in Jax's voice and the admission that he wasn't pushing him out. He never believed Jax was doing that anyway; it was only the heat of the moment that made him say it.

"You shower next. I'm going to put this stuff on Airiella," Jax held out the little container.

"You probably haven't seen her chest yet. It's a little hard to take in. At least it was for me. Still is." Ronnie closed his eyes, trying to will away the memory of the brutal fingerprint shaped bruises on her perfect chest.

"Thanks for the warning. Does our angel still have you shut out?"

"Yeah. I couldn't hear any part of the conversation Airiella had with the herbal demon." Ronnie had hated it too. Winnie was a good distraction from it, at least. Jax had just sat there watching, tension flaring out from him.

"Think she put up that blue fire to protect us?"

"I know she did. She did it after the herbal demon showed up. My guess is because she was distracted by the demon talking to her, and wasn't paying attention to anything else around her, she figured that would at least keep us somewhat safe." It was always her goal. Keep them safe.

I walked back into the bedroom to find what looked like an in-depth conversation between Ronnie and Jax. They stopped when I walked in. Ronnie stood and brushed a soft kiss across my lips. "My turn."

Jax tugged on the hem of the shirt I had put on, another one of Ronnie's. "Pull this off, siren. I want to put this stuff on you."

He needed to do it more than I needed it on me, but I didn't argue. I lay on my stomach and waited while he perused all the bruises. His touch was gentle over each injury, the silky feel of the lotion, and his fingers became sensual.

"Okay, baby, turn over," I heard the husky tone and knew he had felt it too. I flipped over, and his breath caught. Shit. I forgot he hadn't seen the marks yet. They looked far worse than they felt, the ones over my ribs the only ones that bothered me.

He didn't say anything else and rubbed the lotion lovingly over each one. I was utterly horny by the time he finished. I slid my hand up under his shirt and ran it up to his chest; he trapped it when it was over his heart. I could feel the thuds under my palm.

"Sleep naked," he whispered and stood up, walking into the bathroom as the shower stopped, and Ronnie got out. He came out and saw his shirt crumpled at the foot of the bed and chuckled.

"Did you steal all my shirts?"

"Only three," I smiled at him as I slid under the covers. I knew the sight of the bruises bothered him, and I was trying to cover them as quickly as possible.

"Glad you left me a few," he crawled in next to me and planted his body on top of mine. I wrapped my legs around him so he couldn't move without taking me with him. "Mmmm, you feel good," he said softly and kissed me. "I'm going to taste you too, just to make sure you are okay."

He slid down my body as I loosened my legs for him, groaning at the contact of his tongue right where I wanted it. I became so lost in the magic he created, I hadn't felt Jax get in next to me, and my eyes flew open as he kissed me.

Instant orgasm. Between Ronnie's tongue on me and Jax's kiss at the same time, I was gone. Ronnie came up, chuckling, "That was easy, angel."

My eyes locked on Jax, "Is this happening?"

"Do you want it to?" he asked me back, his eyes dark with need.

"Yes," I whispered. The men needed no more encouragement than that. I was overwhelmed with the sensation of both of those mouths on me, all their hands, those bodies. "The door," I said between breaths. Ronnie stood and went to lock it.

"They won't come in," he climbed back in, his hand already smearing my juices up the crack of my ass. I stiffened only a moment before my body recognized his touch and relaxed into him.

"They might try if they feel an earthquake," Jax answered between kisses. I could only nod. Ronnie had started sliding his cock along my folds, getting himself wet.

Are you sure, angel? Ronnie's tone was sensual and gentle.

With you, yes. Just go slow. I trust you.

Jax had slid me up over him, and I shifted a little until he was right where I wanted him, and with a quick movement, I had him buried inside me, both of us groaning in pleasure, the connection at an all-time high with the three of us touching.

Lean forward a little, angel. I leaned forward. Jax captured my lips as I groaned at the feel of Ronnie behind me, rubbing slowly. *Stay relaxed; it might be uncomfortable at first. Probably for all of us.*

Jax reached his hand between us to rub slowly, as Ronnie pushed in gently. Maybe it was the connection we shared. Because the adjustment came more quickly, and the initial feeling of wanting it to stop became needing more. I had never been so full feeling before in my life.

I needed them to move; the more Jax rubbed me, the tighter my body held them, and I was going crazy. Both men were hissing out their breaths with each move I made until Ronnie grabbed my hips and stilled me. "It will be over before it started if you don't hold still a minute, angel."

"I can't," I gasped. "Please," I begged Ronnie. Slowly Jax moved his hips beneath mine, and they soon found a rhythm that had me screaming my release into Jax's mouth as I heard the crack of thunder booming outside. They gave me no time to come down as they increased their pace, the pressure building right back up inside me.

It was so intense I sobbed, my body strung tight with every stroke, electricity snapping between us. I couldn't take much more. It felt like I was splitting apart, the pleasure was unraveling me so rapidly I felt the third orgasm start to take over. Ronnie came with me, grunting as a silent scream tore through me, the room shaking around us.

My body clamped down tight around Jax, pushing him over the edge as the whole house shook, the room lit with blue light. I collapsed down on Jax, sobs still tearing from my chest. They rolled as one, both of them held inside me. We were lying on our sides, both of them holding me while I shook.

"Baby, are you okay? Why are you crying?" Jax rained kisses down on my face.

I couldn't speak. The pleasure of both of those men at the same time was more incredible than I had imagined. I dropped my walls. It was all I could think to do to let them know I was more than okay with what had transpired.

"Jesus," Ronnie whispered roughly behind me. "You're going to kill me, angel. Fuck, I love you both so much."

Jax stole the last of my breath with a soulful kiss. "What he said, siren."

Sleep had never been so peaceful.

Chapter Thirty

What the fuck happened last night?" Aedan fired off the minute he saw Jax and Ronnie come down the stairs.

Mags only giggled. "I know what happened. How was it? Wait, the house shook, a random lightning storm took place, and the entire hallway was blue, that tells me how it was."

"That's why the house shook?" Aedan looked gobsmacked.

Smitty chose that moment to walk in. "I'm guessing that's also why we all broke out in spontaneous sex and were unable to control ourselves."

Mags didn't even blush. "You got that right. Poor Aedan didn't know what hit him."

"He doesn't look like he is complaining," Ronnie dropped a kiss on Mags's head.

"Not if he knows what's good for him," Mags smiled. "Airy still passed out?"

Jax only smiled. Aedan was flummoxed. Jax was not a three-way type of guy. Aedan blushed. The same could be said about himself unless Airiella was involved. He kept his mouth shut and ate a bowl of cereal.

"Jax, the agent called. She's bringing the keys out. Mags will sign in front of her as the last signer," Aedan said, changing the subject. "Anyone going to fill me in on Kalisha?"

"Us. Fill us in," Smitty pushed him as he sat down at the table with his bowl.

Jax told them all he knew between Taklishim and the little bit Airiella had revealed. "Today, we'll do interviews in the town that's there now. If you want to see the location, we can go there first; just wear hiking shoes."

"Will she be able to walk?" Aedan heard Jillian say as she came into the kitchen. Ronnie laughed, and Jax was back to smiling only, while Aedan could only blush. "Well, jeez, you guys aren't exactly small."

Smitty's mouth fell open, and Aedan finally laughed. "It's not just Mags that looks then."

Jillian barked out a laugh. "I mean stature, not dick size."

"She's lying," Mags grinned. Aedan knew the ribbing from the women would be more brutal than what Smitty could dole out. Poor Airiella.

Smitty looked around, "So back there, it forks to where the town used to be, and that way is the cemetery?"

"Yeah," Airiella shifted her pack off. "We can go back there if you want, it's not super far. It's just tricky terrain and narrow at times."

"Might as well get the lay of the land. It will give me a couple of days to try and figure it out, at least. Lead on, fearless one," Smitty bowed.

"Fearless? Since when?" she argued but pulled her pack back on.

He followed her lead, the rest trailing behind as Jax pointed out things. "Baby girl, you okay?"

"I'm okay. Why?"

"Uh, those were pretty potent emotions last night," Smitty wasn't trying to embarrass her, he wanted to make sure she was okay.

"Sorry about that. It happens a lot when Jax is involved. Both of them were overwhelming," she admitted, not shy in the least. He supposed there wasn't a point to being shy now. She turned and looked behind him, then stepped into him, hugging him close. "I'm fine. Promise."

"Then why did you check to see where they were before you hugged me?" Smitty asked, suspicious.

"Because they would assume something is wrong," she informed him.

"Why would they assume that?"

"It made me cry," she said softly, looking up at him with those big eyes of hers.

He dropped a kiss on her lips. "I can still do that, right?"

"You don't even have to ask." She slid her hands up under his shirt and pulled him tight. "I'd miss it if you didn't."

"Everything okay?" Smitty heard Jax ask from behind him.

"Yep. Just wanted an angel hug," Smitty released her and patted her on the ass. "Quit slacking, get back to hiking." He felt her heartbeat go wild through the pulse in hand. "What's wrong?"

To his utter amazement, she blushed, and he felt Jax go still behind him. "Siren? What's the matter?"

Baby girl, do you feel something? Smitty switched to talk this way because she had been right about Jax being concerned.

If I tell you, do you promise not to make fun of me? Came her hesitant reply.

No. I can tell this is going to be good. Spill it.

Damn it, you ass. Fine. Jax takes my breath away and makes my knees shake. Especially the way the light just hit him.

"Ells, baby, what's going on?" Jax pushed his way around Smitty.

He couldn't help it. He burst out laughing. "Chill Romeo, she was swooning over you." He laughed even harder when she glared at him for revealing her secret.

He saw Jax smile, "Is that true?"

Smitty pushed him out of the way. "Get over yourself," Smitty laughed as Airiella blushed again. *Sorry, baby girl, but that just made his day.*

Payback will suck for you. I guarantee it. I'll let Mags and Jillian think up something evil.

"That's just playing dirty." Smitty smiled and

followed her, leaving a grinning Jax in his wake.

innie smiled in satisfaction as she walked away from Marco. She was well and truly in love with the Italian man. Winnie walked right into Giuseppe; she became so lost in her thoughts. "Well, young lady, are you done corrupting my uncle with your unladylike ways?" he smiled, so she knew he was joking.

"Nope. Well, for the moment, I am. What can I do for you?"

"Some colored lady is asking around for you," he put his hands on his hips. "She was a right strange one."

"A colored lady?" Winnie was confused. It hit like a bomb. Kalisha. "Where is she?"

"Back there. I didn't know who the lady was, so I didn't want to tell her where you were. She might have been bad."

"No. Kalisha's the one who has been helping Airy and the crew. She made them their necklaces that protect them. A demon killed her." Winnie rushed past him.

"Hold up there, young lady. I'm coming with you. If this is about Ella, I want to hear it."

Winnie slowed down to wait for him. Today was the filming of the first live show. If Kalisha was here, it might mean she was expecting trouble. She let Giuseppe direct her to where he had last seen Kalisha.

"She knew who I was, how is that? I'd remember meeting her."

"She's very powerful." That is all Winnie was going to say.

"Can't be too powerful if she went and got herself

killed," Giuseppe muttered. He was in rare form today.

"Would it change your mind if I told you it was the number two most powerful demon in Hell that killed her?" Winnie smarted off.

"It would make me wonder what she did to get on his radar," the old man fired back.

"She had just finished making a weapon that can help Airiella defeat him," Winnie defended Kalisha, right as Stolas appeared in front of her.

"They are gathering. It begins now; I will warn Airiella. Find Kalisha," then Stolas disappeared.

"Shit!" Winnie yelled. "Kalisha!"

Giuseppe was startled enough not to chastise her for her language choice. The demon had surprised him. "Kalisha!" Giuseppe joined her in calling out.

"Hush now, child, I'm here," Winnie heard the musical accent she remembered from Airy's interview. Even in death, that woman was startlingly beautiful.

"Stolas was just here," Winnie started.

"Yes, we spoke. Stolas is quite besotted with your friend," Kalisha smiled.

"Uh, er, okay. Stolas said it's started, what do we do?" Winnie wondered where Onida was. No sooner than she had the thought, she spotted the hawk.

"Yes, Onida is here too. Take us to her," Kalisha held out her hand, and Winnie took it, thinking only of Airiella, and she popped in where the crew was setting up. Winnie saw Father Roarke and Degataga.

"Will they be able to see you?" Winnie stage whispered.

"You can speak normally. Degataga can see me. Stay put; you will be in danger here." Winnie watched Onida circle overhead in both worlds and jumped when Giuseppe spoke.

"We are in danger?"

Shit! She'd brought him! Airy would be pissed! "I need to take you back. If she knows you are here, she'll be furious."

"I'm not leaving here." He crossed his arms stubbornly. "I'm not fond of being in danger, but that colored lady seems to know her stuff."

"Her name is Kalisha, stop calling her that colored lady. It's not polite," Winnie chastised him for once. "I don't think we will be able to get inside the building. I think this is as far as I can bring us due to the charms Kalisha made them."

"It's close enough; I can see my beautiful granddaughter right now."

"You can? Where is she?" Damn those necklaces!

"With the Indian fellow."

Winnie sighed. "His name is Degataga. If it's too much to remember, call him Dega. You can't refer to everyone by their race." If she concentrated, she could see Airiella's outline. "Now might be a good time for you to start praying."

"I already was," Giuseppe said quietly.

Kalisha," I breathed. "I'm so sorry."

"It is me, yes. I heard your vow. You still have healing to do. There's no time to waste."

"I know. Things have been a little hectic," I defended myself. Honestly, I still didn't know what to do about it.

"This weapon keep it on you. Always. You must hit Bael in an organ, preferably in the heart, though the stomach or liver would work too. There is a risk, which means you must get close to him, which is very dangerous. This weapon will only work for you, and you must feed your power through it."

"It's a knife, why wouldn't it work for anyone else?" I was confused.

"They can stab him with it. It won't banish him unless it is you powering it."

"Can I kill him?" That was my most important question.

"If you heal, you have a chance. Use all available tokens," she pointed at the amulet and bracelet I had yet to use.

"I never got a chance to thank you for all you've done for me, for us," I started, feeling the grief well up.

"The words you don't need to say. I feel it here," she tapped her heart. "Don't let down your guard. He will use every means possible to get you. I will be close by."

She popped out, and the tears fell. Father Roarke and Degataga put their arms around me, one on either side. "You said a vow?" Degataga asked quietly.

I nodded. "I vowed to serve justice for the wrong done to her."

"Potent words, if she heard it. Be very careful, Airiella, it can be used against you," Degataga warned me.

"Are you sure you want to kill?" Father Roarke asked.

"Absolutely. I feel in my bones that it's the right thing to do. It wasn't Kalisha's time," I said firmly. Father Roarke handed me several vials of holy water. I slid them in the pocket of the hoodie I swiped from Jax. "Please stay safe."

"No one will die tonight, Airiella," Degataga promised me. "Go do your walkthrough; we'll be right here. Tak and Tama are out there," he nodded to the woods surrounding us.

I headed back to where Jax was waiting with the crew while they cued up the interview sequence filmed earlier. I sent my raven up to fly with Onida; my nerves strung tight.

Angel, I need you over here now, Ronnie's voice blasted through my head, making me wince.

Where are you? My eyes flew over the grounds in front of me, searching for him.

I'm behind the hospital.

Jax broke out in a jog towards me. "What's wrong?"

"Ronnie needs me behind the hospital," I said, running towards him. He smoothly switched directions and grabbed my hand.

As we rounded the corner, the tangy scent of blood filled my nose, and I gagged at the smell of death under it. Staked out before me was a dead deer. "I didn't need to see this," I turned away, my heartbreaking for the poor animal.

"It wasn't here ten minutes ago," Ronnie said slowly.

"Fuck." Jax turned away as well. "Jesus, did you call security?"

"Yep. Right after I called Airiella, sorry, angel, can you take a look around and see if you see any souls hanging around out there?" Ronnie sounded remorseful. I knew he didn't call me out here to view the poor creature.

"It hurts looking at it. If I close my eyes, can you get

me around it so I can look without seeing it?" I asked quietly.

Onida, there's a mutilated carcass out here that wasn't here ten minutes ago. Behind the hospital, I informed her.

I haven't seen anything. I'll look closer on the other side.

Ronnie led me around until I was behind the deer and I opened my eyes. I didn't see anything, but I could feel a vibration to the air. "I can feel something was here. The air is vibrating like it's trying to tell me something, but I don't see anything."

It's a message. The demons have already left, Onida told me.

"Onida said the demons have already left, that it was a message." I relayed the information, feeling sick.

"Do not drop your guards. One of you stays with Aedan the entire time. None of you go this alone. Please," I begged them as Tom came around the corner, saw the grisly scene, and promptly puked.

"Come on, let's get out of here," Jax led us back around the other corner, so I didn't have to see it again. We met Aedan and Smitty inside the entrance, where Aedan silently handed me a bottle of water.

"Security was here, we heard," Smitty explained at Ronnie's questioning look.

"Why was security in here?" Jax stiffened.

"He was telling us that he and the others had cleared the area, and local cops were posted at the entrance to the grounds to keep people out," Aedan said, watching me. He brushed some loose hairs away from my face. "Sorry, you had to see that."

"Do you feel anything in here?" Ronnie touched my lower back as I walked around.

"Just the same air vibrations that I felt outside. Something *was* in here. And recently. Dammit! You guys promise me to stay together," I said fiercely, anger lighting my blood on fire.

"I promise, siren," Jax said solemnly.

I stomped back outside, angry tears stinging my eyes that were blinking like crazy so they didn't fall. I went past a startled Father Roarke into a lightly wooded area. "Stolas!" I whispered loudly.

"I'm here." He appeared next to a tree in his raven form.

"Who did that?" I referenced the deer.

"A couple of lower-level demons. Bael wants you scared," Stolas calmly said.

"I'm not scared; I'm downright pissed. Are the demons coming back?" I growled out.

"I'd expect them to. Those aren't the brightest. Stay prepared." He popped back out.

I turned to find Degataga behind me. "I don't want you off alone," he explained at my startled expression.

"Technically, I wasn't alone," I argued. "Didn't you say Tak and Tama were out here?"

"Somewhere," he nodded.

"They didn't see anything?" I pushed him.

"I don't know; I can't speak to them as you can."

"That poor animal was innocent," the angry tears were back. Degataga led me quietly back out to the group, not saying anything.

"You didn't feel them arrive?" he sounded concerned by that.

"I've been feeling the air vibrating, but I haven't felt any immediate danger to the guys or me."

"Are you going to be in the hospital while they are in there?" His eyes felt like they were probing my brain.

"I am now. I'll stand behind one of the static cameras," I told him firmly.

"Good. I think you need to stay close to the team."

I expected an argument, not an agreement. It threw me off. "Jax might not agree."

"Agree with what?" he said from behind me.

"She's going to be in the hospital with you. Behind one of the cameras." Degataga gave him a look. Jax simply nodded.

"The one behind the entrance door in the corner will give you the best view of the surroundings," he kissed my cheek. "I'll feel better knowing I can see you."

You could have knocked me over with a feather.

Aedan almost felt good that they were halfway through the investigation, and nothing had happened. They were all wound tight, and they had gotten considerable evidence that the hospital had paranormal energy, but no demons yet. Not that Aedan was going to complain about that.

They'd made several trips down the near the entrance to check on Airiella, and Aedan and Ronnie were on their way back through there when Aedan got violently shoved, his head bouncing off the wall he'd crashed into with a crack.

"What the hell?!" he heard Ronnie shout through the buzzing in his ears. Another loud crash reached his ears, and Aedan saw Ronnie stumble.

Jax and Smitty came running. Jax helped him up, whispering in his ear, "Demon. Smitty will kill it. Commercial in two minutes."

They filmed and collected evidence of the attack, emotions were running high, and cameras pointed elsewhere other than Smitty while he cleanly turned the demon to ash with a stab of his knife before rejoining the shot.

Aedan's head swam as Jax explained to the camera that Aedan was going to get checked by the standby medical team and how dangerous these investigations were. He then mentioned the massacred animal they had found earlier and tied it all neatly together.

Degataga met them at the entrance as soon as the commercial came on and looked at Aedan's head. "Concussion," he confirmed quietly. "I can fix it, someone please block me from sight," he requested. Aedan saw Ronnie move and act like he was examining a piece of equipment in the light that shone down on the entrance.

Aedan felt warmth radiating from the hand Degataga had on his head, and soon his dizziness and vision cleared. "Is my head supposed to hurt still?"

"I left the bump and cut, just fixed the concussion. It'd be a little hard to explain the cut disappearing and the bump." Aedan nodded, accepting the ibuprofen he handed over and swallowed them dry.

"Thirty seconds," Jax said, reappearing by his side. "She said there's two more."

"Then let's kill the fuckers," Aedan growled. He was pissed.

"Four more outside cornered by Tak and Tama,"

Ronnie whispered as he walked by.

"I'm calling it out," Jax decided.

Aedan groaned but didn't disagree with him. It's precisely the evidence they needed to push the show forward if this was their duty now.

Chapter Thirty-One

I had counted. Twenty-seven demons total came for us that night. Eight caught by Taklishim and Tama, two by Father Roarke, and the rest in the hospital with them. Four of them after the filming ended. Each of the guys took one while I had to sit there and watch.

I understood how they felt then, watching me head right into the shit hole of danger. My nerves felt shot, frayed, and raw. Degataga had to heal each of them, Smitty had a broken bone that thankfully hadn't gotten caught on camera. I had silently thanked Stolas for that magic pain formula, so he didn't feel it as Degataga moved the bone back into place.

I crawled into my bed after my shower and waited for Ronnie and Jax to finish up. All of us were flat out exhausted, and if this was just the beginning, I didn't want to know what Franklin held for us. Seeing Aedan's head bounce off the wall and hearing Smitty's arm break had made my wings come out, and I had started to glow.

Ronnie climbed in the bed and curled around me, his solid body gave me more comfort than he could possibly understand. "You're wrong, angel, I do know. It's the same comfort I am getting from you." He kissed the back of my neck.

"That episode is going to top the charts for evidence collected, especially after Jax said it was the work of demons," I told him. "I thought I was going to lose my shit in there and light the place on fire."

"Sucks, doesn't it?" he chuckled into my neck.

"If you are referring to watching you guys get hurt, yes."

"I'm surprised my ears didn't bleed, you were yelling in my head so loud," he stroked my side.

"I can't really say I'm sorry for that since you listened and ducked at least."

Jax walked in then and slid in under the covers. "I'm wiped out."

I rested my hand over his heart, pushing love into him and Ronnie. "Sleep. We'll need it to get through tonight."

Smitty hadn't quite gotten over the sound of his arm snapping and the burst of pain that had come with it. He looked around the parking lot and saw Asher talking to Tom, as a quad was rolled out of a trailer. The pansy wouldn't even make the short hike up.

I'm already feeling the danger.

Smitty tensed and looked at the other guys. She'd

sent that to all of them. Fuck, they hadn't even set up yet. He instinctively ducked as he heard the flapping of wings over his head, Airiella's raven startling him as she flew up to meet Onida's hawk.

Camera's aren't rolling; please do not leave my sight. Father Roarke is going to ride up there with this pussy that won't stop glaring at me, she sent.

Smitty snorted and heard Jax laugh. So they'd gotten that one too. *Don't let him see your wings, baby girl.*

He'll be lucky if I don't shoot a bolt of lightning up his ass. He told me to let the professionals handle this; her temper was right at the surface.

Let's see how he handles a demon. You're going to see his pasty white ass running down that hill, Smitty told her.

Smitty gave a genuine smile at her laughter. She walked past him with her pack on, and another gear bag strung over her shoulder. "I'm not dumb enough to say race you since you run, but I'm getting a head start."

"Didn't you just tell us to stay in sight of everyone?" Smitty trotted after her.

"I'm just going to the bottom of the hill, relax. I want to get a sneak look up there before Father Roarke goes up. I don't give a shit about Asher."

Smitty grabbed all the gear he was supposed to carry and got it situated so he could bring it. The rest was getting taken up on a second trip by the quad. Smitty at least had a smile of satisfaction that Asher would have to hike up the steeper hill to the mine since they were leaving the quad by the coal car.

He headed towards Airiella, who was eating berries

straight from the vine; he laughed at her juicy smile. "Are those safe?"

"They are blackberries, why wouldn't they be?"

"How the hell do I know? You're the nature girl, and we're out here in the wild," Smitty cattily replied, plucking a berry and popping it in his mouth. "Damn, these are good."

"My ex called them dead body berries," she said, then stiffened. Smitty hated the shadow that fell across her beautiful face.

"Don't, baby girl. He doesn't deserve any attention or thought from you." Smitty pulled a big fat berry and held it out for her to eat.

"I'm fine," she lied.

"No, you aren't. I know that was a lie." He dropped a kiss on her lips. "You do taste good, though."

That got a smile out of her. "I still owe you payback. Maybe I'll let Jillian taste me."

Shit. Smitty got hard thinking about it. "That was plain evil. Hiking with a boner isn't fun. Better hope I don't tell her you said that she'd snatch that offer up."

She gave him a calculating look. "I know you didn't want to share me with her before; I think it's still the same. Even though I'm not the one taking care of that matter now," she pointed at his crotch and picked some more berries.

"You might be right, but I won't admit it. Instead, I'll tell Jax and Ronnie that you were getting depressed because of thoughts about your asshole ex. That should make for a fun hike up." Smitty leveled a look at her.

"You win. Asshole ex is not in my thoughts. I'm only thinking about you hiking with a boner and eating berries now."

Smitty laughed. "You know I wouldn't do that. I don't want you thinking about him, and now I also wish I hadn't made that no sex with you pact, because damn it, you made me horny."

Ronnie walked up to him in time to hear the last part. "She does it to me all the time."

Smitty watched as she sidled up to Ronnie and pulled him down for a berry kiss that left the poor guy panting. "I can pull *you* off into the bushes and have sex with you, though, while poor Smitty has to hike with a boner."

Smitty roared with laughter at the hopeful look on Ronnie's face. "That's an option?"

"No," Jax said, walking up. "Not unless you want thorns in your ass. Nice purple smile, siren."

"The berries are good and ripe," she stuffed one in his mouth.

"Is the way clear?" Smitty nodded to Asher and Father Roarke, who was getting on the quad.

"As far as I can see, yes."

"You still feel it?" Smitty looked over at her.

"Yep."

Jax looked around again. Logistically speaking, this location was a pain in the ass to do live. They'd have to be moving their base as they went along, and it was a lot of work. Luckily, they had a full signal on their connections as a cell tower wasn't too far away, and they had Wi-Fi hotspots for the weaker areas and boosts. Smitty had his work cut out for him on this one.

He decided to do the cemetery part first so they could at least hike back there in some manner of daylight. They'd get the rest on the way back. Smitty kept the base to bare necessities to make it easier to move.

Where's Degataga? Jax asked Airiella.

He's with Taklishim out in the woods. They were on the trail of something. I think it's Bael, she responded.

Fuck. That wasn't good. *Why do you think that?*

The feel. It's a different level of danger I'm feeling.

Asher was following him around, questioning every move he made and arguing about all of it. He was rapidly running out of patience. "Asher, if you don't stay out of my way and back off, I'm going to shove you into a patch of poison ivy."

"There's no poison ivy here," Asher continued to argue.

"Wrong." Airiella appeared next to him. "It's all over. Keep it up, and I'll help him. I'm quite familiar with this area and these woods. Been hiking here all my life. I can even tell you there are cougars in the area. For an uneducated person about nature, that's a mountain lion."

Jax bit back a laugh because he knew Tama was in the area and would be more than happy to make an appearance just to scare the shit out of Asher. "You should do more research before coming out on locations like this," Jax fired off, leaving Asher standing there looking around him nervously.

Ronnie hid his smile, having heard the exchange. "I've read about cougars. You never hear them coming."

Smitty joined in. "I saw that most hikers of places like this never know that they are getting stalked the entire time. I think the article said if you've hiked out here, you've gotten stalked by a cougar. They don't scare the same way bears do."

I'm almost ready to ask Tama to show up, Airiella sent to him.

If you do, I'll film it.

Asher had moved to stand near Father Roarke, his eyes darting everywhere. Jax went back to check the links to the cameras and got the one strapped to his chest secure and his handheld ready. They'd start in a few minutes. Airiella stood near Father Roarke out of the shots of the cameras.

Onida said Degataga is coming up behind me, Airiella told him.

Good to know. Have I told you today that I loved you?

If you count that time, then, yes. Love you too, Zeus.

Jax waited for the cue from Tom, started introducing the location, and pointed out the difficulties associated with sites like these and showed the camera placements. He then introduced Asher as a guest on the show and called out the demon problem they had the night before. Adding that he hoped Asher would be safe from possession.

He saw the bright smile Airiella gave him. Asher had no idea who he was dealing with now. He got a few residual energy hits around some of the headstones, pointing out that so many of the dates were the same, recounting the tragedy that had taken so many lives.

As they moved carefully closer to the mine shaft, Jax saw Asher stiffen up and focused the camera on him. Smitty was moving cautiously around to get Jax in his shot,

Ronnie and Aedan both behind him. They had prepared for this and suspected Asher was about to announce his supposedly surprising find of Airiella's relative.

He didn't disappoint. "My spirit guide tells me there is a relative of someone here trying to get through."

Ronnie jumped right in as planned. "That's right, in our research, we found an ancestor of Airiella's she hadn't known about, through her family, we learned of his tragic story."

Asher's face gave away his shock, but he couldn't stop once he started. "Yes, he feels like a negative entity. Very angry and unhappy, seeking revenge."

"Do you speak Italian?" Ronnie asked, his tone of mock surprise.

"What? No," Asher fumbled, his very pronounced British accent coming through loud and clear.

"How would you be able to understand him? He didn't speak English," Smitty asked.

"I feel something very evil, energy trying to come through," Asher's fear was real this time, and Jax glanced over to Airiella who nodded. The computer screen in front of Tom lit her face, somewhat masking her faint glow that was starting.

"What about her ancestor?" Jax broke in. "Where did he go?"

"Marco is there, but there's something else," Asher backed up, and Jax stopped him.

"Unless you want to fall down a cliffside, you might want to stop moving backward."

Father Roarke had moved in front of Tom, and Airiella moved a little to the side, and behind him, on the genuine chance that her wings popped out. Jax felt the energy building. "We should leave here," Asher warned, his head swiveling from side to side. He almost looked possessed.

Jax heard the cawing of the raven and the screeching of the hawk. Fuck. Bael was here. Somewhere. *Will you be able to wipe his memory?*

If I can't, one of the medicine men should be able to help with that, Airiella responded.

"Tell me what's going on, Asher, we'll start heading back to the mine shaft," Jax tried to herd him forward as the others moved safely out of the shot.

"Jax, something is coming through, my guide is scared," Asher's voice shook.

"It's not Airiella's ancestor, Marco?" Jax pressed him forward. "You just said he wanted revenge."

"This is not Marco," Asher repeated. "Oh my God, Kalisha," he started visibly trembling.

Shocked, Jax uttered, "What?"

"Kalisha is here; she called me a fool. She said I was playing with forces I could never hope to understand," Asher was blindly repeating what he was hearing. "I didn't agree to this, Jax. Not this."

Jax felt a chill go down his spine. It was as he had expected. Someone was forcing Asher into this. "Agree to what?" Jax asked.

"I didn't agree to this!" Asher shouted, turning to run and instead tripped over one of the thick steel cables still present. "Marco isn't evil," Asher cried, picking himself up off the ground.

"We know he isn't," Smitty tried to calm him down, seeing this was going wildly out of control.

"Kalisha was murdered!" Asher sobbed. "She said

someone murdered her."

The only good thing about this was they were getting this breakdown on film on live TV. "Asher, turn around and walk back towards the mine," Jax told him calmly.

"A demon is going to take your girlfriend from you," Asher said, woodenly.

Father Roarke stepped directly into the shot and started reciting a prayer while he marked Asher with holy water. "Fight it, Asher, don't let it control you," Ronnie called out.

Is he possessed? Jax asked urgently.

I think something is trying to possess him. I haven't seen anything yet. His soul is still his own. If Bael is here, he's invisible and in the dark where I can't see him.

"In the past three days, we have dealt with demons, poltergeist, gentle spirits, and agitated ones. Possession, sexual assault on all of us, a murder, and now you are implying there's a larger conspiracy at play?" Jax listed off things as they walked. Father Roarke having finished the blessing.

Asher tried to play it off, but it was too late, he'd either have to get caught lying, or implicate himself in the scheme. "I think we were all played," he tried the path of least resistance.

"None of those things Jax listed are playing matters," Smitty pointed out. "Is there still something trying to come through?"

"It's already here," Asher said flatly. "It's as dark as can be, and it wants her. I will not stand in its way."

Jax felt the chill again as they broke for commercial and tried to get down the rest of the trail as quickly as possible. Tom was stunned at the turn of events and not sure what to do. Asher was finally near the mine shaft and not in danger of falling down a cliff when he let out a blood-curdling scream right as they went live on-air again.

Smitty, Aedan, and Ronnie were near him and spun around, looking for the reason he screamed though Jax saw nothing. "No!" he heard Airiella in front of him but didn't see her. Instead, he saw Bael, his evil face sneering at him.

"Jax! No!" Aedan shouted.

Rage took over his brain, and he felt the darkness in him trying to break free. Jax shoved it back down and drew his fist to smash it in the demon's face, only before his fist connected, the beast disappeared, and his fist crashed into the side of Airiella's face. His camera captured only her stunned expression before his fist connected, her head snapping back as she dropped straight to the ground.

In the background, he could hear Asher chanting maniacally, "He's here, he's here, he's here, the demon is here."

Chapter Thirty-Two

Ronnie felt the tension ratchet up. "What the fuck?! Break for commercial!" He bolted for the crumbled form of his angel. Degataga beat him to it as a cougar burst through the bushes, landing with a roar.

All hell broke loose as Asher lost his mind to fear. He was screaming like a mad man as he ran into Tom, who fell backward, while all the cameras still filmed the scene. Even Smitty and Aedan froze at the sight of Tama in her animal form. Easily the largest cougar anyone would ever see.

She wasn't facing any of the people, though. Her body pointed to the hillside. Her roar deafening and ferocious as Degataga and Ronnie lifted Airiella. Father Roarke was trying to calm Asher down, while Jax picked Tom up off the ground.

Smitty was trying to cut the live feed off, but his

hands shook so badly it took him a while. Tom was finally able to get a commercial break. Ronnie sat on the rock by the mineshaft while Degataga had his hands on Airiella's face. Ronnie switched off his camera.

Jax looked wholly shattered. Ronnie knew Jax's state of mind broke after that, he had just committed a cardinal sin in his eyes, against someone he loved more than life itself. If Ronnie had thought Jax looked broken after Jax hit him, this was a thousand times worse. Ronnie had seen the demon; he knew what Jax was aiming for with that punch.

They heard a wicked cackle break through the chaos, and they all went silent. Tama's cougar tense, still facing the hillside. An eagle tore through the sky, followed by the hawk and Airiella's raven, landing next to Ronnie as Tama leaped up the slope in a roar.

"They are telling me to go back on the air," Tom's voice was quaking, and he looked like he was going to pass out.

"Then film Aedan and me," Smitty stepped up. "We'll go down to the other part of the town, away from this."

Tom nodded mutely, following Smitty's lead, Aedan looking sick. Ronnie heard Jax sobbing behind him, "Do you got her?" he asked Degataga.

"Go, I can't fix him," he told Ronnie kindly. "This is a broken jaw. I can fix that."

Ronnie set her gently down on the ground and squatted next to Jax. "She'll be okay." He reached over to switch off the camera. Once he was sure it was off, he pulled Jax into a hug. "I saw him too, Jax. So did she."

"You didn't see her face," Jax shook violently.

"We all know you weren't hitting her, come on. Anyone who knows you will realize that. Pull it together enough to finish the show. Break down later. We've got to try and salvage this, or it will all have been for nothing."

"How can you not hate me?" Jax shuddered as he sucked a breath in.

"I know you weren't hitting her. I know what you were aiming for with that punch. I don't know why you thought a punch would stop him, but I don't hate you. She won't either. Jax, you've come too far to let this drag you back down. All this was pure demon setup and trickery."

Go and try and fix it, they'll use this to try and discredit Jax. I've got him.

Fuck. Angel. Are you okay? Ronnie asked frantically.

I have a bitch of a headache again, but Taklishim told me he had some of that pain stuff in his car. I'll be fine. My jaw's fixed now.

I love you, angel. He's shattered.

I know; I feel it. I've got Jax. Take Degataga and try to make it believable, she urged him.

Ronnie stood up, Jax hardly noticing, and he stepped over to Airiella, his eyes roving over the swollen face and spreading bruise. He kissed her softly and headed down the hill at a fast pace with Degataga. This night wasn't going to be easy.

J ax, baby, look at me," I pulled on his arm.

"Siren, oh, God. I'm so sorry," he crushed me to him.

"You didn't lose control," I pointed out to him. "You should be proud."

A bitter sound tore through him. "You don't call that losing control? I broke your jaw!"

"You weren't aiming for me. Let me put it this way; I was about to pull the knife out to stab him when he disappeared, I would have stabbed you instead. I'm guessing that was his plan all along. Get us to hurt each other."

"There is no way you should be so forgiving right now," he sobbed into my neck.

"If you had been aiming for me, I probably wouldn't. Ronnie doesn't blame you either. None of them do. Especially me. I'll take it to social media explaining it. Don't let him win by giving in to this. Come on, baby, let's get up." I extracted myself from his arms even though I didn't want to.

I held out my hand to him and heard a noise from the bushes behind me. Me spinning around, got him moving and standing in front of me. I almost laughed, like I'd let that fly if it were Bael. I wasn't using soul sight and only saw the glowing eyes reflecting the moonlight, and my wings burst free.

I wrapped one around Jax, the other folded in front of my body as I switched to soul sight and saw it was Tama. She took her human form while still in the bushes. "He's still somewhere around here. Don't let your guard down and get back to the others. They are an easy target without you."

"Got it," I leaned over and grabbed the camera that Jax dropped. "Come on, you heard her. We can fall apart later." I gripped his hand as we headed down the trail. "It's nothing more than a bruise, Zeus."

I felt the danger again as soon as we neared the coal

car. Now, we were in an open enough area now to call the lightning, and I did, letting it fill me. My anger was fueling it with more energy than usual, thinking that I could have stabbed Jax.

I looked for the dark spot, and finding it, I unleashed the lightning's full power. Bael's inhuman roar filled the night air, letting Tama, Taklishim, and Onida know his exact spot. I heard Tama charging through the woods and the swoop of the wings of the two powerful birds as they attacked.

Father Roarke started the exorcism prayers as my wings burst out again, and I fired more lightning at the enraged demon. I pulled the knife allowing the electricity to flow through it; it's glow matching mine.

Stay behind my wings; I warned Jax.

Thankfully, Smitty kept all cameras pointed away from me. But it didn't stop their heads from turning at the downright terrifying scream that ripped through the night. I felt the earth's energy drawing into him. He was going to attack.

Brace for the earth to move! I shouted at them all.

Thinking fast, I called the air asking for help. It swirled around me, ready to join the fight. I asked it to lift everyone safely from the earth and smiled inwardly, as I saw all of their feet leave the ground right as a tremor tore through where they had all been standing.

Fight back, I told the earth, keeping the rest suspended in the air. Drop a tree on him. I fired the lightning when I saw the tree move; Ronnie chose that moment to throw a star from his elevated position.

All three strikes landed perfectly, and he disappeared in a cloud of sulfurous smoke, his stink polluting the air. I put everyone down and made my wings disappear. I wasn't dumb enough to think this was over, but I figured he was hurt at least a little.

"Stolas," I whispered, and his black raven landed in front of me. "Is he gone?"

"Temporarily. I suggest you finish what you need to do here and go. The container I gave you will help with your face." He flew away without another word, his tone sounding somewhat irritated.

Finish up; we don't have a lot of time before he's back, and I'm running out of energy. I sent to the guys. Jax quickly joined the group, Father Roarke and Degataga, carrying the unconscious form of Asher away.

Aedan finished reading what Airiella had posted on social media in response to the night's incident. Support for them all was overwhelming with the evidence that they had captured. He'd seen some of the haters speaking up and loved how the rest shot them all down.

He didn't think he'd ever want to do a live show again. They'd all pretty much traumatized him beyond belief. His awe and respect of Airiella soared even higher as her love patched them back together after seeing Jax knock her right out. The sound of her jaw cracking still echoing in his head.

He couldn't wait to crawl into bed with Mags. If he was honest, he wanted to drag Airiella with him. Even if only to make sure she was okay. Ronnie and Jax glued themselves to her; she was taken care of by them. Both men looked rough.

When they pulled in the driveway, he saw the front door open, and Jillian's frame silhouetted in the doorway. She didn't come outside, and Aedan figured Smitty had told her to stay inside where it was relatively safer than it was outside. It also probably meant that Mags was trying to get out, and this was Jillian's way of stopping her.

Once he got out and saw her trying to peek around Jillian, he knew he was right. He turned to Jax and Airiella, "She's going to want to check on both of you. Humor her."

Airiella gave him a tired smile and let Ronnie lead her in the house while Aedan held Jax's arm. "Don't treat her like a porcelain doll. It's just my advice, take it or leave. She hates it, and she's one fierce woman. I know what happened hurt you, but Jax, even I saw him in front of her."

"Easier said than done, but I get it. She's drilled it into my head that she's fine. It'll take a while for me to let go of the feeling of my fist hitting her face."

"Try to sleep? We are leaving for camping tomorrow, and we've still got Bael out there somewhere. Do what you need to do to forget. I'm sure the rest of us will be doing the same," Aedan said softly.

"Thanks, Aedan." He watched Jax trudge in, and he locked up the car, glancing cautiously out at the street behind him.

Chapter Thirty-Three

Jax showered quickly, she had insisted they all go before her, and he wanted her to have some warm water. She got in as he got out, trailing her fingers across his wet chest with a crooked smile, her perfect face swollen and discolored from his hand.

"Stop," was all she said.

Jax dried off and leaned against the counter, waiting for her to finish. He wasn't ready to face Ronnie alone yet. He knew he'd get more of the same as what Airiella had been telling him. Between Ronnie and her, they'd spun the situation so that the team and Jax had come out winners. He certainly didn't feel like a winner.

He grabbed her towel as soon as the water turned off and held it open for her. She let him wrap her up and dry her off, her bruised back almost healed to his amazement. "We are for sure, putting that stuff on your face," he kissed her forehead before hanging the towel up to dry. He watched as she brushed her hair and shook some of the excess water out.

He followed her back into the bedroom, where Ronnie already had the container out and was putting it on her face before she even sat on the bed. "Does it hurt?" he asked her as she settled in.

"No. Degataga healed everything but the bruise which was just bleeding under the skin. It doesn't hurt. I promise," she repeated.

Jax locked the bedroom door and shut out the light. "Siren, remember how you asked me to make you forget?"

"You know that I do."

"I need you to make me forget," Jax whispered roughly.

"Want me to leave?" Ronnie offered.

"No, stay, please," Jax pleaded. "I need you both."

"Then I'm going to start on the lubrication process," Ronnie growled. Jax felt him slip the covers off them, and her hand slid against Jax, stroking him.

Do you want me to pull it from you, Zeus?

No, siren. It might have been an accident, but I still did it. Feeling you like this, knowing you don't blame me, helps, but I'd like to be where Ronnie is right now.

She stopped stroking him and pulled Ronnie up, Jax taking his place, reveling in the feel of her shattering under his tongue. He came up to kiss her, dragging himself along her folds and then moved, Ronnie, pulling her on top of him, burying himself in her with a groan.

Jax slid in slowly from behind, letting her adjust and worked on bringing her as much pleasure as he could. When they all drifted off to sleep, Jax managed to let it go as she turned into him as if there was nowhere else she'd rather be.

I woke up slowly, stretching my body, and smiling. Saying last night had been good would be the biggest understatement of my life. Maybe too good. The connection we had wasn't something that anyone could easily ignore, and I was absolutely positive everyone around us felt it also, no matter who they were. I rolled over, finding no one and the sheets cold where Jax had been sleeping, his scent lingering. Stifling a groan of disappointment, I sat up.

Fourteen seconds later, the man I was missing came back in the room, a soft and enticing smile on his face. He slid into the bed next to me and pulled me up against him. Even with him being fully clothed, where we touched, the air sparked bright like it was alive and electric. He buried his face in my hair and breathed me in, which I had to admit was sweet and quite hot. I loved it when they did that to me.

"You are like a drug to my soul," he said, his voice breathy in my ear. "Thank you for not giving up on me after yet another disaster." Yep. I fell further down that damn, always present, rabbit hole, no doubts about it. I was getting ready to tear his clothes off when the door opened, and Jax muttered hotly, "I knew I should have locked the damn door."

Grinning, I looked over to see Ronnie leaning against the wall with a smirk on his face. "Happy to interrupt. Mornin' angel. I'd love to have another Airy sandwich, but we have a slight hiccup."

I liked the sound of that sandwich and flushed, remembering how it felt to have my body pressed between these two. I needed to make that happen again. And again. "What's the problem?" I managed to ask between my dirty thoughts which, I know they both heard.

"We have company out on the porch," Ronnie said slowly. "In the form of an ex, it appears." Jax was out of bed in a flash, his body rigid with tension. I was a bit slower. "Hers," he nodded at me, "not one of yours, Jax."

I froze, standing there naked, my thoughts scattered and pinging around in my head. "Which one?" My voice had gone cold, and both men watched me, Winnie choosing now to pop back in. Jax, the only one with a necklace still on.

"The last one," she told me, having seen my memories, she knew.

"Not sure, angel," Ronnie stated, ignoring Winnie because Jax didn't know she was with us. "You are kinda closed off about putting faces to your past."

I could feel the rage bubbling out of Jax and threw myself across the bed to reach him, sliding my hand up under his shirt to touch him, skin to skin. "Fuck, why now," I muttered under my breath.

Winnie replied, "Because he saw the live show." Ronnie nodded with minimal movement as I did my best to calm Jax.

"I'll take care of this," Jax ground out, his jaw clenching and ticking.

"Nope. No. You won't. I will. I need to do this. Though you both can come with me," I said with an edge sharpening my tone as I headed to the door. "The moral support will be needed."

"Not without clothes on you won't," Jax growled. Ronnie barked in laughter, even Winnie snickered.

Blushing, I walked in my closet and quickly got dressed, as Ronnie came in behind me and whispered, "You smell like sex. I like it. Which one is this, the one out there?"

"I don't care what I smell like; he needs not to be here. He shouldn't even know where I live. Winnie said it's Michael. You heard her," I shot back.

"I wanted confirmation. You know, I can make the asshole leave," Ronnie blocked the doorway, his voice hard and cold. He knew all about Michael. Of course, I knew that he could handle it, but it wasn't his fight, this was my battle.

"I got this. I need to heal from it anyway. The universe is just upping the time frame," I said evenly, pushing against his chest so he would move. Jax still standing there, coiled in tension. I kissed them both on the cheek and headed down the stairs. I had to laugh as I reached the front door. Aedan and Smitty stood there like bouncers with Jillian and Mags behind them looking equally fierce. "I can handle this," I assured them.

"Oh girl, don't think for one moment we don't got your back," Mags spoke up, her voice tinged with steel and her inner gangster coming out. I knew they did, and I loved them for it. They all took a step toward me as I went to open the door. I smiled and held up my hand to stop them.

"How about I leave the door open so you can watch the show?" I suggested wryly as a compromise, so they didn't all follow me out.

"You aren't going out there alone," Ronnie said, leaving no room to argue. I wasn't going to fight him on it either; I needed him behind me. I yanked open the door.

Stepping out on my porch and down the first step, I felt Ronnie and Jax behind me, like giant walking brick walls. "Michael. Care to explain why you are here and how you know where I live?" I asked menacingly, my voice bitingly cold.

"There's my girl." Michael exploded in a bitter laugh as his eyes fell on my men. "Fuck! This guy? Really, Airiella?!"

"Funny," Jax said darkly, "I was just thinking the same thing." Both he and Ronnie stood shoulder to shoulder behind me.

"You fucking knocked her out on live TV, asshole!" Michael shouted at Jax.

I crossed my arms tightly across my chest and leaned back against them, drawing strength from their touch. I wanted to let them loose. "I'm not your girl. Why are you here, and why do you care?" I repeated, noticing neighbors coming outside to see what the noise was. Let them look; no way was I inviting Michael inside. My house was my safety zone.

"I can smell you from here. Are you fucking both of these guys now? Fangirling all over them?" He spat, advancing a step towards me. "Him, I get," he said, looking at Ronnie, "but this other asshole hit you! Given your history, I'm surprised to see him. But I guess you have sunk to new lows." He sneered at them, "Too bad I got the best of her; she's used and dirty now."

At that, I heard the screen door open and knew they were all on the porch behind me now. Michael's eyes widened slightly, and I felt the anger of all them, allowing it to bolster my confidence. "Last chance to answer my questions before I call the cops," I warned. Jax shifted behind me; I could hear his knuckles pop as he tightened his fist. Ronnie was radiating lethal levels of anger; he knew some of the bitter details on this one. How badly Michael had broken me without laying a finger on me.

"Don't, he's a coward," I whispered so both of them could hear me over the sound of Ronnie's teeth grinding together; Aedan and Smitty breathing equally hard. "How long have you known where I lived? Have you been stalking my house?"

"I looked up your license, you idiot; it has your address on it. Do you honestly think I couldn't find you? That you are *that* much smarter than I am? I'm here to check on you. To make sure you're okay, but it looks like a regular orgy going on. I'm surprised to see you've added girls to the mix. Guess I shouldn't be though, you always were a freak." He threw his hands up in the air. "I can't believe this. I came back for you. Yet you keep making these stupid decisions to fuck guys that like to use their fists. Now it's all over the TV and the internet. I keep getting calls from people about it. What makes you think you are important enough for me to stalk?" Michael fired off in a random jumble of words and sentences, answering questions and leaving me with more.

I turned to look at the people I loved behind me, "I've got this, stay put. But please, don't leave me." I turned back to Michael and stepped down the next step.

"Why now, after two years, do you care about anything or anyone that I am doing?" I stepped another step closer, observing his facial expressions carefully. "You didn't give a shit about sex then. Why do you care now? Considering you have *nothing* to do with me, it is exactly zero of your concern. As for guys hitting me, don't speak about what you don't know. In fact, don't speak about Jax at all, ever. You think *you* were a smart choice for me? Just because you didn't use your fists doesn't mean the damage wasn't real. Bruises heal, the wounds you left caused permanent damage. *Permanent.* Let that sink in your thick head. I'd take a punch from him any day over the shit you did. And since when do you give a shit about what people think about me?"

A wary looked appeared in his eyes as I pulled more energy to me, drawing on the bonds I had created. I moved forward another step, barely holding in my temper that I longed to unleash at him. The years of emotions and damage he created building a storm in me that begged me to let it go, to wash him away. He wasn't used to my fighting back, and it was throwing him off.

"You broke up with me in the most cowardly way possible. You left. You broke me worse than anyone else ever has." I let some of that energy go, and the wind picked up around me.

"You hurt me more than any punch ever thrown at me by anyone. You, who saw the bruises from others. You, who told me you'd take care of me, to trust you, that you'd never hurt me. I fell for the lies."

More of the storm inside me leeched out with every word, the wind whipping my hair at my face in a perfect mirror of the violence contained inside me. "Why now? You verbally abused me because I was upset with the way you chose to break up with me. Yet, here you stand, causing a scene, in the driveway of *my* house, where *you* shouldn't even know where it is. You wanted to check on me? Right. You stand here flinging insults at people that treat me like an equal, instead of like unwanted luggage or an old appliance. People you don't even know enough about to form an adequate insult, people that love me for me. You can leave *now*. Do not come back. Do not contact me," I snarled. I could feel the energy around me make my hair float, the wind carrying it away from my face now instead of the stinging whips.

"I came because I care," he whined, trying to play on my empathy. "I miss you."

I laughed darkly. "That's a fucking joke. No. You don't. It took me a long time to see that. If you are here, it's because you think you can get something out of it. You don't seem to understand; you already took everything I had to give you. You chose to throw it all away, and then blamed it on me. I wasn't good enough; I was stained and reminded you of ugly things. I never did anything right for you. You have the audacity to say you care? That you miss me? I know better. Leave. I won't be held responsible for what those that love me and wish to protect me do, nor will I hold them back," I motioned behind me.

"They don't love you. These people don't know you the way I do," Michael spewed, his voice dripping with venom; the same poison that used to take me down a dark hole of self-hate and feed all my insecurities. "You aren't as lovable as you think you are. Look at all the shit you put me through."

"What I put *you* through? You *never* knew me! If you had, you wouldn't have said those words. It's because of you that I don't think I am lovable!" I yelled, a sharp edge to my words.

I turned my back on him before I lost myself to the rage. I blinked rapidly to keep the angry tears back. He didn't deserve my tears. My eyes settled on Jax first, then Ronnie, silently pleading with them to stay still. I saw the need both of them had to end this, to close this once and for all for me. Violence brimmed in their eyes.

Michael's words were impacting these two men I loved so much. He was a coward and wouldn't try anything physical, even if they hadn't been standing there. I was damn sure happy that they were there, though.

I love you; I told them both through the connection.

"You'll regret turning your back on me, Airiella. Especially when they find out how fucked up you are, and they leave you," he yelled at me. "They'll run from you, just like I did. You and your smug attitude and fake good deeds, trying to make everyone else feel like shit because they don't do what you do. She's a sham," he yelled at my safety net from behind me. "She wants you to think she loves you; then she just uses you. I gave you everything! You should be thanking me! You're fucking them to make me jealous; it won't work. They are garbage."

I spun back around and let my temper fly. Michael had gone too far, and I snapped. I opened my senses fully and unleashed the storm inside of me, all those emotions now free and heavy in the air around me. The sky darkened with thick clouds, the wind now howled through the trees, electricity crackling through my veins.

"Do *not* insult them! You aren't even worthy of breathing the same air as them. Plus, if you are going to accuse me of something, you need to do better than that. I've never turned my back on *anyone*, including you. I fought your demons, ignoring the ones you hoisted off on me calling them mine. Telling me I needed to fight my own battles. I took them on, and let them eat at me. Killing things inside me that I planted in hopes of saving myself. You never fought for me," I hissed, holding nothing back.

"You gave me everything? You sure as fuck gave me many lifetimes worth of insecurities. You gave me sleepless nights, while you snuck around in the dark trying to make me think I was paranoid so I would come crawling back to you because I was scared. So you could tell me I need you, that I can't make it on my own," I flung back at him.

"You gave me the ability to question every decision about myself that made me feel good, thinking I was selfish instead of helping people. You gave me a broken heart and shattered my soul. It took these people behind me to show me exactly what you gave me. So, thank you for that gift. I guess I do owe you a thank you for leaving me as well. Thanks."

I felt hysteria slipping in, and I couldn't hold back the words that I'd bottled up and hid for too long. "Thank you for being the reason I'm as strong as I am now. Thank you for making me see just how much the sight of me disgusted myself. How far I'd fallen for every lie that you told me so that when I looked in the mirror, all I saw was a sickened and broken creature unworthy of love. Thank you for showing me who I was with you is a shadow of who I really am. Thank you for being the reason that forced me to face every despicable thing in my past with a microscope and wondering where I went wrong." I felt my words land on everyone around me, showing them just how much he had hurt me and their anger at him ratcheted up another notch.

My own emotions were crashing like the stormy ocean waves inside me now that I let them loose. "You. Left. Me. What does it say about *you* that someone like *me*, who *never* walks away, never gives up on anyone, chooses to walk away from you now?" I said.

My voice was deadly calm. Michael would never see what was under it; he was too blind. "I don't need you. I never did. You needed me, and you destroyed me, someone, who would have died for you. Actually, you know what? I did die for you. Never again. I've rebuilt myself with the pieces you left, and they love those pieces and what I've made from them. Leave. Now. Like the coward you are." I gave my final warning as hail started pelting down.

His face paled more when he realized I wasn't afraid of his words, and he ran to his car, unable to even fight his fears much less the truth of my words.

"You'll fucking regret this! I was the best thing that ever happened to you. Stupid bitch!" Michael screamed from his window. I stood firm until he peeled out and was no longer in my sight.

Then I crumpled, the adrenaline went just as quickly as it came. I never hit the ground. I felt Ronnie's strong arms catch me, his warm embrace one of my favorite things to be wrapped up in and feel safe.

"I've got you, angel," he said warmly into my ear. Then he kissed me, one of those kisses that could melt all the clothes right off of me. "I'm so proud of you. You stood your ground, squared up, fought for yourself, and you won. I love you so damn much. That was amazing; you looked every bit an angel standing there."

"It doesn't feel like a win. If you guys hadn't been behind me, I don't know that I could have done that. Put me down," I protested weakly, my body shaking as if it would never stop. The storm that appeared outside in the morning sky now dissipated, the blue skies reappearing. "I'm too heavy for you to keep carrying me like this. I'm not fragile."

"Fuck that," Jax growled, pulling me from Ronnie and wrapping my arms around his neck. I gave in and wrapped my legs around his waist letting him bear my weight. "You inspire me. You are perfect," he whispered in my ear, and I let go. "Those words, those emotions, they betrayed your fragility, siren."

I broke down in sobs, wrapped around Jax. The remainder of the deadly and toxic storm that had grown in me washing out with my tears. Ronnie moved in behind me and wrapped his arms around both of us, Aedan, Smitty, and the girls joining in on the sides, me in the middle. The connection of all of us together filling me with all the beauty they brought to my life, fighting against the dark that Michael tried to deliver and had left me with two years ago. They all held me while I cried, and I felt their love rooted deep in me, it was real. It wasn't anything like Michael's version of love.

"I'm changing every day because of you, and not in ways that are bad like he insinuated. Ways that make me who I should be," Jax whispered in my ear again. His hold on me just as tight as I was gripping him. "I'm fucking proud of how you stood firm and didn't let him manipulate you, fucking gaslighting asshole. You are beautiful, extraordinary, and so strong. I'm so in love with you that no one else exists for me but you. The inspiration that you light in me burns brighter every day."

"Mags and I love you to the moon and back; you know that. We just watched you face the person who hurt you the most. You stood tall, defended yourself, defended us. I've never been prouder, you earned this release," Aedan praised me, taking his turn in soothing me.

"Baby girl, I've got no words that can take away the hurt he caused you, or the hurt he just tried to add to it all. But I can say I'm fiercely proud of you. Not once did you back down. You fought like a champion, on your own. All we did was stand there. You go ahead and let those wounds weep in the tears you cry. It means you are healing. You've got all our love." Smitty's words settled into me in only the way he could.

"Aedan, the girls and I are headed to the Costco down the street to stock up for our camping trip. You do you. Let these two buffoons take care of you. Love you, baby girl," Smitty said with a smile and a kiss on my forehead.

Jax, not even close to letting go, sat down on the porch with me wrapped around him and rocked. His arms the most welcome steel cage I've ever had locked around me. When the sobs quieted down, he stood and carried me upstairs and into my bathroom. He released me to undress me, and gently led me to the shower, stripped his clothes off and joined me. I was still trembling and he just took over and washed me. He was cleaning the toxic tears away. Then dried me and carried me back to my bed, laying there holding me as I shook and cried in the aftermath of letting go of the pain I'd held in for so long.

Wiping my tears away, I sat up. "I need to pack my clothes up and check the supplies in my pack," I said, trying to distract myself from wounds that still bled, but now had a much better chance of healing once and for all.

"Please look at me," Jax said brokenly. I looked at him, my eyes filled with tears I didn't want falling anymore.

"I'm going to be who you need me to be. I'm going to be the one you need."

I cupped his cheek, and brushed my lips over his, "Jax, I don't blame any of this on you. This breakdown was Michaels doing and a long time coming. Not yours. You didn't bring him here. You are exactly what I need. You got me through this." I touched the visible connection that shimmered in brilliant colors between us. "This was what I needed, and you gave it to me. You did more for me standing behind me out there, letting me fight for me, than he ever did in the years I was with him. This is a forever thing, Jax. I can't do less than that."

"You are always what I need, but not what I deserve. My promise to you is I will work on fixing me so that one day I will deserve you." He'd already fixed him; last night had made him lose sight of that.

"Just don't leave me, Jax. This bond, this right here, if you leave me, will destroy me," my voice was shaking, and I felt so utterly weak. I needed to snap out of this, Michael had no power over me anymore. He made his choice two years ago and it brought me to this place right now. "If you stay," I put his hand over my heart, "those scars he gave me, they will heal."

"You are hands down the strongest person I know." I could feel his fears battling him, keeping him from promising to not leave. This latest episode shaking him, though his eyes held a promise that made me hope. "What was he scared of back there?"

"He is a coward through and through. Maybe the weather? That seems to happen when my emotions get out of control. My life was never in danger, so no lightning." I thought about it. My life hadn't been in danger, but my heart certainly had been.

"It was enthralling to watch. You are fucking beautiful," Jax smiled the sweetest smile I'd ever seen on his face. I kissed him then, a real kiss to show him how I felt. "Ronnie is right; your capacity to love is your biggest strength. The depth of the feelings I felt in you while you were out there scared the shit out of me. I felt how he made you feel, and under it all was this crazy love that had an amazing color to it. When I touched it with my mind, I knew it was the love you had for us. For me. How you keep that alive and in front and center in the middle of all that blows my mind."

"It's always there, Jax, it never goes away. I'm so glad you can see it now." Ronnie came in the room then and put his solid body behind me. He never failed in being the support that I needed. "Thanks for catching me."

"Always, angel. Always. Now please let me feel you because I am not okay after witnessing firsthand the shit he throws. He didn't even deny that night stalking shit he used to do to you. He didn't once mention the assault the other day for all his ridiculous claims about being worried. That got broadcasted, too." He pulled his shirt off, and I watched Jax's face to see if he was okay with this again. To my surprise, he gave Ronnie a fist bump, and they squished me between them. My two most powerful connections were flowing freely and bathing my room in blue light. We lay there until we heard the others come back.

"Now, let's get packing so we can get out there, and you can see how inadequate and little girl like in the woods I truly am." Jax pulled me up, dressed me slowly and gently, and gave me a kiss that curled my toes.

When I was completely breathless and ready to

strip back down again, Jax turned me to Ronnie, and another potent kiss got planted on my lips. If I hadn't been standing between the two of them, I'd have dropped straight to the floor; they left me so weak-kneed.

"I think we need to talk more in-depth about another Airy sandwich," I told them as I held on to them both.

Jax laughed. "Oh, trust me, baby, that's already on my agenda." Ronnie nodded his agreement. Oh, fuck yes, I thought as my knees wobbled again.

Chapter Thirty-Four

Smitty drove and kept looking in the rear-view mirror. Airiella was on the phone almost the whole way up to where they parked. As soon as she hung up with one call, another came in, countless texts while she was on the phone. By the time they got there, her battery had already needed charging.

Between her family and the few calls from friends that she had answered, she was exhausted, and they still had a five-mile hike to go carrying camping gear. Smitty wanted to ask her if she was okay and correctly guessed it would annoy her because Aedan asked her as soon as she got out, and she snapped at him.

She also got irritated with Ronnie when he tried to remove the stuff she was going to carry. She had her backpacking pack loaded up with everything her setup needed, and two extra bags. She had to be taking at least a hundred pounds.

"She doesn't have to be so stubborn," Ronnie grumbled, falling in next to Smitty.

"Look how much she has already dealt with today. Isn't nature her thing? Doing this is probably exactly what she needs to feel normal again. Okay, maybe as normal as she can feel while having to worry about demon attacks. Just relax. If she needs help, she'll ask for it."

"More likely, I'll figure out she needs help when she drops out of pure exhaustion," Ronnie hitched the bag he was carrying up farther on his back.

"Possibly, but she did give you a heavy bag to carry. That woman is no weenie, let her be. Even Jax didn't try to stop her, that has to tell you something right there."

"Yeah, yeah. I just hated seeing Airiella hurt so much this morning after that asshole."

Smitty had a hard time with that one too. Shit, even Jillian, was about ready to tear into him. "I'm right there with you on that. He's a piece of work."

"She told me about him in her usual understated way. It wasn't until I heard her tone of voice and saw her face, did I truly understand how badly he hurt her. Thought I was going to break my fingers, I clenched my fist so hard."

"She did it. She did exactly what she needed to do to let it out and bring herself to a place she can heal. She's scary as fuck when she's pissed. Did you see the size of the hail that started pelting down? I almost hoped her wings would pop out. Imagine that idiots face if he'd seen that?" Smitty laughed.

"His face? He'd have shit himself." Ronnie looked around them. "It's beautiful here. Did you see that mountain this morning? Huge. And this forest. It reminds me of her, so full of life." Ronnie mused.

"Too much of a change for you?" Smitty observed his response.

"Nah. Airiella wants to go sky diving, she said. Her words were, it can't be any scarier than fighting Bael."

Smitty laughed. "No matter what she says, she's fearless."

Mags was uncomfortable. Five miles is not a long way to go, but she underestimated the number of times she'd have to stop and pee, and carrying these babies was no easy task. The beauty of the place was indescribable, and she understood why this area was one of Airy's favorites. Mags let it distract her from the discomfort.

She felt guilty sitting on her ass while Airy set up three tents in under fifteen minutes. She even baffled the guys who had been struggling with the one she took from them. She'd sent them off to collect firewood while she got everything else situated.

Jillian stuck close to Mags. "Think she's okay?"

Mags studied their angel. "I think she doesn't like the extra attention and is trying to adjust."

"Well, she's certainly giving off a stay away vibe right now."

"It's not personal. See how many calls Airiella got before she shut her phone off? She even posted she wouldn't be reachable, that she was fine, and everything was good. Look at the comments if you have a signal." Mags leaned back soaking in the sun.

"Are the animals that were helping them close by?"

Jillian had kept looking around.

"I'm almost totally positive they are. The hawk circling, I am sure is Onida watching over me," Mags gestured to the sky.

"How are all of them going to fit in that tent?"

Mags laughed. "Is this your first-time camping?"

"This kind of camping, yes."

"It's a lightweight backpacking tent. It's a three-person tent, but in case you hadn't noticed, those three are sleeping a little closer the past few days. Trust me; those men will not be complaining about lack of space."

"Are you worried about something happening out here? We are kind of remote," Jillian looked around them.

"I am a little bit, but I know Taklishim, Tama, Onida, and Degataga are close. For that matter, Father Roarke is with them too. Airiella, in action, is quite the force as well. She's more powerful than all of them combined. My worry is more that I'll go into labor."

"Should the tents be closer?" Jillian continued to wonder about everything and worry.

"Girl, relax. Look at this view! And do you want to hear us all having sex? You know that's what happens, right? All this fresh air, the sound of the waves, the stars overhead, puts you in the mood for some down and dirty time."

Jillian broke out in laughter. "Okay, the tents are well spaced then."

R onnie decided to try again. *Angel, are you going to keep up shut out for the entire trip?*

What?

You've had us shut out since you got in the car. What's going on?

Oh, nothing. Sorry.

Ronnie felt her walls drop; it was only a small consolation. The chaotic emotions swirling around in her were dizzying. "What do we do if it rains?"

"You get wet," Smitty called across the campfire. "Really? You can't think of something to do while it's raining?"

"There's no rain forecasted, you're safe," Airiella said evenly.

Jax dropped a hand on Ronnie's shoulder, "Take her for a walk, maybe? I think this morning threw her after the debacle of last night."

"Wouldn't you rather do it?" Ronnie was more than happy to, but he didn't want to intrude.

"The others are coming to have dinner with us. I want to get prepped, I've never cooked over an open fire like this before."

"Here, I'll help you," Airiella said from behind Ronnie. "It takes a bit of getting used to."

"Oh, hey, I told Ronnie to take you for a walk," Jax was flustered.

"I heard. I'm fine. Besides, I needed to talk to you about that energy in you."

Ronnie was on instant alert. She was going to pull it from him. "Angel, is this the best time to do this?"

"Yes. There's magic here. I can feel something

different in the energy of this place."

"You can't be serious?" Jax fell back on his ass.

"I won't force you, Jax. With the ocean here, the extra energy, and our medicine people, I think it's the best opportunity we will get."

Ronnie felt stuck. He was on the fence for this one. "Let's wait until the others are here before we think about that." Ronnie didn't know how to argue this with maybe the most powerful person on the earth. "I'm not for or against the idea, angel. I just think we should wait for the others if you need them."

"They're here," she said quietly and stood.

Ronnie could barely make out their forms in the distance, heading towards them. He looked back at Airiella and cocked his head; this was new.

Aedan laughed faintly. "Okay, I agree, it's slightly funny to watch. I swear, though, when Tama burst through the woods, I almost pissed myself," Aedan recalled.

"I almost pissed myself watching it!" Mags exclaimed. "Then it was because of the look on Asher's face. That, to me, was the most comical thing. Not the experience as a whole because I thought I was going to have a heart attack watching that."

"She's not joking, she damn near broke my hand," Jillian remarked.

Aedan pulled Mags closer to him. "I wasn't sure who to be more afraid of, Tama or Bael."

"My fear hit an all-time high when my feet left the ground," Father Roarke added.

Aedan laughed. "At that point, I wasn't sure what to expect anymore." He looked off at Airiella, sitting alone closer to the water.

"She's fine, Aedan," Taklishim saw him looking. "She's fully healed now. The scars remain and will still cause her moments of grief, but they no longer hold power over her. She's adjusting."

"She told Jax she felt magic here," Aedan looked back at them and saw everyone looking at him. "Is there something special about this land?"

"She's feeling her magic," Onida stated.

"Did one of you tell her you had arrived?" Ronnie asked.

"No," Tama joined in, her gaze on Airiella though. "She knew, didn't she?"

Ronnie nodded silently, and Aedan looked back out. "Can she defeat him then?"

They all shrugged. Degataga spoke, "We don't know. She's different now. The power coming off her is in far greater magnitude than I expected, and her energy feels resolute."

"Resolute?" Aedan wasn't following.

"Unwavering," Jax added. "Firm. It has a meaning and a purpose."

"You feel it too?" Degataga looked surprised by that.

"I did. I do. I got stronger after this morning too. I'm guessing you all did to some degree." Jax shrugged.

"He's right. My link to Airiella is faint, but what bleeds across when I am near her makes me stronger," Onida said casually.

"She wants to pull the energy from Jax while we are here," Aedan looked back out at her.

"It's not a bad idea. We are all here to help Airiella if she needs it. We can help Jax, too," Taklishim looked over at Jax. "She won't do it if you don't want to."

"The idea has merit?" Aedan needed more information before he threw his weight on either side of the issue.

"Yes," Father Roarke weighed in. "She has the saltwater here. Maybe, combined with the holy water, it would be easier for her."

"You want to do both?" Aedan started having flashbacks and shivered. "What about Jax? Is he still at risk?"

"You saw what happened to her; you honestly think whatever risk is there for me is more concerning than what she goes through?" Jax burst out in a wild whisper.

"No, that's not what I mean. If there is even a small chance of it killing you, she won't do it, and it becomes null. I'm gathering information," Aedan stood firm. "Shit. Her wings are out," he bolted to his feet, looking around wildly.

"Sit. There's nothing here," Onida's tone was mildly amused. "She's still sitting down; if there were a danger, she'd have been on her way back over here."

"She's crying," Aedan stood back up. He didn't know how he knew that, but he did.

"She's talking to Kalisha," Taklishim informed them. "She's fine."

Chapter Thirty-Four

J ax knew they were all on edge except Airiella, who was as Jax had described her. Resolute. She was currently asleep, sprawled across the top of both Jax and Ronnie, and he was doing his best to enjoy the moment. He would assume half the risk of getting rid of this energy; their future could be drastically altered today.

He'd already talked to Father Roarke about it, who had said he would speak to Taklishim after they had left. She had told him it was his choice, and this was his choice.

Please stop thinking about it. I'm not going to argue with you. We will need sleep if we want to make it through this.

"I'm sorry, siren." Her glowing angel eyes settled on his. "We are in this together."

"I won't argue with your decision."

"Someone care to tell me what this decision is?

What if I want to argue with it?" Ronnie asked sleepily.

"I'm going to drink holy water before Airiella pulls the energy to try and kill it more in hopes it will be easier on her."

"Yep, I'm going to have to argue with that one," Ronnie tried to sit up but was prevented by Airiella. "Jax, that shit fights back, what if it does to you what it does to her?"

"Don't, Ronnie, let him be. It's his choice. I'll do everything in my power to keep him safe." Jax heard it again, the resolute tone.

"Fuck that. I stand to lose both of you in this asinine scheme." Ronnie was angry, and Jax understood why. "Why are your eyes glowing?"

"I didn't know they were. It's not like I can see my eyes," Airiella slid off Jax a little, pinning Ronnie more.

"Stop trying to distract me, I protest this idea," Ronnie's voice weakened.

"Jax might be on to something with this idea. Also, Kalisha suggested that I use an open flow of energy while doing it so that I am pulling at the same time I am releasing. I'm not saying it won't be without pain for either of us, but we have a good shot at making this work."

"Then we go for round two tonight," Ronnie said, grabbing her face and pulling her down into a bruising kiss. Jax had to admit it was sexy to watch.

"I agree with Ronnie. Round two," Jax said huskily. "Ronnie, we will both be here tomorrow night too."

No. Absolutely not," I told Taklishim.

"Will you just listen to me?" Taklishim shifted and tried to persuade me.

"You want me to subject Smitty and Ronnie to that pain; I heard you the first time." I crossed my arms, glaring at Taklishim.

"I don't think they will feel what you do. It's a connection thing, a blood bond thing. They lend you strength."

"They also feel the same shit I do! If I hurt, they feel it. If I am hurting while they are touching me, they'll feel it even more!"

"Isn't that our choice to make, baby girl?" Smitty said from behind me.

"No!" I spun around to see the subjects of my argument with Taklishim behind me.

"Oh, angel, he's right. We choose if we want to feel it or not. You don't get to choose for us. Isn't that the argument you use on us when we protest you running straight into danger for our benefit?" Ronnie wasn't about to budge.

"Siren," Jax ran a frustrated hand through his hair, "I don't like it either, but if there's a chance it works, shouldn't we try it?"

"No." My voice quieter this time. "No. Please don't do this," tears stung my eyes. "I'd rather die for good than to have you feel this."

Ronnie surged forward and cupped my face with his hands. "Not an option. If we can help, it's our choice. Don't take this away from us."

Gandalf, I swear on all that's holy they better come

through this whole or the wrath of an angel will be released.

Can you try to have a little faith, please? His dry tone came back at me.

"Fine. If this goes badly, you are all stuck with a pissed-off angel. If I die, then a pissed off angel ghost."

"No one is dying, Raven. I would prefer it if you protect the rest." He gestured to Aedan, Jillian, and Mags.

I conjured up a ring of blue fire around the camp and strode off into the cold ocean water up to my knees. Each of us had a vial of holy water, and Ronnie and Smitty drank theirs down first. Smitty stood in front of me, Ronnie and Jax, on either side of me, all of us touching each other, and I opened my senses entirely.

I asked the water, earth and air for help in ridding us of Jax's dark energy and purifying it. I felt each element respond and flow through me in a circuit with each of the guys. Then I called on the lightning. I asked it to fill my body with a continuous flow of purifying power to kill off that which is dark.

Taklishim confirmed with each of them that they felt the energy flowing through them and then had Jax tip his head back and while Taklishim emptied the vial in his mouth. I felt the moment it started to fight back and started to pull it out of him slowly.

The elements in me were responding. The lightning was doing what it was supposed to do, but it didn't stop that energy from fighting every inch of the way. The open flow helped, but not enough. I felt the agony in each of the guys, called more lightning, and pushed the energy out of me faster. I didn't want them feeling this.

"Raven, slow down," Taklishim warned. "Tip your

head back."

I opened my mouth for the holy water and tried to brace for what was going to hit. I didn't have time. Bael chose that inopportune moment to show up, cackling. Power surged through me in a blast of energy that shoved Bael backward.

Can I pull it from Jax? I asked Taklishim immediately.

You won't be safe if you do.

Better me than him. I pulled it from Jax fast and broke the connection. *Help them, please, Tak.*

I stayed in the water, pain tearing through my body in excruciating waves as my wings blocked the men from Bael. I wasn't going to make this easy for him. I pulled the water's energy into me in large doses begging it to purify that energy as I released it, my skin sparking as the lightning scorched the darkness.

I pulled the knife Kalisha had made. "This ends here, Bael."

"Such confidence for someone in so much pain," his handsome face smiling evilly.

"Pain is temporary. Light will always shine as long as it has a power source; love will always win."

"Don't be a fool; all you have to do is come with me. You'll never want for anything," Bael sneered.

"I'd always want for love. Going with you would be turning my back on the purest love I have ever known. That's just not going to happen. Not today, not ever." I advanced towards him slowly, the water flowing around my legs.

Bael blinked out and reappeared behind the guys. *Sorry,* I sent them all. Then I lifted them with the air and floated them over, landing them inside the ring of fire. I launched at Bael, swinging the knife out for his side while I tucking my wings around me for protection.

I scored a hit, and he blasted out that poisonous energy of his with a roar. Like water rolling off a duck's back, my wings repelled it, and I splashed down in the cold water. The dark energy in me was not liking being submerged like that, striking back painfully.

Take it from me; I begged the water as it worked to do my bidding. I called the lightning down to strike the water as I held my breath, allowing more time for the water to clean that energy in me. I asked the earth to keep him in place as I came up, gasping for air, fighting back against the sickness rolling inside me.

"You can't beat me," Bael boomed out, though he sounded less sure now.

"I'm not going to beat you. I'm going to kill you. For Kalisha, for everyone, you've hurt. I will be the tool that justice uses to make right the wrongs."

Bael narrowed his eyes at me. "You will die."

"Then, I die. But so will you," I said firmly.

"My legions will kill all those you are trying to protect," he warned me as the earth rumbled under my feet, and the air filled with the sulfurous stink I associated with Bael. A scream from the beach sounded, and I saw the shadows of demons surrounding the fire.

I lunged again for at Bael, aiming for a kidney shot at least, hoping it would slow him down. *You need to power the weapon, Airiella;* I heard Kalisha tell me.

Shit! I pushed my power through the tip of the blade as it sunk in his skin, a direct kidney hit. Bael staggered, shocked. "You will pay with your life," the demon grabbed hold of me, his hand burning my throat as he squeezed.

My vision was blacking out, and suddenly I was back in the water, and there was an arrow through Bael's arm. Then another. Mentally I was cheering as Mags scored strategic hits, allowing me time to stagger to my feet. My soaked clothes were trying to drag me down and the energy in me trying to consume me.

The knife slipped from my hand as a wave of agonizing pain swept through me, my hair wrapped around Bael's hand as he yanked my head up. "I'll make your past feel like a children's princess party compared to what I will do to you."

I used the water to sweep his feet from under him and frantically searched for the knife. I could hear the sounds of fighting from the beach, and I needed to keep my focus, I'd never survive this if I couldn't. They wouldn't survive.

The tips of my fingers brushed against the blade and I fumbled for the grip, and stabbed it down into Bael's leg. "You have no power over me!" my voice screamed out, impossibly loud as I shouted at the energy inside me, at Bael, at the darkness lurking.

Power surged through my veins again, and I lurched to my feet drunkenly. Fire danced across my skin, and I looked down, confused and pushing against it, then sinking back in the water to douse the flames. I looked up, and my heart stopped, Jax was running towards me.

Bael disappeared and reappeared right in front of Jax, his hand shaped like a knife as he stabbed it into him. The world fell away from me, my focus only on the man I loved and the demon that was killing him. Jax's blood was spilling on the ground around him, his gaze locked on me.

An excruciating noise filled my ears, and somewhere in the back of my brain, I knew it was me screaming. I don't know how I went from knee-deep in the ocean to halfway across the beach in a blink, but there I was, a furious rage tearing my heart apart.

Lightning split the sky in a blast equal to a bomb as I lit up Bael with bolt after bolt driving him backward away from Jax. I was vaguely aware of the demon slicing my gut open, but I didn't stop. I called for justice from every element sending the power through the blade that I jabbed down into his black, evil heart.

I didn't hear his roar of anguish; I only recognized my own. I rained down blow after blow. I didn't feel the pain of my injuries; I only felt Jax. I experienced the rage of Kalisha, the love of my family. I let it all wash through me, channeling the energy and begging it to end Bael's tyranny.

I didn't stop until he turned to ash, his astonished face vanishing from my sight. "Stolas," I whimpered. "You promised."

I felt Taklishim coming up behind me. "You save him. Save him, Tak."

"He'll be fine; we need to help you. Ronnie, grab her!" Taklishim issued orders.

"No! You save him." I moved out of their reach.

"Raven, he will be fine. The world needs you. Let me help."

"Save him first. Without him, you won't have me." Tears blurred my vision.

"We can't fix this," I heard Onida whisper.

I threw myself to the side again as Taklishim tried to grab me. "Fix him first," I avoided their touch.

"Angel," Ronnie pleaded, trying to grab me as I left a trail of blood behind me. "He needs your blood."

I snatched a star from Ronnie and sliced my hand open, dripping it over Jax. "Promise me; you save him." I shoved whatever energy I had left in me to Jax. "Promise me!"

"He's going to be fine," Onida tried to console me. "We need to help you, Airiella."

"I promise you; we will save him," Degataga's voice came from behind me.

I heard the promise. "I've avenged you, Kalihsa." I dropped, blacking out.

Chapter Thirty-Six

Ronnie lost his mind. "Fucking do something!" Ronnie shouted, his life falling apart before his eyes in a bloody mess.

"Tak, we can't fix this. Not here, not like this. She needs surgery," Onida sounded panicked.

"How are we going to get her to a hospital?" Degataga asked softly.

"We do what we can," Taklishim's voice was hard, and he vibrated with an anger Ronnie had never seen before. "Stop the bleeding first."

Ronnie stumbled backward at the appearance of the demon in front of him. "Fucking help her!"

"She extracted a promise from me to save you both before I helped her," Stolas said sadly. "I must help him first."

"He'll be fine," Taklishim shouted, his anger

intimidating in a way Ronnie hadn't experienced.

"He has demon poison eating at his insides; he won't survive that. Where is the recipe I gave you to fight it?" Stolas glared at Taklishim. "The sooner you help me, the sooner I can help her."

Ronnie fumbled through his pockets for the container Degataga had given him and handed it over. "Here's mine."

Stolas looked up at Onida, "Are you going to help him?"

"You promised her?" Onida's eyes were wide and expressionless.

"I did." Stolas reached for Airiella's bleeding hand and squeezed her blood into the gaping wound in Jax's side. "Help me, please, before it's too late."

Degataga stepped up and put his hands on Jax, Tama joining him as Ronnie looked over at Taklishim, who froze in shock and devastation, tears falling on Airiella's crumpled form. "Tak, she would never forgive you if you didn't help him," Ronnie choked out, hating every word falling from his mouth.

"And he will never forgive us if we don't save her," Taklishim cried. Ronnie had never seen the man emotional; it was pushing him past the point of no return.

"Love, help me. Hold that faith," Tama called to him.

Another scream tore through the air, stopping Ronnie's heart yet again. Mags. He tried to stand and fell over, Onida streaking past him. "I've got her, this I can help. Airiella needs a hospital if she is to survive. You all know this!"

Stolas moved back from Jax and looked helplessly

down at Airiella. "Seir!" He bellowed.

Ronnie scrambled out of the way as the big black Pegasus appeared. "Yes?"

"Can you get her to a hospital without injuring her further?" Stolas issued an order in that question, Ronnie was sure of it.

"Appears they both need one," Seir said, cheerfully. "She was successful, Bael's dispatched. I'd be happy to help."

"Take me with them," Ronnie dragged himself to his feet.

"Lift your angel," Stolas told him, nodding at Seir. Ronnie found himself in front of a hospital holding his dying angel at the touch of the demon's hand. The next second, Taklishim was there with Jax and Tama. Shortly after, Degataga and Father Roarke appeared. Lastly, Onida and Mags.

"Let me speak," Taklishim ordered Ronnie, leading them in. "Get Dr. Bagley, now," he shouted as he walked in. "They've been attacked!"

Onida grabbed a wheelchair and got Mags loaded up. "Get her to delivery. Tell Dr. Ashland I sent her. We will be accompanying these two. Go now!"

Ronnie followed Taklishim and lowered Airiella on the stretcher that appeared, his body sagging as they wheeled her away. Father Roarke led him over to the chairs as the remaining council members followed his angel and Jax.

Stolas strode casually in the front doors and bent to speak to Ronnie. "I've upheld my promise. He will survive. Your friends are packing up and will be here soon. Her danger is not over. If she makes it through this, she will still be sought after. The fear of her power is great, especially now that she has defeated Bael. We remain on your side, but can't be in sight of you. Call me in an emergency only." Stolas walked back out the front door, leaving Ronnie gaping after him.

"Close your mouth, son. There will be many questions from authorities on this. Those wounds are serious and they will report them to the police. Say nothing. Defer to Taklishim or me," Father Roarke advised.

Smitty threw his hands up in the air, "How the fuck does this goddamn thing come apart?" he shouted in frustration.

"My wife is in labor, our friend and brother filled with demon poison, our angel dying, and you are worried about a tent?" Aedan choked out.

Jillian's ear-piercing scream tore through the air as a giant bear ambled up to them. "Are you fucking kidding me right now?" Smitty screamed at the sky, hoping the noise would scare the bear. To his shock, it shifted into an older man, a very naked older man.

"I'm Chief Tyee, Taklishim asked for help. We've got ATV's coming. Let me help you tear this down," he walked over like it was every day they saw a big bear turn into a naked man after an angel killed a demon that had just stabbed his friend and sliced her open while a black Pegasus took them away.

Smitty blinked slowly, processing. "Uh, thanks? I'm Smitty. Aedan," he pointed, "and my fiancée Jillian. I'm sorry, this is a lot to take in." He stood there blinking. "I'm losing my mind."

"I understand. Let's get busy; you'll want to be with your friends. We owe the Raven a great debt," he bowed slightly and tore the tent down with ease, getting it halfway packed before Smitty could even process that it had happened.

Jillian scrambled around the campsite picking up things and throwing them in bags while Aedan grabbed all the luggage out of the tents. Together they got it done quickly, and by the time the ATVs arrived, they were ready to load them all up.

Less than an hour later, they pulled up to the hospital, and Father Roarke repeated his message of not speaking about anything. They had no word on Jax or Airiella, and Aedan went to Mags. Jillian was sitting on his lap, curled into him crying, and Ronnie was barely holding it together.

"Father, will praying help?" Smitty asked.

"It's never hurt," the priest said gently, taking his hand and Ronnie's.

Jax woke to find Ronnie asleep in a chair next to the bed, his upper body sprawled across the lower part of the bed. He was in a hospital. He looked at the window to see what time of day it was and saw Tama sitting on the sill.

"Airiella?" he croaked out.

"She made us promise to save you before she even let us touch her," Tama said, her face downcast. "I don't know how she is. They are still in surgery. Tak will make sure they bring her here when they are finished."

"Bad?" He didn't want to ask.

"Very bad. Jax," she walked over to him, "I believe

for you, she will fight to come back." Tama's eyes shone bright with tears. "Her words to Taklishim were that without you, they didn't have her."

"What does that mean?" his voice was faint.

"Taklishim told her the world needs her. That was her response." Tama wiped at the tears. "The good news is, your niece and nephews were born, all healthy and perfect. Mags is doing great."

"Is it over?" he wasn't sure what he would do if her answer were no.

"She killed him. They will always be after her, though, they will think twice now."

"Smitty and Jillian?" he asked.

"They are out in the waiting room; they are fine, a little distraught but not injured. Airiella made Stolas promise her to keep you and Ronnie alive. Do you know the power that carries? I believe she will make it through this."

Jax nodded numbly and closed his eyes. "How long has he been asleep?"

"You've been back in here for three hours; he hasn't left your side once. He only fell asleep a bit ago."

"Are you and the other council members all okay?" He blinked rapidly, fighting the feeling of loss that was trying to set in.

"We are all fine physically. Emotionally is a little different. Taklishim is taking this hard; they've lost her twice on the operating table already. Tak said she only brought herself back once. She's quite important to him, you know. To all of us. Onida has shut down a little and Dega, well, he's a little frantic." Tama sat on the foot of his bed. "We are all invested in this, Jax. Please don't be angry with them."

He closed his eyes again. "I'm not angry with them. It's hard to argue with Airiella." Jax tried not to shudder. "She's going to make it, Tama. I won't believe otherwise."

"How'd you get out of the circle, Jax?" she asked him quietly.

"She needed me. I walked through it. Nothing more to it than that." Jax continued to reach for their connection needing to feel the spark.

"It's something, none of us could get through, not even Taklishim." She paused, then continued. "If the authorities get through, say nothing. Defer them to Tak or Father Roarke. I'll tell Smitty you're awake." Tama kissed his cheek. "Keep the faith, Jax." She walked out of the room softly, not making a sound. Jax closed his eyes again; her words were circling in his head.

"Seeing Bael hurt you gave her the power she needed to kill him," Ronnie told him quietly after Tama had gone. "It wasn't for nothing." Jax opened his eyes again to see Ronnie's pain-filled ones. "I'm so happy you're alive. Fucking hell, Jax, I've never been so scared in my life."

"You've got to stay here with her while I go back. Don't let her give up on me."

"You know how much it's going to hurt to leave?" Ronnie warned.

"I do, but I'm coming back. I'll wait until I know Airiella's okay. It has to be you that stays, Ronnie."

"I know. The backers already demanded you back. Asher is trying to blame you. It's a mess, Jax. I wanted to tell them all to fuck off." Ronnie rubbed at his eyes. "The babies are beautiful, by the way."

"I don't have a wound; if they healed me, why am I here?"

"Demon poison. They wanted to watch over you to make sure it all got out of you," Ronnie sat back in the chair. "It was Stolas that stemmed the poison. Tama sealed up the wound and then finished when they admitted you and got you hooked up to antibiotics."

"Can I do this Ron?" Jax blinked back tears.

"We all can, Jax. It will take all of us."

Jax fell back asleep, only waking when Airiella arrived. "She'll be okay?" he asked Taklishim.

"Yeah. I know you have to go. The backers called all of us. It's going to be very painful for both of you." Taklishim bowed over her still body. "I'm lucky she's still here. Are you sure you don't want to tell her? You know this will hurt her?"

"I know. Get me out of here so I can get back quicker."

Chapter Thirty-Seven

I woke up to a room full of people, but no Jax. Fear shot through me, and I started to panic. My eyes fell on all the sleeping people, and I wanted to scream to wake them all up and demand answers.

"Angel, he's okay. He had to go back. He waited until he knew you pulled through," Ronnie stepped up and settled down next to me. "He didn't want to."

"He's alive?" My throat thickened up, and my eyes started to sting.

"Stolas kept his promise. So did the rest. They lost you twice on the table, angel. Only once you came back on your own."

"How long have I been out?" The pain in my heart was borderline intolerable.

"Only a day. Tama has had a close eye on you and wanted to keep you out for at least a day. Onida has been in every hour. Taklishim and Dega haven't left once."

"He left me?" I couldn't hold back the tears.

"Not by choice, angel." Ronnie held me gently. "Don't you dare give up on him. There's so much happening right now."

He'll come back to you, Ella. He'll be back, don't lose faith, my grandpa's voice floated through my head. I flashed back on watching Bael stab him, his blood pooling in the sand. "Tell her to put me back out, I can't deal with this," I whispered hoarsely.

"Baby girl, he didn't leave you. He only had to go back for a bit," Smitty sat on the other side of me. "I know how much it hurts."

I closed my eyes and shut down the connections. "Get me out of here," I said, my voice cracking.

"In the morning, Raven," Taklishim sat down next to Smitty. "I'll get you released in the morning. Do you want Tama to put you back out?"

I nodded, unable to process that Jax wasn't here with me. What we had wasn't a lie, I wouldn't believe that despite the voices of my past screaming at me in my head. Jax lying in a pool of his own blood; Jax holding me while I grieved for my grandpa. Jax kissing me; Jax loving me. Jax running to save me from Bael. He was all I could see.

Countless images of Jax flying through my head made his absence even more painful. I couldn't open my eyes and bear not to see him. I couldn't keep my eyes closed without seeing him. I couldn't even feel him. There was just a void.

"Sshh, Airiella." I felt Tama's cool fingers on my head, and then thankfully, nothing.

R onnie was out of his mind with worry. "Jesus, he better fucking hurry up." Ronnie paced, "She's not even remotely okay. Like a shell of a person," Ronnie whispered into the phone.

"Is this how you felt while she was gone?" Chrissie asked him gently.

"Not like this. It hurt, and it hurt bad, but I could function. Mostly. The only time Airiella shows life is when Mags puts the babies with her in the bed. Even then, it's so heartbreakingly sad. She's shut us all out, but I can still feel it. This empty nothing that's swallowing her."

"Take her to the ocean," Chrissie told him firmly.

"Seriously?" Ronnie stopped pacing.

"Yes, seriously. It won't take the pain away, but she will be able to cope better."

"Where? Anywhere?" Ronnie was willing to try anything. Even *he* hadn't heard from Jax.

"No, her beach. I'll text you the name of the hotel she usually stays at, rent a room for a couple of nights, pack up some of her clothes, and get her in the car. Use the hotel address to get the GPS directions. From there, I can text directions on how to get to her beach. Trust me on this," Chrissie sounded so sure.

"She won't even talk to her family."

"Ronnie, think about everything she has been through in the past two weeks. Even for her, it's a lot. For the rest of us, it would be damn near insurmountable. Add in the pain of being separate from someone you love desperately. I can't speak about the bond or that stuff because I don't know about it. She needs a safe place. Her beach is that place," Chrissie reminded him.

"I'll do it. Text me the info. I'll call Airiella's dad and let him know."

"Do it today. Go today. Airiella's birthday is in two days. I'll be there, I'll meet you there at her beach," Chrissie instructed him.

"Thanks. See you soon." Ronnie hung up and called Airiella's dad, filling him in, so they didn't worry. Then he did precisely what Chrissie told him to do. He let the others know and went to get her. She dressed today, at least. He scooped her up out of bed.

She didn't even say anything. Smitty had pulled her car out of the garage and he plopped her down inside and took off. She didn't even respond to music. He'd take the gut-wrenching pain she'd been feeling over this empty feeling.

He followed Chris's directions, and as he turned down the street that led to her beach and parked, she stirred. Robotically she got out of the car and walked down the road and onto the sand. This was killing him. There wasn't anything he could do to ease this for her.

He grabbed a blanket that he thought to bring and followed, stunned to see her balled up and laying on the sand. At first, he'd thought she was hurt; then he realized she was just connecting to the place.

He kept his distance, letting her be. She laid there for hours, well after dark, until he went to get her, his stomach growling with hunger pains. This loop was their routine for the next two days. She didn't change out of Jax's hoodie she had been living in. She just lay on the sand.

Chrissie was almost there, and for the first time, Airiella was sitting up. He'd sang happy birthday to her, fielded phone calls from friends and relatives, and finally had heard from Jax. Even though his message was to do what Chrissie told him to do, he was relieved to hear Jax's voice, and he'd laid into him pretty severely for the distress she was experiencing.

"Wow. You're even better looking than I remember," Ronnie heard Chrissie say as she sat down next to him.

He grinned. "I can say the same for you. Nice to see you again."

"So formal. No change?" Chrissie glanced at Airiella.

"She's sitting today. Well, just in the past half an hour anyway."

"Let me tell you the plan," Chrissie started and filled him in. Ronnie was amazed. "Wish me luck; I'm going in." She leaned over and kissed him on the cheek.

"My first kiss from you, and it's on the cheek? I feel a little cheated now knowing you've both been scheming like this."

"You'll get over it. Right now, this is for Airiella." Chrissie stood and headed to Airiella.

Chapter Thirty-Eight

Ells, happy birthday," I heard a voice next to me say. "Are you here, or have I lost my mind completely?" I looked at my best friend. Her arms wrapped around me, and I broke down. "Chris, you're here," I sobbed against her shoulder.

"Ssshh, Ells. Of course, I'm here. This ghost you've become isn't like you, come on, let's go get cleaned up," Chrissie pushed me back and tugged on my hand. "We are going to go out for a birthday dinner."

"I can't believe he called you here. I'm so sorry," I sobbed. "It hurts so bad, Chris. It's eating me."

"That's why we are going to go out and celebrate your birth. The woman who saved the world and no one knows. The strongest person I have ever known. I came all this way; don't deny me dinner with my best friend."

I chuckled weakly. "Guilt trip? Really?"

"Whatever works. Come on. I have a new outfit for you to wear and between the two of us, we can figure out what to do with this sandy mop you call hair. Maybe put enough makeup on to showcase those eyes that have called me out on my bullshit for years."

"If you care enough to lay it on that heavy, fine. I'll do what you say." I broke down in tears again. "I still can't believe I see you. Thanks for coming."

"You get babysitting duty. You drive the rental; I'll drive Ells car. I need a break from the boys anyway," Chrissie took charge as we walked back to Ronnie, handing him her keys and taking mine. I ignored the hope in his eyes at seeing me. I couldn't promise him anything.

"He's hurting too, Ells."

"I know. I feel like an asshole. Ronnie's held me every night, and I've done nothing but ignore him."

"Yeah, he told me. So stop. Apologize to him. I know you can talk to him in your head, so just do it. Give the poor man a bit of relief; he's doing the best he can."

Thank you. I'm sorry for being an asshole, I sent to Ronnie, taking Chrissie's advice.

I love you, angel.

I love you too, Heracles.

As we got to the room, Chrissie looked me over. "Do you need help showering? I know you still have stitches."

"Yes, she needs help," Ronnie pushed his way in with Chrissie's boys and the bags that had been in the car. "I'm on it. I believe these humans belong to you."

Ronnie got me showered and dried, rebandaged, and Chrissie came in and took over. "Out." Within an hour, we were both dressed up, made up, and I felt foolish.

"I look like a clown," I argued.

"You look like an angel. Knock it off. Keep up that attitude, and I'll send him back in here," Chrissie threatened.

"I'm not afraid of Ronnie, that was a ridiculous argument."

"How happy will he be knowing you are putting yourself down again?" Chrissie propped her hands on her hips and glared at me.

"Fine. I look like an angel."

We walked out of the bathroom and got a wolf whistle from Ronnie, who himself was dressed up and looking incredibly sexy. "Hottest dates I've ever had," Ronnie looked us both over.

Chrissie winked. "Ditto."

We left, cramming into Chrissie's rented SUV, and drove quite a ways. "Where are we going?"

"It's a surprise, can it," she told me.

Ninety minutes later, we pulled up to a gigantic black iron gate with Rabbit Hole Estate over the gate, much to Ronnie's amusement. "Nice." He entered a code and drove in, the electric gate closing behind us, and he followed the driveway to a large palatial house.

"Wow." I was a little in awe. It was a mansion, the grounds sprawling for acres on either side of us.

"I heard they have great steaks and fabulous Italian desserts," Ronnie said with a smile as he helped me out. The pain in my chest eased up as he led me in the doors, and I stopped dead in my tracks. We were in a grand room, a stone fireplace lit and crackling peacefully, and above the fireplace mantle was the picture of me from the beach.

"Ronnie?" I looked at him, seeing his eyes sparkle with unshed tears.

"Ells, that might be the most beautiful picture I've ever seen." Chrissie clutched at my hand, and the boys hovered around Ronnie's legs.

"Jax took that picture," I murmured.

Ronnie pushed me forward a little. As I stepped in, I heard the music start playing. I didn't know what was happening, but it was making Ronnie emotional. "I'll Be" by Edwin McCain was playing, the love song was one of my favorites. "Ronnie, what's going on?"

My eyes strayed to the view from the windows of the mighty Pacific stretched out majestically across the horizon. Then I felt him, my heart beating out a staccato rhythm in my chest, love blooming wildly. Standing off to my left, wearing a suit without the jacket on, his white shirt with the sleeves rolled back, looking impossibly beautiful, his bottomless eyes locked on mine. "Jax."

J ax's palms were sweating, his heartbeat erratic, and he thought he was going to be sick. The second his gaze landed on her, it all went away. "Welcome home, siren." He wanted to run to her.

He dropped to one knee instead. "I will walk through any fire with you; I will slay as many demons as necessary. I will let you save me as often as you need to for the single promise of forever with you. I know our lives won't ever be easy; we seem to be in death-defying situations every other day. But you've shown me time and time again that love wins out, and I know we can get through anything with you by my side. I will spend the rest of my life every day proving to you that there is nowhere else I'd rather be than in this rabbit hole with you. Please,

Airiella, will you marry me?"

Jax watched the emotions play across her face; the hope flared to life in those angel eyes he missed so much. "Rabbit Hole Estate? This house is yours?" she whispered, her eyes drinking him in like she was dying of thirst.

"Ours," Jax corrected her, holding out the ring he'd had made with Chrissie's help. Tears were streaming down both of their faces. "I want to wake up with you forever, siren. Hear your voice saying my name in that tone that drives me to the brink of insanity, seeing your eyes glow the way they do when you look at me like you are looking at me right now. There's nothing else for me if I don't have you with me."

"I thought you were mad at me, that it was too much, and you left." She stepped closer to him unable to stay away, whispering. "You want to marry me and live here?"

Jax nodded. "We all picked this place together. We all will live here. A family."

"Everyone?" she whispered again, looking back at Ronnie, who was unabashedly crying.

"I didn't know he was doing this part," Ronnie said quietly, gesturing at the ring. "This is all him, angel."

She looked back at Jax and the ring he still held out to her. There was a large diamond in the center, the setting an intricate pattern of lacework in the shape of wings with brilliant gemstones embedded in the band running down the sides. "Well? Answer the man, put him out of his misery," Chrissie prodded her.

"Yes, I will marry you," she said so softly he wasn't sure he heard her right until Ronnie whooped. He stood and slid the ring onto her finger. "Kiss me as if you missed me," her eyes shone with the love he knew and needed.

"Like that's a stretch, I thought I was dying every day we were apart," he slowly lowered his head until his lips were separated from hers by nothing more than a breath. "I didn't leave you, siren. I was moving in here. This is a forever thing," he quoted her.

"Damn it, if you don't kiss her, I will," Ronnie headed towards them.

Jax settled his lips on hers, claiming her. The room erupted with cheers that had the beautiful angel blushing as she realized they weren't alone. "My family is here," she breathed against his mouth. Ronnie wrapped them both in a giant bear hug pulling them closer together.

"Everyone is here." He led her hand in hand, to the fully furnished backyard where they all waited; her parents, brother, nanie, cousins, aunts, uncles, friends, producers, the remaining council members after the fallout, and the rest of their little group.

"How did you pull this off?" she asked him after all the congratulations finished, and they had eaten a dinner full of the food that people had brought with them. There hadn't been one moment since he'd put the ring on her finger that they hadn't been touching. Jax intended to keep it that way.

"Love. The hope of a future with you. Ben and his real estate agent wife. Taklishim and Tama, Aedan. It was a group effort."

"But what about the house you already have? The show? Your family?"

"Ronnie and I owned our house together. We sold it, my mom packed everything up and shipped it here. This is my family. We all bought this place together. There are two other separate houses on the property, one large enough for Aedan and Mags and their new family; they called it a mother-in-law apartment. The other smaller, but Smitty claimed it. Ronnie will live on the other end of the house. There are eight bedrooms here, five of which have their own private bathrooms. There's an indoor pool over there," he pointed, "I think the smaller house Smitty claimed was a pool house. There's even a separate gym. Our own beach. I have a feeling we will have lots of visitors and guests."

Chrissie walked up to her then, and Jax hid a smile. He knew what was coming. "He offered me a place to live," she nodded at Jax. "That awful job I had? I quit. He connected me with people that found me a job here and helped me move. He offered it either as somewhere I can stay or use temporarily until I found a place of my own. I'm back, Ells."

"Did you tell Ronnie that?" she cried, throwing her arms around the striking woman that was her best friend.

"I just did. That future you told me you saw, well, it actually has a chance of happening now. Hope you broke him in good for me."

Jax burst out laughing. "That she did." Jax thought fondly of their shared nights together.

Jax led her down to the beach after a little while, where he'd sat a lounge chair and a blanket. He sat down pulling her down between his legs and wrapping the blanket around them. "You did all this for me?"

"I'd do anything for you, Ells. I'd give everything up for the chance to be with you. To keep us all together as the family we are. I don't have to, though. The show will continue, the focus being on helping people as well as investigating to keep gathering evidence of the paranormal. The show also includes you on a permanent basis. The council is undergoing changes, as well as formal charges against Stone and Fields. Taklishim is the new head. There are a variety of new money men wanting in after those live shows. Enough so that we can get rid of the one that keeps trying to set us up. We will be able to pick and choose assignments and whether we do another live show again."

"Ronnie was right. He said everything was changing, and it is." Her voice was quiet awe as if she wasn't sure this was all real.

"For the good, right?" Jax kissed her neck. "And it's all solidly real, love. Leaving that hospital was the hardest thing I've ever had to do. I'm sorry you thought I'd left you. They'd all told me how much it would hurt, and nothing could have prepared me for how much."

"For sure, changing for the good. I can't believe you want to marry me and move us into this gigantic place."

"You belong here. I knew it when I came back here with you for your grandpa's funeral. It just took me that long to make it all work. Not one of them hesitated at all in the plan." Jax felt her drop all walls she'd had up, love flowing freely.

Winnie sat there on the sand next to Airy and Jax and clapped her hands. "Marco, isn't it beautiful?"

"The view?" he hooked his arm through Winnie's. "Very."

"Not the view, them!" Winnie pointed to Jax and Airy, who snuggled together.

Giuseppe paced behind them. "Awfully fancy if you ask me."

"Oh, hush, old man, be happy for your granddaughter. She deserves a fairytale castle and prince," Winnie admonished him.

"She does, and she's so beautiful it hurts my heart that I can't hug her right now," he looked sad for a minute but then cheered. "Plus, all my family is here!"

"Go see them!" Winnie tried to get him to go back.

"I can't. I'm chaperoning. Someone needs to make sure Marco doesn't take advantage of the romantic setting here." He gestured at Marco, and Winnie smothered a laugh. He should be more worried about Winnie taking advantage of Marco.

"Come, Giuseppe," Kalisha joined them. "Show me your love; I'd like to see who was able to capture that charm of yours."

"She's a beauty, that's for sure. Come along, then; we'll leave the lovebirds here." Giuseppe held his arm out to Kalisha and headed for the house. Chatting about the day he met Florence. The love for her evident in every word he said.

"She's going to do great things," Winnie said, leaning her head on Marco's shoulder, watching the angel that had changed her afterlife.

"I think together, they will all do great things," Marco responded with a smile.

"As a family. Love wins," Winnie whispered into the wind the words carrying past Airy's ears, making her smile as Smitty and Jillian walked on to the beach, followed shortly by Aedan and Mags, each carrying a baby, and Ronnie carrying the third.

"Happy birthday," they all chorused to Airy.

Winnie brightly smiled as Ronnie handed baby Angel to Jax and a wrapped present to Airy. "This is from all of us." Winnie went and stood behind Airiella to watch her open it.

She unwrapped a beautiful leather-bound book with the words "Love Wins" embossed on to the front. Winnie gasped as Airiella opened the cover. "Marco, come look!"

It was full of pictures the group had taken of each other that filled the pages with countless images of love and family, all featuring the angel that had made them all closer. Winnie gave Marco a teary smile, "See how important she is?"

"I see love," he corrected Winnie. "Lots of love."